Hey, Joey Journal

Colleen June Glatzel

ISBN: 978-1976190711

Credits
Cover Artist: Cherith Vaughn
Editor: Christine Young

Dedication

I dedicate this novel to my family for always sticking together. Mom, Dad, Maggie, the whole gang. Not everyone affected by mental illness is as lucky as I am to have unconditional love in their life. Their support for my book was an added miracle. I especially want to thank my Grandma June and Grandpa Gordy for always telling such vivid stories throughout my childhood. They made me want to tell my own. The antique community in my hometown is another part of my family that warrants many thanks.

I would also like to dedicate this book to my writing coach and friend, Kathie Giorgio. I never altogether stopped believing in *Hey, Joey Journal*, but having a writer I respect believe in the story pushed me through to the finish line. AllWriters' Workplace & Workshop and the individuals involved have blessed my life with more miracles than I can count. I now consider them part of the aforementioned family.

Finally, I must thank Christine Young and Arlo Young and the entire Rogue Phoenix Press team for the biggest miracle of all—a published novel.

August 17, 2012

Hey, Journal,

  That "Dear journal" shtick is overused, so I'll address you with the word "hey." Hey, journal. I usually write exclusively on scraps of paper. Underneath my bed is my literature's habitat and the paragraphs are seldom about anything. Last year, I discussed career goals with my high school's counselor. Once my writing aspirations were revealed, Counselor became giddy and asked about my writing style. She said, "I'd love to hear about it, Rosie."

  "It's disorganized," I said. Then she handed me this ginormous journal and I witnessed a disgusting "I'm-a-cool-adult" wink.

  This is the first time I've cracked you open.

  Time seems to have decelerated. The slowing of time is the only gift August 2012 has coughed up. There's been a drought, among other eyesores. I'm beneath our backyard's oak tree, its gargantuan arms stretching far, shade encompassing the entire lawn. Many leaves are dehydrated. It's as pleasant to lie beneath as *Magic Mike* is to watch. Allow me to explain that analogy. The film's previews had me expecting a rollicking rom-com...something less serious. It differed from the ads. Still, every scene featuring scantily clad men made it worth the cash. That's what happened with this shade. I'm below it, experiencing a full body itch, but it could be worse. Due to lacking rain, the ground isn't summer turf in the slightest. Imagine wearing a pantsuit crafted out of hay and sandpaper. The shade is nice, though. Makes me able to bear my eyes being open.

  Jumping Jesus on a pogo stick. I kid you not, as I placed the period after "open", a bird landed in my eye line and inched toward me. Soon, it was atop this journal. I thought, *Birds are flighty. Timid. Not this one.* Its eyes were a familiar mess. I was confronted by the undeniable fact that birds were my dad's favorite animal. I blinked, eyelids capturing wetness and holding it hostage. Moisture subsided and the bird was all kinds of nowhere.

I wonder what it would be like to sprout wings. To be gone. My pencil is begging me to release it from my monstrous grip and my legs are screaming, "Let us run far away, Rosie."

I'll do what I do best and let my impulses win. Run until I get scared and retreat. Run until I realize it's not the same as flying. Run.

August 18, 2012

Hey, Journal,

I'm not counting the days that have passed since it happened. When a person starts counting the days following an event, it becomes part of a timeline. Then, by consequence, it is cemented in reality. I'm fortunate. My brain is still too immobilized to visualize random numbers floating in space. I'm unable to make numbers relate to each other, events, time or anything at all. Because of this, I don't know how long it's been since he died. It's messed up, but I prefer this ambivalent uncertainty.

I'll speak of something I know for sure. Today's bike ride destroyed me. August is going too fast. It's only the 18th, but it feels like the month is nearing its conclusion. The weather is far too chilly, honestly. Deflated bike tires carried me down the sidewalk of my street. I normally ride in the road, but I haven't been in the mood to care about the well-being of pedestrians lately. Those tires were spinning, moving like the earth's orbit around the sun, constant and circular, at least seemingly so. Home was in sight. My eyes were on the trees above. I was gliding. Gliding. The leaves were rustling. The world was unsettled. God attached a handle to the South Pole, stuffed the globe full of beads and shook this planet like a giant rattle. God's infant-like cries resonated and the wheels came to a screeching halt, all because the malicious fates placed a tiny, dauntless bird on the sidewalk of Kale Avenue. I ran over the motionless bird. Accidentally. Then I pried my fluttering hand from my mouth and threw my wheels into the street. Seconds later, a police car demolished the bike and veered to the roadside.

Fun.

The uniformed man shot out of his vehicle, completely uncentered. There was a restricting quality to his aura, accompanied by an unprecedented ability to snap. Light brown is the color of a traditional rubber band, and when it comes to auras, it's a color associated with discouragement. His body language was discouraging me the second he exited the car.

No, I'm not a psychic. I don't see colors framing the forms of people. However, I do see people for who they are and enjoy describing this reality I perceive with the same language aura seers use. I heard all about auras growing up under the care of parents who lived to study metaphysical concepts. Much of the gobbledygook they taught me is too much for my logical brain to handle. Both my parents underwent past life regression, for example. Listening to my dad talk about his life as a Vietnamese peasant girl creeped me out. But auras? I was somehow able to get on board.

While laying eyes on me, the uniformed man eased. He's one of the cops who came when my dad's body wasn't doing things it should be doing. Like, you know…living. I was the girl the cops found in the disheveled garage, after I found…Nope. No. Nope.

I remember the cop's face well. Upon finding me in the garage, he seized my shoulders. The eye contact we made snapped me out of my blackout for about fifteen seconds. He had warm brown eyes. His eyes couldn't meet mine today. Words friendly, tone stern, the cop said,

"What's the problem, champ?"

"I'm fine. You fine?"

"You tossed your bike into the street, Miss."

"There's a quality explanation. I…"

He rubbed his forehead and relented. "Won't write you up. I was there. Remember?"

That day is drawn into my mind with zigging Etch-a-Sketch lines, the difference being no matter how hard I shake my head, those drawings aren't disappearing. He told me he was aware everything must feel impossible. Couldn't help but let out a light chuckle. "Nothing's impossible," I said. "Truly. Observe my face. A coping individual, right?"

"I'm not licensed to make that judgment, but I can say throwing your bike into the street isn't—"

"Explanations exist, Mr. Cop."

"I believe you," he said. "I'll let you off with a warning. Need help getting your bike home?"

I reminded him I was incredibly close to La Casa Dwyer as I heaved my pulverized bike into erectness. A fully capable woman, I was. He answered with a suspicious stare and earnestly instructed me to send my family his regards. The cop swiveled, heading for his vehicle. A back turned toward me is the perfect canvas to splash a big "eff you" unto. My middle finger went up and I whispered, "Send this up your ass." He pivoted, narrowing his eyebrows as the finger went down, lickety-split. Mr. Cop asked if I said something. My hands were in prayer position. "This too shall pass."

Mr. Cop was unconvinced, but gave a sturdy nod. His car was soon out of sight, and the mutilated bird corpse continued being dead. I vomited then thought to myself, *Damn birds with temporary paralysis, why can't you learn to move?*

However, it should be noted that as much as I was disgusted by this particular bird's stubbornness, I related to the creature. Related to its unending capability to move and related even more to its dedicated desire to act against its own nature. Once the cop car was long gone, I caught a glimpse of the tree firmly rooted next to me. Unlike the bird and myself, "not moving" were two words crucial to defining the tree's true disposition. In spite of this difference, the leafy giant somehow managed to stand in solidarity with us. I situated myself at the tree's base and analyzed the ramshackle house in front of me.

The house is currently green, but the paint is chipping and even the simplest being could determine it used to be red. Some elderly lady supposedly lives there, but the kids on the block make jokes she may be dead because nobody ever sees her. The back of my head made forceful contact with the tree trunk as I said, "My aged darling. Are you dead?" I threw a stone at her walkway. "Good on you, lady. Dying subtly is the way to go."

Once I was done verbally assaulting an old lady, I noticed my eight-year old sister Willow a ways down. She was hiding in a hedge in our front yard. *Shit,* I thought. *We started our game of hide and seek two hours ago.* I forgot. Then came a sharp whistle from me. "Wow, Willow," I yelled. "So hard finding you, I needed to ride my bike around town."

She darted out of her hiding spot and straight at me. Soon the gangly thing was standing over the vomit, arms crossed, head waggling. Willow hasn't spoken since the event happened an undisclosed amount of days ago. Willow loves speaking to a fault, so she's been having a hard time being mute. "That puke is nasty," I blankly said. "Something to say?"

Her lips squirmed for a fraction of a minute. Finally, it was too much for her. She quietly said, "That old lady is dead. She doesn't need your puke."

My stomach warmed as I heard her voice for the first time in far too long. I said, "Now that you finally speak, how do we get you to shut up?" After a dramatic eye roll from the kid, I told her to pull me up. Willow begrudgingly followed my order and I carried on. "Lug my bike home now, or I'll slap ya so hard, you'll be mute for life."

Her eyes bulged but she got straight to work. Didn't quite have it in me to physically grin from cheek to cheek, but I did somewhere inside my body. Maybe my gut. Sure am going to miss this sort of response when she's mature enough to have self-respect and the knowledge to know I'd never slap her in a million years. In case you're curious, Willow has an aura like Elmer's glue. Pure white. Loose and cold when you first meet her, but once Willow gets used to a person, she'll stick to them like glue. Following her, I hollered back over my shoulder, "I'll be back. For the puke. I respect ghosts."

While passing my neighbor's perfectly kept home, the sixty-something owner looked up from his bed of petunias and pointed coolly in the direction of the old lady's house. Stuart told me to pick up the vomit. By the way, he doesn't have an aura. You need to have a soul in order to have one of those. I thought our Dennis the Menace/Mr. Wilson vibe would have eased during this time of turmoil. "Stuart, why sit back and watch as I almost get arrested?" I said. "Surprised you don't have buttered popcorn and Raisinets."

Stu is a perennial pain in the ass but still managed to look conflicted for a moment and said, "I've always held the opinion you're the kind of girl who would benefit from a stern talking to from a cop. Might make you think twice before acting on your impulses."

"My dad just died," I said, trying my hand at milking my situation for the first time. "It's only been, well, I can't remember how many days because I'm not at the counting stage yet. But still, have you no humanity?"

Stuart folded his arms over his tucked in Hawaiian shirt and calmly said, "I gave a gift basket, okay? It had Godiva chocolates in it. I care about your family, but I care an equal amount about the upkeep of this neighborhood."

"Eat a petunia, Stu," I said.

Godiva chocolates mean nothing to me. Hold on. Fifteen days! It's been fifteen days.

Fuck.

September 4, 2012

Hey, Journal,

Thirty-two days have now happened. Today was the first day of my senior year. My creative writing teacher is so hackneyed that she's practically a walking, talking corn on the cob. This teacher instructed us to write a creative piece of nonfiction. *What was your best or worst first day of school? Why?*

Not very creative of her. The school should put her on probation. Here's my worst first day of school, since I have nothing better to do, like, I don't know, *grieve.*

I know this is a space designated for journaling, but I'm going to draft the assignment in here. I would do this elsewhere, but I haven't had time to buy school supplies yet. Blame it on my family being in total upheaval. Sit back and deal with me stabbing my pen into you.

Cornrow Captivity
a story by Rosie Dwyer

He had a Twinkie in his eye. Don't re-read that sentence. I didn't mean to say, "he had a twinkle in his eye," or any gushy-mushy crap like that. Meant what I said. A Twinkie was in his eye, and I was the reason it was there. His name was Logan Fields. He had a green aura. Still does. Seafoam green. Somewhere deep inside, there's always been a healer in him. That's the kindest thing I'll say about him in this story. You see,

Logan is the kind of person who acts against his aura to extreme extents. Logan has eyes that say, *I wanna help.* However, the day I met him, he wore an unnatural smile that said, *Peer pressure is happening. A disease, one that's spreading through my higher self. My aura is now inky black.*

We were ten. It was my first day at St. Agnes Catholic Elementary School. I'm not Catholic or anything. My parents were raised Lutheran and we never had time for church. My folks also reared us bearing in mind Buddhist principles. The Dwyers are a true novelty. St. Aggie's was the only school within walking distance of my house. Convenient, really. We never owned cars. I could only go as far as my feet and the bus would allow. My kin firmly believes we should keep our carbon footprint nonexistent. At least that's the conjecture we've maintained up until August of the year I'm penning this. Mom and brother have cars now. Sellouts. "It's a high stress time," they say. Vexation and public transportation inherently don't mix well, but I'll never drive. When we moved to Wisconsin from California, my parents almost used an Oregon Trail style wagon. I miss that.

Every day, I'd hoof it to an establishment that preached something contrasting what my parents believed. Didn't matter to me. Religions are the same at their cores. People must believe in something. Anything. Even Stuart, my atheist neighbor, is unshakable in his convictions surrounding our corgi, Mr. Bojangles. Our furry friend is named after a song with the same name by The Nitty Gritty Dirt Band. Was my old man's favorite tune. Man, that dog lit up my dad's life. He even engraved Mr. B's bell with the words, *Spell the word 'dog' backwards.* Stuart, on the other hand, doesn't equate dogs with God. He believes Mr. Bojangles is a lowly entity who should only relieve himself on our lawn. Never his. Adversely, Mr. Bojangles forever believes it's his doggy right to urinate wherever. Beliefs. Everyone has them.

I believe battering people with baked goods is beyond justifiable. My mother believes it's also admissible to passively batter people's emotions until they're no longer recognizable. My mother is Melanie. Her aura was always mixed. Bit of lemon yellow dominated by a deep violet. Like Logan, she's found a way to act against her natural aura. Since August, it's been inky black——my way of saying she's a goddamn piece of work. I'm not saying this because I'm a stereotypical teenager, and teenagers sometimes slander their mothers when writing about them. In my case, it's the truth. Much can change in a single August. This is the first time I've allowed her into my mind since everything went to shit. I'll set my mind on a time when she wasn't made of excreta, to a time when she was hemming my new uniform in the kitchen.

I stood on a kitchen stool, tapped her shoulder to attract her attention and asked her for a more interesting hairstyle. Just watched John Travolta in *Battlefield Earth*. She told me I'd regret it. I could've said, *I'll take your advice seeing, as you're an expert on regrettable decisions. Polyester pants circa 1978?* Went in another direction, saying, "My individuality is developing."

She caved. Mel was an occasional interior decorator and made doohickeys out of Popsicle sticks for craft sales. Since mid-August, Mel has toyed with the idea of becoming a secretarial temp. She's been working toward doing this after her grief reduces to a functional size. As of this moment, it's only been thirty-two days since my dad's passing. I hope this job change doesn't happen, but I understand it might have to, for the sake of my family's financial security. My dad had a life insurance policy, but Melanie says it's not enough to sustain us forever.

Her career aspirations may be mad boring these days, but I'm sure if she were given the chance, she'd still encourage my unique mind. In the past, I could sway her to eat Bugles out of Mr. Bojangles' butthole if I insisted it was for my imagination's sake. I like to assume that hasn't changed, even though everything else has.

Enough of her. I've realized she's extraneous in the context of this story, and also the context of my life. This is not about my messed up family. It's about my first day at a new school. St. Aggie's. That Catholic schoolgirl getup was unbecoming on a goober wearing beady glasses and sun-bleached blonde cornrows. I leaned against the monkey bars, looking like a nerdy version of Christina Aguilera during her "Dirrty" phase. Logan Fields had big ears, shaggy red hair and annoying audacity. He welcomed me by tying my cornrows in a knot around the playground equipment. Logan tied a wad of chewed gum around his work for good measure. Didn't notice it happening, since I might have ADD and the cornrows numbed my scalp. The bell rang. My eyes closed. I inhaled. Exhaled. Eyes popped open, zoning in on the line forming in the distance. I whispered the mantra my dad gave me that morning. "Confidence is key, kid. Confidence is key."

A stride forward was taken, but I didn't travel far. The pain inflicted upon my scalp was comparable to childbirth. Never pushed a lifeform out of my lady parts, so all I know about the experience is what I heard while my sister came into the world via water-birth. My cries were identical to both mother and daughter. Then Logan jumped out, proud to have forced me into cornrow captivity. "Welcome to St. Aggie's, kid. Welcome to St. Aggies," he cockily said, smile cocked sideways, the trademark grin of cocky cocks everywhere. He ran off as the bell rang again.

My arms flailed something awful, and the youngsters inside gathered around the window to laugh at me. This was a Dark Age, and I was a medieval peasant in the shackles. The teacher sprinted toward me, frenzied. Then she tried undoing Logan's handiwork. The disruptive child must have been a boy scout. This is based solely on the knot tying prowess. His expression indicated he was incapable of earning badges for helping the elderly cross the street, but knots! Knots, he could surely do. "Certainly something," she said. "A Boy Scout perhaps?"

You don't say.

"I can't undo this, really—"

"You can't?"

"Sorry, sweetie."

I'm no sweetie, I thought as my hands shot at my coiled hair. I knew the implications of what would happen if I didn't make like most Hollywood celebrities and quickly untie the knot. She said, "We have to cut it, hon."

My arms wilted. I was a rare flower in bloom. Chopping the cornrows was like plucking my unique petals. She asked if that was alright and I nodded, giving the go ahead. After that day, anytime someone called me "hon," I've transformed into Attila the Hun. It's not a great look on me.

The only thing more unpleasant than the teacher's word choice was her breath, which smelled worse than my brother's fart-in-a-jar collection. And her aura was a black and white picture with all the white parts cut out. No purity left in her soul's architecture. Gray and black, together in holy matrimony. She snipped and snapped as I wiped salty, yet subtle tears away. Once it was over, she handed me my braids. The clump was eight inches in length, gum still on it. I shoved the mess in my backpack. As we walked to class, Teach asked me to describe the delinquent and I told her I hadn't a clue.

The avenging was my job.

Once inside, I digested my new educational digs. All there was to be found were turds in gray uniforms. The teacher stood near the gray chalkboard, name written out, "Ms. Smith." She sure resembled her name. Perfect picture of normality. Gray button-up, long pencil skirt, tightly pulled back hair. Ba-bam! Basic. However, on that day, Ms. Smith's face didn't look ordinary. Her cheeks were inflamed by her pure hatred for her job, the cockamamie bastards she was forced to teach, and life in general. She said levelly, "Meet Rosie Dwyer. She moved here from California. Say hello."

They mumbled a collective and barely audible greeting. A saddening age. When most young folks enter fifth grade, they become drained of the childhood enthusiasm they once glowed with. I gave an expansive smile and a flourishing wave. My peers were about as reactive as the noble gases.

"Would the person responsible for her haircut reveal themselves?" said Ms. Smith. "Confess now. You'll get in less trouble."

Pushing my glasses up, I worked my magic. "Smithy, let's forgive and forget. I needed a trim. The baboon who did this did me a favor."

"I prefer Ms. Smith. You will call me Ms. Smith, okay?" Smithy crouched in order to make direct eye contact with my short self. Shot me one of those squinty glares teachers give as a means to intimidate facts out of children and scare them into calling them by the correct name. Too bad her crouching act had none of the grace a woman should have while daring to wear a pencil skirt and heels. Her pose brought monkeys to mind. In fact, I envisioned her in a circus monkey costume, one complete with finger cymbals. My cheeks turned red in embarrassment for her. I told the woman I was heading into ragamuffin territory with my old hair. "Long live my new look, Ms. Smith."

My response was absent-minded as I studied a bird on the telephone line outside. It was completely red and entirely free. I was wearing grey, sealed up inside a colorless classroom, a dire life period dawning. I yearned for my florid scarves and shoulder-padded neon jackets. Made a mental note to brace myself, knowing that achromatic is what elementary school would immovably be.

"Positive?" she asked. Mixed in with her question was an underlying tone, as if Carol meant to ask, *Positive? I'm a Catholic schoolteacher. I get high off punishing students.*

Smithy repeated herself, asking if I was sure once more. I squinted back and said, "Look at my face." The corners of my smile expanded elastically. "Is this the face of a jilted woman?"

I heard that terminology on the *Lifetime Movie Network.* I've always been a fan of difficult words and other people's issues. Carol stammered out a single 'um'. Her failure to articulate forced me to say, "Gotta take a seat, Smithy. Might have early onset arthritis."

"I could punish this whole room," she said to the mass of children, hands trembling. She was a weak one, I could tell. She was the kind of woman who probably cried during every commute, to and from work. Poor Smithy. "I could easily punish everyone. I could."

I pulled her sleeve and waved her back into a bending position. Then I whispered in her ear, "Smithy, don't make them hate both of us on the first day."

When she backed away and stood up straight, a resentful look fell across her face. However, it quickly disappeared. Next came confusion, then understanding, and finally a feeble nod. "It's the first day," Smithy said to the class. "And you have given me reason to watch you extra carefully this year. My increased attention to every action in this room is punishment enough." I was proud of her. Although there definitely wasn't enough bite in her delivery to freeze the room into a brand new Ice Age, her performance was adequate. Smithy reached for her clipboard and said, "Rosie, your seat is in the back, next to Logan Fields. The redhead. And stop calling me Smithy."

way, they pretend to be in a relationship. No build up.

Logan didn't destroy my hair because he 'liked me'. Instead, he was a satanic imp with a mean streak. Even at ten, I understood where I fell within the romantic caste system. I was…interesting. A kind way to put it. Logan, although a soul-sucking ginger, was of high quality if you took into account his dimples, his almond colored eyes, his naturally acquired 'swagger'. Little dude was *GQ* at ten.

I let him sit in discomfort. When Logan was about to retract his offer, I eagerly cut him off and told him I'd date him. His face looked like a blissful dog, sticking its head out a car window. In a wind tunnel leading to his first taste of tween courtship, he said, "What now?"

"Lucky for you, this isn't my first time at the rodeo. I've dated a lot. There's tons of stuff couples do."

Ha. More lies.

"Kissing?" He could barely contain his excitement as he leaned forward.

"Slow down, Skippy," I deadpanned. "Let's share our lunches."

He emptied his paper bag as I spread out the contents of my Alf the Alien lunchbox. My parents were on a health food kick. We're talking lentil. My arteries nearly ruptured as I examined his goods—fruit roll-ups, chocolate pudding, a Twinkie, processed goods galore. It crossed my mind to maintain this charade so I could eat his food daily, but the image of my chopped hair beat its indignant fists at the back of my eyelids. "Start with the Twinkie," I said.

He split it in half, examining it. Logan wanted it for himself, as is the way of a person with a Y chromosome. "Feed it to me if you want," I said with another wink, using my wily woman ways to service my agenda. He bit his lip, cheeks reddening, eyes dilating. I've always been charming. The way he fed me, however, was hardly sexy. Logan shoved the snack down my throat, gagging me. He had a pressing question. "Can I eat my half now?"

Despite choking, I didn't spit it out. I swallowed. Spitters are quitters. Soon, I moved the Twinkie in slow motion toward his open mouth. It almost entered, but I speedily brought my hand up, forcefully shoving it into his eye. From all the studies I've read about Twinkie injuries, the eye is the worst place to have one crammed. He yelled, "My eye!"

I pulled him in by his tie until his face was two inches from mine. I said, "Tell on me and I'll tell Carol what you did, pinhead."

The lunch supervisor approached in my peripheral vision and I let go, pretending to panic as well. The teacher surveyed Logan's eye, asking what happened. Logan gravely gave me the look—the look on a young ginger's face upon realizing their relationship was a sham created to facilitate an elaborate revenge scheme. That look. Then he told the adult what happened. "What happened" happened to be a lie. To kids, lies and truths are synonymous. Logan solemnly said, "I was laughing at Rosie's joke and put my head in my hands. She's hilarious. Couldn't handle it. Forgot I was holding a Twinkie."

"Want me to walk you to the health room?" the adult asked.

"Whatever."

"Don't worry, dearie," I said. "I'll guard your food." Once they were gone, I packed my health food in his lunch sack and gobbled his fruit snacks. Tasted like victory.

September 4, 2012

Hey, Joey Journal,

It's the same day as the previous entry. Still only thirty-two days since it happened. Knowing the number is keeping me awake. I wish numbers were floating in the air again, unrelated to anything of major importance.

Sorry if I'm depressing you, journal. Consider us even, because you've been nameless and that depresses me. From now on you are Joey. Joey Journal. Your namesake is Joey Gladstone from the hit television sitcom *Full House*. Why? Because that character was outrageously corny. Journaling is like Joey Gladstone in that respect.

Earlier today, I composed a true story about a Twinkie. I was ten. I'm seventeen now. Today was the first day of my senior year at Wira North High School, which I can thank the universe is a public institution. I've been a public school student since middle school. No gray plaid skirts for me today. I went all out with a bright green harem jumpsuit, paired with a cropped eighties windbreaker, just because I could. Memories of my first day at the hellscape known as St. Aggie's flooded in when I was walking to my first period science class and slipped on a stray Twinkie. Who in their right mind would leave a Twinkie on the ground? If I dropped one, I'd still consume it. Those bad boys are magic.

My feet were victimized by the goodie, body joining it on the floor. "Curse you, universe," I said into the linoleum tiles. Stares came my way, but I didn't give a flying yoo-hoo. My peers have seen me mortify myself on much grander scales. You wouldn't believe what happened during last year's science final.

There was a party the night before. River, my brother, was back from college while my parents were in Florida. They were celebrating their 25th wedding anniversary. River invited over a few old high school friends. Those friends invited a few of their friends, so on and so forth until River's unabridged graduating class was at our house. The living room was congested with inebriated imbeciles and I said, "I can't sleep!"

River ignored me, continuing to drink with his rowdy friends. I eventually punched him in his tummy and tackled him. We landed on a huge beanbag, his friends laughing and cheering as he wrestled me off. Then I rushed to my room and yelled at a kissing couple to scram. While reviewing my science book, I recalled two facts. Number One: Science books aren't thrilling reads. Number Two: Even on quiet nights, I have trouble drifting off. So, I threw my cares to the wind, playing video games until 2 am. The next day, I arose with a penis drawn on my leg. No time to be found. It was a t-shirt and sweats kind of day. My gnarled blonde waves were tossed into a bun while I sped into the bathroom to freshen up. I discovered one of River's homeboys puking in the toilet. As I prepared my toothbrush, I said, "Get it together, sir."

During my teeth cleanup, the guy came up for air and called me a certain four-letter C word. And no, he didn't call me Cher. I spit, threw my brush into the medicine cabinet, and then promptly gave him a swirly in his putrid mess. Once he was gone, I examined the toilet, which was covered in regurgitated food, and decided I wouldn't be using it. That's when I went to my parents' bathroom and walked in on a constipated River. He threw my mom's magazines on his lap and begged me to grab him the Funnies section. I promptly stuck my tongue out at him and went to eat cereal while sitting on the kitchen counter. I personally eat breakfast every day, even when late. When I was done, I bounced on the bellies of some people sleeping in the kitchen, then sprinted to class, chugging an energy drink.

My house is positioned across the street from Wira North, so I made it under the wire. I crushed the can and chucked it into the bin like my name was Kobe. Nailed it. Strutted to my desk, feeling sexy. This false pride was an energy drink side effect. A sigh of relief was unleashed

though I'm in bed thinking solely about screwing you senseless. Here's what I'll do. Masturbate. Yep. Masturbation. But I won't do you."

Silence fell on the line for a lengthy moment. *Shit*, I thought, *He doesn't want me around anymore. He's weirded out. His penis has needs I can't meet. Hurry, Rosie, say hollow words that'll keep him around even though you don't plan to act on them. Sound polite, if you can.* "Now, Eliot, I overheard you saying your penis has needs. This true?" The line was silent. "Your penis has needs?" More silence. "If you need it, I'll perform oral favors. Gotta find out if your aura can get passed onto me that way, though."

"Okay," he said, breaking in. "Whoa. You don't gotta suck me off. I told you. We're only gonna make out."

"But your penis needs, Eliot. How will they be met?"

"I…I don't know."

"Can't have you pressuring me."

"Fine," he said. "Fine. We'll be sorta together, right? Friends, of course. That's what we'll call it, for now. Maybe more later. Me, you, and we got this 'Don't ask, don't tell rule'. A rule where we get to see whoever the hell we want, but we keep it our own business."

The puzzlement hit a climax. Suddenly, I realized my hand was in my pants. Voice shaking, I said, "Solid. Have to jet. Let's meet up tomorrow. I'll be in touch."

Then I hung up and masturbated for the first time ever. The whole time, I was thinking, *I hardly think about this kind of thing' my ass*. And that's how I came to know Eliot Buxton, in all his mind-boggling glory. The last day of last school year. Today was the first day of the current one, and we began it with me flat on my back in the hall and him hovering above me. "Dude, need help?" he said, laughing.

Soon I was up, Doc Martens hitting the tiles. Eliot slung my backpack over his shoulder and I reclaimed it because I'm an independent woman, strong enough to carry her own books. We strolled to class with our fingers interlaced. He smelled like a forest. Eliot and I are complicated now, even more so than in the beginning. At first, we were 'just friends' who had 'fun' together. By June's end, we were Facebook official. But he still refers to me as his friend in most circles. I don't know why I haven't concluded this sham. Maybe I'm still in it because being in a relationship on Facebook feels nice, even when it means nothing. Maybe I don't wanna give up the confusion because it makes me hot. Or, possibly, I'm addicted to people I can't decode. Facebook official. His idea. We're still allowed to have 'fun' with other people. I myself haven't had 'fun' with anyone, but I'm fine with him seeing other girls because of our rule. And polyamory is stylish these days.

"You kay, Rosie? You ate it hard."

"Damn Twinkie," I said with vigor.

"Probs karma, troublemaker."

"Hmm?"

"You smashed a Twinkie into Logan Fields' eye. Fourth grade?"

I smirked, remembering. "Fifth grade."

"The guys teased Logan at soccer practice," Eliot said. "He got kneed in the head by Lenny "Thunder Thighs" Olson. The kid shed tears. I told Fields to stop being a vagina. Another dude said, 'Got something in your eye?' and Louis said, 'Normally, Fields only has Twinkie cream in his eye.' Another dude said, 'And dick cream, too.' Didn't know the Twinkie story. They told me. Legendary, kid."

Kid. He's always calling me that one in particular. His use of faddish lingo is constant and irksome, if you haven't noticed already. Eliot rubbed his fist on my head and my hands were a million slaps-a-minute, while my mouth bellowed the word "stop" in abounding variations. When he did that, I fantasized about breaking this shit show that is our love life up in some wildly humiliating way. Like on his birthday. Or maybe I could get a hold of the school loudspeaker and make an announcement about it. These ideas have me more hot and bothered than he's been able to make me since late July. However, the truth is I'm too overwhelmed with my life to find the time to break up with him for the vexing quality of his existence. Once the noogie ended, Eliot held back chuckles. "A Twinkie? You smashed that shit in his eye?"

"Had to," I said, pulse quickening, disposition transitioning into rage. "He's a calamity."

Once my hair was fixed, Eliot grabbed my hand and said, "Chill, girl. That dude is mad funny. We're bros."

Bro. Hate that word so much. I gave him an incredulous stare as we entered room 152 and venomously made a declaration. "Trust me, Eliot. Logan Fields is devil spawn."

When my focus deviated forward, Satan's offspring was standing before me. My eyes beetled while meeting Logan's briefly, then united with the beige carpet. Couldn't see his expression, but I could feel it—his cocky grin cocked sideways, his smile's malignant smarminess. "Rosie," he said, bowing. "Eliot, my man. Excuse me."

Eliot said, "It's the first day. You skipping already, man?"

"Yeah. This room has got horrible energy. Gonna treat myself to a special first day of school breakfast at Denny's. You two are welcome to join me."

Don't pretend like you care about energy, I thought. *You have the worst energy I've ever come across.*

Eliot was about to accept the offer, but I pulled him into the classroom before Logan and him could—

I just broke my fucking pencil and am now writing with a stub. Pressed too hard. That's how irritated that boy makes me. It's high time I turn in, before I start throwing up flames.

September 8, 2012

Hey, Joey Journal,

Thirty-six days.

There's a Maori legend that says thirty-six gods came together to assemble the parts of the first human before the god Tāne breathed life into the being. I wish each of those thirty-six days were a god. I wish they would rebuild the parts of my dad and say, "Yo, Tāne, come over here and do your magic breathing."

I should probably stop being a naive dreamer and get started on my writing homework.

Me, Jacques, and the Dingy Dojo

My best friend Jacques lives on his family's farm on the less populated side of town. We met at karate class during the sixth grade. The dojo was in this ramshackle strip mall on the corner of Jefferson and Main. He and I quit a few months after my first day and joined jazzercise classes. Jacques had irreconcilable differences with the dojo master, while I was on the verge of being kicked out for consistently getting 'too into it'. Hair pulling, name calling, sometimes scratching. I'd tackle a bitch if I had to. I was always provoked.

On day one, I was paired with Maria, a hefty Mexican chick and a heavy breather. Got on everyone's last nerves during water breaks, chomping her Cheetos, mouth like a garbage disposal. The karate master said, "Maria, you're with Rosie. Floor is yours after Jacob and Al."

Maria asked her friends who I was. One pal was a white girl who fancied herself a thug, but she lived down the street from me. My neighborhood is suburban. Quite decent. I was onto her. Her name might have been Angie. Maybe Miss Thang. The trash's caked on turquoise eye shadow and forced twang was cringeworthy. She was a bit cross-eyed and appalling. "She goes to my school. She's loco," said Miss Thang, directing her bobble head toward me. There I was. Cornrows were out by then, but it'd be another year until contacts and proper beautification skills entered my life. Miss Thang continued. "One time, she crammed a Ho Ho into somebody's eye."

I waved and grinned. "A Twinkie."

Maria cackled and said, "This honky?" It was too much for her, seeing a white person for the first time. She walked toward me. I almost wrote 'like a jaguar walks towards its prey', but that wouldn't be honest. Maria walked toward me like a hippo. Got up in my grill. When I say 'grill', I mean 'braces'. Her breath smelled like the fryer at McDonald's and she had orange dust on her pushed-out lips. Up close, I could smell the mysterious scent of cat piss on her body. "Listen up, twig," she said. "Gonna beat you up and laugh the whole time."

"Damn you," a sharp voice howled, interrupting our exchange. The banshee was a boy fighting on the mats. Tiny, most likely the runt of whatever litter he came from. His karate uniform had the appearance of a white polar bear, one hell bent on swallowing him up. A hand-me-down, no doubt. "You idiot," he said, in a high-pitched voice. "My sister just did a treatment on my nails. Hate sounding cliché, but c'mon." He shoved his pinkie finger into his partner's face. "Broken."

Al was a tall boy and loomed over him, stifling laughter. As our karate master approached the boys, the bigger one whispered, "Yep. Broken, like your dad's dream of having a straight son."

Doug Lee, our karate master, interjected, tapping the short boy's shoulder and saying,

"Jacob, we don't talk like that here."

"Douglas."

Doug was goofy, had Jackie Chan's body, but the face of a sumo wrestler. He said, "Corner. Now."

This scene made me livid. Jacob was a bantam baby and competing with a boy who should've been fighting someone his own size. Back then, I was short, but able to take Maria with my cunning nature. Jacob, well, I didn't know Jacob yet, but he seemed utterly endangered. I now know he fights with words. Jacob glided to the corner, his gorgeous gait becoming apparent. Found out later he's a natural born dancer. His parents made him take karate like his older brothers had, but whenever he got home, his sisters taught him ballet. Nose in the air, he said, "My name is Jacques and you're pretty much nothing."

Doug seemed like he hadn't heard him and told Maria and me that we were up. Heading toward the mats, Maria shuffled by, bumping her fleshy shoulder into mine. "Oops," she said, with a Cheshire cat grin.

"Let's see a nice, clean fight."

Maria wasted no time, charging at me like a bull. I coasted out of harm's way, like a matador, and instead of using a cape, I stuck my foot out, tripping her. Maria sprawled out, resembling the stray Cheetos spread around her gym bag. In her ear, I said, "Oops."

Doug bounded over, yelling, "That sure as hell wasn't karate."

"Master Doug, this is my first day. Don't know karate."

Doug, irritated to the highest degree, brought his clipboard to his face. "Says on your form, you're a yellow..." He looked closer before finishing his sentence. "Misread that. White belt."

I gestured to the belt in question, entirely bewildered. "Exactly," I said. "White belt. Didn't know karate, saw I'd be fighting a bull, decided to play matador."

"Shh. Don't say that. She's big-boned."

Chuckles were suppressed. Maria's bones weren't enlarged. Maria's mom simply packed Cheetos in her daughter's gym bag instead of water. Then Doug said, "Even if you don't know karate, you shouldn't trip people. You're new, but the rules apply. Corner, till class ends, with Jacob."

The fiery child shouted, "I'm Jacques, you fool." Doug didn't flinch. I shot the dojo master a confused look over my shoulder as I passively strolled into exile. It was as if he didn't hear the boy in the deadly corner. Jacques was far, but wasn't in the Ozarks.

My future life as a 'corner kid' didn't leave me concerned. My parents signed me up for karate so I could unleash my "aggression" somewhere. I didn't have anger problems back then, though. May sound laughable, considering my previous description of unfolded events, but for the majority of my early years, I only became violent out of necessity. However, my dad, being an adolescent therapist and all, saw what would come as my teen years drew near in the same way a meteorologist sees a hurricane brewing: a mixture of science and a bullshit shot in the dark. I was twelve. Soon, I'd be thirteen. We had to make sure the angst that comes with the territory had a place of refuge. At least that's what my dad said.

You should probably know I never called him "dad." Called him by his first name when he was alive, like I do with Mel. It was disrespectful in a cute way when he was living, but it feels odd now. You should also know he wasn't a therapist like I just said. That was an inside joke in my family. He played one. Before we moved to Wisconsin from California, my dad was a comedic actor and was an adolescent therapist on a sitcom about a mental hospital. The show was bright and beautiful and not even close to what a mental hospital is like.

The show lasted three episodes. Hollywood is hit and miss. He made money acting in commercials after that, but once Melanie gave birth to Willow, they decided to move the family back to Wisconsin, to be closer to our extended family. He took a job as a drama teacher at a high school in the next town over. But who wants to hear about him, anyway? That sounds awful, doesn't it? Didn't mean any disrespect. I merely hypothesize that if somebody were to read this, they'd rather hear about a vivacious person that's full of life like Jacques. My dad's ashes are in an urn, waiting to be scattered, making him a depressing subject.

Let's get back to my best friend before I give myself a brain hemorrhage. I slid down the wall in the corner, meters from Jacques. Took a peek at him. His aura was like a Sex on the Beach cocktail. Orange-red. Power and confidence overflowed from his small body. His lips were pursed, his face was seething, and it was one of the most hilarious images. A Yorkshire terrier of a boy, shaking in his oversized karate uniform, skin as red as Rudolph's nose. His face, albeit flushed, was like Mark

Wahlberg's in almost everything he's been in after his Good Vibrations era. The kid was straight out of *The Departed*. My laughter began and couldn't end.

"Your problem, whore?"

I flashed a silly grin and asked him where he'd been all my life. Jacques looked at me as if I were a spider inching into his Egg McMuffin. "Nut," he said. Moments passed and something inside Jacques made him ease. He giggled like me. Freely. When we calmed, Jacques requested I unveil the misfortunes that brought me to the corner and I made a reference to my favorite musical, singing, "I just tripped a girl named Maria."

His baby blues became so bulgy, I thought he was suffering from Graves' disease. "Oh my," said Jacques.

"Oh my, what?"

He placed his hands over his heart, breathing in and sighing. "*West Side Story* is my favorite musical."

"Same."

At least it was back then. Jacques still ranks *West Side Story* as number one, but my current poison is *Next to Normal*. Love musicals. If I could sing, I'd audition for every show possible, but alas, I'm William Hung in woman form. I stick to stage crew. But honestly, I probably wouldn't even do that anymore. It would be too unsettling being in a theatre after…you know, since my dad was a drama teacher. Even if I wanted to try out, my school's drama department is deceased. Don't ask. Doesn't even have anything to do with my dad. Someone else. Someone creepy.

"I'm happy Fugly Doug Lee sent you here," Jacques said. "We'll have fun." He waved me in, signaling for me to fill the gap and become his best friend for the rest of the wild blue yonder. Sliding over, I told him I'd do anything to get away from the 'Maria Monster'. He said, "Get this. Douglas is her uncle or something. Horrible is genetic." He extracted a file from his uniform sleeve and went to town on his nails. "Nepotism is why she gets away with everything and has a yellow belt."

"They look nothing alike."

"My dad calls the Lee family a cultural melting pot. They live near us. The whole family is packed in this crappy blue house. Not sure if she's adopted or if they're mixed."

"Doug is a character," I said decidedly. "The kind you read about." Jacques tilted his head and asked for clarification. Told him I didn't know and threw my gaze toward the mats. Half the time, I don't know what I'm rambling about. Dissecting thoughts is useless. Continuing my aimless adventures in speaking is much preferred. I said, "It's cool how his first name is so white and his last name is so Asian."

"Why?"

"Ethnic contrast." I was talking out my arse. I speak from that crevice often. Jacques nodded, buying my bullshit.

"Oh," he said. "He's also deaf in one ear."

"Deaf?"

"Half," Jacques explained. "Had meningitis as a kid. Lost hearing in his left ear."

"Ahh. I see. Y'all say whatever you want, low enough so he won't hear."

Jacques flashed a toothy grin. He was beautiful. He was what I like to call "Catalog Kid Cute." At the time, I thought he looked like a boy I saw in a JCPenney ad. Found out later he was. Child model. The sheer perfection of his blond pompadour suggested he used hair product, but Jacques never over-gelled. Some boys over-gel. Over-gelling is only okay when Hispanic boys do it. I don't make the rules. I just enforce them.

"Is Jacques your real name?"

He dropped his file and said, "Jacob isn't totally lame, but 'Jacques'? It's more me."

"You're French?"

"Yes." Jacques' eyes were intently beholding his hands as they flattened his uniform's wrinkles. My eyes expanded and his face shifted. "Not by blood."

Jacques' eyes stopped analyzing his nails and met mine. Icy blue. Made my body go straight up hyperborean. He was a Draco Malfoy/Jack Frost/Mark Wahlberg hybrid of a child. The iciest, most intimidating kid, well, ever. In other words, he had my attention. "Why'd you change it to a French name?"

"We did reports on foreign countries in the fourth grade," he said, cutting me off, speaking kingly. Jacques sounded like his words were a monologue rendition he practiced his entire life. "We drew country names from a hat. Guess what I got? France. Guess what I found out? Everything about France is beautiful."

The bodily hygiene of its people withstanding, of course. I finally said, "France is pretty, but many places are."

"Let me finish," he said, loud enough for everyone but Doug to hear. Jacques was smiling, so it was a tad more charming than rude. That's him stripped to his core. Always proudly walking a thin line between those adjectives. He breathed, pacified, and said, "Its culture, its people, its food, its land, its language." Jacques was in a Technicolor daydream. "Beautiful."

"And?"

A conflagrant glare came, then his face melted into sheer gorgeousness. "France is beautiful. Look at me. I'm beautiful. My name should be like me. Beautiful."

I was in love. The platonic kind, but still love. "Your last name, Jacques?"

"Blain."

Blain. Jacques Blain. If names could dance, this one would. I asked for his real last name.

"No."

I stared into his haunting baby blues, waiting for him to reveal his hidden truth. "Not telling you," he said. His discomfort was so…there. I kept asking questions. "Tell me, Jacques Blain, what do you like about *West Side Story*?"

Hey, Joey Journal

September 8, 2012

Still thirty-six days and they're still not gods and I'm still awake and so I will write.

Earlier, I wrote a rough draft about Jacques for class. We were supposed to write about our best friends. Jacques is the closest thing I have to that luxury. The relationship between a girl and her favorite gay is a special thing, indeed. We have this game called 'Moon Wars', where we flash our butts at each other when least forecasted. Last December, Jacques wrapped the holiday lights in his bedroom around his bare derriere. When I entered, Jacques was stooped over, swaying his butt to Jingle Bell Rock. I wet myself.

Lately, we haven't been hanging out. Actually, we haven't been hanging out at all. He hasn't decided how he wants to talk to me after this past August's event. Jacques used to be sarcastic with me. Blunt, in this amazing sense of the word. Now, he waters his speech down and his sass-less eyes stare straight ahead. I'm a vase in an antique shop, held gingerly by a shaky customer. That's when he's not avoiding me.

I guess Eliot has been strange, too, but our communication has been wonky and almost nonexistent from the get-go. He's normal at school, but when the last bell rings, he always has somewhere to be. Eliot signed up for polyamorous fun, not the death that happened or the impression of death I now wear on my person like a badge of dishonor. Oddly, I don't care about Eliot, his dreadful aura, or his reaction that is lacking in all respects.

My focus is wrapped around Jacques. Jacques is my closest friend. Known him six years. That's what makes his feeble reaction so painful. My dad was a short guy, about 5'4. Jacques is now long and gangly. Towered over him in the end. If my dad weren't in an urn, he'd get on a stool so he could look Jacques in the eye, and he would gruffly say, "Hey, fucker. Be cool. Be normal. Be yourself. Be around. It's the only way to be her friend."

Then he'd kick him in the nuts. Wouldn't be first time. River, Jacques, and my dad were always kicking each other in that precise spot at unexpected moments. It started when Jacques officially came out to my family in the eighth grade. We were all chilling in the kitchen while River and Mel worked on dinner. It happened naturally. Riv looked up from the pot of chili he was stirring and said, "Ever gonna ask my sister out, Jacques? Been courting her a long time."

Jacques was totally at ease with my family and nonchalantly said, "Can't. I'm a homo."

My mom dropped a stack of plates when she heard the word "homo." Gave him a big hug. My dad smiled and said, "Good for you, bud. I ain't gonna hug you, though."

Then came a kick to the balls and Jacques dropped to the kitchen floor. "What the fuck," Jacques said.

River said, "'That's a hate crime."

"Just showing you you're still one of the guys."

That's practically the only thing Jacques said about my dad during the funeral. Jacques said my dad had the best reaction to the biggest struggle of his young life. That being said, my dad would be mighty ashamed of the reaction my supposed best friend has had to my biggest struggle. I feel that brain hemorrhage coming on. I have to stop talking about it.

Living people. Jacques is alive. My dad isn't. Jacques is breathing somewhere. And I understood even during our first conversation the best way to ease him was to change the subject to musicals. One question drained all strain from our first discussion. *What do you like about West Side Story?"*

Jacques ranted about the excellence of the movie's choreography. The harangue only halted when he displayed his dancing adeptness, imitating the snapping and the gangs' flourishing movements. He grabbed me, attempted to mambo, and became flustered. "You have no rhythm. Sit." I followed the command. Noticing my pout, Jacques abandoned his combativeness and said, "Keep watching. You'll dance like me someday."

I've been observing Jacques shimmy for a while. Yet, when I dance, I manage to look like a one-legged woman at a butt-kicking contest. The show was for me, but Doug saw a high kick in his peripheral vision. Told Jacques to "park his can." Soon, we were singing "I Feel Pretty" from *West Side Story*. I yearned to sing Maria's part, but of course, Jacques filled the role. Claimed he was more leading lady material. By that first encounter's end, Jacques asked if I'd visit his family's farm to watch *West Side Story*. My answer was an enthusiastic, "Holy yes."

When I left the dojo, I found Melanie sitting on a bench far away from the huddle of other moms. Like her daughter, she's never been a joiner. If it were up to her, she wouldn't even be in the same proximity of that many women wearing The Gap, but alas, she always rode the buses with me back then. Comforted by the sight of Mel, I hastened toward her. "Hey, Chicken," she said, patting my head. My family calls me Chicken, because at age five, I'd often flap my arms, yelling, "Look. I'm a chicken. MOOO." Yep. I made my parents look sketchy when I entered preschool with the animal noises jumbled up. It's more common than you'd think. They probably have support groups for folks like me. My brother, River, caused my confusion by teaching me the animal sounds wrong behind my parents' backs.

Once I reached her, she stood up. Melanie is taller than me. 5'11. That's partially why she and my tiny father made such an interesting pair. I was squatty back then. I'm 5'3 and a centimeter now. Average, I'd say. However, I didn't have a growth spurt until age fourteen. I remember what Melanie was wearing when she came to pick me up from my first karate lesson, a knee length poncho and a hat straight from the nineties. I proudly smiled and gave her the rundown. "I have a new BFF. His name is Jacques and we're gonna watch a musical at his farm."

She tentatively said, "You know you're too old for imaginary friends, right?"

"No, Mel, I really have a friend this time and he's really real. We met after being sent to the corner."

"The corner?"

All at once, I was in a pickle, and not the kind that's green and juicy. I said, "Where the winners…get sent? Yeah! A place for the ass kickers. Sounds true, because it is."

"Yeah?" she said, surprised. "Congrats."

My "triumphant moment" was astonishing because sports aren't my forte. My lacking athleticism resulted partially from my refusal to follow rules. Guidelines? Plant your behind on the sidelines if you want me to follow guidelines. Damn straight. Take fourth grade basketball. Referees divested the game's creativity. I once tried, in vain, to convince my teammates that if we made a pyramid beneath the hoop, the other team would be everlastingly screwed. The person topping the pyramid could stand tippy-toed and push the ball out before it sunk. The opposition would be unable to score. My vision went unshared.

"Where's your friend?" said Melanie.

"Jacques is getting permission."

"He's French?"

I shook my head and said, "No. France is beautiful. He's beautiful. Jacques suits him."

Melanie thrust her chin upwards and giggled her envy-worthy laugh. Melodic. Unforced. The reason for my wacky stunts. Her amusement is my catharsis. That's not what it's like anymore. Her rare laughter sounds like a symphony of vuvuzelas. "I don't know," she said. "It's getting late and remember the dating rule." The rule was that we Dwyer kids weren't allowed to date until our fifteenth birthdays, respectively. Pretty sure they gave up on that one, though, seeing as my kid sister had a boyfriend last year named Bae. He was Korean.

"We're friends," I told her.

Mel attempted not to cave. "Chicken, I know, but it sounds like you're crushing hard."

My pointer finger became air bound and I warned her of the

dangers of calling me a hussy. She lowered to my level, eyes dancing the Macarena. That metaphor may seem odd to those unfamiliar with her eyes, but if they met her back then, they'd understand the Macarena was the exact dance her eyes once did. Whimsical. Classic. A must for any jovial gathering. That was her eyes, and somehow they made it okay. Coils of curly brown hair escaped her hat, which framed her face in a way that made her appear younger. She was forty-five then, but looked thirty. "You called Jacques 'beautiful', Rosie. You haven't been this excited about a boy since Davie from our LA apartment building."

"Mel, don't bring up my heartbreak. Took forever to forget that doorman's dimples."

Small fingers tapped me. I turned and there stood Jacques, who said, "My mom can't wait. Barb loves *West Side Story*. She might watch it." He then regarded Melanie, in awe.

"You're Rosie's mother?"

"You're real?" she said.

"Rosie was right. Definitely don't have the skin of a forty-five year old."

Her eyes shifted in my direction. "Rosie Dianne, don't broadcast my age."

Jacques interjected, saying, "Melanie, if I may call you that, can Rosie come over? We need to go. Barb hates waiting."

This is the second time he's called her Barb, I thought. *We both disrespect our elders. We are soulmates.*

"She sure can come over, Jacques. Call me Mel. Rosie has her whole life."

Jacques catapulted toward my lanky mom, squeezing her torso tight. "Yay, Mel."

I embraced them while trying to make sense of her heart's sudden change, unable to comprehend that her gaydar was so effective, it worked on children. Soon I was crawling into his mom's blue Dodge Grand Caravan. The air turned heavy and dead. Barb's aura at that definite moment was not blue like her vehicle, or any other color I could fathom. It was black, in the way Eliot's hair is. It wasn't natural. Even in that moment, I knew this for certain. How could the colorful ball of energy that is Jacques come out of somebody so dead in the spirit department? The answer is he couldn't. No, the blackness was something she took on, of this, I was convinced. His mom was silent while pulling out of the strip mall parking lot. I rubbed my hands together, trying to ignite a conversation. "How goes it, Barb?"

Her eyes overflowed with irritation in the mirror, definitely not dancing the Macarena. "Call me Mrs. Fagg, or don't speak," Mrs. Fagg said. Seconds passed before her exhausted eyes eased. "Sorry. I'm tired."

"That's fine, Mrs. Fagg."

She rolled down the window, lighting a cigarette as an elderly man crossed the street. The gray smoke did a little dance and made me realize there was also some gray whizzing around the car's energy field. "Jacob," she said. "When we get home, watch the musical, but keep it down." I suppressed a dizzying urge to ask for the radio to be put on as she said, "Christ, I need a nap. You understand that? You're being an inconvenience."

"Okay, Mother," Jacques quietly said, focusing on the rolling landscape.

Okay, Mother? Who is he? Norman Bates?

The van coasted up their long driveway as Jacques shot me an uncomfortable look. A sign came into view. It read "Fagg Family Farm."

Once we were watching the movie on the Fagg's leather couch, Jacques looked at me with worried eyes. "About my mother..."

I whispered, "You don't have to explain Barb."

"My last name..."

"Jacques, shush. Blain is a wonderful last name. Watch the movie." And we did. We watched the movie with relaxed smiles, the kind that people make in the company of an extremely important person.

September 20, 2012

Hey, Joey Journal,

It's been forty-eight days. My dad once told me that Siddhartha Gautama positioned himself beneath a Bodhi tree. Some say he stayed as long as forty-eight days in hopes of making sense of the big bad universe. Enlightenment and Buddhism came to be as a result of his awakening. Although I've always been too keyed up to be any good at meditation, I'd like to try what the Buddha did. Like all humans, I wanna face down the universe and ask it my questions. My main question would be, *Are you senseless? Because what you did to my dad was just that. Senseless.*

Speaking of senselessness, earlier today, I endured a senseless urge, one that brought about a senseless decision. Like all the worst choices one can make in this life, mine was made while watching *Glee*. My body was aching hours ago. I spent two hours on the elliptical at the new gym, which is a short bike ride away. It was once a privately owned gym called Frank's Fitness Central. Frank was cool. He was often at the front desk with a brilliant joke ready. "Hey, kiddo," he once said. "What do you call a sheep with no legs?" Frank's face was perpetually deadpan while cracking jokes. I'd shrug, because nothing ever came to mind. His responses were always said in a voice as flat as his baseball cap's bill. "It's a cloud." He never grinned with his mouth, only his eyes.

Whenever Jacques used to follow me to the gym to check out men in the weight room, the gym owner was normally his main focal point. This was gross because although Frank was super fit, he was also sixty. Jacques could only seem to grasp the fit part. *Fit.* Frank once did eighty-three pull-ups. Exactly eighty-three. Jacques salivated. I stood in the distance, pretended to curl ten-pound dumbbells, and counted Frank's movements. I can't even do one pull-up. Jacques has never even tried as far as I know. He probably would be able to, though, being a strong dancer who often elegantly carries full-grown human beings around onstage. The reason Jacques' fingers never wrap around the bar is his tendency to spend all his gym time flirting with straight boys who aren't into him, but love his attention regardless. Ultimately, Jacques would only take to a pole in that weight room if it were vertically positioned.

Forget him, though. Forget Jacques. I called and asked him to work out today about an hour after his dance practice ended. He said, "You know I'd love to, doll, but I got loads of homework."

This would've been fine, had I not heard laughter in the background throughout the call, the kind that sprang forth from multiple mouths. Then a shrill female voice asked Jacques if he wanted to split fries. "Interesting," I said. "I've never tried studying in a full car visiting a drive-through. Tell me how that works out."

After sharply hanging up, I bawled for half a minute like a socially inept seventh grader. I couldn't take my room any longer and ended up at the gym. Frank wasn't there to greet me. It's not his gym anymore. Despite his apparent healthiness, he unexpectedly died a year back. Preexisting heart condition. I was present for his heart attack. Feels like an eternity ago. My phone was glued to my ear while I breezed in and told my dad I'd be home late. As I approached the counter, Frank was perched on his stool, frozen, hand clutching his heart. He hit the floor. Bam, like a bag of muscular bricks. I hung up on Dad and called 911. People soon were surrounding him, but I still got glimpses of his face reddening as his deep red aura left his perfect body. Within a year, corporate America swooped in like a vulture in the desert. A brand name gym was put in the building. *Swoop.*

Watching him die haunted me a bit. Mucked up my dreams for a stretch. Looking back now, it seems like kid stuff. You'd think it'd get me ready for what I saw in August, but nothing can prepare a person for something like that.

Once back from today's deathless workout, I crumpled onto my queen size bed and pulled my orange comforter over my sweaty body. A minute passed, then came a fist knocking on the door, gently. *Shave and a haircut. Two bits.* I said nothing, but Melanie opened the door anyway. My head was at the foot of the bed, watching her from a crack between the covers and the mattress. The hallway was lit behind her and my room was black. Mel was a shadowy silhouette, one wearing an awfully humdrum ensemble. Jeans and a T-shirt, all of which were purchased wherever moms do their shopping these days. That's probably where she purchased her new toxic aura, too. I don't know who Pete is, but for his sake, we need to figure out why losing one's husband means having to shelve your flamboyant wardrobe. Wearing vibrant hats and ethnic gauchos is in no way disrespectful to the dead. I breathed in the buttery popcorn aroma as it invaded. The normally delightful scent made me wanna puke. "Hey, Chicken," she said. "Made popcorn."

"Why would I want that, Mel?"

"I don't know," she said. "You didn't eat dinner, and I thought popcorn would be—"

"Leave it."

She set the popcorn bowl down and evacuated my room as the alarm clock on my dresser glowed with its green numbers. 7:59 pm. For some reason, I started chewing on the remote instead of turning on the television. You don't get out of my room much, Joey. That must suck scrotum, but worry not about never leaving this place. You're lucky. I wish I could be at ease all day, hidden below my blanket. I'd rather be the one everybody tells their secrets to than the person who goes out and accumulates secrets that need a place to go.

What are my secrets? Well, they're not secrets, exactly. Just shit I don't wanna talk about and specifics I don't wanna get into. Don't ask. I received you from a mildly creepy school counselor, not long ago. We're still becoming acquainted with one another. Some words can't yet be written. I'm the gray plunger next to the toilet in the bathroom. Lacking in color. Exposed. A bit naked. It's as if I'm being dunked throughout the day into a whole mess of shit and piss water.

I finally stopped slobbering on the remote and turned on the television. The wacky kids on TV were singing. One of them was trying to shave her head in the middle of class, but her peers forestalled her. And I hurtled to the bathroom. The red scissors were an easy find, situated in the top drawer. Promptly found them and slammed them on the bathroom counter. I clamored through every drawer, the exhaustive search for the electric razor fully commencing. My hands were Urkel level clumsy. It was buried in the bottom drawer. Hands clasping the razor, I stared at it— good, hard and for some time. Analyzed my face. Analyzed the crap out of it. Solemn, gaunt, features tremendously sharp, cheekbones were Ginsu knives. I have no appetite, not even for my morning Fruit Loops. A tear put up a good fight, attempting to escape my eyeball, but I went all Gandalf the Gray, saying, "You shall not pass." The tear conceded and my face was unmovable marble. With chaotic waves parted, I grabbed a fistful of hair from the right side. There was a little less than half the hair on my head in my hand. Secured it tight to my skull with an elastic band. Snip. Snap. Only shaking on the inside.

"Gotta pee," said my kid sister through the door.

"Not now."

She screamed my name on repeat and *The Catcher in the Rye* came to mind. It used to be my favorite book. The main character, Holden Caulfield, has some sort of beef with practically everyone. One of the only people he doesn't classify as 'phony' is his younger sister, Phoebe. I'm not like Holden in that respect. My sister, Willow, bugs the living crap out of me. Remember...she's eight. Children with only eight years under their belt have that effect on the heartless. I keep telling Willow about my plans to tie her to the other Willow for a night. The other Willow is the willow tree in my neighbor's backyard.

Willow believes everything I say as if it were the law. Never cries when trade threats are made. However, her eyes swell as reticence becomes her and her Elmer's glue aura beams all around her. One time, I checked on Willow after warning her, searching for emotional stability. Willow's door was ajar and she was on her knees praying. She's annoying, but she listens. Though, for some reason, she wouldn't heed my words tonight. Willow banged on the door, harder and harder and harder. I could feel her aura temporarily turning a muddy red. "Let me in!"

"Shut it, you hag child," I said, pulling out the elastic from my head's right side. A nub of hair remained. Stroked it. Soft. Comfortingly soft. The razor was plugged in and releasing its electrical roar. It made contact with my head as the knocking subsided and tufts of hair fell to my shoulders.

"What's that noise?" This time, it was Melanie's voice—a perturbed voice, indeed.

"Buzz off," I shouted, grin coming about. My pun was too much for me. Then the door swung open, ricocheting off the wall behind me, giving my hindquarters a good smack.

"What're you doing?" Melanie said. I looked at my reflection. Looked at my dead face. The electric razor. *What the hell am I doing?* I released the razor from my rigid grip. It came close to falling in the sink before doing a noisy jig on the counter. My fingers seized the plug and plucked it free. Because my unshaven side had been facing her, Melanie hadn't yet seen the number I did on my hair.

I rotated and our eyes met briefly as her bottom lip fell. Willow was staggered behind Melanie, hands glued to her mouth. Willow is a Minnie Mel—tall, gangly for her age, dark curls. Perfect picture of mother and daughter, shocked and shaken. Willow asked if I was okay and I flashed a mild smile, then gave a rapid explanation about how shaving half your hair is all the rage. Threw the word 'trendy' in for good measure. Melanie nodded with an overwhelmed expression on her face, like 'trendy' was the magic word. She mentioned decorating for an edgy client, who wore the same hairstyle. Mel said, "Leave it. Stay home tomorrow. I'll make an appointment."

"Kay," I muttered, ambling toward my poorly lit bedroom. Sitting on my bed, I listened to the house become still. My eyes fixated on the popcorn bowl. The room was dark, but I could make out the bowl's shape due to the hallway light penetrating my bedroom. After countless minutes, I rose, legs carrying me to the popcorn bowl. I chucked it at the wall.

"What the what?" said River through the wall. I don't know if I've mentioned it, but he's moved home. River is back, with all his LPs, his hookah, his blow-up doll that I hope is for decorative purposes, and his aura that I don't feel like heavily describing. It's blue. It's soft blue and too much like my dad's. So, Riv is home. He's twenty-two and says that college debt is a debilitating affliction. However, we all know he'd still be living on his own, had a deplorable incident not developed over the summer.

And so River sleeps most of his free time away in the next room, while I always stay awake the majority of the night in my own. I think River secretly hopes to enter a coma and wake up when life sucks less for us Dwyers. Tonight, my antics fully rattled him into a conscious state. "Willy already woke me once," he said. "Screaming about pissing. I get back to sleep only to hear more of this shit." When River enters crotchety old man mode, his aura fights to remain calm blue, but forever fails to do so. It was gray in this moment, and the same shade as the one constantly surrounding Mr. McAdams. River said, "Seriously, Rosie. What now?"

"Fell," I said. "On the wall. Night."

And don't you dare call her Willy. Only he did that.

"Go to bed, weirdo." River's voice was muffled, a pillow surely over his head. His transformation continues to confound me. He's no longer himself. No time for cartoons—not even the funnies section of the newspaper. Cut all his shaggy hair off, like I mentioned in an earlier entry. Shaved his beard. Grungy to clean cut. He even put Belinda the Blow-Up Doll in his closet instead of proudly on display where she belongs.

My brother also started doing a workout program called Insanity, and his flab is rapidly vanishing. No longer plays War Sticks with his friends at the park. War Sticks is a game where the players dress in medieval ware and hit each other with giant rods. No. It's not Live Action Role Play, Joey. This is a contact sport, where people lose teeth. Only bad asses allowed. But River gave it up. Wakes up at six am daily and eats oatmeal, the planet's blandest food. That, and couscous, which has become River's favorite dinner meal. He's waved microwaved pizza rolls goodbye and introduced himself to couscous. It's the food so nice, they named it twice, but it's no kinder to one's taste buds than pizza rolls. It's not.

But I'm sure he's there, deep down. Last time I checked, his fart-in-a-jar collection is still stashed in his closet. And I've been tallying his chuckles on this notebook's inside cover. He laughs freely at least once every three days. River inherited most of my dad's appearance, but his display of elation is all Melanie's.

Still, it's disheartening to see this total metamorphosis, and all to get a "quality" job. In other words, he's not currently making much as the sensei of the gas station up on Park. Says that job is the most temporary thing of his life. For the first time ever, he wants to make something of himself. My dad isn't around anymore to say, "Chill, son. Don't rush. It isn't a race. You do you." That's how Dad was. No pressure. Like I've said before, I won the parental jackpot. Until August happened. We never worried about the future because he never did. It was vastly important to him that we not sweat events that may or may not happen, which makes the last thing he ever wrote so confusing.

That brain hemorrhage is coming again.

Mel's not exactly forcing River to try harder, but since the death, her subtle pushes for him to get a better job have become more persistent. It mostly happens at the dinner table. *"Hey, Riv, I have this friend that's hiring for insert yawn of a job here. It's not exactly what you're looking for, but—"*

My parents used to encourage my siblings and me to be whatever we dreamt up. Willow is adamant she will be a CEO. I want to be a writer, so we already know something isn't right with my wiring. It's unbelievable, but River's dream career is even more laughable. When he was five, he and my dad went on a fishing trip. Dad asked him what he wanted to be someday, and he said, "Plato."

My dad broke into laughter. "Dude, you're five. Do you even know who that is?"

"You talk about him lots."

My dad smiled and broke it to River that he couldn't be Plato entirely, because Plato already did that. River started pouting, so my dad smirked and said, "Hey, kid, smile. Can't be Plato, but you can be River and a philosopher."

River grinned and shouted, "Gonna be a falafel!"

By age ten, he was correctly pronouncing the name of his future occupation and reading all the greats and probably understanding little of their texts. When he was fifteen, he landed his first girlfriend by quoting

Johann Wolfgang von Goethe. Can you imagine? Floppy-haired River stroking his lab partner's arm while whispering in her ear, "Hey, beautiful, did you know we don't have to visit a madhouse to find disordered minds? Our planet is the mental institution of the universe." The way River tells the story, his love interest blushed before he cinched the deal by saying, "Wanna come over to watch Ace Ventura?"

I'd be repulsed if some guy did that to me, but apparently it worked for her.

He is Socrates Jr., alright. When he finally turned eighteen, he got a tattoo to prove it. It's a Nietzsche quote that spreads across both ass cheeks and says, "When you look into an abyss, the abyss also looks into you."

My dad gave him a high five after he mooned the family during dinner.

What did River expect to find with a philosophy degree, anyway? If you're going to pick a major that's difficult to market, at least get decent grades. Dumbass. Sensitive dumbass. And if you've been a sensitive dumbass your whole life, you should probably stick to it because that's what your loved ones have finally gotten used to. It seems changing drastically sends the cosmos into a frenzy.

I'm not like Holden Caulfield when it comes to my sister, but the way he feels about his brother is all me. Holden's brother stopped writing short stories and started working in the movie industry. Holden thus saw his brother as a whore. River cut his hair and quit cartoons cold turkey and stopped quoting philosophers incessantly. Works out and has the sleep schedule of a well-adjusted adult or toddler. He gets off on going to bed early. Whores, whores, whores. This world is filled with them, and you'd be surprised by how many are menfolk.

The blackness of my bedroom had my open eyes in its clutches for fifteen minutes. When I had enough of my mind, I climbed out of bed and went downstairs. Everybody was asleep. Nobody heard me digging for a flashlight. Once outdoors, my brain surrendered control to my limbs. Soon I was heading toward the far corner of my backyard, where the compost bin is located.

My hands dug into the compost and my back inched down the

fence until my behind was banded to the ground. In my lap was a heap of dirt, coffee grounds, apple cores, orange and banana peels, green grass clippings, Tofu, egg shells, tea bags, sawdust, dryer lint, possibly Mr. Bojangles' poo, God knows what else. As my hands pressed the mess into my scalp, it became clear my actions were conclusively idiotic. Compost is for plant growth, not hair growth. However, I'd seen nothing but a sad clown reflected back earlier, and nobody likes a sad clown. My desperation to fix my folly was asphyxiating me. As I fondled the substance into my head's bare side, I softly sang, "I Dreamed a Dream" from *Les Miserables*. I imagine you don't know the jam, as I'm not sure journals can hear or communicate. That's why people feel so comfortable exposing themselves to their notebooks. Ink sinks in, leading diary keepers to believe their secrets have been heard, but there's no way of knowing if a journal is deaf. This is because, if one thing is certain, all journals are mute.

In *Harry Potter and the Chamber of Secrets*, Tom Riddle wrote back to Harry and Ginny through the Horcrux journal. That shit doesn't happen in real life. If you can write back, Joey, please refrain. Would love to hear from you, but a reply would make me poop myself. Spoiled undergarments are beside the point. What I'm trying to say is that I sang into the darkness that beset me. Off key, truly. An abstract singer. Screw any eavesdropping neighbor who doesn't understand my art. I was tearing up, you know, but Joey, sometimes you have to quietly sing songs from *Les Miserables* in the darkened outdoors. By yourself, pajama clad, no matter how off key, until you're crying and impervious. You must.

By the time I was inside, the tears were cleared. I reverted back to 'stare into the blackness' mode. My eyes fixated on the glowing green numbers of my alarm clock. It was now 12:11 pm. Not late, but I knew sleep and I wouldn't be fraternizing soon. That's why I'm still writing. 2:22 am. Starting to feel drowsy. Only a bit.

October 4, 2012

Hey, Joey Journal,

The great philosopher River Dwyer is full of fun facts about the greatest minds our world has seen. *Did you know Honoré De Balzac drank fifty cups of Joe a day? Did you know Descartes thought apes and monkeys could speak, but didn't out of fear of being made into servants? Did you know Sigmund Freud had an irrational fear of the number sixty-two?*

Joey, did you know it's been sixty-two days since he passed? Did you know I have a fear that I'll never wake up again without the knowledge of how many days it's been? Did you know that this fear is causing me a brand of unrest I'm incapable of describing?

Instead, I'll detail a simpler unrest. Today's bout of anxiety was mostly caused by a woman who enjoys drinking noxious amounts of energy drinks and singing show tunes under her breath. Her other hobbies include wearing her black box braids in side buns and smiling all the time. This creature is my creative writing teacher, Bette Perkins. She's a 'young, cool teacher' who prefers being called by first name. Short, plump, a bubbly bubble that's about to pop any second, there's only one Bette Perkins.

A Bette Midler CD played while Baby Bette high-kicked out of the womb, so the name seemed appropriate. We're a month into school and I have her class eighth hour. I normally don't mind her. Bette isn't currently in my good graces because she cast an unprovoked punishment upon me. At the top of today's class, there was a new seating chart on the board. My picture was next to Logan Field's picture, and so I plopped a squat at my new front row desk.

Logan and I have been seated next to each other multiple times since our first encounter. We've grown to be above cornrow tying and Hostess snack weaponry. We have the maturity to ignore each other and avoid eye contact. That's what we did today as Bette began class with a random fun fact. The class was too checked-out to react, so she carried on. "Let's move on to my latest creation—Imagination Collaborations. You've written two short stories and here comes feedback. You're paired up based on strengths, weaknesses, common interests. Partners are as follows. Günter, you'll be with…"

Günter Kappel is our German foreign exchange student. He's obese and has a grizzly beard. I wanna be his partner. Never have I had an opportunity to befriend a foreign exchange student. Bette paused, squinting at her clipboard. "Can't read my handwriting," she said. "Oh! Okay, Günter, you'll be with…."

Please say Rosie.

"Anastasia."

Bette, anyone but Anastasia. Anastasia Moretti-Slocumb called me "Whore Face" throughout middle school and freshman year. After that, she dismissed me altogether, making me a poor nameless slob. Anastasia has two names the one her parents gave her and the one her classmates call her behind her back. That name is "Mouthful." We call her this for many reasons. First, her name is a mouthful. Second, she never shuts up. Third, she's a hopeless gossip. Finally, we've come to the fourth and sauciest reason. Let's find the classiest way to say this. Guys at school say Anastasia Moretti-Slocumb always has a mouthful of love potion. You know, man yogurt? C'mon! Surely you've heard of baby gravy. I suspect my drift has been caught.

If we had anything in common when I first met her in middle school, it was our determination to remain sweat-free during gym class. Seventh grade gym class. You remember, don't you? Course not, Joey. You're a journal. Your physical activities are limited to opening and closing. Because you've never experienced the perils I'm alluding to, here's a synopsis. Sit ups, pacer tests, dodgeballs slamming into faces.

Picture hyperactive boys with stinky pits and sagging clothes. Girls with shorts rolled up four times and large shirts cinched tightly, below the navel. Can't say I was in Mouthful's gaggle of bitch-faced Chiquita bananas, but I'd cower a few feet from them during dodgeball games as the boys manned the front lines of the game. Ahh, dodgeball. The great equalizer.

As for the boys, they always savagely pelted each other with balls, occasionally hitting each other in the balls. I witnessed many a male child enter the fetal position back in the day. Still, it was the girls who were hiding in the back. And so that fateful dodgeball game began in the same way as every other. We had a while until our gym teacher would mandate that we ladies get in the game. "You know Jacob Fagg?" Mouthful asked her group.

I overheard this, tapped her shoulder and said, "Jacques. Jacques Blain, He's a kindred soul."

She discounted my response in favor of speaking more. "The Faggot family is in Florida for two weeks. Kevin is getting people together to trash his house."

"What do you mean by 'trash'?"

Mouthful's answer was cavalier. "Who are you even?"

"Rosie Dwyer, if you must know."

She said, "Well, Rosie Dwyer, if you must know, we're toilet papering, egging, and tagging the words 'Jacob is a faggot' all over their huge front lawn. The usual."

I said, "I wanna rip off your trash smile and make you eat it. That's only the 'usual' for psychos."

"What'd you call me?"

"Psycho."

"Well, you're a whore face. And a faggot lover." My eyes went in circles as I walked away until Mouthful called my name. I turned and she said it again. "Whore-faced faggot lover!" As the little slut completed her slur, a small dodgeball flew toward me. Without peeling my eyes away from her, my arm shot out. Caught it one-handed. It was the single most badass moment of my life. A tense second passed, then I tackled Mouthful, repeatedly whipping her face with the rubber ball, counting aloud the times it made facial contact. Nine times. Would've gone for ten, but our burly gym teacher lumbered over and pulled me off before I could wale on her an even number of times. He yanked me to the school office. That principal loved me. No suspension. Didn't even call my parents. I charmed my way into getting off with a warning, in typical Rosie Dwyer fashion.

I awoke at 6:00 am on Saturday morning to Melanie's voice screaming for my father to wake up. My pillow smothered my head. River sprinted in and I said, "Weekend, Riv."

"There's been a vandal."

"Your dumb friends."

He said, "You're a 'faggot-loving whore-face'?"

I cascaded down the stairs, nearly bit it on the welcome mat, and in no time, my body was outside. There it was. Toilet papering, egging, the words, 'Rosie is a faggot-loving whore-face,' were spray painted across the lawn. The usual. When I turned, the spray painted words, "Die Rosie Dwyer," clung to my white paneled house. My parents interrogated me to find out who did it. They said, "Who would want to do this, Rosie?" Over and over and over again. Played dumb. I ain't no rat. They almost made it a police matter. I assured my dad that my punishment would be more devastating than the cop's. He patted my head and said, "Atta kid."

Got my revenge the next week of school while in math class. During silent study time, Mouthful asked to go to the bathroom. While she was gone, I stealthily spooned mayonnaise onto her seat, which was next to mine. When she got back, Mouthful sat in it. She immediately stood up and said, "What the hell?"

One of the most immature kids in school was seated behind her. He laughed heartily. "Yo, Anastasia, is that jizz? Did ya get it up the butt?"

Laughter roared as she ran out of the room.

Although the score is now even, I'm still jealous that she and Günter got paired up. And it still isn't the worst part of today's class. Mouthful was all Günter's. Don't have to deal with her, but I have to deal with someone else. "Logan, you're with Rosie," Bette said.

We looked at each other out of the corner of our eyes. Of course I don't abhor Logan Fields for merely tying my hair to playground equipment. He's sleazy. That's all. I know some would say the same about Eliot, but at least that idiot is open about the openness of his legs. Logan plays dumb when he's called on his shit. All month long, it's been common knowledge that he's been simultaneously dating Mouthful, Ashley and Emma. He was never official with any of them, but the girls verbally sparred during Drawing and Painting earlier today. Logan left for the bathroom during the altercation, passing the girls as they nearly came to physical blows in the hallway outside the classroom. He moseyed back to class ten minutes later when everything died down. Logan was quiet as his pen made contact with his sketchbook, acting like nothing happened.

He parades about as if he's not made of excrement. Girls feel loved when he's around. Even hefty ole' Emily Hayes is embraced when she opens her arms to Logan Fields. Emily Hayes has a quarter-sized mole on her face. Guys never get within spitting distance. A medieval rat, through high fives and come-ons, a plague is spread, a love plague. For every uninfected, liberated chick, there are a thousand dicks like Logan. The statistic, although unproven by a formal survey, is frightening to the core.

Logan has even led guys astray by unintentionally sending vibes. According to Jacques, Logan once embraced him during home economics. My best friend claims to be in the throes of passion, while I ignore Logan like my fat cells neglecting my chest in favor of clinging to other body parts. Unfortunately, this stupid 'Imagination Collaboration' invention is now happening.

"Time for a 'get-to-know-each-other' activity," Bette said, navigating the rows, passing out a worksheet. I informed her that we're seniors, and that we know each other too well. Little Miss Sunshine smiled, unbothered. "Yep, but to collaborate, you'll have to know each other better."

"Bette—"

"Go with it," she said, eyes like lasers... beaming and whatnot. "Explore your partner's true character. Characters drive the best stories, not just plot." Bette sat in her bright yellow swivel chair that matched her aura perfectly, opened an energy drink, and started grading papers.

The classroom filled with chattering noises. Every mouth was moving, aside from the ones belonging to Logan and me. I could especially hear Mouthful's mouth moving as it loudly gushed in the exceptional presence of Günter. That mouth was supposed to be my mouth. My eyes were on Bette's motivational poster. She's a big fan of motivation. Silly seconds ticked by until Logan spoke slowly and softly. He's always been soft-spoken. The slow part was because he was nervous or simple. You pick. He said. "Why are you here?"

"Huh?"

"The first question."

"Sorry. Forgot," I said. Logan asked for my answer again, and I wiggled my eyebrow upward. "Why are you in this class?" he said once more. Told him I didn't know, shifting my eyes to my lap, analyzing the lacey dress. Red, moderately short, only one sleeve. The concept of a one-sleeve dress irks me. It made me feel like my new hair makes my head feel unevenly warm. "Go first, Logan. My brain is farting."

"Um, we had to take Creative Writing or College Composition. Heard College Comp. has a cool teacher, but more assignments. So, um, here I am." I wrote his answer down, word for word. Ums and all. Logan said, "You?"

We made brief eye contact. His eyes were relaxed, almost sleepy looking. "Same," I hastily said, doodling a picture of SpongeBob SquarePants in my worksheet's top margin. "I also wanna be a writer."

"Really?"

I scowled. "What's so surprising? Didn't peg me as being literate?"

"No, Rosie, I didn't," Logan said, famous smile present. The cocky cocked sideways smile of cocky cocks everywhere. I instructed him to get rid of it or I'd slap it off. He pretended like he was wiping his grin off his face and threw his imaginary balled up smile toward the window. Logan whipped his head back in my direction, face placid. Soon his lopsided smile reemerged. "Sorry, Rosie. Tried, but my mouth has its own mind."

"I won't fall victim to your charms," I said stoically.

Slightly taken aback, he returned his eyes to his paper as the next question was vocalized. "Where do you see yourself in ten years?"

"Stop," I said.

"Why?"

"The questions are routine." Bewildered silence encapsulated the boy as I went on a calm rampage. "Why don't you tell me where I'll be in ten years? Hell if I know, man. This world is changing fast. Robots and computers are gaining power. I prophesize that they'll one day take over all the posts belonging to the world's writers, not to mention every other career field. I'll be shit outta luck."

He gently ripped the top edge of his packet, giving it a fringe effect while saying, "Creativity can't be computerized."

"Doesn't matter," I spewed. "Still don't know where I'll be. Not now, not ten years from now, or ten years after that. And I don't like this question."

He apologized, eyes rolling. "Gotta ask them."

"Don't like it."

"Rosie, answer the freaking question like a freaking normal person," he said, grinning and exasperated. I had a major 'I'm-about-to-cry-bitch-ass-tears' expression going on. He relaxed, falling into his seat. "No clue where you'll be either."

"I know where you'll be," I said.

Logan was still, vulnerability washing over him. In my mind, he was abruptly sitting across from me at lunch with Twinkie cream smashed into his youthful face. The images were so similar, except his current face was now harder and completely vacant of creamy traces. Although Logan is older, his youthful energy remains prevalent. Concurrently, I could sense his quietly existing anxiety, a component of his aura that contrasted a great deal with his out-of-season Christmas sweater. His persistent silence ended and he smiled while leaning in. "Where will I be?"

"Stripping."

After a guffaw, Logan said, "Not a man-slut."

I sighed. "Whatever you need to tell yourself to get through the night."

Our vocal tones were muted and uncomfortable. The conversation turned into a game, one that we were both subtly attempting to win. It went on in this fashion for the class' duration. At the period's end, Bette was suddenly before us. As students packed up inventories, she stood on her stool. "Announcement time," she said, voice rich with irritation. Our classmates continued to chit n' chat. "Yep, you're busy packing up, but let's not forget the assignments." The sounds of conversation kept up the good fight. Bette said, "I'm gonna sing an annoying song till you all shut up and sit your asses down."

Quiet didn't come, so Bette resorted to wildly shaking her arms above her head while singing some obscure showtune. Once we were seated and silent, Bette was deeply, spiritually and physically invested in the song, and in no way able to stop. She belted the words like singing was her real job. "Earth to Miss Perkins," Mouthful said, smiling.

Bette snapped out of it and lowered herself. Once her boots were on the floor, she brushed lint off her purple frock. "Thanks for quieting down." Walking around the room, passing papers out, she continued speaking. "One out-of-class assignment this week. Read your partner's first short story and the one they wrote about summer. Sink your teeth in. We learn the most about our craft from those learning alongside us. The peer review packet is due Monday."

When the speech ended, Bette's behind was adhered to her swivel chair. She said one more sentence, that sentence being, "Bell's about to ring." It did, and Bette grinned, experiencing the relief teachers feel when everyone shuffles out of the day's final class. Everyone was gone, aside from Logan and me.

I said, "This isn't going to work," as Logan synchronously said, "We need to switch partners." Then we both said, "What?"

"What's the *problemo, muchachos*?" Bette asked, speedily packing up. Before I could speak, she said, "Gotcha, Rosie. You're wondering if I noticed you didn't hand in the summer story. I did. Send it to him by Wednesday night and you're in the clear."

"No," I said. "This partnership is a toxic arrangement and we motion it be absolved at once." I shot Logan a frantic look and asked him if he agreed. He nodded as panic pulsed in my veins. Our first prompt asked us what our worst or best first day of school was, and to describe it.

The day this was assigned, I slipped on a Twinkie and called Logan 'devil spawn' to his face. The fifth grade was on my mind. As a result, I wrote about Logan. Didn't like him, but I also didn't want him to read "Cornrow Captivity" and have reason to sue me for defamation of character. I wouldn't have written about him, had I known he was going to read it. My past English teachers let us pick our peer editors.

"C'mon," she said, smile sympathetic. After fastening her laces, Bette slung her bag over her shoulder. "Rosie, Logan, the partnership plan is a fragile balance."

"Miss Perkins," Logan politely began.

"Call me Bette."

"Bette, I can't be with Rosie. Just can't."

She said, "Not gonna tell ya to trust me. Instead, I'll tell a quick story. I used to be known as Heavy Betty. I'm still heavy, but only half as heavy. My physical trainer, Bernardo, never tells me to trust him. He repeats the words, 'Trust the process.' Now, look at me. I'm in tiptop shape. Sorta."

"What does that mean?" I asked.

"I'll never say 'trust me'," Bette said. "Trust the process, pass the class. *Capisce*, kiddos?"

I gave assent with a slight head jerk while Logan rubbed his hand through his short waves. His hair has somehow changed since age ten, no longer a shaggy orange mess. It turned dark auburn over the years— nearly brown. It was foliage hair, changing like the leaves do. Never noticed until now. He finally nodded and Bette sprang toward the door. "I teach Zumba at church on Thursdays. I'm late," she said, locking the door. "When you leave, kill the lights and shut the door. It'll lock. *Ciao*." Once out of sight, the crazy lady sang in a falsetto, "Trust the process."

Bette was gone, but Logan wasn't. "Sorry," I said.

"Why?" he asked, all friendly. "Sorry is a shitty word."

"If you're the homework type, you'll find out."

With that, I strode toward the door. He told me to wait and I slowly rotated to face him. "Don't read into it," he said, leisurely unwrapping a piece of gum, smile cocked sideways. However, it wasn't cocked sideways with conviction. It was cowardly and contrite. I walked out the door as Logan chewed his gum, which must have been four separate pieces wadded up just to annoy people.

October 4, 2016

Hey, Joey Journal,

Home from school. Read Logan's story. Gonzo journalist Hunter S. Thompson is said to have retyped the works of his favorite authors when he was young, so he could know how it felt to write great fiction. I plan to rewrite the writing of Logan Fields, so I may know how it feels to be a complete tool.

First Day
by Logan Fields

My best first day of school was the first day of the fifth grade. It was also the worst. Saw a girl next to the playground that morning. She was cute, but not like other girls. 'Interesting' is a good word for it. The girl was unique despite her gray uniform. Probably the blonde cornrows. Seven years have passed and she still doesn't give a rat's ass.

The boys stopped when they saw her. Brad said she just moved in near his house and Trent called her a weirdo. They laughed, and so did I, but deep down, I didn't like it. Brad suggested we tie her 'stupid hair' to the monkey bars she leaned on. David always had to throw in his two cents, so he pointed at me and said, "Him." The dick knew I never say no to dares. I dive in, head first. This was different, though. I said, "I don't know, guys."

They started chanting the word "pussy." That's hard for a young dude. I caved and approached the girl, staying close to the fence behind her, walking Native American style so she wouldn't hear me. My brother taught me how to do that when I was real little. While walking, I rationalized my actions, telling myself she might think it was funny. I told myself she might like funny guys. But I wasn't funny. Just an ass hat. Sorry if my language is inappropriate for a school essay, but you said in class we could swear if we needed to. Ass hat. That was me. Maybe that's still me.

Somehow, the closer I got, the weirder she became. She reminded me of a baby duck. Sounds weird, but you'd understand if you saw her. Gawky limbs, a real scrawny thing, mouth gigantic compared to the rest of her. She has a duck mouth. Scrunched up lips, sorta smiling, sorta scowling. Thinking hard, it seemed. Oh, and bush baby eyes. Bush babies have big, scary, intense eyes. Eyes like hers. None of this sounds like a compliment, but I think it might be.

I grew stupider with each quiet step until my brain was on autopilot. Soon her hair was tied, tighter than I wanted. And it had bubblegum in it. That happened spontaneously. My mouth hung down and my body froze when I realized what I did. When the bell rang, she took a breath and said something to herself. "Confidence is key, kid. Confidence is key."

I'll never forget that. Then I jumped in front of her and mocked her mantra. Said, "Welcome to St. Aggie's, kid. Welcome to St. Aggie's."

Ms. Smith didn't see me race in before the last bell. I was at my desk a minute before she even looked up from hers. She did the "Welcome back" speech every teacher does on the first day. While she spoke, Trent turned and whispered, "You do it?"

I nodded like a little bastard. In the blink of an eye, everyone was at the window, laughing at the girl as she struggled with her hair. Before I could blink once more, I was watching Ms. Smith from the window as she ran to the girl. Soon, other people pushed their way to the window. Couldn't see a thing, but heard my classmates saying absolute crap. "She's cutting her hair," the kids shouted. Some pricks high-fived me. I high-fived back.

She walked into the room, hair falling below her chin instead of down her back. That's a lot of hair to lose, especially when the person's not expecting a haircut. She seemed unfazed as she smiled and told the class it was a favor because she needed a haircut. The girl got vengeance, though. I don't blame her. She told me she thought I was cute, tricked me into becoming her "boyfriend" and pulled the rug out from under me by smashing a Twinkie into my eye. All anybody has to know is I still have more respect for her than I have for any other girl in this town. It's something about her strangeness. It's intimidating and demands respect.

The first day of the fifth grade was wild. I destroyed someone's hair, was led on, and got cream filling in my eye. However, I remember that first day. The rest have escaped my memory.

October 5, 2012

Hey, Joey Journal,

I'm barely into day sixty-three. It's three in the morning. Still haven't done most of my homework, all because of Logan's goddamn story, which I read hours ago now. Sleep hasn't been in the cards for this evening. I keep getting out of bed to turn my light on and off and on again. Can't decide whether being an insomniac is better when I'm in the pitch dark or the stark light. I reread that nightmare twenty-five times. I counted. My restlessness isn't because of the revelation that Logan might actually have a redeemable side. I'm not awake because my faith in humanity has been restored by reading somebody else's perspective on a shared event. I don't care about my strange cuteness, or his guilt, or the respect he has for me. I'm livid, and not about his entire essay. Pathetically, I'm being haunted by the silliest detail. Why did Logan have to compare me to a bush baby? That's the problem. Can't stop looking at the front-facing mirror on my phone. I've never noticed how scary my eyes are, and I can never forget the observation. At school tomorrow, I mean today, I'll be an extremely squinty person. And it's Logan's fault. Solely his doing. I'm laughing. Okay. I'm now giggling and writing and psychotic. I need to laugh into my pillow. Until I fall asleep.

October 5, 2012

Hey, Joey Journal,

And now I'm almost done with day sixty-three. I will write yet another rough draft for creative writing inside you because I'm too lazy to look for my backpack and the correct notebook it contains. My body is in bed, and it will stay that way if I can help it. We were instructed by our teacher to write on a broad subject, summer.

What I Won't Write About

I'd like to start by listing the things I won't write about, at least when it comes to the subject of summer. I won't write about the nasty family friend who shoved an ice cream cone in my face when I was eight. I won't write about my cousin sliding an icy pop down the back of my one-piece swimsuit when I was ten. I won't write about my brother emptying my grandparents' freezer when I was five, tricking me into climbing inside it, then sitting on top of it for a minute. And I'm definitely not writing about spilling a slushie on the seat of my dad's rental car when we went to up north two summers ago.

Won't write about anything cold. Chilliness during times when life should be warm is all I'm experiencing lately, and I don't want to think about unwanted low temperatures. Those were the moments of summer I came to know well, and they only deserve one or two sentences each. What I'm going to write about is the summer that sweltered and sweated and lived in sweet tea before I happened across permanent coolness. It's now the only summer that matters. In the same way I don't want to talk about the icy mayhem of my youth, I'm also not ready to write down the specifics of what happened. I can't cough up any sentences on the chilling event that came at the end of the summer in question.

However, I can tell you what happened before, and with full force. But before I do so, we need to address something. I don't know how many people will one day read this class assignment. I assume a great many will study my early works long after I'm gone. For now, I know of two definite people. Hi, Logan. Hi, Bette. You'll surely read this as a result of the class we all belong to. At this point, Logan, I don't give two shits about our preteen feuding or the fact that you think I look like a goddamn duck/bush baby mutant. You get to experience my messed up life, and not because you did anything to deserve the privileged information that is to come. You may wonder why I don't leave out all personal details. Well, I'm not getting familiar because I trust you. I'm giving these details because consistent candor is my prerogative. I cannot stress enough that it has nothing to do with you or the level of trust I have toward you. You're smart enough to realize Bette simply read our first stories and thought, *Well, looky here. These cutie patooties wrote about the same gosh darn day. Let me put my Noah costume on, pair these adolescents up, and get them on my ark straight away. Serendipity.*

More like *serendipshitty.* Again...Bette, hello.

Look, Logan, she's probably already planning our wedding. In Bette's world, she's singing show tune standards at the ceremony and is my maid of honor. We must resist her fantasy until we're blue in the cheeks. This is business, boy. Read this example of what last summer was like. Try to not get in the way.

The third official day of this past summer, my best friend Jacques and I made plans to hang out after his early morning text woke me up. He's a morning person to gross extremes. I got gussied up, remembering that Eliot and I agreed this was the day the two of us would get in touch. Crop top and high waisted shorts, because there's no better way to showcase my complete lack of a figure. Jacques shot me another impatient text. There was no reason I needed to hurry up other than the fact that he knows telling me to do so makes me want to yank all my teeth out.

I blitzed through applying makeup. Makeup is something I normally don't do. Simply knew it was likely I'd see Eliot at some point. When I went downstairs to eat my morning cereal, I walked in on my sister sitting on the counter and I jumped in the air. Then I asked if she was aware that it was 7:30 am. Her smile stretched eagerly and she said, "Couldn't sleep. Keep thinking I got school. Heard ya on the phone with Jock. Can I come?"

Her inability to pronounce his name used to be adorable, but now I think she's milking it. Speaking of milk, as the skim milk met the colorful cereal, I admonished Willow for spying on me and denied her request. Willow continued to beg and even threw herself on the floor at my feet. I couldn't cave, though. 'Jock' had a word of the week and that word was 'Pussy'. *Pussy this, pussy that.* Even if I told him to censor himself, there'd still be a slip. I told the girl she'd have to cover her ears the whole time. "Don't mind," Willow said, spinning on her tummy.

"Willow, you'll still hear stuff. Want me to cut off your ears?"

She dutifully slapped her hands to her head and ran back upstairs to her lair. Jacques sent me another text, warning me to hurry, so I slurped up the remaining cereal and the tasty tinted milk the food floated in. Then I glided on my bike to Fagg Family Farm. Jacques couldn't pick me up because he wasn't able to drive at the time. Unlike my situation, he wasn't licenceless out of fear. He's distractible and failed his driver's test five times. Jacques finally passed it at the end of summer, a week after what happened with my family. Maybe that explains the radio silence. He's too occupied with driving matters to be a proper friend.

When I reached their winding driveway, I dismounted my bike and let it lay haphazard on the asphalt. No cars were parked, indicating that Jacques was home alone. When my fist danced melodically on his family's rustic door, nobody greeted me. My intuition led me right to him from there, body striding quite a stretch, through dewy grass and toward the stables. My sandals invited wetness to fully meet the soles of my feet. Soon I heard singing, as Jacques was riding his horse and rounding the corner at me. The big guy's name is Cary Grant. Jacques isn't as amazing at singing as he is at dancing, but he's working on it. He even meets with a vocal coach. Jacques was off-key, but his voice still rang out the opening song from Oklahoma.

Oklahoma is in his top ten favorite musicals. It's the farm boy in him. I rolled my eyes. "Jacques, you've never been more gay."

Jacques hopped off Cary and said, "Bull. I was Cher two and a half Halloweens in a row."

Last year, he was Cher the majority of his party, but changed into Lady Gaga gear to mix things up. "C'mon, Cary Grant," Jacques said while leading the horse and me into the stables. He gave Cary a smack on the rear, so I did the same to Jacques. He flinched dramatically. "Why?"

"You did it to Cary Grant."

"He's a horse."

My eyes bulged. "Wait…you're not a horse?" Jacques wasn't amused. I said, "This explains so much."

Soon, we were in the stable. Jacques got Cary situated and took to caring for The Other Rosie. Gave her carrots and everything. The Other Rosie was an elderly donkey that once was named Beatrice. She didn't respond much to her former name. A bit after Jacques first encountered me, he decided to try calling her by my name, seeing as I was the "biggest ass he ever met." Beatrice acclimated to 'Rosie', and so that became her name.

During the time in which this story takes place, we couldn't ride The Other Rosie, given the fact that we were full grown humans and she was as brittle as the bristles of the brush he used on her. As I stood there, Jacques kept his loving focus on her every second. He adored her. The Other Rosie became his world when she was around. Finally, it came time to interrupt the tender scene. I asked him where he wanted to venture. When he didn't answer promptly, I kept speaking. "Wanna wander?"

"Aimlessly?"

I nodded.

"Have to change into socially acceptable clothes, but sure thing." Jacques arrived at a quality quitting point and I blew The Other Rosie a kiss. Then we closed up shop and advanced down his sprawling lawn. That was the last time I saw The Other Rosie. She died in her sleep two days later. Last summer was her last summer.

I wish that was the most dreadful happening of those three months, but as I established at the start of this hot mess, it wasn't. You know. Both of you know. You have to know. Everybody knows. You're not everybody, but you're Logan and Bette. The people reading this are comprised of you, and maybe I'd continue on with that shitty tangent about what happened as if you weren't Logan and some teacher I hardly know, but since you're somebodies I'm unsure of *and* I feel a brain hemorrhage coming on, I'm going back to Jacques in 3...2...1...

When you and your best friend are without licenses past the age of sixteen, two phenomena occur. First, you'll exceed the amount of steps your body needs to achieve in a day by frightening sums. Second, at least one of the friends will complain incessantly about having to walk everywhere.

That friend was Jacques, as I secretly felt that journeying in this fashion made our time together more adventurous and drawn-out. On the day I'm writing about, Jacques was moaning about it more than usual. He flat out refused to ride bikes since he still had ass cramps from our last ride. That sounded dirtier than I intended. Anyway, I walked mine as we meandered and he griped. After annoyance finally got the best of me, I unleashed my grip on the bike and bulldozed him to the lush green lawn we were walking by. I attempted to lunge away, but he latched onto my leg like a screeching, blue-assed baboon and hauled me to the grass to join him. My body hurled itself onto him and we entered wrestling mode. When he bit me, I screamed and said, "Stop it. I'm a girl!"

"And I'm a gay man. This is a hate crime." I pinned his face into the grass and straddled his back. He yelped a whole slew of sentences, but the only one I understood was, "Off. Now. I'm wearing white."

At that moment, I felt a downpour of cold water. Icy cold. I know I said I wouldn't talk about coldness in this story, but I guess I lied. During this sprinkling, I smiled because I thought it was raining while the sun shined. My dad spent time in Liberia during his time as a volunteer for Clowns Without Borders and he brought home a saying that described the sun being out during rain. "Too bad your face is in grass and you can't see this," I whispered into Jacques' ear. "The Devil is fighting with his wife over a chicken bone."

Alas, it wasn't Mother Nature being sweet. It was you, Logan Fields, proudly poised on the greenest grass, menacing hands clutching a hose. You smiled that stupid smile of yours and said, "Hey, you kids. Get off my lawn."

Corny as shit.

Jacques, who has always been friendly with you, charged toward your wiry figure and hugged you most outlandishly. He jumped on you and wrapped his legs around your torso. You let him do this and didn't call him names and sort of bounced him about as if he were a big baby. You seemed so comfortable with yourself. And I admired that about you. Wow, those are kind words. Never thought I'd say kind words to you, Logan. Maybe I'm in a sentimental place. Maybe it's because I'm writing. Maybe this is my best self. Maybe I can say things here that I can't say aloud.

Still don't trust you, though.

When it seemed like you'd break, I lightly called out, "Seriously, dude, his knobby knees are buckling."

My best friend climbed down. Spoke fast and desperately, as if he was being reunited with a great love after a great war. He said, "Mad that you hosed me, Logie Bear, but that hug fixed everything. Already miss seeing you at school, love."

"Miss ya too, man," you said. Jacques squealed and rushed back into your arms for a more normal embrace. You looked over his shoulder and directly at me. I was in a lotus position, attempting to garner the patience necessary for dealing with your reunion. You said, "Wanna get in on this action, Rosie? Or do you wanna keep sitting on my client's lawn like a giant dog turd?"

"Going the dog turd route."

Jacques released you and said, "Client? What's this now?"

"My uncle is a landscaper. Hired me for the summer." You lifted up your shirt. Said, "Look, already got a farmer's tan."

At first, I rolled my eyes at you for being a ham. But you looked so…happy. I hated you, but wanted to spread your happiness on bread as if it were savory jam and eat it. Being the bitch that I am, it took everything inside me not to congratulate you. And I didn't. I'm only letting it out now because, like I said, writing makes me good.

You continued to catch up with Jacques for what was the longest minute of my existence before I had to interject. "Jacques and I are super late."

You said, "For what?"

"Top secret. Has to do with my menstrual cycle."

You told me to say no more and fiercely meant it. In case you didn't have the people skills to understand my words, I wasn't actually bleeding out my tampon tunnel. In truth, I didn't want to be around you.

Once we were a block away and you were out of earshot, Jacques said, "You crazy? How dare you pull me away from a guy like Logan? Hot and nice and—"

"Stop listing arbitrary adjectives," I said, leading the way with dignity. "Let's introduce you to a hotter, nicer guy named Eliot Buxton. Hurry now. We're meeting at 3:00."

Jacques whipped me around. "How? How do you know him?"

I sluggishly said, "From that time I was in his pool and my tongue was in his mouth."

Jacques giggled for a good while and finally said, "No."

I brushed my hair off my neck to reveal a hickey.

"No!"

I shrugged.

"Rosie," he said. "One doesn't casually shrug about this. Nobody 'knows' Eliot. He's too new. I mean, everybody knows him like, 'Oh, that's Eliot, he sits by me in class. Cool guy. Wanna bone him.' He's new. That's why he's dreamy. Here you are, getting to *know* him, almost in the biblical sense, and you're shrugging about it?"

Logan, you're probably wondering why I'm being so open about my love life. Let me point out that you parade your affairs all about and nobody calls you on it. Why should I be guarded? We're adults. I don't trust you, yes, but I'd share my relationship details with any goon plucked from our school's hallways. It means little to me.

Jacques continued to freak out behind me for the rest of the walk until I was knocking on the Buxton's front door. My friend waited at the bottom of the driveway, pacing. Jacques never gets nervous, so this says a great deal. Eliot answered the door, beaming. I said, "Parents out?"

His response was to dip me slightly and lay one on my face. Notice I said face, not mouth. Eliot missed his aim and gave too much tongue, if you must know. Jacques finally screamed, "What universe is this?"

A startled Eliot dropped me in the hydrangea bushes and, without even checking on me, rounded the corner to find the voice. I climbed to my feet and followed. Eliot nervously said, "Sorry, who are you?"

For a moment, Jacques wore an expression that's made when falling in love with the wrong person. Being one of few openly gay guys at Wira North, this face occurs often. Jacques caught himself, shook his head and playfully said, "Name's Jacques. I'm with The Hickey Queen."

Eliot smiled, but didn't know what to say. I was too discombobulated from my fall to think of anything to insert into the uncomfortable conversation gap. Jacques smirked and delicately said, "You have such white teeth."

This spawned a thirty-minute conversation about teeth whitening. I made a frittata in Eliot's ginormous kitchen while the two of them chatted in another room. Maybe they were on his deck. Don't know. My entire mind was wrapped around each breaking egg, every cabinet I dug through, and all the spices I played with. When they came into the kitchen, Eliot wrapped his toned arms around my waist, kissed my neck and whispered in my ear, "Dude, man, fucking love eggs."

Then he set my body free and grabbed a handful of eggs with his meaty claw. Ate the food like an ape. And I thought, *Wish I used the eggs to crack over his head instead of the pan.*

That was what most days were like, leading up to the last ordinary day. Eliot and Jacques. Jacques and Eliot. That was summer. And now that the coldness came, now that the imaginary ice bucket in the sky has turned over, I can't help but wonder if I spent my last days of normalcy in a proper manner and with the right people. The sun is out and it's raining and I don't see beauty. Because it's cold now. And Jacques and Eliot aren't here like they were when it was warm.

Bette and Logan, you're not completely evil, so please don't hassle me too much about what I've written. You know how patients and doctors have codes of confidentiality? Can we have something like that? While creating this, I've discovered that writing doesn't merely make me good. It makes me honest. Don't make me regret not editing this story.

October 8, 2012

Hey, Joey Journal,

Today was day sixty-six and it was still incredibly painful and it was somehow made better by it being the first day of homecoming week. Yes. I said better. Not best. Not good. Everything almost went to shit. Bullshit. But yes, it was better. I'm knocking my fist on my wood desk. Better.

You might not have pegged me as being the school-spirited kind. Bingo. My pride arsenal is barren. Can't wait to depart to a faraway land. I'm not positive as to where 'faraway' happens to lie on a map, but it's out there, and once there, I'll be gone beyond any doubt.

I went to one football game during my entire high school experience, the first game of freshmen year. It was like hearing a crappy song on the radio. I sat for a while, nodded my head, attempted to get in sync with the beat. However, no matter how badly a person wants to dig something that is unable to be dug, they simply won't be able to dig it. Ya dig? When presented with an unlikable radio song, one will switch the station and hope for the best. In the case of high school football games, I simply stopped attending.

Eliot is on the soccer team, so Jacques and I have gone to some of his games. All I got out of it was butt pain from the bleachers. Stares were subtly cast in my direction, for I was a blobfish in a sea of sharks. I focused on my nacho stack to get through those late summer nights. Ahh, staring fools. They know things about me, yet they don't know me, and they don't know what to say. I'm just a blobfish who's been telling people she volunteers with the elderly on her boyfriend's game days. Technically, I don't kick back at the old folks' home, but I do hang with River on weekends. His youth is eroding, so, in a way, I'm chilling with a geezer.

I'm most alone when surrounded by countless, cheering people. So, let me lack school spirit supply. I'm equipped with the essentials: clothing, food, a roof over my head, every CD Jewel ever made. And although I'm school pride deficient, homecoming week is still soothing. It's the one week where elaborate costumes are encouraged at school. My outfits have been planned since July. I knew what the theme days would be early because of Emily Hayes, the hefty girl with a quarter-sized mole on her face. Even though she's physically unappealing, she's proven herself reliable when it comes to matters of information and gossip. I have this theory that her mole can read minds and predict the future.

Today is Monday. Decade Day. The seniors dressed like they were from the 80's. I splurged on an old Victorian style dress at a flea market. It was matched with a beehive wig from the drama room and my face was powdered until it looked like a Pop 'Ems donut. All day long, I declared to onlookers that when I heard the seniors were to wear '80's clothing', I thought they meant the 1780's.

Mostly everybody was wearing neon spandex and their heads were drenched with hairspray. Those wearing American Apparel were an insult to Decade Day. Half the school didn't even dress up, boring me silly. Fortunately, an envelope threw a wrench into the spirit week machine.

It was delivered by an office aide at the top of first hour— Anastasia Moretti-Slocumb. Mouthful slithered into the science room while Mr. McAdams told us how disappointed he was with our latest test results. Was so fired up, he didn't notice Mouthful at first. She stood patiently, out of place and unwilling to interrupt the teacher's vociferation. Her perfect black hair stretched down to her shoulder blades. It was slightly teased and '80's-esque' without being '80's grotesque'. Leave it to Mouthful to pull off hair that made the other girls look like they had mangy sloths residing on their heads. She got a fake tan for the dance, but didn't look as if she used Nutella as bronzer. Fresh glow, nothing more. The girl didn't wear what other girls wore for 80's day. No Olivia Newton John 'Let's get physical' threads for her. Mouthful opted for a hot pink Malibu Barbie business dress suit, and even had a clunky 80's cell phone in her free hand.

McAdams was peeved that an office aide was derailing his speech about the 'time commitment that AP Bio demands.' If AP Biology were a girl, that ho would be having her period 365 days a year. I met the requirements for science last term, thus I could've spared myself the agony of having to dissect a cat. I'm clearly dense.

Mouthful had fans in the class. Her pals waved at her, making playful faces. This douche named Aaron said, "Anastasia! Whatchoo doin', baby?" A provocative wink was hot on the heels of his exclamation. Aaron is Wira North's self-proclaimed 'class clown'. Some say I'm the school's 'female' class clown, to which I dryly reply, *Stop. Clowns are creepy. Like Aaron.*

McAdams grew angrier as the room's attentions shifted from the falling grades lecture to the smiling bimbo. She handed him white envelopes while the teacher's pale face grimaced. Mouthful waved at Aaron as McAdams caustically thanked her, then softly nodded and exited. Everyone knows students take on 'office aide' spots only to get class credit a study hall can't provide. More importantly, they aim to walk around school during class and socialize in the halls. Can't stand that. Get to class. We're behind China, children. God, office aides. The worst kind of aides. Scratch that. Thought it over. Office aides aren't actually the worst kind of Aids, but you get what I'm saying.

My science teacher's hand nervously pushed back his lengthy dark hair. McAdams' then massaged his temples, stressed out eyes closed. He peered down at the envelopes and said, "Homecoming week is fun, but…"

You're about to assassinate our fun.

"School is for learning. Costumes and joking around are a privilege."

McAdams distributed the envelopes. One was for me. The exterior read: "For Rosie Dwyer. Open after class." A pleasant feeling mixed with my apprehension, creating an odd chemical concoction. This was the best kind of envelope. A cryptic one, like Harry Potter's acceptance letter to Hogwarts. *Hold on*, I thought. *Is this from Dumbledore?*

When 'after class' came, I tore into it zealously. The paper inside provided a mission—to either accept or decline my Homecoming Court nomination by lunchtime. I audibly laughed at the words contained. The senior class must've been smoking dope on voting day.

After class, I stood before my open locker, trying to remember what I went there to get. My hands threw my supplies into the bottom half, then I felt two delicate hands on my shoulders. My skin lurched as I whipped around to find Eliot and Jacques. My eyes bulged in shock, since it's now an unfamiliar situation to have either one of them showing up at my locker. When I realized my eyes had grown, I started squinting, because I don't wish to be a bushbaby. Dammit, Logan. I said, "What are you doing here?"

Jacques asked me why I looked like I was standing before a pair of ghosts, and I shrugged.

"We're here to say congrats, bro," said Eliot.

I asked them how they knew, since court nominations hadn't been on the announcements yet. Jacques bragged that he knows everybody, including the girl who tallied the votes. Told me he was also nominated, grabbed my hands and tried to do a victory dance with me. It was lackluster on my end.

I hadn't thought about the dance until my place on court was revealed. Never been asked to one. By my fourth year of high school, I'm just over it. You know, even Jacques gets asked to every dance by various straight girls aiming to have 'fun' all night. Those ogresses always get to him first. Nobody has ever propositioned me, not even when I'm finally "seeing" someone. That person is Eliot, and this was honestly our meatiest interaction in a long time.

Eliot was a sight and a half during this conversation. Almost soiled his bright turquoise skinny jeans. When my lame victory dance completed, Eliot gave me a bear hug, lifted me in the air, and declared his 'girlfriend' to be 'the world's best'. My little phony. Embarrassingly boisterous, truth be told. He said, "Give me a day. I'll ask you, big time. It'll be dope."

Jacques cut me off before I could flirt back, saying, "Okay, Rosie, Eliot and I have to jet. Math class calls." Then my best friend kissed my cheek and floated off, Eliot following close behind. And I stayed, still and in place, thinking. Overthinking it all. Despite acting like I'm not the 'typical teenager', I'm just that. This girl exudes a tough exterior, but let's not forget that *I write in an effing diary*. I'm average. A regular reverie of your matter-of-course minor is to be among the ten seniors parading around in sashes at the pep rally. Sashes are sublime. They're right up there with Butterfinger bars and *Bringing Up Baby*.

We all desire our peers' admiration. For a pretty little second, a trivial sheet of paper made me think my classmates dug me. Homecoming court is a ridiculous tradition that unfairly puts a limited amount of people on a pedestal, but I needed the lift. However, while gathering supplies from my locker, I plummeted from the cloud I was cabbage patching on. *Did the idiotic student body vote for me as a joke? Or worse, out of pity?*

My body used to be in constant motion, but now I'm constantly going through the motions. I've been sensing everybody sensing me slipping into this senseless place. By no means do I intend to take a giant dump on myself. It's only reality. I'm not popular or well-liked. I'm more of a novelty item people wish to possess when it's fashionable for them. People call me a social butterfly. I'm not one. I move from sentence to sentence with zero grace. And I'm not social. Lately, I've been more isolated than the Sentinelese tribe. Not a butterfly. Instead, I'm a bird shitting as it soars through the air. A bird ramming head first into a glass window. Butterfly, my butt. My being takes the form of a boorish bird.

I don't want to be a bird.

Sure, I can never shut up. The diagnosis is in. It's not diarrhea of the mouth. I suffer from terminal vocal dysentery. However, talking nonstop doesn't mean the speaker is skilled at communication. Chatting with classmates, I'm a robot malfunctioning. Random words surge from my mouth hole. *Bee-boo-bop-beep-now-inserting-foot-in-mouth*. People grin and deem my phrases 'funny'. It's not funny. Nope. Artless, I am. People enjoy me, but there's a corresponding number of people who firmly refuse to give me the benefit of the doubt. They notice uncouthness. Let's call them truth seers.

Everybody is oafish in their own way, but there's a faction that's only one percent awkward. They make up the top one percent of teenagers. Normally, those belonging to that percent are the kids who get voted onto homecoming court, and not as a prank. The rest of us, us extraneous weirdos, who are ninety-nine percent awkward, and one percent unknown, we can never be one hundred percent sure of ourselves when something amazing happens.

I'd rather it be a joke than pity. When the sympathy vote notion surfaced, I swiftly made my way to the bathroom. I checked the perimeter, peeking under stalls. The coast was clear. My hands shut the stall, boxing myself into a makeshift panic room. The routine began. I silently cried, hands quashing my mouth. Typically speaking, I'm a clattery crier. Still, I'm highly practiced at 'The-Public-Bathroom-Silent-Sob'. At least once a week, I ask for the potty pass, but not for whizzing purposes. I weep, becoming a limp noodle over trivial matters. Like, if I lose something or forget an assignment. This heightening feeling wrecks my being, but if I freak out in class, everyone will think my dog died. Can't have that. Mr. Bojangles is my sweet prince. I can't handle anyone asking, "Did your dog die?"

That's what all the idiots ask in-class criers. And if the cause is actually frivolous bull crap, the person crying becomes nothing but a common Cry Baby. I'm seventeen. Nobody wants to be that at seventeen.

Sometimes, I'm tardy because I spent passing time in a stall, biting my lip, attempting not to shake too much, and coming way too close to pressing my whole melancholy body against the stall's corner. But I don't press my body against the stall. Although life makes me fussy, germs make me ten times fussier. So, I stand there, biting my lip, attempting not to shake too much, and coming way too close to pressing my whole melancholy body against the stall's corner, but not all the way, because please remember, germs make me sadder than life does. I do this until my eyes open and find a weird stall drawing. Like a distressfully detailed wiener. I strive to muffle my giggling, but cannot. It's rip-roaringly hilarious because…think about it! What sorta girl sits in a bathroom, drawing a hyper realistic wiener on the wall? That belongs in the men's room. What an artistically talented nympho. Did she work from a picture?

A live model? What? Suddenly, I'm wiping away tears and weakly smiling. After a breath, I journey to class, grinning at the fact that a penis drawing is a symbol of hope in my world.

The stall. That's what snapped me out of it after the pity-vote hypothesis. This time, it wasn't a penis drawing. That was last Friday. This time, it was words carved on the stall's left side. "Fuck the bullshit. Just do you."

The little voice in my head screamed to the heavens, *Who are you, girls' bathroom philosopher, and why do you just get it?*

That's the only reason I accepted my nomination. And that's the only reason today was better.

October 10, 2012

Hey, Joey Journal,

It's been sixty-eight days since he's been gone. Dad loved getting all us kids together to cheat on the family's various health food kicks behind Mel's back. Big Macs. We always got Big Macs. Fearing River would make steamed vegetables tonight or worse, couscous, I stopped at the McDonald's after school let out. Eating by myself took it out of me, man. My siblings weren't there, for one. And my dad wasn't there to rattle off the millions of McDonald's facts he acquired during his lifetime of being a fat ass.

Kids, did you know the Big Mac was originally 49 cents? What a travesty. Still...I'd pay up to twelve dollars for one if I had to. Ask anybody else what was the best thing to come outta the year 1968, and they'd say Apollo 8 or the White Album. Ha! Shit for brains, every one of 'em. The only true answer? The Big Mac, baby! Long live '68.

Silence at today's table. Curse the number sixty-eight.

I shouldn't have eaten that pile of grease anyway. Got a food baby I fear it won't be delivered from my belly by this weekend. I wish I would've turned down the court nomination. Not looking forward to this weekend. At my school, nominations are revealed only days before the actual dance. No time to properly prepare. And why do I even care about being properly prepared for something I properly disparage? Every dance is the same. It begins. Shitty pop music plays. Students 'grind'. Personally, I don't call their movements 'grinding', opting for the term 'jungle humping'. Chimpanzees, the whole lot of 'em. Jungle humping is easy. Girl shoves her gluteus maximus into Guy's junk, gyrating up, down, around, all the way to funky town. When I say funky, I mean *funky*. Subtract the dress clothes and it'd be called "Anal Sex."

You wouldn't believe some stances on this epidemic. Today, Bette had us to do a 'Quick Write' about our opinion on grinding and opened the floor for discussion. Always chatty during in-class conversations, I asked the class straight away, "Grinding? You mean jungle humping? If so, my answer is no. I don't dance like a glorified cave lady."

That's when a wench in the back scornfully said, "Hell, your chastity belt on too tight, honey?"

I turned to face the callous chick, who was Angie, the faux-ghetto best friend of my former Karate partner. Both Angie and Maria skip class so often, I completely forgot they went to North. By the way, Angie still wore too much eyeliner and eyeshadow. Without faltering and with a smile, I said, "Hey, Angie. Or would you prefer I use your full name, Angelica?"

With the face of a rabid beaver, she said, "My full name is Angel."

"Angel, tell me, if you wouldn't dance like an escort at your cousin's wedding, why would you at a school dance?"

Bette said, "Let's stop using terms like 'escort'. Now."

Then 'Angel' dropped another intelligent remark. "Course I don't want my family seeing that, but hey, my nana ain't gonna be at the dance with me. Don't blame me for dropping it low."

I looked incredulously at everybody and said, "Newsflash, folks. Teachers chaperone…and silently judge you."

She said, "Bitch, you sour because no guy is ever finna grind with ya ragdoll looking ass."

Finna. I'm sheltered, but that means "fixing to", right? The class was rendered mum until my laugh happened. It was my full one. My actual laugh is mayhem. When my sister was a toddler, she'd become fussy whenever I chuckled. River says it sounds "like a seal on cocaine." So, I force myself to laugh 'cuter' when around other humans, my family and Jacques withstanding. Wasn't able to hold back today. "You're a strange girl, Angel," I said between heaving breaths, but I was incomprehensible. Soon, everyone joined in, even Miss Finna herself. Bette still sent her to the office, though. As the room mollified, Logan leaned over and whispered, "Don't worry. You'll find someone who's finna grind with your ragdoll-looking ass."

We aren't buddies, so I pursed my lips and kept my eyes on a motivational poster. Almighty, I can't stand watching grinders as I attempt to enjoy myself with the few who share my opinion. Some even start grind lines. Boy, girl, boy, girl, boy. Shake that booty and it's a slut sandwich.

I remember St. Aggie's annual dances. I slow danced with this weird kid at the end of the sixth grade. Jeremy. He uncontrollably farted in class every day after lunch. Daily. People mercilessly made fun of him. When he asked me to dance, he seemed decidedly defeated. I wanted to give him one decent elementary school memory. I'm not a heroine for doing it. At least he controlled his flatulence for the entire song. His body was eight inches from mine. A safe distance, but a shrewish teacher didn't agree, pulling us apart an additional six. "Save room for the Holy Spirit," she said. Then he let one rip. Aw, memories of me and my first love.

Where's the happy medium? Room for the Holy Spirit shouldn't be required. We also shouldn't treat our dance partners like scratch posts and we're kittens with itchy butts. And even if I wanted to dance like that, I wouldn't have a partner. Earlier this week, Eliot assured me that his homecoming proposal would be "dope." Today, he video-chatted me to give the news of his ailing health.

"That bad?" I asked, masking my piercing disappointment and blatant selfishness, cultivating a concerned tone. I'm quite used to the "hiding my emotions" shebang. Eliot nodded, expressing that it was *that bad*. Without a single shred of self-consciousness weighing on his voice, he revealed that he was suffering from diarrhea. My eyes grew and refocused themselves on my desk. Eliot's one handsome King Bee, but he's mastered the art of decreasing his hotness via words. He said, "It's exploding. I'm like a...I don't know, a liquid poop fountain? You know the computer game, 'Oregon Trail'? The one from elementary school? They have it at yours?"

I nodded and noticed that he was compulsively drinking from a water bottle. Next, Eliot said, "Remember how you could die of diphtheria in that game? On the Oregon Trail? I might have diphtheria. I think I'm dying."

I said, "You don't have diphtheria, dipshit. That's an upper respiratory tract disease. You mean dysentery?"

"Yeah! That!"

"Eliot, you're not dying. You have the flu."

He nodded, reluctantly agreeing, but then his cheeks puffed and his finger escalated. The boy blew chunks all over his computer screen and webcam. As I stared at my own screen, all there was to be seen was his dripping, curdled, yellow vomit. My hand clamped my mouth.

"Rosie, you still there?"

I was speechless. After a few silent moments, he asked again. When I didn't answer, Eliot started talking to someone who I think might have been there the whole time, only off camera. The puke was obscuring the visual image, but I could still hear Eliot say, "Yo, she's gone. Who would've known drinking warm salt water would do that? The Internet, man. Missed the bucket, but needed a new laptop, anyway. My mom likes treating me."

A distant, feminine voice was difficult to hear properly, but it sounded exacerbated and said something like, "Why couldn't you just go with her?"

"Told ya," Eliot said. "I should've never told her I'd ask her. Something came over me. It seemed like the thing to do, I guess. But the more I thought about it, the more I just can't. She's a cute kid, but her energy right now is like this leech. Ya know? It's dark and sucks everything out of a guy. Understandable, but it sucks. Shit, I even sound like her, with her aura crap. I mean, we've been so casual, so how am I supposed to be there for her when something serious happens? I've tried, but we're just not that kind of thing. Let her have her night. She'll have more fun if I'm not there, half-assing it. And I'll have more fun if I'm home and playing video games."

The other voice in the room seemed to have said, "You're a prince." Then came a slamming door, which made me jump. After realizing my hand was still on my mouth, I slowly shut my computer. Any normal person would have a serious talk with their "boyfriend" immediately after hearing something like this. I'm not a normal person, though. I'm the kind of person who can't fully blame a "casual" individual for malfunctioning when his formerly "casual" girlfriend heads into a more complex life period. I guess I'll just smile more? That should appease him. We all know that my priority during this fragile time in my life is making Eliot comfortable around me. So, if he wants casual, I'll handle this in the most casual way possible. I won't speak to him. He won't notice. And it should be known that I myself feel like drinking warm saltwater.

October 11, 2012

Hey, Joey Journal,

    It's been sixty-nine days. Don't feel bad. I understand your mind quickly went from my dad's death to a dirty, dirty sex position. You filthy animal. But if I'm being honest, I imagine sixty-nine is the saddest of the all the numbers that ever numbered in addition to being the raunchiest. "I'm so much more than what you know me for," whispers the soul of sixty-nine.

    I know another person like that. Never-Leaves-the-Street Steve is homeless and perpetually seated on the library's front steps. Even when it's freezing, his homeless backside is planted there. The man's appearance is slightly skuzzy, but he never begs. Talk to him a second and you'll see he's only void of a house. I wait for the bus with him often and we've had countless conversations. People typically advise young ladies to avoid street people, but Wira isn't completely an urban setting. Steve is only a humble man, hopping from city to city. During our first bus stop discussion, Steve told me he consciously decided to experience the ragtag lifestyle of a rambling man. As a kid, he heard "Like a Rolling Stone" by Bob Dylan. Steve said it woke up all his senses and senses he didn't know he had. He began craving the realization of one goal: to roam "with no direction home."

    In high school, he read Jack Kerouac's *On the Road*. More senses were discovered. Soon, his diploma was in hand and summer was present. He was a young man with no plans. While his classmates buckled down at their chosen colleges, Steve was already traveling Europe. Odd jobs, constant motion, no direction home. It stuck.

I frequently bus myself to Wira's Public Library. Today was one of those days. Like every other excursion, I waved eagerly at my favorite rambling man and he pensively nodded. His soul whispered, "I'm so much more than what they know me for."

Damn. I wish I were a rolling stone.

Last year, the library was where I studied, hoping to claw my way out of abusive AP classes. The land of the book stacks was my oasis, a place that replenished my brain. Studying was purposeful, the quiet felt relaxing, everything seemed right. This year stands at variance. Studying is insignificant, the quiet feels far too loud, everything seems wrong. What I now do is wander. Becoming lost in a purlieu of printed text is a sensation most prodigious. It's a game. Whenever library goers walk near me, I stroll the other way. Normally, I avoid humankind altogether during my wandering sessions, but today, I bombed at being a book hermit. When this failure occurred, my location was the self-help section. Fingers grazing book spines, I drifted down the aisle, mind in a secret memory. My everything was impaled by an image that can't be unseen. I wasn't in the self-help section to better myself, but to forget. More importantly, I was there to be forgotten. Nobody ever comes down that aisle, after all.

I first visited the section after Eliot said his father writes Christian self-help books. Wanted to see if they were in stock. They weren't featured, but what keeps me coming back are the ridiculous book names. I spied a figure walking past as I picked up an oddly titled book that seemed misplaced. The figure in my peripheral vision was an itch in a place I couldn't reach. Initially, I didn't budge, because the person moved on. Then they backtracked, entering the section. My body rocketed in the opposite direction, and a moment later, a voice leisurely whispered, "DJ Rosie Dwizzle, in the house."

That's the 'rap name' I tried to make everybody call me in middle school, teachers included. As I sharply whipped around, sheer delight shimmied across Logan Fields' face. "Why are you here?" I asked. He was confused and told me the sign on the building says 'public'. I told him he was a wise guy, longing for him to leave, but not because he's Logan. Truthfully, I didn't want anybody there. He's not awful anymore.

He's anybody. Confused? Well, I'm mixed up myself. School effortlessly muddied up my views on Logan.

Bette's Thursday classes are now called 'Peer Review Periods'. The two of us turned our desks to face each other as he said, "Rosie, you look..."

"I look what?" I asked, voice as bland as the couscous dish my brother made for dinner the previous evening.

'Ridiculous' was his descriptor of choice. He was driving at the green dinosaur costume I sported in celebration of Class Color Day. I growled and introduced my butt to my chair. Logan's eyebrows arched as he peered down at me, gently repeating himself. "Ridiculous."

My head swayed in disapproval. He was sporting a green screen jumpsuit and running shorts. On a typical day, he bears the appearance of a string bean; what with his long, gangly figure. In today's outfit, he literally became a legume. I said, "String bean calling the dinosaur green."

"Naw. I'm just dripping pure liquid sexiness."

"Good God, man. Nobody wants to hear about your liquid drippage."

Once seated, Logan dived straight into business. "My looks were 'GQ' status good? Even when I was ten?" Logan flipped to the page in my story that complimented his childhood appearance. The kid had the paragraph circled and a luminescent gold star beside it.

Forgot about that description in *Cornrow Captivity*, so I tapped my dinosaur foot, trying to force the discomfort away through movement. "Don't go there," I said. "Your first story was an ode to me."

Abruptly, he stopped drumming his fingertips. "At least I didn't name names. Also, you wrote about me in both stories."

Fearing he'd rip on me further, I let him off the hook, saying, "You know, Logan, it's too bad you're not as enjoyable in person as you are in your writing." One of his thick eyebrows raised suspiciously as my mouth kept moving. "The simplicity. I reveled in it. Was left wanting more." He told me I was a very funny liar, and I replied, "Honest. It was aesthetically pleasing."

Logan gave a closed grin as he scratched his scalp, reddening cheeks contrasting against the neon green hue of his jumpsuit. "Rosie, don't worry about robots out-writing you."

"Shucks."

He said, "Both stories are too long. Unorganized. But hey, it's creative stuff. Real creative. Can't teach that." I didn't know what do with my face. Logan's additional comment was, "Reading it was like talking with you. You do the bulk of it, but you're stupid good at the job." He was goofy looking, but I started understanding the appeal. Logan was befuddled by my blank features and said, "Whoa. I think I just complimented you?"

I broke our eye contact to draw Patrick Star at the top of Logan's story. Once finished, I pushed it toward him and said, "You deserve a star, too. I guess."

"Screw peer editing," he said, obviously pleased. "Let's draw random shit on each other's sheets, kay? Bette will love that."

A laugh sprung forth, but it wasn't my full "seal on cocaine" one. It was soft and lightly controlled. "I see," I finally said. "I know what you're looking for."

Patrick was joined by a veiny penis doodle before I silently pushed the sheet onto his desk. Without taking a single beat, he brought his pencil to the paper and shoved it back. There was an arrow pointing to the cartoon penis, accompanied by the words, "What Rosie's soul looks like."

"True," I said, dully smirking. I could tell by his eyes he was physically holding his amusement in by force. I burst into laughter. Full out, disgusting, unstoppable laughter. This chick seated by me, gave us dragon lady death glares through her Ugly Betty glasses. Logan removed his hands from his face to 'laugh'. When amused, he bites his lip, closes his eyes, and laughs without making much noise at all. It's breathy giggling. Weird, cute, but mostly weird. But really cute. I fell out of my chair. He also toppled over. We were overreacting, but you have to while you're young. Mostly everyone was rowdy, except Dragon Lady. I blame Homecoming Week for our energy shift. Bette was sitting at her desk, plugging her right ear so hard I'm surprised her finger didn't get lost in there. Completely miffed. However, because Bette is the 'young, cool teacher', she was conflicted about whether to lay down the law. Finally, she gave up her internal battle against discipline and said to us, "Don't make me regret pairing you up."

We sat in our seats, noiselessly tagging weird shit on our papers until the bell rang. The two of us quickly packed up and raced out before Bette had to chase us out as she usually does. Once standing in the bustling hallway, we smiled at each other. "Cool with confidentiality?" I asked. He breezily asked if he would be the doctor or the patient. I said, "Not sure yet."

My hand extended out to Logan. He swatted it away and hugged me instead. "Come from a long line of huggers," he said.

After embracing me, Logan departed in a new direction. So did I.

Despite the unspoken accord between us, running into Logan during my library jaunt wasn't on my To-Do List. When I got home earlier, I changed into an airy muumuu, removed my makeup and spent an hour dancing. Then I power napped before journeying to my 'by myself place' with a torn apart bun drooping on the side of my head. I was bloated. Greasy. Gross. I don't know why I was feeling so insecure about the way I looked when Logan popped up. It's not like he was better dressed than me. His jeans were ripped at the kneecaps in a way that made it obvious he didn't purchase them like that. There were a few grass stains, too. And his multi-colored drug rug hoodie also had this aroma that wasn't exactly terrible, but it was the kind of strong scent that leaves bystanders thinking, *What is that smell? I kind of like it and kind of don't.* Peeking out from the hoodie's neck hole and the gaps in his jeans was familiar shiny neon green fabric that made it clear he was wearing the green screen jumpsuit underneath.

Logan had no intention of shifting, so I said to heck with it and contorted my facial features. I often do this when I run out of things to say. My eyes crossed and I couldn't see Logan clearly, but it was apparent he hadn't walked away due to my strangeness. Grinning, he said, "What you doing, cuckoo?"

I grimaced for a moment. *Cuckoo. Don't call me cuckoo. Birds say that. He liked birds. They were his favorite animal.* Then I shook my head and my face normalized. *Let's be a normal human person.* All of sudden, I had this idea to play 'moving hide and seek'. Revealed it as soon as it formed in my mind. Logan asked what that was, and I said, "I hide, but I can move, even if you see me. You don't win by finding me. You win by tapping me."

Logan did his mostly cute laugh. "That's called tag, dum-dum."

"Truly?"

He inched closer, whispering, "Yep."

Logan's eyes were sleepy. They're always a wee bit comatose, eyelids constantly hanging halfway down his pupils. Sometimes, they're basically closed. It's a comfy variety of drowsy, though. The eyes are amber, coinciding nicely with his hair.

I winked, but it wasn't sexually provocative. My wink said, *About to run and hide. Care to play a game?* So, I ran. Logan joined. I hid. He searched. We had fun. This time, I'm not using that word as a sensuous euphemism. Fun means fun. When I lost Logan for the last time, I was fresh out of hiding spots. I hightailed it to the ladies' room. If Logan discovered that the girls' bathroom concealed me, he'd be unable to come in and tag me. I'd win. Many minutes slipped by before I grew bored and chucked my head out the door. Logan was in the middle of the lobby, gaze transiting all over. I teased the lost boy by calling out in a hushed tone, "Yoo-hoo, pussy!"

Logan pounced toward the door and I slammed it in his face. Seconds later, his tentative fist knocked. As I opened up, Logan breathed the words, "Found you." All the running our reindeer games required had him exasperated. Ridiculous, really. He's a soccer player. Running is all those guys ever do. They're a team of hamsters.

"Logan, this is moving hide and seek," I said. "Gotta come in and tag me in order to win."

"I don't think—"

"Na-na-na-boo-boo, stick your head in doo-doo," I said, hitting all my consonants, like a big girl. The door shut once again as I lunged into a stall and locked it. Then he shuffled into the bathroom and crawled under the stall. I stared, dumbfounded. "Logan, you mad man."

His pointer finger landed on my nose. "You're it."

We had a moment. Our eyes locked for the entirety of it, until his finger glided from my nose to my bottom lip. As it moved, I flashbacked to those tramps arguing about Logan in the hallway, and him escaping to the bathroom. I didn't want to be another girl. I wanted to be *the girl*. Not for him. For anyone who so much as laid a finger on me.

My eyes closed as I tilted my chin upwards. Logan's finger grazed my neck until it reached my clavicle and the one finger turned into all five. He brushed a stray hair out of my face with his other hand, thumb brushing along my cheek. Then I took his hands in mine and threw them off my body. "Nice catching up, but it's undignified to spend one's time chatting with boys in bathroom stalls."

Logan's smile was pinned to the side as usual, but this time, his expression was laced with the words, *"Shit. I'm a shithead."* His apology lay in his weary smile and worn down eyes.

"Whatever," I said, not a single eye making contact.

Logan unlocked the door and held it open. "Ladies first."

I left the stall and Logan followed. Humiliation stood waiting for me in the form of Mrs. Buxton. Forgot it was Thursday. I always see her arriving for book club on this day of the week. Why does Eliot's mother only see me when in compromising situations? Like... damn. I mouthed the word 'hello' while her eyebrows rose high above her sealed shut eyes.

As I left, Logan explained that we were playing 'hide and seek'. My legs were gelatin, but still, I rushed out, and Logan quickly followed. We both ran through the library's security system without checking out our books. Weewoo. Weewoo. Wee-freaking-woo. Suck a big one, library security system. When the security guard approached us for a chat, Logan said, "We didn't mean to, our minds were..." As he trailed off, I finished his sentence with the word 'elsewhere'. When the guard asked where exactly our minds were, Logan heartily said, "A distant land called 'Stupid-Teenage-Crap'."

My eyes were glued to the green tile that lay beneath my feet as the guard warned us not to make it a habit. Next, we walked to the self-checkout machines, all of which were occupied. We stood in the shortest line, but this woman and her son were taking out twenty items. Time needed killing. "What are you checking out?" Logan airily asked. "Besides me, of course."

"Not checking anything out," I said, sneaking a quick peek at the bizarrely titled book. In a flash, it was behind my back. Although I put up a fight, Logan successfully yanked the book from my grasp. He held it out, squinted, and read the title aloud. *"Why Do Men have Nipples? 100's of Questions You'd Only Ask Your Doctor after Your Third Martini."*

The sheer delight seeping from his pores was unbearable. "Cute book choice," is all he had to say. His facial muscles tried to suppress his silent laugh as I wrangled the book from him and told him it wasn't worth explaining. Once the lady in front of us was done, she whisked her son away. As they walked, the kid cried and his mom said, "Quiet, Julio."

While Logan scanned his books, I placed the man nipple book next to the machine, planning to forsake it, but Logan checked it out for himself. "Rosie, I've always wanted to know why I have nipples." Once outside, we smiled at each other and silently went in different directions, that is until he asked where I was going.

I turned and said, "Home?"

"You're walking?"

"To the bus stop. I'm allowed, right?"

"It's dark."

"Don't have a license, hombre." As the words were routinely spoken, my focus shifted to the streetlights behind Logan. They built new ones in that neighborhood. The old ones were yellowish in tint. These new lights were icier, glowing with blue mixed in. I don't care for them.

"I'll drive you," he said. It was cold. Last year was an Indian summer while this fall has been chilly. I'd forgotten a sweater and didn't want to wait for the bus in a muumuu. The goose bumps on my arms yelled, *Say yes or we will revolt.* So, I gave him an unenthusiastic 'sure'.

Logan's car was the same color as his aura—seafoam green. A clunker, a real junked up Honda Civic. It was only ugly on the exterior and was pristine inside. As I buckled my seatbelt, Logan grabbed a red hoodie from his backseat and tossed it at me. "Put that on. You're shivering like a damn Chihuahua." I said no, but he told me it wasn't romantic. Goose bumps gross him out. That's all. I put him out of his misery. The sweater smelled wonderful. I didn't give it a creepy sniff or anything. The scent naturally worked its way into my nostrils. Couldn't figure out the aroma, but it was alluring.

Logan held out a stack of CD's and told me to pick my poison. As he exited the parking lot, I went with the first one. There wasn't a single familiar band or artist. The CD was called *A Brief History* and it was by The Penguin Café Orchestra. As the instrumental music played, my stomach growled and my mind tried placing where I'd heard the song before. Soon, Logan explained that his affinity for the group stemmed from his preference for wordless music. "The music says everything. It takes the words out of a person's head instead of putting them there."

"That's why 'Like a Rolling Stone' is my favorite song," I said, eyes glued to Logan's firm grip on the steering wheel. "Bob Dylan asks us 'How does it feel?' instead of telling us how we should be feeling."

Yielding at a red light, Logan relaxed his body and pivoted his head in my direction. "Your taste in music is solid," he said. When Logan's attention redirected to the road, silence hung about for three minutes and my mind moved quickly. *I wonder how many girls have worn this sweater. Shut up. Logan has nice hair. I wonder if he uses Herbal Essences. Why is he cute and so abruptly? Shut up. He's not. His chicken legs are so…chickeny. Look at him for one second, but don't be obvious. Okay, I lied. That boy is all eyebrows, but he's everything. Look out your window. Much better. I wonder if he knows that while I lean my head against the window and study the passing scenery, I'm secretly wishing I was leaning my head on his shoulder and looking up at him. Shut up! That's nonsense. He's driving. Putting my head on his shoulder would be dangerous. Stupid. I wonder if he can read minds. Oh, no. Logan, if you read minds…*

He asked me why I didn't have my license. I jolted, quickly collected myself, and told him about my parents striving to raise me with as little impact on the environment as possible. He said, "Neither of them ever had licenses?"

"No, both could drive. Just never did it much. We started taking the bus and cabs when I was five. Sometimes we used rental cars for longer rides and vacations, but it was rare. My mom and brother have cars now. It's only out of necessity." I explained it like it was a painfully obvious answer. "Didn't I touch on this in 'Cornrow Captivity'?"

He nodded as his mouth moved in a way that suggested he was carefully considering the phrasing of his words. Logan eventually settled on saying, "Does your mom not want you driving?"

"No, even if I wanted to, I wouldn't have a car."

"Rosie, did you say, 'Even if I wanted to'? You don't? Not ever?"

"Not hot to trot on the idea."

Logan shook his head, facial expression indicating that wasn't the end of it. I told him to just say it. My eyes rolled, dice off the table after shaking them too violently during Monopoly. "Say what, Rosie?" He was either playing dumb or just plain dumb.

"Logan, say whatever is festering away at your brain like a no good gerbil."

"Change your mind," he said. "Freedom and licenses are besties."

"Fallacies, Mr. Fields. I'm free."

"Free as a bird?"

With that, I was taken aback. *Just remembered I don't wanna be a bird anymore.* "No. Not that. Never that."

"Glad we're on the same page."

"Incorrect," I deliberately said. "No, I'm not physically air bound, don't metaphorically possess wings, but rest assured, I'm both loosey and goosey."

He said, "Hate to break it to you, but gooses are technically—"

"Don't say the B word, Logan."

"Either way, you're not free." Logan smiled, standing with his opinion. "I'm liberated, knowing I can get in a car and go anywhere."

"Public bus system."

"Not the same."

I've heard the "car equals freedom" speech from my peers on repeat for years. The second everybody approached sixteen, they became obsessed with obtaining a license. Except me. Whenever I envision myself cruising, feeling 'free', the fantasy soon turns into a nightmare featuring a gory car wreck. I don't get nervous in the passenger seat, but the thought of driving and causing an accident makes me shake. My dad used to say, "This might be symbolism. By not taking the wheel, you're living out a metaphor for your passive approach toward life."

My dad would always apologize for "psychoanalyzing" me.

As Logan pulled over in front of my house, he noted that he lives nearby. "Let's hang out sometime. To be clear, 'hang out' is Logan code for 'go on a badass adventure.'"

"Nope."

I'm second guessing this whole beginning-an-impulsively-formed-friendship thing. Why start a new one?

"A dangerous journey for awesomeness," he said, eyes lighting up despite the car's darkness. "A legendary time, one that involves... what do seriously dope adventures involve, anyhow?"

"Don't know," I said, while thinking, *What I do know is that even true friends, like Jacques, can't handle friendship when life gets tough. Logan's aura is flimsy, at best, and I know he'll essentially be cardboard if I lean myself against him.*

"Course you know, Rosie. Here are a few adventure ingredients to jog your mind: parrots, hot air balloons, twerking, juggling knives, interject at any time." All I gave back was an unamused stare as my mind raced. *Logan is naive if he thinks parrots and twerking are enough to distract me from life.* "We could build a raft like Huck Finn," he said. "Float down a river?"

"Am I Jim?" I asked.

"From that book? Course not. You're Tom."

"Hell no, Logan. Tom is by far the densest of the three."

"Precisely why you're Tom Sawyer."

I said, "Dammit, I'm Jim."

"No, no, no, Rosie. I'm more believable as Jim."

"You mean to say that you'd make a better black role model to wayward youths?" He nodded joyously, so I said, "We're both white."

"I have that stand-up guy thing Jim has," Logan said. I reverted to a dead silence. A non-physical bitch slap. "C'mon, girl, our adventure. Let's map it out." I wanted to say, *You're gonna disappear on your own accord, disappear when somebody new appears, disappear when somebody else does, disappear.* Saying that would make me feel like a pouty victim, so I instead gave him dead silence. "Okay," he said, "No more Huck Finn talk. I'll suggest more activities. Tell me if you like any." Dead silence. "Whitewater rafting?" Dead silence. He grew louder. "Horse surfing?" Dead silence. His voice boomed. "Nude skydiving?"

Dead silence. His voice was ever enlarging, as were his eyes. "Let's direct a porno. Fight a pack of lions, like gladiators. What about a prostitution ring? We could do it all." Dead silence. Then he simmered down. "Bowling?"

Why does he want to befriend me so badly? Is this a joke or pity, like my homecoming nomination surely was? The only type of bowling that will happen here is the metaphorical kind. Logan is the ball and I'm each one of the pins. God is the bowler and a total ace. This doesn't end well for me. I finally said, "Doesn't sound adventurous."

His nutty smile shot sideways. "But it got you to talk. When we bowl, it'll be straight up Looney Tunes. Children will one day tell urban legends about it."

"That so?"

"So, you'll bowl, Rosie?"

"Nope."

I wish I could.

Defeated, he turned away, looking straight ahead. "That was Eliot's mom, wasn't it? In the bathroom? Seen her at soccer games."

I leaned back, jaw dropping. The boy operates on a wavelength of sheer irregularity. Logan had the urge to say more words, but fought them as they tried fleeing his throat. He lost control and asked, "What's going on between you two? Dude is a dick."

My crazy smile came out to play, as my eyes turned crazy themselves. I sucked in air and made a long high-pitched sound. He was baffled for sure as my crazy smile transformed into a crazy scowl. I said, "Nope, nope, nope."

"Listen. Eliot fools around with other girls and brags about it to the team."

I slammed the back of my skull against the headrest, irate eyes closing. "Not an idiot," I said, eyes unfastening. "Our relationship is open. Open! Wide open. Open wide. The dentist is ready to stick his tools into our relationship. That's how wide the openness is."

"You're swingers?"

I peered at him like I was the most mature young lady to ever be young and a lady and explained that we're allowed to see other people as long as we don't ask or tell each other. "If the 'Don't Ask, Don't Tell' mindset didn't last in the military, what makes you think it'll work for a high school relationship?" he asked.

I made another strange high-pitched noise and only halted when he flicked my shoulder. "Stop that alien crap. You do stuff with guys who aren't Eliot?"

A doubtful glare was sent his way. He was more awake than I'd ever seen him and I reluctantly told him no. Logan stared in the mirror, took a deep breath, and explained that it wasn't fair. Then I asked him who he was to judge. Logan's eyes went straight to his lap, knowing exactly what I meant. I listed off some names. Anastasia. Ashley. Emma. Dead silence. "Huh?" Dead silence. "Huh?" Logan was about to combust, but reined himself in enough to say he wasn't official with those girls. Apparently, he'd been 'single' on Facebook for months. "Well, whoopdy-doo, Logan. Your trophy will be here shortly. I'm having it engraved."

"Never asked any of them to be my girlfriend," said Logan. "Hanging out. What don't girls get about just hanging out?"

"You get romantic with them?" I asked.

He diverted his eyes, fiddling with the cup holder, avoiding the issue. I slapped his hand and gave him a stern look. "Fine," he huffed, in the manliest way a person could possibly huff. "Anastasia and I did stuff at a party last summer. She started it. We were both drunk. I guess we hooked up other times. Was gonna ask her to be my girlfriend after a while, but she won't talk to me, not since…"

He broke off, attempting not to laugh. "What'd you do?" I asked.

Logan's hands went up while he shook his head and said, "Promise you'll never tell anyone."

"I solemnly swear."

"Rosie, this goes to the grave with you."

My nodding became more urgent. I said, "I'm being cremated when I die, but I comprehend."

"Swear it'll go to the urn with you?"

"It'll go to the urn with me."

"Haven't told anyone this," he said. "The last time we were together, it was August. I was over when her parents were out of town.

We were smashed on Mike's Hard Lemonades and UV Blue. Long story short, Anastasia straddled me. When she did, yeah, she…she farted."

"Mouthful farted on you?"

"Mouthful farted on me." We busted out laughing, in our own weird ways. Logan continued, "Really, I was gonna overlook it. It was almost cute."

"Cute?"

"Almost, but she's too embarrassed to look at me."

"What about the other girls?" I asked.

His face was nonchalant and it was pissing me off. "Flirted with them. I'm an indiscriminate flirt."

"No, you're defective," I said.

"I wanna be a nice guy."

He seemed overwhelmed by the conversation's hasty change in tone and had the face of a distraught child. I grasped his chin, turning his head to face mine. Once our eyes met, I sternly said, "You're a nice guy." His smile reemerged and I let go. "But you're authentically nice, Logan. You don't have to constantly flirt to prove the quality of your compassion. It's unnecessary. You lead girls on. Don't like a girl? Don't brush hair out of her face. Or touch her lip. Or her clavicle. Understand?" His disorientation invited me to keep speaking. "The greatest flaw of my gender is that the members of it are often so insecure, we allow ourselves to cling to guys who shell out charm like Casanova Pez dispensers."

He rubbed his temples for a second, then removed his hands and focused his eyes on the mirror. "What about you? If girls are 'fragile', why hasn't Eliot destroyed you?"

"Been through worse recently," I said. "You know what I mean."

My mind was once again deep in that image that refuses to be erased and my face did that whole "I'm-about-to-cry" shit. Logan's mouth fell open, eyes immense and apologetic. They shifted from my eyes to my mouth, then back to my eyes. I thought he was gonna do something stupid like kiss me in attempt to retrieve my mind from its journey into a dark place. Logan thought better of it and returned his head to the headrest, instead. "Let's be friends," he said. Logan pivoted and his smile was the easiest smile I'd ever seen. A boy was sitting next to me, and he was relaxed. I had a relaxed smile on my own face, the kind one makes when in the company of a person who is extremely important.

Looking at my watch, I pointed out that it was getting late. 8:45 pm, on the dot. The car door flew open and I realized I was still wearing Logan's red hoodie. My fingers began unzipping it, but he smacked my hand. "Have it. A 'first day of friendship' present."

I zipped the sweatshirt all the way up, put the hood on, and knotted the drawstrings tight. My pointer finger went toward his face as I made an ET voice. "RD…phone home."

Logan, who was drowsy, silently laughed as much as possible and said, "Crazy girl, leave my car, before I make you."

Once I was on the grass, my head went back in and I thanked him. Logan told me it wasn't a problem and winked before driving off. It wasn't a provocative wink, or a friendly wink, or even a hide and seek wink. This wink said, *Like Steve and the number 69, I'm so much more than what you know me for.*

I'm in bed, wearing his hoodie, realizing what it smells like. Body spray, cotton, Sweet Baby Ray's.

October 12, 2012

Hey, Joey Journal!

It's been seventy days. When a person lives to be seventy, they are called a septuagenarian. My dad would've loved to assume this title. He'd probably make some joke about finally achieving his lifelong goal of being a lizard. Septuagenarian. I wish I could've seen him at seventy, looking like a shriveled-up newt.

I'm going to make it to seventy. I swear it. I'm determined to make it to the shriveled-up lizard life. And I'll be a lizard who dances better than all the other lizards. You bet your ass.

In my teenaged human form, I always participate in our school's annual pep rally dance-off. I've been in a funk, but I couldn't disappoint my fans by not shaking my funky stuff. Plus, my odds of winning increased this year. Jacques triumphs yearly via the hip hop moves in his repertoire, but he sprained his ankle at dance practice. He has a competition coming up and wishes to avoid effing up his anatomy further.

Every year, I don a wild costume. Winning is hard, but garnering attention isn't. This year, I was an elderly lady. Being a representative of the senior class, it was only right I resemble a senior citizen whilst making my booty clap. Inching onto the floor with my cane, I surveyed the competition. My achievement chances were squashed. Nicole German, Jennifer Muelly and Anastasia Moretti-Slocumb were competitors. They began dance training at three when I was still mastering walking. Jennifer and Nicole have been on varsity Poms since freshman year. Mouthful is even more gifted, belonging to the same professional troupe as Jacques.

And on this particular day, the girls had a joint aura that was the shade of a poop-shaped potato.

My feet wigged out as I became one with the art of gyration. Logan walked out dressed like an 80's B-Boy, while two sophomore guys came out in cowboy hats and short shorts. The music began. The first song was Bootylicious by Destiny's Child. My rump shook like an epileptic Weebles Wobble. I'd describe the dance movements further, but there's a famous quote with anonymous origins that says, "Writing about music is like dancing about architecture." Shuffle the sentence, and it still makes sense. Writing about dancing is like music about architecture.

The judges lowered their standards this year. Busting out my white woman's overbite typically fails me and my shoulder gets tapped instantaneously. When this happens, I refuse to concede, forcing the judges to drag my flailing body off the court. Not this year. Nicole and Jennifer's tap and lyrical dance skills went unappreciated and they were eliminated early on, receiving the ax within seconds of one another. The two walked away with their arms over each other's shoulders, because they're like totally best friends forever. Both were wearing borrowed football jerseys, tied at the waist. They also wore spandex dance shorts over blue tights. Two proud hoochies. I was too busy cutting footloose to gouge my eyes out.

The contestants petered out until it was Mouthful, Logan and me. Mouthful sported the same harlot uniform as her friends. She was lucky lack of style wasn't grounds for removal. In other words, she was schooling us. I have two left feet and Logan only had three moves: pelvic thrusts, slow motion nipple rubbing and what appeared to be the Oompa Loompa dance. Repeat process. Mouthful was the indisputable front runner, until Bootylicious ended, and Gangnam Style commenced. The crowd was familiar with Psy, the South Korean singer and viral sensation. Mouthful's clueless expression suggested she's been living under a rock this past month, Patrick Star style. Or maybe, because she has a life, she hadn't spent her free time learning dance moves to maddening Youtube songs. Logan and I, on the other hand, had those moves down pat. We Gangnam-ed the fuck out of the pep rally.

Bette eliminated Mouthful and each senior yelled one of two

names: "Rosie!" or "Logan!" We faced each other, lit up by unsettled strobe lights, slaying it, as if we were colleagues who'd been practicing the art of Gangnam Style for years. The song ended and McAdams tapped my shoulder. My fans booed in response to my defeat while Logan's brethren celebrated. My hands were glued to my knees as I tried to suck up air that memories are made of, deep inside my lungs. I was completely Gangnam-ed out. Bette grabbed Logan's hand, bringing it as far up as her squatty body would allow.

When Bette unleashed Logan's hand, he did the funky chicken for a moment before suddenly stilling his legs. Logan then brought my hand upward, sharing the dance off title. His aura was no longer messed up by foreign colors. It was the healthiest shade of green ever seen. After he dropped my hand, I hugged the crap out of him. His arms wrapped around my waist, bringing me in tightly. As I ran to the senior section, I screamed because my dance partner caught me off guard by picking me up. While being transported off the court, I asked him what the hell he was doing. "You looked kaput," he said. "Not my fault you can't handle Gangnam style."

My smile grew outrageously as I called him a douche canoe. After he threw me down, people high-fived us before the pie toss stole their attention. We blended into the crowd as I realized my old lady cane went missing in the heat of twerking. Didn't care much, honestly.

I congratulated him. Logan said he couldn't hear me, so I repeated myself in his ear. He lazily grinned and yanked off my gray-haired wig. Then he grabbed my hand and shook it. As he did this, I fought the oddest craving. The feeling of his palm, the energy of the pep rally, his eyes. Fuck. I was fucking into it, and the most fucking painful part of the whole fucking thing is knowing that I can't pause life. Fuck. There are these moments that move us, but time makes us move along to the oncoming moment. It sucks. He and I lingered, with stubborn hands. Impulsivity regularly courses through my bloodstream, making my actions unexplainable. We were etched into that scene, shaking hands for a ridiculously long time. And…Jacques and his brilliant interrupting skills came into play, saying, "Time to change for court."

I released Logan's hand, turning toward my "friend." His mug was a Jacques Blain classic. Lips pursed, eyebrows skyrocketing to his hairline, large eyes equal parts regal and astonished. I clenched my fingers into a fist, one that I longed to catapult into the center of his expression. What gives him the right to look at me judgmentally? The only people with any right to an opinion on my actions are the motherfuckers who are actually in my life. Still, breaking habits is torture. I bid Mr. Fields adieu and followed the command of Mr. Elevated Eyebrows like I was his puppet. Soon, I was in the bathroom and Jacques was entering behind me, something that I can only imagine would happen at a school as sloppy as ours. He unzipped the back of my paisley frock, kindly saying, "You and Logan. When did that—"

"Not happen," I said, icily cutting him off and turning to him as my unshaven hair became a bun. I thought, *Why am I letting him be in here? I'm capable of getting dressed by myself. By myself…like how I've done every last thing by my bloody self, for weeks.*

Jacques folded his delicate arms and tilted his unamused head in a way that made me able to hear the unwarranted transcendence in his voice before he even spoke. "I'm a dancer, Rosie. Much of my time is spent watching people move in unison. The way people move together reveals a lot about—"

"Toss me my dress," I said, dipping my toe into black tights.

My little black dress soon went over my head, besieging me with darkness. Jacques did what he does best and kept talking. "We dancers know chemistry can always be found when two people dance together." I pulled my head through as an exuberant smile emerged on his face. "You two have chemistry! Passion! Romantic potential!"

"You were watching us perform the Gangnam style, not *Paso Doble*," I said. "Why are you pushing him on me?"

"Hello, you have potential to someday be in love."

"No. With Logan, I'll always be in hate."

"Did you say 'in heat'?" asked Jacques. "Like a cat? Damn, girl, you're randy."

I threw my arms into the air, attached my hands to my head, and irately said, "If you insist on being in here, shut up and zip me, before a teacher catches you," to which Jacques replied, "Dress is backwards." I corrected it, then Jacques marched over and executed my command. Once my hair was cleared away, he sounded uncharacteristically concerned. "Whoa. You lost weight?"

"Don't know, Jacques. Why?"

"Your back is all bones."

"Nobody asked you to come in here. We're going to be late if you don't shut your mouth," I said, throwing my black heels on and making haste through the doorway. He chased after without objection and we barreled toward the line of nominees in the hallway and speedily located our spots.

We had a few moments to spare, so Jacques turned me around, placed his hands on my shoulders and whispered, "You're a hot mess." I used his button up shirt as a towel, rubbing my face all over his chest, leaving an impressive sweat mark. Then I sent him a sizable glare. Jacques said, "How nasty." I shrugged, then Jacques shifted from perturbed to emotional. Voice fluttering, he said, "Chicken, I hope you win." He was near tears. I sternly warned him not to call me "Chicken" and advised him not to get his hopes up. We had the typical conversation that carries on after a statement of that nature. First, his eyebrows raised once more as he was surely weirded out that I was shooting down my long standing nickname. Not wanting to get combative, he simply said, "Don't be modest."

"Ain't going to be me. I'm not delusional, Jacques-y Chan." When it was time for the court couples to parade onto the court and do our cute poses, I was ready to not be surprised. I still received a shock, though. Mouthful was crowned queen. I bet ten dollars the tiara would go to a chick named Sofia. People enjoy her presence, while they only tolerate Mouthful's. I'm talking about a pure white aura that is so angelic, it could only be compared to that of a newborn baby. It balanced out in the end, though. I made ninety-five bucks betting various people I wouldn't win.

Jacques was named king. Yes, I was mad at him deep down, but my instincts had my fist so high in the air, I thought I'd break through the ceiling. The jubilee pressed on when the senior class won the pep rally. They rushed the basketball court and confetti exploded everywhere. Pure pandemonium. It's a total brouhaha every year, but it feels better dancing atop the totem pole. Amid all this chaos, Queen Mouthful advanced toward me, face happy, yet sad. She said, "I don't deserve it."

"What?" I'd heard her, but didn't understand.

She shouted, "I voted for you!"

I smiled and said, "Don't sweat it, Anastasia. I voted for me, too."

We laughed. Like old chums. And hugged. Wow. Pep rallies have an odd way of forcing weird shit to go down in the toilet bowl that is high school.

I can't wait to look back on this odd day as a wise old lizard.

October 13, 2012

Hey, Joey Journal,

It's been seventy-one days. Last night, I wished I was as fast as that one famous spy plane—SR-71 Blackbird. I would've gotten so far away. It's now the next morning. Saturday morning. Last night's football game was a farce. It all went to shit after I finished writing about the dance off and left the house. Crossing the street wearing school colors, body heading toward the football field, a sky-high bird shit on my head. Birds are a symbol of freedom. When "freedom" passes a bowel movement on you, consider it an omen. Once on the sidewalk, I stood still, the substance seeping into my scalp like an unwanted deep conditioning treatment. My eyes dejectedly sealed shut. When they unlocked, they fixated on three delinquents staggered before me, going har-de-har and all that bull. I'm not one to crawl inside myself and hide when presented with a steaming mess of humiliation. That said, I gently shook my head and quoted a movie to the heavens. "Please, lock me up. I'm gonna hit someone and I don't want to."

They were a sack of potatoes. Lumpy. Plain. Bland. Expressionless. Potatoey. Potatoey is a word if I say it is. And that's what their auras were about. Poop shaped potato coloring, the same shade as the girls in the dance off. The boys were so different in form compared to those girls, but so similar in spirit. I eventually said, "*Rebel Without a Cause*, anyone?" Their stares were blanker than professional card players at the World Series of Poker. "Haven't seen it?"

Their faces suggested unawareness of the 50's film referenced—

a seriously great film about a generation trying to find their place in the world. I exploded. "It's a shame you don't realize your whole devil-may-care attitude was originally pioneered by James Dean in a movie you've never heard of. Before his movie character, it was developed by countless others throughout history. Ever hear of Laozi, the founder of Daoism? Look into his teachings. Dude had to have been high off his ass."

They remained a sorry mess of silly putty.

"No comprende? Whatever. You know, it's depressing how amazing movie quotes are lost on so much of our generation because they're too busy watching *That's My Boy*. And…are you understanding me? No? Well, looking at you makes me realize none of what our generation wears, does, or stands for is new. It's all recycled. That's not the sad part. The sad part is that clowns like you three don't realize what you wear, do and stand for is recycled. You saunter about like you're the first young adults to ever exist. The first ones to have listened to alternative music, forsaken showering, done drugs, and been 'different' from everything that's come before you. You're not different. You're buffoons. Recycled matter that doesn't matter."

The three stooges exchanged looks with straight faces, then busted out laughing, completely stoned, mind you. One of them was this chubby knob wearing too many strange trends at once. Blue hair, drug rug, immense gauges, even bigger hipster glasses. He had equally huge undereye bags and looked more bummy than Never-Leaves-the-Street Steve. Finally, there was a tattoo on his neck. An infinity symbol. Let's call him Chubbers. He stopped his chuckling long enough to ask two questions. "You on crack? If so, can we have some?"

He was making a joke about the way I talk. My speech becomes accelerated. Booms. Can't help it. The tempo and volume increase when I'm nervous, excited, or pissed. In this case, it was the latter. "I'm not on drugs!" I yelled.

The scrawny, floppy-haired one finally registered my face, body language transforming as his friends continued to laugh. The twerp elbowed his chubby friend in the stomach, and muttered at him to 'shut up' because I'm 'that one girl'. The acne-covered, gangly guy said, "Fuck does that mean, bro?"

Yeah, bro. Fuck does that mean, bro? Better not be what I think you're talking 'bout, bro. Bro. Bro. Bro. Bro. BRO, said my inner voice. Damn, that voice hates the word *'bro'.* Once Stretch examined my facial features, he bit his tongue and looked off into the distance, finding a place to focus his eyes. Anyplace that wasn't my face. Chubbers was slow to catch on, however. Judging from his physique, he was most likely the slowest at many other activities. His mind was abroad, his chuckle persistent. The kid was the kind of kid who is forever the last kid to understand the punchline when someone is kidding. In this case, he was the last to realize the joke was over. "Why'd you guys stop laughing?" he said.

He squinted his bespectacled eyes at me until his cheeks puffed out and his eyebrows inched up his forehead. I felt bad for him as he felt bad for me. "You're that girl," he said. "Your dad...I'm sorry. I should just...shut up. Oh, no! Not saying you should shut up. I should shut up." As he apologized, his eyes volte-faced to the sidewalk. Mine glassed up. Lips and hands trembled in unison as I headed home to wash the poop out of my hair.

"Look what you did, fat ass," said Short Fry, admonishing his pal for failing to yank his fat foot out of his fat mouth. I could hear Chubbers' paralysis in his voice as he yelled after me, apologizing and congratulating me on making court. My legs kept moving as I told him not to apologize. Once home, I immediately hopped in the shower.

Being bombarded by droplets is the world's greatest sensation. A steaming hot shower is a goddamn oasis. Once in, you want to stay in. It's like a gang. Or a cult. It's difficult to work up the courage to get out and face the cold. I could live inside a hot shower for eternity, my languid body becoming raisin level wrinkled as a disconnect forms between my problems and me. To be a prune void of issues would be a superlative reality. There's only one reason to get out. Showers don't stay warm. They turn cold eventually.

Later that night, Melanie escorted me onto the football field. Parents walking with their children is a Homecoming Court tradition. I felt valued, but something was missing. It was a charade. As the football field lights heated me, Melanie squeezed my hand and whispered in my ear, "He'd be so proud." I wanted to rip her hand off her wrist, wave it in her face, and say, *You don't get to speculate on how he'd react to things. It's your fault.*

I'm tired of trying to write kindly about her. Reflecting on her, in any sense, is a charade. And high school football games are an immense charade, too, unless you attend a school that isn't "Wimpy Wira." That's what the other team's fans cheered during the slaughter fest. "WIMPY WIRA!" Repeatedly. Lame, I know. Jacques screamed back at the other team's horrible fans, "Suck your own wieners, Hamilton High!"

I joined him. "Suck your own wieners, Hamilton!"

Then Jacques and I chanted together: "SUCK YOUR OWN WIENERS! SUCK YOUR OWN WIENERS! SUCK YOUR OWN WIENERS!" Soon, everybody was staring. Our chant mildly caught on for a solid minute and the crowd crumbled into laughter. Other than that, tonight was awful. We didn't win. We can't. Not our homecoming game or any other game. What blows even more than our guys blowing it was the "fans" blowing off the team. The student section trickled throughout the game, migrating to the line outside the school. By the third quarter, the score was 42-6, and the numbers weren't in our favor. There was an Ice Cream Social to be held after the game. Everybody wanted a hot spot in line for the sugar fest. Fatties. Obviously, I live in Wisconsin, a mystical land where food always comes first. We all have Velveeta cheese coursing through our veins in the place of blood.

People kept dwindling. I was the last student to depart from the bleachers. Guys on the sidelines glanced back frequently at the nearly empty stands. The players shook it off as if it didn't bother them, but of course it did. We abandoned them. When the last strain of fans got up at the beginning of the fourth quarter, hefty Emily Hayes, with the quarter size mole on her face, asked if I was coming. My eyes surveyed the premises. I was cast away on an exotic island called Empty Metallic Bleachers. Didn't want to leave, but I'm a teenager, and an average one, at best. I've decided to not be a bird anymore, but my body follows the flock. Followed it all the way to the end of the Ice Cream Social line. But first, I pulled my camera out of my bag, snapping a photo of the forsaken bleachers.

Others only keep pictures of school's lovely memories, but I keep pictures of ugly ones as well. I hoard them so that years from now, when I sit before a box of memories, I will stumble upon the photograph of vacant bleachers. As the picture lies wilting in my wrinkling hands, my inner voice will speak up and say, "Being a teenager was great sometimes, but wow. We were a bouquet of pricks."

Sad pictures mean I'll never covet years I can't regain. I'll grow up.

October 14, 2012

Hey, Joey Journal,

Seventy-two days now. Throughout my parents' couplehood, they bonded over their shared obsession of mythologies from all over the world. In fact, my dad was set on River being named Osiris, after the Egyptian god of the afterlife. Melanie thought this was messed up. She told him a name representing the dead is no name for a baby. "Apollo is much better."

"Apollo is a total nerd," said my dad. "Osiris is darker. Edgier. Trust me, Smelly."

Luckily for the Dwyer kids, my parents ultimately chose a name scheme revolving around nature.

Somewhere along the line, I was told the good god Osiris was placed in a coffin by seventy-two evil disciples and accomplices of Set. He was then sent down the Nile. Not the most ideal send-off. My dad was cremated like he wanted, but that was the only thing about his actual funeral that matched his dream one. He used to joke that he wanted puppet strings attached to his limbs and for some sort of crane to make him fly and dance through the funeral home. He would be dressed like Beetlejuice and everybody else would be required to wear a costume of their own. Told us only fun music would play—The Bee Gees, Madonna, Flavor Flav. And he didn't get any of that. When I protested, Melanie said, "How can you plan a fun funeral for a death like this?"

I understand there are a few cut and dried impossibilities, but it's like Melanie didn't even try to give him any portion of his dream. There was all black and not a dry eye in the funeral home. He would've hated it. You know, the Egyptian goddess Isis used her great love for her husband Osiris to bring him back from the dead. She breathed life into him by turning into a bird and flapping her wings above him. If only Melanie could be like Isis, having enough love in her heart to breathe new life into someone. To her, what's dead is dead. Death is stereotypically sad, and she let it be sad on a day that should've been filled with The BeeGees, Madonna, and Flavor Flav.

The dance was last night. The Bee Gees, Madonna, Flavor Flav—none them made it to air.

We got dolled up solely to take and upload our pictorial hoard to Facebook. I only vaguely remember a time when pictures were taken to make memories last—to capture moments. Some folks still photograph as a means to remember, but those ranks of camera-wielding soldiers are dissipating. I salute them. All there is to be said is, "Tweet, tweet, bitches. Welcome to the age of Instagram."

Most pictures my friends upload are only in online circulation to receive 'oohs' and 'ahhs' and 'Facebook likes'. I'm fine with candid shots, but the posing is like somebody popping bubble wrap in my ear. It's only okay when I do it.

The setting is a Saturday night party. A kickback, or a rager. From my limited experience, it's all the same. Girls run up to random guys they've spoken only two words to in math class 'that one time'. These girls say, "Oh my God, David! It's been so long. We have to take a picture!"

Who is David, you ask? I sincerely don't know him, and neither does she. The phrase "It's been so long," is code for "Saw you yesterday during third hour." "We have to take a picture," means "This is going up on the Internet because I must keep up appearances."

"Oh my God" Girl and David pose, his arm slung lazily around her shoulder as she becomes a boa constrictor. Barely knows him, yet she squeezes his abdomen like they were roommates, way back in the We-Still-Live-in-Our-Mother's-Womb Days. Twinsies! Goofy faces are made and deuces are chucked up. The pictures fill their Facebook profiles, ear splittingly singing, "Look! Look! Look! I have friends! I have fun!

I'm not phony at all!'"

But everybody is.

Some candid gems can be found in last weekend's pictures, but it's like finding a needle in a stack of duck faces. As we search for that needle, we seldom remember anything from Saturday night. Date rape drugs weren't slipped into our systems. We were simply under the influence of a smart phone's flash. Technological sheep...only able to recall a bunch of posing. That's what it means to be a teenager in 2012.

We're posing for the picture instead of living.

Maybe it's always been this way.

I solemnly swear by the scrapbooks piled in my closet, which are tangible. The mementos guide my hand, silently stealing me away into yesteryear. I say "yes" to yesteryear. *Yes, you can have me. For a while.*

However, I'm glad yesterday's calamities are slipping away. After I'm done recounting it all, I vow to never revisit the memories.

10:00 am to 5:00 pm—Shaved legs, nursed the nicks, shaved the pits, lotioned the limbs, and beautified all of it. Melanie's friend came over, did my hair and gave me a vintage hat to pin on my head's hairy side. It matches the black flapper dress I conveniently found in the back of my eclectic closet the day I was nominated. I hardly wanted to go to the dance, let alone shop for it. The dance's theme was 'Night at the Speakeasy'. Nobody ever dresses according to the theme, but that doesn't stop me from parading about in attire that coincides. I reapplied my lipstick for the seventh time, and ha-chee-cha...I was sort of a hottie.

5:00 pm-6:30 pm—Pictures were taken to commemorate the milestone. Pre-dance photos have been a tradition long before the Internet existed, back when our caregivers were in their prime. Once upon a roller disco rink, our parents were us, illuminated by their parents' amateur photography. And now they're the camera-holding adults. My parents never come, though. Always urged them not to. They complied. I like that. Not because I'm embarrassed of them, but because my solo situation is mortifying. They were teenagers during a different era. I'm pretty sure that if you didn't have a homecoming date back in the 70's and 80's, you didn't go. If you went dateless, you'd be pinned to the wall, left to fraternize with the other withering wallflowers. Nowadays, it's acceptable to go stag to a dance.

Herds of people go in groups of friends, but I always end up tagging along in a posse of couples. Normally, it's because I never fail to wait until last minute to decide about my attendance. This year, it's because I have a blockhead boyfriend who prioritizes video games over me. A few days before each ball, my 'gal pals' beg me to go. Not because they're relying on my presence, but because if a person says, "I'll sit this dance out," people pity them. They feel it's their duty to save me from a Saturday night spent crocheting sweaters for Mr. Bojangles.

"It won't be fun without you," they cry.

My internal voice shrieks back, *You'll manage!"* My mouth, however, says, "Don't have a group."

"Come with us and our dates!"

This year, hefty ole Emily Hayes, with the quarter-sized mole on her face, told me I was going in her group the second she heard I was on court. Didn't fight it because I was too busy trying to figure out what kind of witchcraft she used to get a date. I'll be tagged in a fatuous amount of Facebook pictures. That's plenty. It's better this way. If I was somebody's mama-paparazzi, I wouldn't want to see my kid alone in a whirlpool of paired-up adolescents.

The pre-dance photoshoot is always in somebody's backyard, at a park, by the river, or on a lake's dock. The poses range from classic to goofy. Throughout, my mug becomes the spitting image of *Young Frankenstein's* Igor. There's about ten photos with everybody, ten with only the girls, ten with the boys. Once the group shots wrap, fifteen minutes are spent running around, getting singular pictures with only specific people. This year, Jacques approached me for our "annual picture" and when he tags me in it later, I bet you he won't realize I'm frowning.

Every year, I spend a lot of time standing with the about two other girls who shared in my dateless misfortune. We talk amongst ourselves as we avoid watching everybody else posing with their dates. We laugh intermittently, not positive if we're pretending to have fun or actually having fun. The lonesome doves don't need to watch the couples to know how it goes. We've been dateless before. This scene has set in many times. The corsages, the boutonnieres, the romance. All that jazz. The same lucky girls get all the corsages, while the others wish they could don a mess of flowers on their wrist. Only once.

6:00 pm-8:00 pm—Dinner time. The restaurant can either be fancy or fast food. It's the best part of the evening, but not because of the cuisine. I barely ate, aspiring to avoid stomach bloat. This is the point in the festivities where discussion takes place. Food makes people's true selves come out. Engaging words flow out of mouths as morsels are shoveled in. Not all at once, preferably.

8:00 pm—Jungle humping happens. As you know, jungle humping is one of my least favorite movements on the planet. And you should also be made aware that I'm a hypocrite. Logan started talking to me while we waited for beverages. He said, "Rosie, you know what's better than standing in a hot gym full of sweaty punks that are, in your words, jungle humping?" I faintly smiled and gave a slight shoulder jerk. His answer was the word, "Bowling."

I lightly backhanded his stomach and we continued to chat while he drank Sprite and I downed water. When we tossed our plastic cups, I thought he asked, "Wanna dance?"

The gym was booming, leaving me unsure if I heard him right. I said, "You wanna dance?" And I meant it like, *"You asked me to dance? Can't hear you."* Fast. He grabbed my hand fast, pulling me into the crowd. Because it was the dance floor, we were obligated to dance. We didn't just dance. No salsa, no tap, no Macarena. None of that. We grinded. Jungle humped, as I'm known to call it. I liked it. It's tiring dancing in the black hole of single ladies, reminding myself to turn my head away from the couples. Your eyes can't help but fall on people making bodily contact.

Most girls don't slut-shame themselves for dancing with another human, but my mind makes everything paramount. In the moment, life was infinity on the highest of highs. Wanted, I was. Noticed, too. Largely, I felt nothing. When the song was over, Logan kept dancing, but I pulled away and into the hallway where I perched myself against a locker for the longest time. Logan was probably off with another girl by the time my sitting body was surrounded by a group of happy dancegoers who probably had no idea I was zoning out their jabbering. My mind was racing. You know you like someone when your heart's racing, but when your mind is racing, it has nothing to do with another person at all.

My brain entertained the thought that at that damn dance, I was Logan's Jeremy. I was a flatulent and fat Catholic schoolboy. Logan was making it okay. It's the Homecoming Court nomination all over again. I can handle tomfoolery, but cannot hack baseless philanthropy. I didn't find a place to cry this time, instead remembering a time where I silently sobbed in the bathroom and read the words etched on the stall. "Fuck the bullshit, just do you."

Don't think about Logan a second more, I thought. *If you think about that bonehead, I'll do my duty as the brains and punish your body by developing a 24/7 menstrual cycle and a mustache for good measure. Be independent. Fuck the bullshit. Fuck it up.*

I tried to eff the bull crap, got up, bounced from group to group, entertained the masses, left a trail of funk behind my shimmying physique. But for the first time ever, getting funky wasn't fun. My intestines were mangled like a handful of silly putty being clutched and twisted by a fifth grader. A spoiled, devilish, impossible, immature, stupid fifth grader. *Fuck the bullshit. Just do you. Fuck the bullshit, just do you. Fuck the bullshit, just do you. Why the fuck isn't this bullshit working?* The mantra lost meaning to me.

You should've seen Jacques during the King and Queen dance, though. He fucked the bullshit. Hard. Queen Mouthful was MIA when the DJ stopped the music and summoned only the royalty to the floor. Rumors spread around the dance. Apparently Mouthful left to get a mouthful of her date so she didn't have to dance with Jacques. She snuck back in later on. Weasel.

Jacques told me Mouthful hates him for a "silly, bitchy, insignificant reason." He heard from one of their mutual dance friends that she bombed the ACT. Got a 14. Jacques told everyone and not for revenge. Truth is he still doesn't know what Mouthful called him in middle school, or what she did to my lawn. People kept mum about it so they wouldn't become her next target. I don't think I'll ever tell him. Jacques didn't repeat her secret ACT score because he hates her. He repeated it because his case of vocal dysentery is far more fatal than mine.

During the King and Queen dance, the other court couples joined a solo Jacques on the floor. Aaron from science class and I were forced to dance together because our partners received the crowns. As soon as we were in slow dancing formation, he grabbed my tush with one hand and made a thumbs up at the student body with the other. I nearly ripped his ear off as I said, "I'm done with your needle dick antics, Aaron!"

We resumed our dancing silently. I leaned past Aaron's bored body to watch Jacques. If this situation would've happened a year ago, I'd have joined Jacques. I would've danced with him. Hard. But this is now. And right now I liked seeing Jacques alone. He needs to know how it feels. He put on a spectacular solo show in the middle of the gym floor, stepping up, being queen enough for both of them. It was beautiful. I'm starting to hate him, but I can admit that a lone Jacques is beautiful.

All in all, the dance was about as fun as my dad's funeral.

November 25, 2012

Hey, Joey Journal,

I accidentally abandoned you, but you haven't missed much. It's been forty-two days since the dance and 114 days since he died. Triple digits. People who live to the age of 110 and up are called supercentenarians. Had my dad made it to age 114, he'd constantly dress like a centaur and wear a cape. Half-deaf in his old age, he'd think people were calling him a Super Centaur. I pictured this while fiddling with a bag of grapes in the cafeteria. I was sitting next to hefty ole Emily Hayes and her wiggling quarter-sized facial mole. Since the first day of freshman year, I've made it my daily mission to never sit with the same group of kids in the same spot. I've eaten at every table in that cafeteria. I've also had lunch in hallways and classrooms, not to mention all the off-campus locations. Today, for God knows what reason, I chose to sit next to Emily. Her mole's wiggling sped up as she ranted about college apps. And that's when I imagined my dad, trotting in dressed as the wrinkly Super Centaur. In my daydream, he gently tapped Emily on the shoulder. "Hey, Mr. Dwyer," said daydream Emily. "You look well."

"Thank you," he said before smashing his hooves into her face multiple times. Somehow, this act of violence made the mole fall off. Before galloping into the distance, he said, "You're both very welcome."

And we all lived happily ever after.

Back in the real world, real world Emily became real serious. "This is no time to be hysterically laughing, Rosie. I told you I got put on the waitlist for my backup school and—"

That's when I made a dead sprint for the bathroom. Had my first ever silent laugh session.

114 days. I can hardly believe it.

The most tumultuous event since my last entry was Hostess going out of business. Twinkies are off the market. It's been more than a month since I've beaten you silly with my pen, and our separation had a reason. Today, I walked past my little sister's open door. An odor exuded from Willow's wilderness. My room is untidy, but her room is grotesquely messy. This trend began in August. My dad would've yelled this chaos away. He was never diagnosed with OCD, but he often acted in accordance with the main traits of the disorder. Other disorders, too. You wouldn't imagine if you didn't know him well, but those problems were always there.

In his absence, her Hannah Montana bed sheets are forever unwashed and her clothes moonlight as her carpet, leaving the floor invisible. It was lost. I thought about reporting it missing. All the milk cartons in America would feature a picture of what Willow's floor formerly looked like, accompanied by the words, "Have you seen this floor?"

My nostrils trailed the smell over to her bedside table, where a rotting banana peel was cemented to a bowl of yogurt. I yanked the eyesore off her nightstand. It was sticking to the wood. Once it was detached from Willow's furniture, my hands shook the bowl, and the strawberry yogurt refused to jiggle. Spiraling into fear, I headed toward the door before I could find an animal carcass on the premises, which isn't an unlikely premise. Two years back, Willow's hamster died. Otis. She told nobody and somehow captured a chipmunk for the newly empty cage. Willow named him Chuck Berry. I don't know where she heard of the 1950's singer at age six, but she treasured the name. Willow put Otis' corpse in a shoebox and shoved it under her bed. Because it was Willow's responsibility to feed her 'pet', nobody realized her actual hamster no longer had a heartbeat. Four days passed before my dad smelled the box. When asked why she didn't tell anybody Otis died, her eyes embodied misery. She said, "Didn't want to upset anyone."

Leave it to Willow Dwyer to turn the insanely gross into the innocently charming.

When I turned around, I saw you, my only confidant, sitting on Willow's unmade twin mattress. I was panic-stricken for weeks, thinking my private thoughts were floating around somewhere in the school. Honestly, I felt an odd sense of relief when I saw you opened and face down on Hannah Montana's crotch.

"Why are you here?" Willow was in the doorway, donning her Nicki Minaj costume. Pink wig, fake nails, overabundant egotistical air. Her latex leggings were even stuffed with butt padding. It was a Halloween costume. Even though today's date was November 25th, she still finds excuses to wear it on a near daily basis. For instance, she often claims her friends are starting a Twerk Team. Apparently, they won't let her join until she perfects her "booty bounce." She says she dances her best in the get-up. Melanie needs to reevaluate her parenting style. Whoa. Weird. *Her parenting style.* Her. Not "their." I just threw up in my wastebasket. There was no food in it. Just water and bile.

In addition to looking wacky, the insidious witch child was also red with fury. Despite treating her room like a garbage can, Willow is quite protective over her stanky environment. However, I was more incensed than she, so I demanded the kid explain herself. Her eyes refocused on the rotting food and she plunged into self-defense mode, saying, "I was gonna bring that down. I promise!"

"Don't explain your savageness. I'm aware you were raised by apes for the first three years of your life until that fateful family safari."

"Stop being mean!"

"Stop reading my notebook, Willow."

She gasped upon realizing what was sitting on her bed, then leapt toward her mattress, planting her stuffed bum my notebook, nonchalantly crossing her legs. Joey, I'm sorry you had to be in close proximity to her butt. Even through inches of padding, it must have been an ordeal. She toots often. The scent persistently lingers.

"Don't know what you're talking about, Rosalinda," she said.

"Not my name." My hands squeezed her wrinkled comforter and pulled it as forcefully as possible. She went flying, transforming into a weeping Willow. I didn't think it would work. The apologies promptly began as I knelt down next to her. "You okay?"

Bam. The turd popped me in the nose, inviting a trickle of blood out. She's been so violent lately. There's holes in like three walls of this house. I grabbed my Joey Journal from the floor and lightly hit Willow in the head with it. "Stop," I said. "You're eight. I can't fight you." She threw herself on her bed, propelling her lanky limbs everywhere. Her wig soared across the room, her dark curls convulsing something awful. Soon she was punching and screaming into her unicorn Pillow Pet named Peta. Yes, its namesake is from *The Hunger Games* books. She has a God given gift for naming pets, be them alive or stuffed. And her jabs grew more powerful. I said, "Peta doesn't deserve that, Willow!" She threw the unicorn at the wall and dramatically collapsed, shoving her face into her mephitic mattress. I leaned in, staring menacingly. "Shit Queen," I said. "Why do you have this?'

Willow reluctantly turned her face. Her voice was soft and guilty as she whispered, "I was reading?"

"You can read?"

She sat up and her vocal pace increased. "Loads of kids my age read, Rosie. I'm halfway done with the second *Hunger Games* book."

When her tongue popped out, I grabbed it while saying, "You'd be done by now if you weren't spending your spare time reading my writing."

After she made a string of pathetic noises, I let go. "I'm a slow reader, Rosie."

"No. You're just slow," I said, jumping up and starting toward the door.

"Wait! Can I read a bit more?"

I turned dramatically and said, "What the hell are you on?"

"C'mon. I'm on chapter four. It's getting juicy."

I paused, tilting my baffled head. Then I smiled marginally as I hoisted the journal. "What do think this is?"

"A book. Your first book." I fell quiet as Willow stared at me, toting a youthful grin. There were gaps, because some girl punched the two front baby teeth out during recess the other day. Willow started the fight. Mel keeps getting these loaded phone calls from the school.

Moments passed by as I gaped incredulously at her. She quickly filled the silence, speaking with her odd little expression. "You shouldn't name characters after yourself and family and friends and stuff. That'll make people think this stuff is real."

"Willow, do you sincerely think I was born yesterday?"

The child giggled before becoming rather serious. She said, "I don't like what you wrote about me. You made me sound like a child."

"You are a child."

She let out another chuckle. "But really, a diary?"

"What's funny?" I asked.

"Diaries are so nineties. Get a Tumblr like a normal teenager."

I dashed out of her room, slammed the door, and shouted, "Bring down your damn dishes!"

"I was gonna!"

No, she wasn't.

Right that second, I so wished I could see my dad in a super centaur costume, properly disciplining her.

November 26, 2012

Hey, Joey Journal!

115 days since it happened, and that's exactly how many minutes it took me to respond to a question Bette asked me. She pulled me out of the hallway during passing time a week ago and said, "Will you stage-manage the school musical?"

"You convinced the board to let you do it?"

The strange woman jumped about, victoriously karate-chopping the air. I told her to let me think about it until the end of the day. Fifteen minutes into creative writing class, I had the urge to get it over with. I went to her desk and gave the most unsure sure ever served.

Musical auditions start tomorrow. As the karate chops suggested, Bette is charged and ready to take over our disheveled drama program. When I asked her why she chose me to be stage manager, she noted that I've worked crew before and I'm bossy. It works. Since I'm stage manager, I have to view auditions.

Bette tried her luck on Broadway after high school and had trouble finding jobs, but not for lack of talent. When she sings in class, she's quite the virtuoso. Bette attributes her Broadway misfortune to being 103 pounds heavier back then, not to mention black. Minds are widening, but too many concretely narrow ones still exist. There were limited parts for her to play. Bette lasted two years in the wildly expensive city before it was time to dip. Temporarily abandoning her aspirations was torture, because Bette always considered Broadway her destiny, seeing as she was born with a huge voice and Bette Midler as her namesake. "Failure" made her question her belief in fate. When Bette moved home, she hardly believed in destiny anymore, or herself, for that matter.

One day, while swaddled up in a blanket on her parents' couch, Bette saw the movie *Dead Poets Society* on TV. Robin Williams' character is a prolific English teacher who says, "Seize the day. Gather ye rosebuds while ye may." When Robin Williams speaks to you through the television, it's an abomination not to listen. She wasn't positive that teaching was her true predestination, but she wanted to see if it was. And so Bette came to realize her true destiny was accepting that we must try out all different destinies before the right one swallows us up and says, "Ready for this ride? Fasten your seatbelt."

While in college, she stopped chasing her future and kept her eyes open for opportunities, instead. All she had control over was how she reacted to what she was given—the present. Bette says, "The next moment of your life will be monumental if you do what you can with the present moment. Trust the moment. That's the first step of the process. And you know what I say about the process."

You have to trust it. Bette says she might not have a Tony, but she has stability. And that's something.

I love what Bette has to say, but it's painful listening to her. My dad spoke like that. Exactly like that. Do all drama teachers work from the same script?

Teaching. How's that stable? If I were to ditch my ultimate dream, I wouldn't surrender and take on this nation's most underappreciated profession. I'd go for an in-demand, high-paying job. Like a nurse. I'd puke eight times daily because blood is…bloody, but that cash flow is something else. To me, it's either chase your dreams until you're ragged or go make some bank. I'll never teeter between extremes. I've discussed this with River. He told me I'm not old enough to understand.

We haven't put on a production at Wira North since last fall. Our former director was a piece of ~~crap~~ work. Arthur B. Cummings was his stage name, and he refused to reveal his given name. By 'stage name,' I mean 'deodorant commercial name'. He was in one ad for Arm and Hammer in 1985, and never missed an opportunity to boast about it. Arthur had an infinite supply of flared trousers in assorted colors and always wore a matching ascot. The man would've looked like Fred from Scooby Doo if it weren't for his voluminous gut and white beard. Arthur sure had facial hair, but his hair follicles forwent his head's top. He looked like a truly special Kris Kringle, a Santa experimenting with 1970's fashion.

Arthur was a drama queen, flipping out around the clock. Nobody talked. Not even an occasional whisper was uttered. Not even during breaks. The fall show last year was *Death of a Salesman*. Arthur Miller was Arthur's favorite playwright. I had a part because the characters didn't sing. I was The Woman, which is the character Willy cheats on his wife with. My first part ever. Even though none of us were having a swell time, we still wanted to make it great despite our director.

He spent the first month of rehearsal having us do 'character research' and nothing else. Arthur denied us our scripts until we "understood" our characters. Foolish. How can we get acquainted with our characters if we aren't permitted to know what they say? There's nothing wrong with research, but we had two months of rehearsal. We should've been exploring characters on our own time. But no! Arthur forced us to make dioramas depicting each character's "internal struggle" during valuable practice hours. When the first month ended, the "method exercises" began. Arthur assigned each actor an animal. We were to act like our given animal for a week of rehearsal. Sammy Hruska was a senior last year. His part was the demanding role of Willy Loman, the salesman. What was Arthur having him do the week before tech? He had Sammy acting like a God forsaken walrus.

Arthur was scary serious about the 'method' drills. I was made to act like a flamingo. When I became bored with arm flapping, I started singing "Copacabana" by Barry Manilow. My flamingo bodily movements continued as my voice grew louder. The other animals onstage giggled. Arthur climbed onstage, wobbling treacherously in my direction. Never thought I'd ever use the words "wobble" and "treacherously" in the same breath, but that's what he did. He wobbled treacherously.

When my eyes opened, Arthur was inches from my face. Disgruntled authority figures like doing that. They invade personal bubbles, fold their arms, and stare at people like they're the crust on the underside of life's butt cheeks. Arthur's breath exuded the scents of alcohol and beef jerky. His eyes were crystal blue, nearly white. Under-eye bags swelled beneath them. He hadn't slept in days and had the appearance of a depressed, listless ghost. "What exactly are you doing, young lady?" he said, voice unwavering, yet deflated. Arthur knew none of our names. All the girls were "Young Lady", and each guy was called "Young Man." He was too self-important for simple name memorization. I gawked at him. He said, "Must I repeat myself? What in the name of William Shakespeare are you doing?"

"Being a flamingo."

He shut his eyes, shook his head, then addressed the cast. "This exercise will be treated with respect or my name is not Arthur B. Cummings."

"Your name isn't Arthur B. Cummings," I said, sass swirling in my capillaries. The way he flattened his little hair tufts indicated he was about to smack me.

The theatre kids quieted. Arthur staggered offstage, but thought better of it. He came toward me again, eyes feverish, awkward steps weighed down by animosity. Pillaging my bubble once more, he whispered a most painful insult, with hate lacing each word. "You, young lady, are a disgrace to flamingos everywhere!"

That's Arthur B. Cummings in a nutshell. Emphasis on the "nut" part. When tech week arrived, the action wasn't blocked and we were yet to act with each other. There was one read through. A mess, for sure. The cast walked into the theatre on the first day of the last week of rehearsals, hoping for a miracle. Instead, there was Arthur B. Cummings, lying lethargically dormant onstage. He was passed out, drunk, and bathing nearly naked in a puddle of his own piss and puke. Turns out Arthur suffers from Bipolar Disorder and was having an episode. I'm glad I'm only the fun kind of crazy, not the batshit kind.

You know how they say 'the show must go on'? Ours didn't. The productions that were supposed to follow *Death of a Salesmen* didn't go on either. It was a *Death of a High School Drama Program*. Arthur resigned or was fired. Probably fired. Nobody knew for sure. I heard talk the school didn't want to fund the detonated drama department any further. But Bette, who was in her fourth year teaching at Wira North last year, fought the school board for months to bring it back. She gave up teaching Zumba classes at her church to take this on.

Our show is *Urinetown*. It has a terrible title, but I couldn't be more pumped to put it on. It's about a city facing a drought. Definitely one of my favorites. The story is about love, uprising and freedom. Satirical, witty, perfect. As a result of lacking water supplies, private bathrooms are nearly extinct. The town's people are forced to pay to urinate, because in their community, peeing is a privilege. Sounds like somebody we know? Looking at you, Mr. McAdams, the man who made me piss myself in science class.

I'm a disgrace to flamingos the world over. Here's to hoping I don't fail stage managers everywhere.

November 29, 2012

Hey, Joey Journal!

118 days. The number of elements on the periodic table. Blegh, science. I should be doing homework for that class, but I gave that up cold turkey. Instead, let's discuss auditions. They just ended. Watching them was... shouldn't say "watching." The proper word is "witnessing." A select few auditions were like witnessing a supernatural phenomenon, while the rest were like witnessing a crime, a crime to musical theatre. On the real, a girl wore a pink leotard and a feather boa while singing 'Lady Marmalade' by Patti Labelle. Her "Gitchi-Gitchi ya-ya's" slurred together. She also thought it would be sensible to throw her boa around Bette's neck, playfully pulling at the ends. Insobriety was possible.

The first day of tryouts, the musical hopefuls performed choreography to a segment of the *Urinetown* song, "Run Freedom Run." Mostly everyone was spent by the night's end. Exceptions to exhaustion were the dancers and athletes. Jacques could do the choreography in his sleep. Some girls from the Poms team auditioned, too. We need as many dancers as we can get, but still, it's like they're foreign spies infiltrating a sacred place. I blame *Glee*, and also commercials encouraging us to "keep the arts alive." The arts should be kept breathing, but only by enjoyable people.

A few new faces belonged to a herd of senior guys, on their athletic off-seasons. They must've seen *High School Musical* as kids and thought, "Totally felt that. Gonna be Troy Bolton someday." The beef heads have few similarities to the character in question. No Disney

Channel charm. Just a whole row of left feet paired with elitist attitudes. Logan was among these jocks. He's not like them, though. A member of the sporty sodality, yes, but inside him beats the heart of a dweeb. During art class a while back, he asked for help picking out a monologue and I coughed up a watered-down giggle. "Don't laugh in my time of need," he said.

"Isn't soccer your thing?"

"Hell no. Just a game. The season's done. My last season. I'm not playing in college." Logan sat in the empty chair next to me, agitated. The pause lingered as he bounced his knee. His expression was considerably far off. Siberia far off. I was about to sass him back to reality, but he lightly jolted, smiled and said, "Never played much. Ever. That bench and my butt were faithful to each other. Now, this butt and its beloved are dunzo. My tush is ready to explore new relationships."

"Can your tush sing?" I asked.

He looked down, half smiling. "Maybe, but my mouth does a better job."

"You dance?"

"Who won the dance off?"

"Logan, the school dance off was different this year. The top two were God awful. Wasn't about dance ability. It was about who was the most entertaining."

"So, you admit I'm more entertaining than you?"

"Fine," I said. "I'll send you monologues. Need a song? Something from *Book of Mormon* or *Avenue Q* would be—"

"I already have a song memorized."

Shocking. "You have songs at the ready in your brain space?" He told me his brain space was full of them. "What song, Logan?" He slyly shook his head. "Don't make me rip the answer from your larynx."

Logan laughed in a freaked-out way, holding his hands up, like a criminal when a policeman is approaching. He said, "Calm yourself, killer. Just a song. My parents went to New York once and they dragged me to a Broadway show. Thought I'd hate it, but it was cool. Wasn't all glitter and high kicks. There was this song that made me feel the way Salisbury steak tastes."

"You felt soggy?"

"Kinda."

I said, "What musical? What song? Who the hell are you?"

I guessed nonstop for days until Logan threatened to throw a blunt object in my direction. So, he danced with the rest of the auditionees, and was only half bad. Logan told me later he prepared by using an elite training program called Dance Dance Revolution. No wonder he looked so robotic.

Once Bette finished teaching the moves, she reclaimed her seat in the house. Small groups filtered in to perform what they learned. A purple-haired chick in the first group was doing amazing, but closed her eyes a second too long and got too close to the stage's edge. *Boom!* Home girl toppled off the platform she was boogying down on. I felt for her. Ineptitude is also an illness of mine. After checking on the girl, Bette clapped her hands and said, "Thanks, ladies! Send the next group in."

As they evacuated, I whispered, "That chick is so me. My sister from another mister."

Bette looked confused and asked, "Isn't she your sister? Your faces are identical."

I sighed. "Bette, this may surprise you, but just because we're both white doesn't mean we look alike."

I considered her comment to be merely a crazy quip by crazy Bette, but became a believer the next day during the monologues. Freshman Mackenzie Hemperley entered, wearing a tie-dyed sweater and acid wash jeans. The pants appeared to have encountered a hungry wolf pack. Her makeup was extreme, tragically dark around the eyes. Horn-rimmed glasses sat casually on her nose and frizzy purple hair framed her face, her face that looked exactly like mine. "Holy," I said. "That's me!"

She was chubbier, but we still matched. I impulsively climbed onstage, grabbing her face and squishing her cheek into mine. "Freaky. A doppelganger, Bette! Doppelgangers!"

"Sit," Bette said. "Put your doppelganger at ease."

Then my duplicate spoke, voice outrageously different from mine. Mackenzie soulfully said, "Takes much more to make me uncomfortable. Like falling offstage." Then introduced herself and did her monologue. Phenomenal. While performing, she transformed from lai d-back to perky, with a whole onslaught of heart. I don't remember what her monologue was about because Bette and I were laughing so hard. She was one of the only girls to make us authentically laugh. When people try too hard be funny, it tends to inspire low amounts of amusement in those subjected to it.

I especially hate when girls aren't funny. Looking at that written out, I can see how that sounds anti-feminist or something, but I don't care. I'm not saying men are naturally more amusing. Just think abo ut it. Women have been oppressed since Adam first told Eve to shut up and make him a sandwich. Until the 1920's, ladies weren't allowed to vote, let alone have a voice. Many women are still striving to make the voices our oppressors granted us sound humoro us. Progress is happening, but many have a long way to go. As for men, the non-funny ones somehow still make barbaric people laugh by being denser than a neutron star. If a woman is funny in this way, they're told to read a book and stop being a stereotype. None of it's fair, but that's why women have to be better than "fair." We have to be on our game, always.

When it comes to humor, women are shifting out of puberty and rapidly ripening. Previously, there were few female comics on the scene. Those women were like girls who get their periods in the third grade. Rare, but they exist. Betty White, Joan Rivers, Whoopi Goldberg, Roseanne Barr, Phyllis Diller, Mae West, Lucille Ball, Carol Burnett, Jackie "Moms" Mabley. They got their 'humor periods' prematurely, but now we've got Tina Fey, Sarah Silverman, Amy Poehler, Kristen Wiig, Melissa McCarthy, Ellen Degeneres, Chelsea Handler, countless others. Women are turning the comedy scene on its head.

It wasn't easy or graceful getting to where we are. When it come s to humor, women are almost there. We're nearly out of puberty. Guys got a head start, but only because they captured the head start and refused to share it with us. However, humor wise, our boobs are practically grown in. Once they're fully developed, women will completely capture the comedy world. And that's one of the top fears of menfolk. It's hard not to be entranced by a big, bouncing humor bosom.

That was an odd tangent. Let me state this more simply. The

unfunny male auditionees were so bad, they aren't even worth writing about. Most of the girls' monologues unfortunately weren't humorous because they're still waiting for their 'humor boobs' to grow. There's nothing less amusing than a girl faking 'humor boobs' by shoving 'humor chicken cutlets' into her 'humor training bra'. Mackenzie was an exception, wearing a 'humor D-cup'. Once she was exiting, Bette whispered, "Let's hope she can sing, because she might be our Hope."

"An unintended pun?"

"Fully intentional," she said, winking.

If we thought her acting was sublime, you should've seen us when that girl sang. Today, she voyaged into the choir room and handed the piano player sheet music. I instantly knew her song. "My Friend the Dictionary" from *The 25th Annual Putnam Spelling Bee*.

Ugh. She's the talented twin. I love and hate her, simultaneously. Her 'humor boobs' grew three sizes today. When she finished, I asked if she got a humor boob job. They shot me curious stares and I told them not to ask. "Wow, look at you," Bette said. Mackenzie smiled before the choir room became empty once more. "Of course we'll have to tame her hair and provide contacts, but we've found our Hope."

Later, we unearthed a boy sinister enough to play Hope's dad, the villainous Mr. Cladwell. Jacques admits he's never strong during vocal auditions, but he has improved because of vocal coaching. This year, he was also honest with himself about what part he'd be best at and didn't go for the hunky male lead that is Bobby Strong. Instead, he sang "Be Prepared" from *The Lion King*. Killed it.

As for Logan's tryout, well, I didn't originally plan to write my thoughts on it. However, I'm beginning to think I must deposit all my thinks into this think space in order to stop thinking about it. His performance wasn't good. It was orgasmic. A strong choice of word, but it's the only word in the English vernacular that properly reflects what he did. I'm not insinuating an orgasm was had while he sang. The word 'orgasmic' has multiple dictionary definitions, one meaning to have an orgasm. The one I'm referring to differs. My orgasmic is an instance or occurrence of intense or unrestrained excitement.

He entered the choir room with shoulders slouched and his entire body bumbling. "General Perkins and Major Dwyer," he said, saluting us.

I took an apathetic sip from my giant water bottle as Bette dutifully asked, "What're you singing, Private Fields?"

"A song from a musical I saw on Broadway. 'I'm Alive', from *Next to Normal*."

My teacher clapped her hands and said, "On Broadway?"

"Original cast and everything."

"Jealous," Bette said. "Rosie, that's your fave, right?"

I smiled. "Yep. That said, Logan better do it justice."

He nodded, handing his sheet music to the piano player. Once settled, he began. I wasn't prepared for what was to torrent out of his pie hole. My jaw dropped as his opened. A sweet, rich, creamy, sensational, *orgasmic* voice was unleashed. I felt alive. His energy was that of person existing, as well. I knew what he meant when he said the song made him feel like how Salisbury steak tastes. I wet my pants a bit, thus I myself was Salisbury steak level soggy. I heard Bette's thunderous applause and saw Logan rub the back of his head, but I was disconnected. She said, "The cliché, 'we saved the best for the last,' couldn't be more accurate."

"Aye-aye, General Perkins," Logan said clumsily. He raised an eyebrow weakly at me before striding into the hall, most likely trying to figure out why I was stacking binders over my slightly damp pants.

Bette scrunched her face in a quizzical manner and said, "You in there, kiddo? What did you think?"

"Ever see *The Little Mermaid*, Bette?"

"What true woman has gone through life without seeing it?"

I softly said, "I can only describe this moment as being like the plot of *The Little Mermaid*."

"Help me out?"

I deadpanned. "I'm Ursula. He's Ariel. My soul's desire henceforth is to steal his orgasmic voice and put it in a nautilus shell." And that was the end of that.

After auditions wrapped, Jacques and I went to a new frozen yogurt restaurant. It's called Yo Mama's. The building used to be the dojo where we met, which went out of business. While sprinkling toppings on our yogurt heaps, I smiled, knowing the pair of us came full circle.

I highly prefer froyo over The Dojo. It's the hot thing right now, which is ironic because it's frozen. Anytime some big chain opens up nearby, the youths go mad. It was packed. We settled by the window, digging into our disposable bowls. Mine was only topped with fruit while my friend's bowl defeated the purpose of it being yogurt. It was practically a chocolate sundae. I didn't say anything about it at first. Nothing sticks to Jacques' bony frame because of his overactive thyroid.

I want an overactive thyroid.

I knew my yogurt allegation would annoy him, because whenever we occasionally talk at school, Jacques says I touch on dietary topics too often. He always says, "Rosie, bring dieting up again and I'll insert threat of violence and bodily harm here."

However, impulses cannot be fought. I said, "Not trying to sound like a harpy, but—"

"Buts are for buttheads," he said. "Express yourself, girl."

"Drowning yogurt with chocolate syrup and candy defeats the purpose of it being yogurt." My follow-up smile was lamb-like. Jacques stared at me as I immediately back-pedaled. "Sorry. I—"

Cutting me off, he brutally said, "Rosie, bring dieting up again and I'll find the filthiest nails in my father's shed. I'll bring them back to Yo Mama's and play a game of darts with your body as the board."

"That's graphic. You need therapy," I joked.

"No. You do." This wasn't a joke.

"Diet is the key to balanced living, *monamie*."

"Balanced diets have room for treats," Jacques said, exasperated. "Moderation, baby. Our fixations finish us."

"Can we just eat our food? Let's stop talking about it."

Jacques nodded, leaned in and said, "Make it a promise."

"Auditions," I said. "Wanna know what I think? That's the point of you wanting to get together outside of school, just the two of us, for the first time in 118 days, right?" He took a bite of his monstrosity, conflicted. I was mad at him, but wanted out of that awkwardness. "It's okay," I said. "Takes two to drift apart. At least we're together now. How excited are you for *Urinetown*?"

He yelled, "I'm dying!" It was booming in there, so few noticed.

Once they went back to ignoring us, Jacques smirked and said, "Tell me your auditions thoughts, boo."

"This freshman was hilarious. Gargantuan humor boobs. We're set on her playing—"

"Rosie, no humor boobs. That phrase is atrocious. And you know that when I ask for opinions, I only care for your thoughts surrounding my audition."

Of course, I thought. *Silly me, thinking he simply wanted my views. He only wants me around when it involves theatre or that bastard, Eliot.* My face was concerned as I gently grabbed my pal's hands and said, "Let's have a serious talk." His face was scared and hilarious. "You on performance enhancers?"

Jacques closed his eyes, shaking his head, grinning fiercely. "Thanks. Thought you were gonna say I sucked." Then he disengaged my hands in order to push his light blond hair back. It's not even long. He just loves playing with it. I'd constantly stroke mine if my askew mane was that baby soft. Alas, I'm too lazy to do homemade hot oil treatments. "The singing was good?" he asked. "You screwing with me?"

"Perfect song choice. Endless improvement. What is that vocal coach teaching you?"

His smile was coy. "Tons, but there's one secret that especially works wonders."

"Tell me," I said.

"Fine." Jacques laughed, rested his head on his arms, and squeakily said, "I don't wanna. It's awkward."

My demeanor entered a facetiously serious state. "Jacques, is this 'coach' making you do things you're uncomfortable with? We can file charges."

"No. Shh. She's my cousin."

"Cripes. That's worse," I said. He blew me a kiss and cracked his knuckles, making me cringe. That's his method for keeping my annoying nature at bay. "Jacques, that's the devil's noise." He continued cracking, finding relief in my suffering. Lucky for me, there was a foolproof backup plan in my back pocket. "Tell me the vocal secret," I demonically said. "Or I'll post fliers all over school showcasing what your room used to look like."

It was covered in Clay Aiken and Ruben Studdard memorabilia. He was scary obsessed with that season of American Idol as a kid and couldn't even bring himself to choose between the two by voting. He even wrote fan fiction about the finalists.

"Fine," he said. "The trick, well, it revolves around the privates. You push on them."

"What the hell. With your hand?"

"No. Like you're pushing out a baby," he awkwardly said. "As I sing, I pretend I'm pushing a baby out my—"

"Out your penis? Dude, you know you can't do that, right?"

"Yeah, Rosie, but acting like I can helps me sing from my diaphragm. Try it. Sing. Push on your vagina. Not with your hand, but like you're in labor. Don't push too hard, though. My coach said she once pushed too hard during a recital and peed herself."

"Noted."

I dived into a Rosie Dwyer classic. "Let's Hear It for the Boy" by Deniece Williams. My hands glided up before I even started my terrible singing, swaying to and fro as my eyes sealed. They remained closed while I sang. I eventually switched to my speaking voice and said, "Love this vagina trick! How's my voice?" He didn't answer. At the time, I assumed he was silently celebrating my spectacular upswing. I carried on, mocking his vagina trick by making a demon voice. Eyes still fastened, I drifted into my booming talking voice and said, "I'm gonna pretend to birth babies every time I sing! It's amaze balls. Do I sound good?"

Unfortunately, my eyes were still closed. "You sound amaze balls," said a voice that didn't belong to Jacques Blain. My eyes sprang open. Jacques' hands were clasped over his mouth. His body convulsed as he struggled to hold in maniacal laughter. Or sobs. My evil eye focused on Logan Fields as he balanced on a stool, as close as humanly possible, grinning winningly. I peered beyond him. Nearly the entire restaurant slow clapped, which grew into a fast, thunderous applause. They saw my whole performance, which grew into a fit. Some weirdo filmed me on their phone. I felt no embarrassment, too busy hoping I'd go viral on the Internet. I hopped off my stool and curtseyed. When everything simmered down, I retook my seat and flatly scanned Logan. His smile was like Barbara Streisand's voice, big and able to fill the room's every crevice.

"Greetings," I said, voice unshaken and hands nonchalantly fiddling with my yogurt.

"I'm here with friends," Logan said, pointing at a table where his three chums were. Two girls, one boy. They're not in our grade, so I don't know their names. I'm not even sure they go to our school. "Thought I'd stop over."

I said, "Enjoy your visit? Observe Monsieur Blaine's breathing patterns." Jacques took a deep breath, fanning himself with his hands. "He's excitable. You sent him into a seizure with your hijinks."

"He's laughing at you, Missy."

"Uh-uh-uh. He's accustomed to happenings of this ilk, Logan. He's laughing because you were inches from me. Almost passed out. Ashamed?"

"I've never felt shame," Logan said and proved it by stealing a bite of my yogurt. "Nasty. Put sugary cereal on it like a normal kid." We made cumbersome eye contact for a few seconds until he took another bite, smiling delicately. "What can I say? Food is food."

I shoved the frozen yogurt in his direction and said, "Have it."

"She's avoiding your germs," Jacques chimed in. "Don't take it personally. A germ freak. Like Howie Mandel, except she's only half bald."

Logan apologized and it seemed genuine, until he followed it by saying, "Sorry and all, but I'm excited about knowing how to get free food from you."

"Germs aren't a problem. Your face stole my appetite."

Jacques stuck his tongue out at me and said, "Shut it. Logan's face is…" He trailed off, licking his lips. "Lord, we all know it."

Logan was touched. He tilted his head, slapped his hands to his cheeks and said, "You're too nice!" Then he looked at me and asked, "When is your kindness going to rub off on Rosie?" My face scrunched as I unintelligibly repeated what he said. Then my mouth made a farting noise. "You're weird," Logan said. Then he looked at the table, doing his weird, cute, silent laugh. Jacques solemnly agreed. "But really, your performance was amaze balls," Logan said with a friendly wink. He took more ravenous frozen yogurt bites. Then, in an instant, he became bashful. "Speaking of singing, how was I?"

Orgasmic! Orgasmic! Orgasmic! I was as frozen as my frozen yogurt. Jacques and Logan exchanged befuddled looks. "You good, Rosie?"

"I'm good."

"Good," Logan said, raising his thick eyebrows. "How'd I do?"

"Good."

Jacques leaned toward Logan, getting his flirt on. "Bet you were flawless."

Logan nodded, smiled big and said, "Freaking love you, man. Thanks."

His friend interrupted the blossoming amour, shouting, "Hurry up! We're leaving."

Logan hopped off his stool, stretched his arms and said, "Nice seeing you." He started exiting, but abruptly stopped in his tracks, flipping around to face us. "A hug for the road?"

Jacques and I rose as he walked toward us. My arms opened, but Logan ran past and into Jacques' warm embrace. Logan spun him around and everything. His friend at the door urged him to hurry up once more. My arms were still open, but they awkwardly receded in as Logan sprinted by. My appearance was that of a perplexed T-Rex. I wanted that hug. I really fucking wanted it. I'd have gladly promised my firstborn child to Rumpelstiltskin if it ensured I would receive that hug. As we sat, Jacques looked dreamily into the distance. "Love," he said.

"If you're so in love, take this yogurt, which he grossly contaminated. It's the only swapping of germs you'll ever do. He's straight."

"You're salty because he hugged me. Not you." I sneered as Jacques finished my treat and became distracted by licking the spoon. This sensuous nonsense went on way too long, until he reminded me that, "Ya know, this spoon in my mouth was once in Logan's."

I said, "Before it was in his mouth, it was in mine. And there we have it, how diseases are spread."

143

"Any disease Logan has is one I won't mind having," Jacques clarified. Once he was done violating the plastic utensil, Jacques asked what I meant when I said Logan's singing audition was "good." I bit my thumbnail and examined a dad at a nearby table as he helicoptered yogurt into his toddler's mouth. "Logan asked how he did, and you were as blank as you are now. He asked again. You were blanker. Were you avoiding telling him he was terrible?"

I urgently whispered, "When I said 'good,' I meant 'good'. Let it rest."

Speaking of rest, I should probably do that. Rest, without looking at the alarm clock first. I fear what the time might be.

December 4, 2012

Hey, Joey Journal,

123 days now. 1-2-3. That was my parents' song. Their wedding song and the song they would play when they needed to escape any anxiety that came about. "1-2-3" by Len Barry. My parents loved it so much, my dad burned a CD that played only that song. And a backup one, too, in case it got scratched. Sadly, in the later years of their marriage, the song played around the house less and less.

1-2-3.

Kenny is my cousin. Kenny sent me an apology note, which I received in the mail today. Kenny's letter was typed on a typewriter. Kenny doesn't know how to use a typewriter. Kenny's mother, on the other hand, is as vintage as they come and loves writing to the entire family using that contraption. Kenny's mother probably nagged him to write me a note and his spoiled ass said, "No, Mom, I'm too busy. Video games, yo. I'm playin' that shit. Like Rosie's awful boyfriend, the one I'm gonna grow up to be just like." Kenny's mother typed a message onto her scented stationary and had him sign it on the bottom, which might be more insulting than what Kenny said in the first place.

Kenny is a little bitch.

I didn't write about Thanksgiving when it happened because I was too enraged at the time. My pencil snapped every time I tried. Thanksgiving was November 22, and it's already the fourth of December. We always spend the holiday with Mel's side of the family. I went into it thinking, *Praise the Lord.* My dad's side is miserable like us. Grandma

Dwyer can't look at River without weeping, because he's a stretched out carbon copy of my dad. A cheerless get-together is a pointless one.

I thought we were in the clear, going up to the cabin that's been in Melanie's family for generations. It was fine at first. Melanie's parents and three siblings are tall like her, and she was the only person who married a shorty. I was enveloped by giants and giants in the making. I felt small and at home.

Once dinner was ready, I took my seat at the children's table, enviously glaring at my brother. He was with the adults. The age requirement for that table was eighteen, and I'm seventeen. I turn the necessary age during December. Kenny's mother, Lana, was the one who was a stickler about the regulation. "If you break the rules for one kid, suddenly, you're doing it for all of them." Bah! Like Lana's precious Kenny is being raised with a single restriction. My ire was already building. All the cousins on Melanie's side are younger than me. They couldn't make eye contact while we ate. Normally, we're jokesters when we get together at the cabin, but they remained silent and focused on their plates. Kenny was installed directly across from me. He is thirteen, has no censors, and took to shifting in his seat. I could tell he wanted the jokes back. Once upon a time there was laughter. Kenny craved that freshly lost era. I was with him there. A dim grin came to my face. "Looks like Kenny has a joke." The other kids exchanged looks. I said, "Go for it."

"You sure?" said my red-headed cousin Lucy.

"You know I love a good laugh."

Kenny unleashed a sigh of relief. "It's not so much a joke as an observation." My smile grew. Ahh, Kenny. He lives for observational humor. I was fully expecting him to put on a Jerry Seinfeld voice and say, *"What's the deal with mashed potatoes? What did they ever do to us?"*

That's not the commentary he made. He said, "When everybody was hugging earlier, I realized there were way more tall people than short people. River took after your mom. Looks like Willow is going to be the same. If the short people are going to die first, that means you're next."

The grown-up table didn't hear it, but my cousins sure did. Lucy hid her face in her little palms, and four others had the same reaction. Bennett, age ten, was a smart cookie and made his way over to the buffet to get seconds. Willow was in the bathroom at the time, thank God. I stared at my mashed potatoes. That visual became what I wanted to do to Kenny. I wanted to make him into mashed Kenny and serve gravy over him. Finally, he defensively said, "What? You said you don't mind jokes."

"Kenny, you little bitch," I yelled. I shoved the spread off the kids' table, pounced over it and hauled off on him. The whole time, I repeated a shouted phrase, "Give thanks to my fists."

Willow was soon out of the bathroom and immediately darting to my aide. Gotta love the kid for assisting me in battle when she doesn't even know why I'm fighting. River and Melanie pulled the Dwyer sister tag team to the side, but it took them outrageously long. Kenny's mother was bouncing up and down, shrieking, "My baby!" Everybody else sat back in their chairs. A heaping bunch of Thanksgiving mashed potatoes taking human form.

Then my immediate family slid out the door in silence, playing the role of the gravy. Late that night, I heard noises while wrestling with insomnia. When I went to investigate, I discovered the sounds were coming from beyond Melanie's door. She softly cried as she played the backup "1-2-3" loop CD even softer. I didn't go into comfort her because I was too mad that my parents royally befouled such a feel-good classic. My stomach felt like mashed potatoes as I snuck back into my room.

That mashed potato tummy feeling is back as I'm stationed at my desk. One second. I'll be back.

There. I just ripped up Kenny's forged apology. I ripped it thoroughly. Ripping paper felt good, so I ripped up half my homework assignments, the posters on my wall, and the picture of my dad on my desk. He made me the only short person. This rips my heart out and he deserves to be ripped to pieces, just like me.

December 13, 2012

Hey, Joey Journal.

132 days since he died. The top definition for the number 132 on Urban Dictionary was uploaded in 2004 by a user named Zimbu. The post read as follows (excuse their lack of precise grammar skills):

"132 is short for 'fuck you' dirived from the way one can count in ten fingers in binary. If you assign your digits from your thumb to your pinky 1, 2, 3, 4, 8 and 16 on one hand and then 32, 64, 128, 256 and 512 on the other hand then the number 132 would be displayed using both middle fingers exclusively."

I wasted twenty minutes of my life trying to work out the math. I struggle in math class, so why bother bringing more calculations into my life. I just like the concept, even if I don't understand it on any level.

Hmm. Binary. An incredibly complicated explanation, coming from a person who can't even spell 'derived' correctly. Although none of that made sense, I have a new favorite number. 132. I'm giving 132 to this year, this month, this day.

Haven't written in over a week. Winter is happening. Life is happening. Too many happenings are happening. December began and I barely can climb out of bed. People imagine Hell as a putridly hot place. Living in Wisconsin for seven winters has convinced me Hell isn't hot. Hell is below zero and located in America's Middle West.

Motivation is a lacking resource. Grades are slipping. Senioritis. I'd eat dinner with my family, but food nauseates me. Minutes ago, River knocked on my door and said, "Wakey, wakey, Chicken. Made a new dinner medley."

He's constantly high-spirited because he recently started seeing a former high school classmate named Kate. I don't remember her last name, seeing as it's utterly forgettable. She's as dull as her name. River brings her around and they play house. They first reconnected when he started working with her. They're training to be 911 Dispatchers. Sometime during River's job hunt, he made the shift from wanting to philosophize to wanting money to wanting to help people. Can't harp on him for that career goal evolution, but I'm able to be peeved by him bringing his considerate work attitude home each night. After his supper announcement, I said, "Does this 'dinner medley' revolve around couscous?"

"It's not the entree. Steak is included and I marinated the granules differently."

"Ate leftovers before you all got home. Nom, nom, nom. Let me sleep."

"Okay, I'll be going," he said, skeptical.

After moments passed, I aggressively screamed for him to stop hovering outside my door. He said he understood and his voice was energetic and it made me wanna vomit. I flipped onto my stomach, planted my face into my pillow and mumbled, "Standing out there...can't stand that." I soon sensed that he left. I can always sense when nosy nimrods are lingering outside my door and when they're not. The only voice left to respond to my moaning was my stomach's roaring. I wasn't honest about the leftovers. I'm not trying to be one of those anorexic chicks in a *Lifetime Original Movie*. When I force-feed myself cereal, biliousness takes my stomach and tangles it, like a teenage boy working at the pretzel stand. Switched to oatmeal. I'm unable to hack that either.

I used to eat normally. Candy and pizza and cheeseburgers. I'd have probably consumed a candy-pizza-cheeseburger if that were a thing. Didn't give two sheep about what I piled into me. In September, my brain shifted. I wanted healthiness. I thought maybe if my dad balanced himself, like inside and out, ya know? Yoga and other healthy crap. Maybe he wouldn't have...I don't wanna be like that. I wanna be like him, but not his end. Weight loss wasn't the goal. My shrinking frame was chasing the word 'healthy'. I run on the elliptical for hours, and don't get any closer to that adjective. I want healthiness desperately. River wants the same. It's working for him. He's fit, yet balanced, and I'm not there.

First, I cut out soda. I felt okay, but not there. Candy, pizza, cheeseburgers, and all of life's greatest offerings were eliminated. Still not 'there'. Then I thought, *Vegetarians! They're Zen. Let's eradicate meat*. Meatless Me found the feeling of "there" to still be unachieved. Phased out bread and cereal. Oatmeal. Couscous. Milk. Not 'there' yet. Bye, bye, butter! Sayonara, salt! Ciao, ketchup! Not 'there'.

By early November, I only allowed myself fruit, yogurt, vegetables and almonds. Then there are the late night kitchen raids on Saturdays. My family is on a health food kick, so peanut butter is the junkiest pantry item. At midnight, I'll eat two thirds of a jar in one sitting. My mind overreacts and I dispose of what went down my throat. There are two disposal methods. Laxatives and puking. That's the only time I do that, don't worry. After Saturday night binges. And after the Ice Cream Social. And after Jacques forced me to get frozen yogurt, which isn't as healthy as people claim. I can't have someone find this, but I need to tell somebody. Since I'm not going to, I'll instead tell some*thing*. Writing it in a well-guarded journal is as good as it'll get.

I feel like being in bed for a long while. Under my covers is an okay environment. I only lift my blankets up to examine my legs as I squeeze them together and witness how wide the gap between them is getting. I vaguely like this. That's what I'm doing now. I'm putting the notebook down to do this for a while.

I'm back. River opened my door sometime after they finished eating and invited himself in. He relaxed on the green armchair in the corner of my room, and I continued writing in you, hoping to do so until he left. He wore his work uniform, khakis and a navy polo with our county's emblem. He's not my brother anymore. River grabbed the book beside the chair and said, "*Heart of Darkness*. Love this book." *Heart of Darkness*. Hate that book. We're supposed to read it for AP English. Don't plan on it. Won't even look up chapter summaries on Sparknotes.com. Failing to sense how unwelcome he was in my room, cheery ole River kept talking. "Your opinions?"

I responded by not acknowledging his existence and sharply turning on the TV, searching for entertaining programming. I looked at what was on the Showtime channels for a bit. *Dammit*, I thought, *I want HBO.*

You see, a blowup happened during today's art class, but the tension started building during the passing time that came before. When I was at the bottom of the staircase, I missed a step. After getting my bearings, I sped around the corner and slammed right into Eliot. The force of our collision knocked me to the ground. He came over to my body that was stretched out on the floor, like it was on the first day of school. As he extended a hand, he said, "A familiar scene."

Once I was on my feet, I gruffly said, "Gonna be late." Then I tried to walk past Eliot, who had no intentions of letting me by. He grabbed my arm, stirred me around and gleefully said, "Come to Daddy."

Soon, regret was in every part of his eyes, even the lashes. When Eliot wanted a hug from me last summer, he'd say, "Come to Daddy." It was this inside joke we had after Eliot, Jacques and I randomly made a music video for the song "Come to Daddy" by R. Kelly. We filmed many music videos last summer. When Eliot used to say, "Come to Daddy," it was corny and cute. This was the first time he's said it since my dad died. He followed it up with, "Rosie, look, I'm sorry."

He pulled me in for a bear hug, as if that would help matters. Next thing I knew, Emily Hayes, with the quarter-sized mole on her face, was taking a mother effing picture of us. After the flash evaporated, I tore myself from Eliot's grip, glared at Emily and said, "What the hell are you doing?"

Emily smiled and her mole danced and she said, "For yearbook! You two are nominated for cutest couple."

We're not a couple, I thought. *We're a confused charade of a relationship, one that only millennials are capable of.* Then she grabbed my sleeve, yanking me toward the art room, and as we traveled, she wouldn't shut up. Emily talked about last night's babysitting job, her college acceptance, and she probably would've covered her menses had the bell not interrupted her as we hurdled through the door.

For most seniors, art class is a studio hour. We do what we want.

If your artistic progress begins to dip, the teacher will of course get on your ass and suggest things for you to do, but I don't have that problem. Today was taxing, though. I sat on my stool, put my head on the table, and replayed every memory I had of my dad saying anything remotely close to, "Come to Daddy."

That wouldn't be his exact phrasing because that sounds weirdly sexual after a kid passes a certain age. But he often said cheesy, nonsexual things like that. When a sweat puddle began forming beneath my forehead, I sat erect and dug through my backpack until I was holding my scrapbook. I've consistently been carrying it with me ever since the event, but haven't been able to open it. Today, I did. I flipped to a picture of him and me in the woods behind the family cabin. He was wearing a corny birdwatching outfit and I was in a colorful parrot costume. I was five. It wasn't Halloween. Costumes were just an integral part of my upbringing. With a sharpie, I wrote, "Daddy," all over the picture until it was completely black. Once I was done, I slammed the scrapbook and conversed with Emily, who was to my right. "Hey, where did you leave off before? Your menses?"

Emily looked horrified for a moment, but then nodded, grinning. "You mean my acceptance to the University of Memphis? Yes. It's my dream school. Where are you going?"

Before I could reply, "No idea," a menace paused her work on a shitty watercolor to talk pop culture. Anastasia "Mouthful" Moretti-Slocumb, the girl who farted on Logan, was wondering if any of us watch the show *True Blood*. Everybody at the table exploded, wailing, "Adore it! Amazing! Ahhhhhh!"

Since HBO isn't in my life, I couldn't contribute. Emily Hayes, with the quarter sized mole on her face, was talking about some character I was unfamiliar with, saying, "Eric gives me tingles and—"

"I watch *Homeland* sometimes." Yes. I interrupted Emily's raving. She's my friend, but all I cared about was finding a way to add to the dialogue. I said, "*Homeland* is also critically acclaimed. Anybody watch *Homeland*?" I've only seen one episode. Not my cup of tea, seeing as terrorism is awfully depressing. Claire Danes' dreadful onscreen crying is even more dispiriting. "None of you watch *Homeland*? Too bad."

Everyone looked at me coldly, and not so much because they weren't *Homeland* fans, but because I was being rude. Finally, Mouthful ended the noiselessness and said, "Looks like someone is stuck with *Showtime*."

"I swear to God, I'm two seconds from giving you a giant mouthful of my knuckles, Mouthful." Yeah. That was me. I said that. Using the name Mouthful was gunfire. Nobody calls her that to her face. Logan was at the next table over, facing me. We made uncomfortable eye contact for a millisecond before my eyes broke away from his dumbfounded self. Everybody was silent as I slowly raised my middle fingers into the still air. 132, in all its glory.

"Think I don't know about that name?" Mouthful said, haughty and fumbling with the ends of her black hair, which was straightened to perfection. "Well, I do. It's stupid. You're unoriginal, Rosie."

I serenely said, "More original than you. Nice North Face fleece, the same one as eight other girls in this room."

"Why do clothes matter? You having your period?"

"No. Your face having its period?"

She said, "Who do you think you are, Rosie? The Dictator of the art room?"

"Who do you think you are, Mouthful? The 'Tater Dick' of the art room? Because you have a dick made of tater tots. Voila! Tater Dick."

The guys at Logan's table laughed at my admittedly feeble quips. Logan was the exception, while Mouthful kept appearing malignant. "Eliot asked for my number," she said, squinting. "I gave it to him, among other things."

There were a few "Oohs" from our audience. Unimpressed, I told her that her claim had no meaning. She suddenly took a deep breath. Damn, was she tirelessly attempting not to blow. Mouthful said, "I'm sorry I brought Eliot into this. Guess I'm just tired of walking on eggshells around you. I know you're going through something, but it's been months since it happened. And it doesn't give you the right to interrupt Emily, or call me names. I hate watching adversity make you a bigger bitch than you already were."

"Shut it," I said. "At least I'm not a slut who drunkenly makes out with guys and ruins it by farting on them."

Her face paled as she grudgingly turned to Logan. After shaking her head, Mouthful bounced up, chucked her paintbrushes in the sink and went toward the door. Logan chased her. Once in the doorway, Mouthful bitch slapped him and punched his eye. Our teacher yelled from the hallway, "Christ on a cracker!" My art teacher is a demure sixty-something year old woman who wears pastel sweaters tied around her shoulders and her gray curls in a bun. Her name is Mrs. Filipowski. We call her Philly, to shorten her monstrous name. It's perfect because she grew up in Philadelphia and has a thick accent to prove it. The woman is a class act, though, and rather soft-spoken, but today, she rampaged into the classroom, Tasmanian devil style, speeding toward the stereo as it played 'Light Classical Favorites'. The tunes were slammed off and Philly said, "I can't go in the hallway to help students for five minutes without this room collapsing?"

When the calmest teacher erupts in a classroom, the explosion leaves nothing but stillness in its wake. She addressed Mouthful and Logan, who hadn't moved since she entered. His hand gingerly grazed his upper cheek and the culprit scowled at the ceiling, eyes watery. Her arms were crossed and the meaner she looked, the more obvious it became that she was about to sob. I felt terrible. "You two. Explain yourselves," Philly said.

They remained hushed until our teacher walked back into the hallway. "Explain it out here."

Mouthful and Logan marched out of sight. Naturally, the class ran to the door, becoming an army of jostling spectators. Philly wasn't pleased, replying to our mob mentality by banging the door shut. We could still see through the glass, though. Logan mumbled, but was interrupted by the Mouthful bomb detonating. "I'm done!" was her battle cry.

She ran out of view, Philly dashing after. My classmates laughed. Even the guys who regularly say, "Mouthful is totally fuckable." Even the girls who would later advise me to "get medicated," even those tarts laughed like the hyenas they are. Even the shy kids, the nice ones who stay to themselves, stifled giggles. Even I, who felt unfathomable guilt, even I laughed. We had to and I hate that. My essence became about the laughter, absorbing it. When my eyes opened, Logan was staring directly at me through the window, shaking his baffled head.

"It's been thirty minutes," said my brother. I jumped in my skin, having forgotten River's presence in my room. This was the point where I abandoned my pencil and chatted with my brother. He said, "*Heart of Darkness*. Your thoughts? Love rereading it, but I always enjoy your take." River's therapeutic smile was in place and I wanted it gone.

"Hate it. Not reading another page." My stare was steely. River asked for an explanation. His stare was sweet and I said, "Its words are antediluvian and the book itself is impenetrable. Don't have time to decode it."

"Shouldn't a girl who uses big ass words like that be able to understand Joseph Conrad?"

"Nope. Not a dictionary, dickwad."

My brother brushed off my bitterness with a shrug. "I finished college and I'm not even confident on the meanings of those words."

"College educated doesn't equate to intelligent! You struggled to maintain a C average." I was out of control, but calmed myself so I could coherently enlighten him. "Antediluvian is synonymous with the word prehistoric. Out of date. Impenetrable has multiple meanings, one being that said 'impenetrable object' is unable to be understood."

"Don't know, kiddo. You sound like a dictionary to me."

With that, I myself became impenetrable, as did the world around me. Moaning is the soul desire of an impenetrable object. That's what I did. "Why'd you have to move home? Go! Leave! Confront the real world!" I threw a pillow at him while a drum beat inside my head.

"Why don't you take time to make sense of the words, Chicken?"

"Don't. I'm not a fifth grader."

"C'mon," he said. "You'll always be our little Chicken. And don't change the subject. Why can't you sit with the words in this book and—"

"Words, words, words. Get off it, Riv. I don't have time for a stupid string of words in a stupid book."

He looked at the novel for a moment, patiently, then spoke,

passionately. "You love words. When you were nine, I'd find you reading Shakespeare with a dictionary nearby. That's why you could quote *Hamlet* just now. Words, words, words. They're your favorite. Gave a damn about them. When you were young, that's the only time you'd be quiet. I'd watch you read for countless minutes, amazed by your quiet intensity. After a while, you'd smile and read me a quote that you considered 'otherworldly'. A strange little girl in a meaningful relationship with strange little words."

"I don't care about words anymore."

"Doesn't sound like the Rosie I know."

I shook my head. My brother. My clean-shaven brother. My brother who cut off his hair. My brother who reads the news and not the cartoon section. My brother who gets his kicks from figuring out fresh ways to incorporate couscous into every meal. My brother, who had been a perfect stranger for months, was telling me I changed. Couldn't handle my brother anymore. He asked me why I was crying. "I'm not!" I was. Not loudly, but still, tears have been streaming since I started writing.

"You are," he said, pausing as I buried myself under my comforter. "This about Dad?"

After a considerable silence, River got on his soapbox and said, "When it happened, I was shaken up. How could a person not be screwed up after something like that? Still am. Still screwed up. Always will be. Back then, I didn't wanna talk about it. Mom made us attend family therapy, but during our first session we bitched. Besides Willy. She cried and got more upset. After that, we didn't put any effort into going back. Mom and I got busy working. Willy and you got busy with school. None of us meant to, but we shoved it under the rug. Enough, though. We need to talk and the discussion can't be me asking, 'You okay?' and you saying, 'Yep'. Real talking. For the good of everyone. You, me, Mom, Willy."

My comforter stopped bringing me comfort. I slapped my hand to my mouth, holding back audible lamentation. He was shortening Willow to Willy. Dad was the only one who called her that. My anxiety increased tenfold when the bed weighed down. "Remove your rank self, River." He gently laughed and I said, "Not joking."

"You won't joke with me. Won't talk with me. What will you do with me?"

I screamed into my mattress. "Beat you!"

"What?" River asked before I threw my comforter off and pushed him to the floor. Sprawled out on the carpet, he somberly said, "Surprised you had the strength for that, seeing as you didn't eat."

"Leftovers."

"Willy was home before you. Said you went straight up. Never came down."

"Stop," I said. "Stop calling her that! You're not him."

"You think I'm trying to be him?" River said, climbing up. "That's it? Nobody could do that. He was amazing and funny and unlike anybody else. I'm trying to be responsible."

"That's not you," I said. "You're supposed to throw parties the night before my big tests and play stupid games like War Sticks and scream out random things at movie theatres. We took Willow to see *Wreck-it Ralph*, a movie flush with opportunities for you to scream funny stuff, but you didn't." I belly-flopped on my bed, hysterical.

Glassy-eyed, he remained tranquil and tried being a man. Tried being like Dad. Voice weak, he said "I'm named River. I try to be like my name, changing my currents occasionally. Keep it interesting." Ugh. River and his philosophical outlook. "Sorry I pissed you off, Rosie."

"You're not the reason I'm crying. This day was crap."

And eighth hour was the crappiest part. Logan was late. It was a Peer Review Period and I was eyeballing a new motivational poster in favor of the clock. When Logan finally arrived, he looked at me like I had an ass for a face, then fleetly traveled to Bette. He handed over his late pass and strolled to our desks, which were already moved to face each other. The second he sat, I apologized. No response.

"I'll say it again, Logan. Sorry."

"You ruined it," he softly said, staring at the papers he pulled out of his green folder.

I glowered, thinking he was being melodramatic. "She called me a bitch."

"We've been flirting nonstop. We're getting close, seconds from happening. Then you ruin everything."

I grew stupefied. Was he talking about us?

"Rosie, I was, I don't know, maybe, gonna ask Anastasia out today," he said.

Shot through my heart. The two of us bonded during musical rehearsals and Imagination Collaborations, but the connection feels imagined now. We monkey around, but don't truly talk. The last time Logan spoke about another female was two months back when he mentioned a 'hot grandma' who pulled dollar bills out of her brassiere while purchasing pretzels at the mall kiosk where he works. When you're around Logan, it's easy to feel like the only girl in existence. As my eyes studied my tremulous hands, I swallowed saliva and apologized again. It was strange, though. It seemed as if Logan was sliding out of a state of anger and into one of regret. I asked if he blocked out the entire exchange in art class. "You saw the way I was treated, right?"

Wincing, he said, "I'm only being fair. Anastasia didn't tell the principal you provoked her. She's in the office right now, starting her in-school suspension. Technically, she's being the bigger person."

I fought the urge to agree and say, *"Body-wise, she is in fact bigger."* Instead, I said, "She forsook that detail because ratting on me meant telling her principal why she clocked you. Why was the punch packed? Straddling boys makes her gassy." He slammed his head on his desk and said nothing. "You're nursing a shiner and you're gearing up to ask her out?" Slamming. Logan took to repeatedly slamming his head on his desk. I looked over at Bette and she flashed me a quick smile, probably thinking Logan and I were simply up to our usual antics. "I implore you to stop. You're making your eye worse." Slamming, slamming, slamming. "Tell me why, Logan."

He halted his head and let it be still on his desk. "The 'why' you want is about what?"

I gazed up at the rectangular light fixture above, hoping its brightness would blind me so I wouldn't have to address him with my eyes. He erected his bludgeoned head and the position of my head neutralized. I was silent and still had my sight, but seemed to have lost my power of speech. His fully capable eyes nearly punctured my equally proficient ones.

"You want me to say why," he said softly. "Can't until you expand on that why."

I considered keeping this eye contact up because his almond color eyes were so tragically beautiful. But if I did that, I'd give myself away. He'd know what I was feeling before I even could understand it. My eyes directed themselves back to the light above me and I hoped for my blindness request to be fulfilled this time. No luck. I slowly said, "Why Mouthful?"

"Mouthful. Anastasia can be a royal pain in the ass, but—"

"Why do you wanna be with somebody you can't stand?" I was almost yelling. Bette didn't notice because the room was loud and she had earphones in. He shook his head. I knew what Logan was about to say and he knew I knew. His face grew more and more sly. Logan's mouth was opening so it could come out, but I beat him to it. "Eliot. Ha! Said it first. Eliot. Can't stand him. I fell into a topsy-turvy semi-relationship and it is hell, but the least of my worries. This is about you consciously choosing to pursue a girl that you consider an ass pain."

My voice became mum when Logan calmly rose from his chair and sat under his desk. I got out of mine and bent down to see what the hell he was up to. Anger coated my every word as I said, "This confrontation has been childish, but this is a new and fully furnished level."

"Come down here or I won't talk," he quietly said. I begrudgingly took residence under my desk and asked him what gives. He said, "Sometimes I get real angry, Rosie. I seem relaxed, but sometimes I wanna scream till all the windows and mirrors in my house shatter. Couldn't do that much growing up after a certain point. Can't explain it now, but I can't just…explode. If I explode, I make it silent. Private. Because I never wanna worry anybody. I'll say passive aggressive comments I don't mean, but explosions are rare. That's why I'm hiding under my desk right now. You're making me want to go boom, as you often do. And I've trained myself not to let anybody see me do this. I was so close to throwing my desk when we were up in the real world. You were so close to slugging me, Anastasia style. I can't go through that public humiliation again today, no matter how much I deserve it. Can we see if this talk goes better down here? Please?"

Logan's ranting somehow eased me and I proposed that we try meditation. He nodded vigorously and mirrored me as my body entered the best lotus position I could get into under the cramped desk. I closed my eyes for ten seconds until he said, "Wow. Isn't it amazing how they're all so busy talking, they don't even notice us? Public school, am I right?"

I shot him a glare that said, '*You're not meditating right.*' Logan went straight back to business and my eyes resealed. Thirty seconds in, I had this feeling that I was the only one with my eyes closed, so I opened one of them. Logan's arms were limp and he was gently smiling. "Hey," Logan said, and it wasn't a normal 'hey'. It was a 'hey' that his mind probably extended into much more. "*Hey, Rosie. We've been saying 'hey' to each other for many lifetimes before this and we will say 'hey' to each other for many lifetimes to come. Also...you look gorgeous when you sit all peaceful and thoughtless like that.*"

I couldn't know for certain that these were Logan's exact thoughts, but his face filled in most of the blanks. At least that's what I thought in that moment. I leaned forward and gave him a slow kiss on the cheek. When I pulled back, his eyes were the size of garbage can lids. *Are they big in a bad way?* Mine expanded even more as I got lost in analyzing his expression. Two goddamn bush babies, staring at each other. My hands clasped to my mouth. I thought, *I was wrong.* Squeezed my eyes shut, hoping the scene would reset when my eyes reopened. When my lids finally inched up, Logan was still sitting there with enormous eyes. "I'm sorry," I said. "Confusing day. Don't know why...why I did that. Forgot how this dialogue began. Mouthful. You're asking out Mouthful. Good luck. With Mouthful."

I speedily crawled out from my desk and made a beeline to Bette's desk where she sat on the edge of her yellow chair. Her earbuds were hooked up to her computer as it played a Kenny G music video. Simply tapped her shoulder. She flinched and exited out of her browser. "How much did you see?" said Bette. I asked if I could go to the nurse's office. She shook her head gravely. "We've discussed it, Rosie. You can't go see Rhonda this often."

"Why?"

"Rhonda says you're never sick and that you're rude to her when she explains this."

"I'm gonna puke," I said.

Bette asked me if she could talk to Logan, and I flatly refused. Overhearing this, Logan finally crawled out from under his desk and stood next to me, fidgeting. Bette rolled her eyes at us. "This is the last time I'm gonna tell you my classroom is not a place for hide and seek."

"And Kenny G has a place here?" I said. If looks could smack people in the face, man, the one she gave me would've left me red. "I'm gonna puke?" I said apologetically.

Bette climbed to her feet and put her hands on her hips. The iciest curves ever seen. "Logan, you know this girl better than anyone in this room. Is she about to puke? Or can we save myself a post-it note permission slip?"

"It's my fault," he said and I promptly vomited on most of her desk. The consistency was mostly water. At the time, I thought it was the animosity inside me that made it happen. I'm realizing that it was probably the fact that I popped three Advil tablets before class and my empty stomach couldn't handle it. My jittery hands fumbled around in the backpack that lay at my feet and retrieved a pad of post-its. I passed Bette the top one and said, "Don't want you wasting another square."

Bette signed away and handed it back, giving a remorseful nod. Then she said the worst arrangement of words possible. "Logan, babe, make sure our girl gets to Rhonda okay."

The second I was in the hallway, my speed walking began. Logan trailed behind and yelled, "Hey, slow down!"

And I shouted back, "You are just too slow, Logan!"

That's the moment I was living in when my brother snapped his fingers and asked what personal hell I went off too. I scrutinized River's blue eyes, ignoring the fact that he inherited them from my dad. "My day was crap," I whispered before my body went berserk on my bed.

"Count to ten."

I rattled off numbers, but as seven approached, I was unable to be understood. An impenetrable object once more, a most impossible state of being.

He said, "Start at the beginning."

I shouted, "*True Blood*!"

"What?"

"It's an HBO show. *True Blood*."

"Never heard of it."

"How?" I said. "It's critically acclaimed and there are sexy vampires in it."

He ignored me, shrugging. I advised him to pay attention to pop culture. My brother replied, "Was not being able to watch some show something to get worked up about?"

"Some show? River, it's critically acclaimed."

He said, "Your paramount dilemmas are what I like to call first world problems."

"You and the rest of Twitter nation would call them that."

He laughed and told me that he doesn't tweet. I didn't laugh and told him he wasn't my biological brother. River responded by walking to the door, hands in his pockets. Then he backtracked, swiveling around to face me. "I'm gonna give you your birthday presents early."

My birthday is Saturday. I'll be eighteen and I'm pumped to visit the porn store with a group of friends. That's what we young people do around these parts when we come of age. The outline of River's gifts could be seen through his pants' material. He gives great presents. Last year, he gave me a travel journal and his old camera, then promised I'd have a cornucopia of voyages. This year, River pulled out a handheld tape recorder. "You wanna be a writer. If you go into journalism, you'll be able to get exact quotes."

'Exact' and 'quote'. Combined, those words furnished my insides with fervor. Then he pulled a cassette tape out of his other pocket. "You love the nineties, and are obsessed with impractical objects. I learned how to make a mixtape. Remember when I was away at college and we'd send each other videos of musical comedians? Well, this is a musical comedian mixtape."

I immediately asked, "Is Bo Burnham featured?"

"Obviously."

"But is 'Art is Dead' on—"

"It's the first song."

"Thought you hated it."

He said, "I don't hate it. It just not as funny."

"That's because Bo said he wrote it to help him sleep at night and—"

"Night, Rosie."

Once River left, I found a cassette player in my nightstand. As my fingers fumbled with the tape, my brother yelled from his bedroom in a *Wreck-It Ralph* voice, "I'm gonna wreck it!"

For a moment, I felt better. Like nothing ever happened. But the moment ended and I looked at my legs. *That gap could be wider.* I don't feel like writing, even for another second.

December 14, 2012

Hey, Joey Journal,

133 days. 133 days have passed and I'm still counting the days and there seems to be no end to this in sight.

Today, something unsettling happened in Connecticut. Nowadays, we don't have to purposely follow the news to be bombarded by it. A monumental event happens and Facebook explodes. Twitter explodes. The world nearly explodes. Our newsfeeds reveal a never-ending stream of condolences and opinions. I was home "ill." Mental health day. All I had to do was login on and it pieced itself together. Horrific events keep happening in this country. In movie theatres, in gas stations, in hair salons, in Sikh temples. This Sandy Hook Elementary School shooting has me shaking.

I remember being a kid, pumped for my first day of kindergarten. My dad insisted on being there to take me. His large hand gripped my tiny one and I felt safe. Over the years, I've never believed my educational environment could be precarious. School has consistently been my sanctuary. I've felt sad at school, even unwelcome, but I've never feared for my life. Now, I'm not sure. I'm questioning the existence of sanctuaries. I keep reminding myself that safe havens subsist. I almost believe it.

Joey, remember how I told you about my journeys to the library's self-help section, not having the intentions to help myself, but to forget? Remember how I want to erase an image from my memory? That image still burns into every crevice of my cranium like a ceaseless bonfire. As I scrolled through today's commemoration status updates and clicked on gruesome articles, that fire blazed from my mind into my whole body, ravaging me. At first, it left me in a cold sweat, but now I'm red and reeling. It's too real. My temperature rises, mind focused on the survivors of the gunman's attack. I can imagine them lying in bed, overpowered by images that refuse to let them rest and counting meaningless numbers in a futile attempt to make it better.

December 15, 2012

Hey, Joey Journal,

    134 days since he lost his life. Today, for the first time since it happened, everybody has been requiring me to celebrate my own life. Yes, it's my birthday. The first one without him was like Alf without fur. Unnatural.

    It's a Saturday birthday this year, which is usually my favorite kind. They normally allow me to sleep in. I also worry less because there's no school the next day. But when I woke up, I didn't feel older or well-rested. I felt like something was missing.

    This morning, Melanie took me to get my State ID at the DMV. I didn't feel annoyance while standing in the long line, because I was too busy feeling something's absence. Later, Jacques took me to the porn store. I didn't feel like laughing at the wild sex toys and magazines. I felt a lost thing being gone too hard. After Jacques dropped me off, I logged onto Facebook and scanned through hundreds of birthday wishes on my wall. I didn't feel loved. I felt like there was something missing. When I became sickened by the Internet and how robotic the teenage condition has become, I went downstairs and ate with my family. We had Kentucky Fried Chicken and red velvet cake. I didn't feel full, but like there was something missing. Happiness, maybe. I also felt like vomiting. And I did.

    Melanie handed me an envelope later, which contained a Hoops & Yoyo card. When one opens a card of this variety, they find cartoon animals that rant in bothersome voices, impossible to follow. I recoil upon experiencing this. My dad bought all the cards for our birthdays, and he'd never pick a Hoops and Yoyo card. Card selection was something he excelled at. It must suck for Melanie, bombing at something so simple. She smiled as I opened it. I anted up a fake chuckle until I saw the money inside. *Four-hundred dollars. Cash.* "Too much," I said.

"That's all you're getting. I don't know what to buy you anymore."

Suddenly, all I desired were new socks and underwear, like she traditionally buys.

Around 8:30 pm, ridiculously early, everybody was holed up in their own bedrooms, including me. I was rolling, writhing, restless until I hopped up and headed to my desk. My hands rummaged around inside the top drawer. I soon had a collection of items in my grasp: the four-hundred dollars I was given, my State ID and a small sketch of a flying bird flock. Doodled them earlier this week. Right then, I wanted them on my wrist. Wanted to force myself to see birds every day. To torture myself, as sick as it sounds. Once bundled up in winter clothing, I snuck out and began my thirty-minute jaunt to the bus depot.

There's this tattoo parlor in Milwaukee that stays open late. I know this because the summer we moved here, the entire family went to see the fireworks. We camped out practically overnight for a spot at Veteran's Park and it was worth it. The water and the architectural majesty that is the Calatrava lit up. It was the first time I was able to admit to myself that Wisconsin wasn't going to be entirely terrible. My dad was doubly inspired by the fireworks. After the last explosion in the sky, he said, "That's it. I'm getting a firework tattoo above my butt crack."

Melanie was pregnant, which meant she wasn't tipsy like my father. Still, she didn't need much persuading. "Fine," she said, after he started chanting 'tramp stamp'. "It's your body." Bear in mind that this is back when Mel was a cool person. She drove the whole family to this place she knew about. I forget the name. I was too young for it to gel into my memory perfectly. Whoever did it, they were willing to work on him late at night. We didn't miss the cutoff point, but nearly did. My dad turned to face us and addressed River, who was fifteen. He said, "Locking the doors. Keep Rosie safe?"

River nodded. My ten-year old self chimed in, "C'mon. If somebody tries to carjack us, I'll be the one stopping them."

My dad giggled while Mel's eyebrows narrowed, lovingly warning me to play nice. They went into the tattoo place for a surprisingly short amount of time. When we saw them come out, River unlocked the car and we rushed out to meet them. River asked if it hurt and my dad told him no. "Picked a simple one, son."

Then he mooned us. Folding up his flag shirt would have done the trick, but we wouldn't have gotten the full effect of the cute firework shooting out of his rectal entrance. Mooning. That was my dad's favorite party favor. It's painful realizing this, but I got that from him. Brain hemorrhage. Let's avoid one of those and talk about my tattoo, not his. Freshly eighteen-years old, I took a bus into the city and walked until I was almost ready to give up. I was naive going into this, thinking I could instantly find a place with a forgotten name in a relatively strange city. My direction providing app made me want to chuck my phone under a passing car. Much to my dismay, I thought, *What would my dad do when he was his best self?*

Meditate. He'd sit his ass down and close his eyes, regardless of his location. My body leaned on a building and sank to the ground. My eyes closed. I sat like this for God knows how long. The city sounds surprised me. They were a welcomed escape. Finally, I opened my eyes. The laugh that came out of me was seismic. Positioned across the street was a shop completely lit up with neon red. There were two neon crosses and signs that read "Tattoo" and "Piercing." My favorite sign was in the middle and blazed with the deepest red tones of all. *Open.*

I jetted across the street. Nearly got slammed by a car. When I got to the door, my body slowed down. My hand tentatively pulled open the door. I found a wonderland in there. It's…I'm having trouble describing it. I was expecting a waiting area of shit-faced folks, ones intent on wasting space. And when I didn't find that, a bright red open sign took over my imagination and every inch of my mind. An open sign was there through everything—through getting the tattoo, through the bus ride back to Wira, through sneaking back into the house. *Open.* Can you hear the vibration of the Tibetan bowls? I can.

December 22, 2012

Hey, Joey Journal!

On this day, it's been 141 days. 134 days after my dad passed, I had to celebrate my own life. I've now transitioned into this jarring mode where I'm hyperaware of my own impending doom. All because last night happened. The False Apocalypse.

I went mad last night, around eleven. It was a Friday, one that was theorized to be the last in Earth's history because the Mayan calendar reached its completion. Many gullible members of the population were adamant that December 21st marked our entire planet's doom. Dunces, the world over, presumed this. An even larger amount of people laughed at the believers. The words on everybody's lips were "the apocalypse." Not mine, though. I didn't mock or even muse on the subject. The day was nearly over and social media updates dubbed the "Apocalypse" a grand fluke. Once in bed, laying in wake, I thanked God for granting me survival. Then the noise happened. It sounded like an explosion or an avalanche. Maybe both. An 'explosalanche'.

Poo nearly exploded from my rear as the roaring 'explosalanche' encountered my ears. My mind went a trillion miles a minute. Typically, it manages only a million. The increase left me suffering from brutal whiplash. I didn't feel myself sinking off my bed or sinking into girlish sobbing. Didn't feel myself sinking. An echo in my brain announced the end, unendingly. My mind's words became tangible, stacking around me, enclosing my body in an edifice I was incapable of escaping. The thoughts that somehow remained in my nearly empty cranium bunched up. Only one thought didn't sound like an agglomeration of gibberish and it devoured me. *I never got to be a rolling stone.*

I snuck into the bedrooms of my family members and shook them awake. When I ranted and raved about the apocalypse, everybody told me to go back to sleep. After making sure they all understood they were going to perish if they didn't wake up, I let them go back to sleep.

I chose to save myself.

After much thought, my quaking hands seized my backpack, which soon became stuffed with clothes, toiletries, my iPod, you, my journal, my Jewel CD collection and the cash stash that's been under my mattress for years. The essentials and I stealthily escaped, torpedoing into the night. My body barreled down the sidewalk, unbothered by the world that appeared no different. My psyche shot above the cement I rambled on, skyrocketing, high on the notion that something as seemingly permanent as Earth could expire. I had no grasp on the origins of the 'explosalanche', but it sounded real to my rattling eardrums.

I stopped momentarily, pulling my iPod out. Then I examined the expansive sky. Snowflakes floated from above, collapsing into my exposed skin bits. My fingers put the headphones in place, playing the song that inspired my voyage.

Many claim that there's vengefulness in "Like a Rolling Stone", but I've never felt that.

When Bob Dylan originally wrote it, his initial product was approximately ten pages. Heard that in a documentary. He kept writing. Freely. The song the public is familiar with is considered lengthy, but it was heavily edited from its infant state. The words traveled down the page like feet on an open dirt road. There's something magical about the image of a moving hand, bringing life to words the mind can't make sense of itself.

Bob contemplated quitting singing before "Like a Rolling Stone" happened. His career had been successful beforehand, but he didn't like his own work. Bob once said, and I believe this is a direct quote, "It's very tiring having other people tell you how much they dig you if you yourself don't dig you."

Amen. I'm fatigued for similar reasons. Confused, too. But in that instance, I wasn't confused. Blank, rather, and there's a difference. One of those adjectives is about experiencing too many thoughts. The other is about the absence of thoughts. Blankness felt good. Last night, I was standing down the street from my house, snow falling on me, listening to a great song. It asked me how I felt. Actually, it asked me how does "it" feel, but I always hear it as *"How do you feel?"* And I considered that a polite question, because most songs aim to convey the musician's feelings or sway me to feel a certain way. Here was a song, taking the time to ask me, very earnestly, to pause and figure out what I was truly feeling. So, I asked myself how I felt. My answer? *I feel like driving.*

I spun around, lunging toward my house. Inside, I rummaged through a kitchen cabinet, ransacking as quietly as one can possibly ransack. Once I had River's car keys, my body was almost immediately in his banged-up white Oldsmobile. Then I was gone, full on Tokyo drift style. Minus the Tokyo part. And the drift. I drove very carefully. Although I've never practiced, driving was simple to pick up. I habitually study people's movements when they drive me places. My journey was aimless for a long time until my focus fell on the tattoo on my wrist's backside. Birds. I cringed. I've been hiding it with bracelets, but last night, it was exhibited. Glancing at the flying birds, I asked myself how it felt to be driving. It felt illegal, but mostly directionless. Then it occurred to me that flying would feel better. Naturally and nonsensically, the word "airport" sprung to my mind and out my mouth. "Airport."

It took fifteen minutes to reach my destination on the outskirts of town. The airport isn't for commercial use, but for private planes. Don't know what I was thinking. The open field and the air station beyond it had my attention, but I hadn't a clue who had my brain. Maybe it got a little lost, chasing freedom. Don't know where freedom is, but I need to be there. Somewhere, at least. Somewhere unrelentingly liberating.

Parking in a snowy patch outside the gates, my eyes diverted to the left, analyzing the typically frenetic highway adjacent to the airport. It was unusually calm, but every so often, a car whizzed by. This should've tipped me off about the apocalypse, or lack thereof. However, it was no longer about the apocalypse. It was about being senseless, giving into all five senses, and newly unearthed ones. None of it made sense.

I wrote my thoughts down on random pages at the end of this journal. When I reread them earlier today, the rubbish frightened me and also excited me. So, I designated a new notebook exclusively for babble. Invigorating, really. Any and all words that come and go. Lovely and ludicrous drivel, for hours. The Nonsense Notebook might be the "unrelentingly liberating somewhere" I've been searching for. Still, I can't help but want to find a physical location to feel free in. An hour ago, I switched back over to you. Hope you don't mind being in an open relationship, Joey. Putting my Nonsense Notebook down takes herculean force. I started writing this morning and now it's almost...balls. It's after midnight.

Where was I? Oh, yeah. My fast, rhyming thoughts. It was like living in a Dr. Seuss book. Soon, I was on tippy toes outside the fence that guarded the field. I unleashed a jumbo belch and did a clumsy pirouette. Jacques has been coaching me on this move since we first met, with no success. Maybe I should say "coached", because an "ing" would imply he's still doing this. He's not, because that twat is avoiding me during the most awful time to avoid a person. I've been sitting often, sitting in the audience for *Urinetown* rehearsals, withstanding the most unearthly sensation. Mackenzie Hemperley, my chubby doppelganger, is the better me. She can sing, but it goes deeper. Her clothes are cooler, her purple hair is cooler, and her overall personality screams, "I'm a freshman and I'm cool. Cooler than Rosie."

Jacques speaks the language of cool, with a dialect of, "I want old Rosie back. Mackenzie is innocent and unbroken and as good as it'll get."

And so they've become fast friends. Selfie friends. Constantly-talking-during-notes friends. Piggyback-rides-through-the-theatre friends. Bette-yelling-at-them-to-settle-down friends. Til-the-mother-fucking-end friends. It would far be less harrowing had he plucked himself a non-lookalike. I don't understand why they can't just show up and be actors. They treat rehearsal like it's this giant social hour. Throwing hard work to the wind and relying on talent alone might obliterate this show.

I wish they'd follow Logan's example. Holy. Holy shit. Wish I could see fifth grade Rosie's reaction to that sentence. It's true, though.

His dedication to *Urinetown* is admirable. During every free moment at rehearsal, he finds a quiet place where he can study his lines and eat candy in peace. I'm under the impression Logan fears he'll be the weakest link. That's what he was on the soccer team. He accepted this because he got to chill on the bench. Couldn't affect the game much. No pressure. And now Logan's the star of the school musical and determined to follow through under those boiling lights. I wish the Logan from the fir st day of this school year could see New Logan study his script. Old Logan would say, "New Logan, ya wanna skip rehearsal to go to Denny's?"

New Logan would lift his script in the air with one hand while tossing a handful of Skittles into his mouth with the other. Old Logan would skulk off, properly rejected.

New Logan. I don't mind him.

It's been nine days since our confusing encounter in class, although it feels like it's been ninety. We've been forced to communicate for our Imagination Collaboration and the musical. We've nodded at each other, but made no eye contact. If we don't have to speak, we don't.

Since the Logan debacle, I haven't spoken at school unless I had to. Teachers live to call on students who have their heads buried in their arms. My patience is tried by my towering awareness of the fact that everybody probably likes me better in a state of total quiet. When I'm not around, they likely sing. *"Ding-dong, the bitch is mute. Which 'ole bitch? The biggest bitch!"*

Nine Logan-less days doesn't sound like much, but this time has left my face long and my eyes begging for a dose of chloroform. The Mackenzie-Jacques bond has been afoot since rehearsals commenced, but it was bearable when I had Logan to play hide and seek with during breaks. For nine days, we hid from each other. Ducking, pivoting, hiding. No searching, though.

Open. Stay open.

I tried the pirouette twice more on the snowy patch outside the gates, for good measure, failing even worse. Then my feet firmly planted themselves in the snow. I felt it in my bones and tendons and the farts forming in my intestines. "It" was a juicy helping of change. I screamed happily. The apocalypse's sole survivor, my arms were thrown up, stretching to their farthest extent. More fun words blazed from my mouth. "Arctic sky! You're only here for me!"

My body spun on the snow and plopped down, eyes attending to the thick blanket falling from above. My hands gathered snow and threw it upwards. My craziness was excusable because I was alone. However, time slid away and I found my perception of isolation to be false when a figure ambled by. His feet were bare and the rest of his body wore nothing but a T-shirt and plaid pajama pants. I shouted a greeting as he kept walking. After watching his dazed and measured traveling, I jumped up and pursued him.

Neon lights in my mind. Open.

It was slippery. My rubbery black boots were made for fashion purposes, not durability. I slid on the ice as if I were cat poop on linoleum, buttocks burning as my face muscles flexed. Barefoot Boy was now far away. I trailed him, being careful not to increase my speed to the point of falling again. Once I neared him, Barefoot Boy stepped onto the highway. The road instantly felt busier than it had before. The first car swerved, missing him by a meter. I charged after him, screaming, "Are you insane?"

December 23, 2012

Hey, Joey Journal!

142 days now, but I have no time to reflect on that number. Love you, Dad, but no time. Last night, I fell asleep writing. Before drifting off, I mentioned Barefoot Boy roaming onto the highway and me yelling, *"Are you insane?"* He continued trudging across the road, speechless. When sounds of an oncoming semi-truck blared, Barefoot Boy was journeying at a snail's pace. My hands hurled outward, desperately pushing him along. We were nearing the road's edge, but not quickly. The trucker's horn did what horns do. For weeks, I had barely the might to get out of bed, but was abruptly robust enough to tackle Barefoot Boy, sending us both soaring. We landed in the ditch. He faced downwards, my body stretched over his. I rolled off. Lifeless, he was. I said, "Dingo's kidneys."

My hand checked for a pulse, finding one present. After a few uncertain seconds, I squeezed his shoulders, shook him, and repeatedly screamed for him to wake up. When I threw him down, Barefoot Boy lifted his face from the snow, groaning the words, "Not again."

"Again?"

In a flash, he flipped onto his back, eyes protruding. Mine did the same. He screamed, as did I. Christ's sake, it was Logan Fields. He said, "The hell?"

"Same to you!"

His deep-set eyes kept growing. Uncontrollably. Then he cried. Again, uncontrollably. I couldn't settle on something to say. You see, I didn't want him to punch me in the face. That's how I've been feeling anytime I've wanted to say something to Logan since the Mouthful incident, like he'd knock me out if I tried. Maybe he wasn't ever mad at me, but he should've been. A knockout should've happened. All he did was say, 'Hey.' 'Hey' under the desk. 'Hey', in a heavy way. A 'hey' worth a kiss on the cheek. A 'hey' to vomit over. Hey. I'm the reason he got walloped by a girl he may or may not have feelings for. And he still followed me into the hallway. Tried to help. Slow. I called him "slow." Logan had nine days to knock me out, and of course he didn't. Society would rightfully frown upon that, but it'd be sweat off my back. *I shouldn't speak.* That's what I thought as I balanced in that snowy ditch. *If I speak, I'll say more foul words that warrant a punch in the face.* Seconds scurried by, then Logan spoke, heavy breaths skewing his words. It sounded like, "I'm so damn sorry."

Why are you sorry? I'm sorry, I thought. *But I won't say it. Hearing your voice has stolen mine. I'm sorry, although it's only in my head.* After a hesitant moment, my voice managed to eke out three words. "Count to ten."

He couldn't and was only able to breathe into his benumbed hands. That's when I grabbed them, warming his fingers up with my gloved ones. Logan stared at our intertwining extremities, squinting and slowly allaying. I said, "Cold?" He gave a tragic nod, reluctantly making eye contact. "Logan, what happened? Why are you here?"

"Can't." After this was said, I snappily released his hands. My migraine minced my patience to a million pieces. He scrutinized a car passing behind me, eyes trailing it until it left. "Don't remember," he said. "Wasn't awake."

"Sleepwalking?"

He solemnly nodded. "Done it before. I piss in the closet. Throw things away."

"You leave the house? How often?"

"First time," he said. His face scrunched before he took to pulling at his hair's roots.

"Know where you are?"

He shook his head, hands now yanking his cheeks down. I told him to follow. Logan removed his palms from his sheepish face and I said, "Trust me?"

He shrugged. "I'm over that stuff."

My heart spasmed, but my elation didn't show externally. "Why?"

"Stop saying why, Rosie."

"Okay. Follow me?"

We hopped into the Oldsmobile and it became obvious that Logan had forgotten about my nonexistent license due to his current dilemma. No questions were asked while the car warmed up. All he said was, "Horsetits. It's cold."

I rifled through my backpack, retrieving baggy pink sweatpants and a familiar red hoodie. I said, "Here, and my name's not Horsetits."

My body turned while he swapped his snow-drenched pants for the dry pair. After a moment, I asked if he was done. Logan said yes and I threw him the sweater. He gravely stared at it, saying, "Gave it to you."

"Goose bumps gross me out, too." Then Logan faintly smiled, pulling his sopping wet T-shirt over his head. I looked the other way once more. He may be a string bean, but his body has charm. It's awkward to stare. Once he was swaddled in fresh sweats, we took off. While driving, solid gold oldies consumed our brains, as neither one of us felt like talking. When we cruised by a truck stop diner, my hunger became apparent and I pulled into the parking lot.

"What's this?" he asked.

"Our systems need food."

He curled into a ball, wiggling his toes, weakly shooting me a grin. "Not wearing shoes."

My hand shot into my bag and tossed moccasins on his lap. "A tight squeeze, Barefoot Boy."

We walked into Andy's Truck Stop Diner. It's open twenty-four hours most days. Andy's only patrons at 2 am are young people and truck drivers. When we entered, it was damn near empty. Those present were the late shift staff, three tables of college students who were home for the holidays, and one burly truck driver sipping coffee. Very well could've been the man who almost plowed us down. We grabbed a seat and mutely looked over menus. An emaciated waitress wearily waltzed over, eyes swollen. She was as friendly as a worker can possibly be during the night shift. Once our orders were taken, Logan finally felt like talking. He asked how we ended up in a ditch. Logan was biting his hoodie's aglet while rubbing his arm. I slowly ripped my napkin as I said, "Got to the airport. You were walking. I ran after. Thought I was alone, completely, like the apocalypse happened."

His hoodie string fell as he sleepily smiled.

"Shh, Logan. I heard an exploding avalanche. An 'explosalanche'. So, I went to the airport for kicks. Chased you, but you walked onto the highway. A car almost got you," I gently said. I hadn't realized how shaken up I was until it was all vocalized. "I pushed you along. A semi blared its horn." He was blank, and not the good kind. "Probably that grizzly bear over there," I said, gesturing to the trucker. Logan smiled lightly, in a compulsory way. "Nearly hit us. Threw my weight into you and—"

Logan's eyes glassed up as he said, "You saved me?"

"No, c'mon."

"You did." His uncertain hands grabbed mine as he said, "Thanks."

Neon lights. Open. Wide open. My eyes closed, wanting to remember only the indents of his palms. He brought my hands to his lips, giving a thankful kiss to both of my hands' backsides. I retracted my hands gingerly as I opened my eyes, overjoyed knowing whatever anger he might have been feeling toward me dissolved. I said, "Right place, right time."

At that precise moment, the door made a dinging noise. Logan and I looked over, but I instantly turned back, astonished. Anastasia Moretti-Slocumb traipsed in with Eliot Buxton. I know we have a "Don't ask, don't tell" rule, and that we steadily avoid one another, but tell me this, what the hell am I supposed to do when I see somebody who calls himself my boyfriend out with another girl? How can I get upset with him when I'm with another guy, even if we're together under strange circumstances? I understood our arrangement at first, but this has evolved into something I can't handle. This Polly wants not a single bite of that polyamorous cracker. Didn't sign up to have Mouthful as a sister wife.

I hunched my shoulders while pulling my hood over my unkempt hair. Soon, I dived under the table. The two walked by, failing to notice us, it seemed. Logan whispered, "Why does awkward shit only happen when you're around?" Then he clambered underneath to briefly meet with me. "Sit on your stool. Hiding under tables doesn't end well with us." Once we reemerged and were in our seats, he said, "At least I'm facing away from my sorta-kinda-maybe love interest." Logan and I made long, numb eye contact until he broke the silence by saying, "It's not what it looks like?"

"It is."

"Rosie, it's not."

"Mouthful has sex hair."

"That's not from sex," he said, way too light-hearted. "Maybe it's just her hair?"

I said, "Mouthful straightens her hair daily. Combs it in class. She once flat-ironed it during art. You think that girl would go on a date with messy hair?"

He crossed his arms, then recrossed them, unable to decide how he wanted to position his forearms. Logan finally clutched the table's edge and said, "Maybe it's not a date?" He said it so breezily. What happened to wanting to ask her out only nine days before?

"Okay?" I said, failing to mask my confusion. "Ain't a date, Logan. They got it on in his car. Now, they're hungry." He silently massaged his caterpillar eyebrows with his index fingers. "Mouthful," I nonchalantly whispered, "Mouthful got a giant mouthful of my pretend boyfriend's Gentlemen's Relish."

Logan was wistful as he said, "Why are you so calm?"

"Same to you."

"This isn't about me."

"Me?" I said. "How can you expect a person to be mad about something that they're used to?"

"You should be a human dagger, Rosie. Dangerous. He uses you. You feel useless. I know it. Get mad."

"Won't get mad. Just even."

He said, "Twinkie level even?"

"Worse, Logan. And when I get around to it, I'll break up with him. Hard evidence that a person is shitty merely means another person is in my past. That's how I operate. Unlike some people at this table."

He snorted and said, "Talking about Mouthful and me?" When he got a load of my smug mug, he smirked and said, "Grand Duchess Anastasia?"

"Course."

"You don't know the first thing about it. I'm attracted to her, but not enough to go there again. I...I lied. Okay? Got punched in the face by a girl and tried to make your heart bleed a bit."

After a cumbersome silence, the waitress delivered our meals. As she placed Logan's cheeseburger, I freaked. "No," I said. "She looked at me!"

The energy deficient server was overwhelmed. "Sorry I looked at you, kid. Just doing my job." She was nice before, but it was apparent that it was too late at night for our bull.

"Not you," I said. "Mouthful." The waitress savagely set my soup down and swiftly departed. "They're holding hands and she keeps looking over here," I said, pushing my meal aside and laying my head down.

"Pick it up, Rosie." I moaned the word 'no' into the greasy table. "Pick it up if you wanna make those swingers jealous." My head ascended and he said, "Ball isn't in our court. Let's get it back. Let's play the game." I looked over at the table. Mouthful was laughing, but her eyes occasionally focused on us. She was being a girl, still caring about what Logan thought. I was also being a girl, giving in to the part of myself that still semi-cared about Eliot.

"Fine," I said. "I'll play, and only because I..."

I didn't want to say it, so he said it for me. "Wanna hurt Skank Bucket's feelings?"

"Hell yeah."

"Remove your hood," said Logan. Then my eyebrows did a perplexed little dance. "You heard me, Rosie. You're not the Unabomber, but a lady on a date."

I slowly pulled off my hood. "You know we're here on accident."

"Mouthful and Eliot don't know."

181

A sly grin came to my face as I adjusted my hair and grabbed Logan's right hand. He sat up straight. I said, "Just two people on a fake date. Act natural and eat." He tried eating his burger with his unpracticed hand, looking entirely uncoordinated as an involuntary grin appeared. I said, "It looks odd. Put it down."

He started silently laughing and tenderly dropped it. "Not my fault I'm right-handed."

"I know," I said. "I don't go on dates, alright?" Eliot hadn't taken me to eat since summer, and Jacques always came along when we did go out. "Relinquish my hand, Logan." He nodded, but I told him to wait, rendering him confused. I said, "Don't be abrupt. She'll know something's off. If Eliot was facing us, we wouldn't have to worry. He's thick. We got Mouthful. Although she's mostly evil, she has a brain. Be smooth."

Logan beamed and said, "Smooth is what I do best." With a wink, he tenderly kissed my hand. When he removed his lips, he gave me a closed smile. His thumb grazed my fingers as he let go. Then Logan took a bite of his burger, swallowed and wiped his mouth with a napkin. My eyes fell on Mouthful, then back to Logan. "She's jealous. Let's keep it up," I said, but it soon dawned on me that my noggin was misinterpreting his every action, every signal, every shift in his nature. The charade needed to cease, so I said, "Never mind. My ideas have expired."

"I've got one, Rosie. Remember the first day of fifth grade? You should feed me."

I laughed and examined my untouched soup. "I couldn't."

"Right. I don't want food on my face," he said, rubbing his eyes, thinking. Suddenly, he said, "I'll feed you." This made me shake my head. "C'mon," he begged. "You look like an Ethiopian child." I stared at his fries as ketchup oozed on his plate's perimeter. "A little birdie on the sidewalk with a broken wing, one who needs help and food."

"You told me I'm not a bird," I said, growing more tense and frantic with each word. "You drove me home from the library and said not having my license means not knowing freedom. I said I was free. You said, 'Free as a bird?' I hated this chat for two reasons, I'm free and 'bird' is among my least favorite words now. 'Bro' is the only terrible word ranking above it. I said I was free, although not a bird. You said I wasn't free or a bird. I remember."

"That's your problem," he said. "You remember too much." I scrunched my face at him and he continued. "I stand by what I said. You haven't been free this year, which I get. You're going through stuff, but part of me thinks you're not free because you've become afraid of the big bad bird word. You're denying yourself your rightful place in this world as the bird you secretly are." Despondency was on my face and slight regret was on his. He sweetly smiled before trying again. "Yeah, I see you as a bird. Right now, you're more of a chicken, because you're grounded, but also loud and afraid of many things. But I know you're able to be a way more amazing bird than a fucking chicken."

"Stop. No birds! No birds. No chickens either."

"I'm kidding. You're a little baby chicken. That's all. Let Mama Bird feed you."

Disgusted, I said, "You know what 'Mama Birding' is, don't you?"

"It's when one person feeds another person."

"Logan, it's when somebody chews up their food and spits it into another person's mouth, based on the feeding habits of birds, which is a topic you best avoid."

He tentatively stroked my arm and told me to relax. I slapped his hand away and Logan said, "I wanna feed you non-chewed up food."

"Fine," I said exasperatedly. "Fry me. Not like frying, as in deep-fried chicken. Oh, chicken! Fuck. Fry. In my mouth. Now. And stop talking about birds."

He leisurely picked up the fry and effortlessly fed it to me. Once I was done chewing, I grumpily said, "Tasted sinful without ketchup." Logan's pointer finger plunged into his ketchup and shot up. "No," I said, laughing.

His finger glided toward me as he sang, "Here comes the choo-choo train." Logan's ketchup covered finger cascaded into my smiling mouth, my eyes drifting shut as I licked the substance off his finger. My eyes coasted open, becoming transfixed on Logan's finger, which rested on my bottom lip. In retrospect, we must've looked more bizarre than romantic. I went spiraling into a memory. I saw us in a library bathroom stall, his finger on my lip. *I didn't want to be just another girl. I wanted to be the girl. Not just for him. For anyone who so much as lays a finger on me.* I pulled my head away, forcing a polite smile, then hit a wall. *But what if I am the girl? The only girl. The girl he truly likes. Frightful. Neon lights. Open. Mind open.*

Seeing double, I ravenously chugged my soup, breathed in my saltines and grabbed a handful of fries from his plate. "Wacko, slow down," he said. I could hardly hear him, like I was in a vacuum. Soon, my plate was empty. I glanced at Logan, who held back silent chuckling. He said, "That was the most disgusting thing I've ever seen you do." I was gonna throw up while Logan kept noiselessly laughing.

"Goddammit, laugh out loud," I said.

He clapped his hands to his mouth, shocked and entertained.

"Laugh out loud or get the fuck out of my face!" Crap, I was snapping.

"You hate my laugh?"

"No, I love it," I blurted out, but caught myself and grimaced. After a deep breath, I said, "I mean, I like it. I like you. I mean, your laugh. I like your silent laugh. Don't change it. Please." I couldn't look anywhere but my bowl.

"'Silent laugh'?"

"You never laugh out loud."

He grinned and said, "You have an interesting laugh yourself." I stared at the ceiling and he said, "Sorry, I personally love your laugh." Then he pretended to be all anxious and girlish. "I mean, I like it. I like you. I mean, your laugh. I like your Janice-from-*Friends* laugh. Don't change it. Please."

"If Mouthful weren't watching, I'd shank you with my cutlery."

"How did you not notice they left?"

I looked over their now empty table. "Hold on. What?"

"Left while you inhaled your meal," Logan said. "I went over to your side of the table for a bit. You know, in case you choked on your crackers and I needed to give the Heimlich. You think our scam worked?"

I asked him how she looked upon leaving and he vigorously

hopped off his stool, bouncing over to where Mouthful and Eliot sat. Logan doesn't run. He casually hops from one foot to the other. These hops never bring him higher than an inch from the floor. A shuffling Peter Cottontail. It's hilarious, especially when he's wearing women's sweatpants.

Once Logan was at their former table, he struck a feminine pose, thrusting his nose upward, face becoming haughty. Then Logan sashayed down the aisle as if it were a catwalk. When he got to our table, he sped up. Logan shielded his face, making it seem like he was playing with his hair. Then he almost left the building before I shouted through my cackles, "Come back!" He shuffle-bounced back to the table, glowing, and I said, "If she left like that, I predict you'll get a text message within three minutes. She'll nonchalantly ask to talk."

"Sounds about right."

I nodded and eagerly said, "How jealous did he look?" Logan's jaw fell open and there was remorse in his eyes. "Oh," I said, smiling away potential tears. "He wasn't jealous?"

He shook his head. "Honestly, he was stoned. Patted my back and called you Becky. Strange fucker. I think he might have mistook you for Becky Adams. She has similar hair."

"Crap," I yelled into my hands. "The money's in the car." Then I sprinted out, but not before commanding him to finish his food. Once in the dark parking lot, I experienced vertigo, which made my movements laggard. Then I grabbed twenty bucks from the car and mustered up enough energy to reenter the building. While seating myself, my hand slammed the money down. I took in the state of Logan, who was gazing at his phone and glowering. Soon, he grinned lazily and handed it over. The text said, *"Wanna talk?"* I sighed, tearing up from out-and-out exhaustion and envy. "I'm a teenage Nostradamus and need a nap. If I have more visions, I'll wake up and tell you." Then I dropped my head on my unoccupied plate.

"Who's Nostradamus?"

I said, "Don't wake me until you're done." I don't know how long my unconscious noggin was laying on that plate. All I remember is a tap on my shoulder, then sluggishly standing up and Logan helping me walk straight. I waved at our server, groggily saying, "Night, kind waitress. Sleep well."

"Shhh," went Logan in my ear.

"You tip?"

"Yep," he said. "I'll pay you back."

Once we reached the Oldsmobile, I stopped leaning on Logan and hopped in the driver's seat. I clasped the wheel as he opened the door and told me to get out. Despite the cloudiness, I could tell he was smiling. I grabbed his lips, smooshing them together and giggling. "Your smile's soft."

Through adhered lips, Logan once again requested I leave the driver's seat. His voice deteriorated into an unintelligible mumble. Then I said, "No, man. I'm good."

As my hand gently fell into my lap, dozing off reached its climax. Logan dragged me out of the driver's seat, carrying me to the car's other side. Then he put me down on my wobbly feet and held my shoulders so I wouldn't fall. He said, "You, my friend, are a license free zombie. Get in."

Once seated, I curled my legs and put my head between my kneecaps. Then I reluctantly gave up the keys. "You gonna buckle yourself, Rosie?"

I shook my arm, but my eyes couldn't stay open. Logan shifted me around and belted me. As the car's wheels began vibrating, my friend busted out laughing. Out loud. I whispered, "I hear your laugh."

"This is real funny."

"No laugh. No you laugh at me."

"Rosie, you got high off soup and saltines. How can I not?"

"Drugs bad," I said. "I no do drugs."

Once we were in front of my house, he said, "I'd walk home, but it's... dark." My mind drifted to the night when we were at the library. When I told him I was waiting for the bus, he said, "*But...it's dark.*"

"Afraid of the dark?" I asked.

"Naw."

"You are."

"Fine. A little," he said. "I'm also beat. I'm so tired, I don't know which way home is."

I slapped myself a couple times in the face, revitalized myself, and asked if he was ready to sneak in. Logan showed me how to Indian walk on the driveway before we successfully executed our noiseless penetration of the house. Once in my room, I cautiously shut the door. When I turned, he hugged me.

We lingered in each other's embrace a second too long. After we released, I unlaced my shoes and climbed under my comforter. I didn't hear movement, so I pulled the blanket off, finding Logan maladroitly swinging his arms. I gave the other side of the bed a careless pat. Once I slipped into darkness, the bed weighed down and the comforter lifted. Minutes passed. When I neared sleep, the image that cannot be erased stampeded into my brain. I cried, gradually growing noisier. Logan tapped my shoulder and I reluctantly rolled to face him. I was now painstakingly awake. The lights were still on and Logan's eyes were heavy with concern. "So damn sorry," I said, sitting up. He sat up, too, eyes studying my hands for a long moment. At last, he grabbed my left one. His free hand traveled along my face, grazing away tears with his thumb as the rest of his fingers caressed my cheek. My eyes closed as his lips softly contacted my forehead. Then Logan hugged me again. Ever so gently, he asked what was wrong, ever so gently stroking the side of my head that has hair. "Nothing," I whispered.

"Nightmare?"

"Don't know." I fell back down while Logan got up and killed the lights. Once he was back in bed, his hand fumbled around until it grasped mine. "Sorry. Really," I said.

"You were a good friend to me earlier. It's my turn."

"Aren't you afraid of the dark?"

"Only when I'm alone."

December 23, 2012

Hey, Joey Journal!

It's still Sunday. Still 142 days since he passed. Midnight is approaching. I can write more because I remembered there's no school tomorrow. Christmas break.

On this day in Rosie Dwyer history, I realized falling asleep next to somebody you're interested in is only half as exciting as waking up to their presence. I thought about the 'waking up' all day yesterday and today. I have to get the moment out of my system.

As you know, The False Apocalypse happened and Logan Fields was in my bed the next morning. My eyes popped open. Pop! 9:23 am. When I discovered a sleeping Logan, I jolted, forgetting how he got there. I gently lay back down, studying him. When he's awake, his face is tranquil. While slumbering, he rumples his brows, grinds his teeth and turns about. He was as tense as a gymnast's muscles during a floor routine. My body faced the opposite direction. After moments of sheer calm, his side of the bed shifted. My whole self spasmed. Before I knew it, I was in standing position.

"Hey," he said.

"Hey."

"FYI, I'm gonna shimmy out your window."

"It's a two-story drop."

I now suspect he does facial yoga because his grin stretched so skillfully. "When there's a will, there's a way."

"Or a broken ass bone."

He said. "Look, last night put me in the mood for more adventure."

We argued back and forth like this as he tied my sheets together. Before he could open my window, I tackled him to the ground. Straddling him, I said, "Front door, you idiot."

Logan and I loitered in this position for an unbearably long time until he broke the tension. "Please, don't fart on me."

I fell on the ground next to him and we stretched out on our backs. Both of us smiled until our lips almost fell off. Then he kissed my cheek. I shot into sitting position. Before I could form a verbal response, he was already halfway to the door. Logan said, "Let's see if I get caught doing things your way."

He didn't get caught. At least I don't think so. I'm unsure. I'd rather write about certainty. Here's something I know. When Logan told me not to fart on him, I knew I loved him. I knew it. The only thing that's unclear is where this love falls on a scale from platonic to romantic. But I fully know I love Logan Fields. And I revel in knowing that every time I hear a fart in the future, I'll think of him. And instead of squeezing my nose, I'll smile until my lips fall off.

You probably assume I haven't felt anything but elation since he left. You're incorrect. My lips are still on my face. Yesterday, fifteen minutes after Logan was gone, the source of the 'explosalanche' became known. Writing nonsense at the kitchen counter, I looked out the window and discovered the noise came from our backyard tree. It's ancient, rotting, and falling apart at the seams. The tree has two huge trunks. One of them couldn't handle the copious amounts of snow resting on it, and so it broke in half and descended upon my neighbor's yard. It scraped their house, mangled their children's playset, took out half their deck and stuck the landing on an electrical wire above their yard. The ordeal removed electricity from eighteen homes. Ironically, our house's electricity was unaffected.

I'm the only person in my family who heard it, so no wonder they told me to go back to bed when I tried to get them to evacuate the house. When I saw the scene, I heaved myself out the back door. Employees from the electrical company were cutting down the wire, which plunged downwards as the trunk balanced. The wire was ready to break. I grabbed my camera from inside and took four shots before realizing my feet were bare. A bout of hypothermia sounded unsavory, so the indoors became my destination.

While inspecting the pictures, I only saw death. Loving somebody for making a perfectly timed fart joke isn't enough to make me see only life.

December 26th, 2012

Hey, Joey Journal,

145 days. On this day, my exhausted body feels like it just ran the Grand Union Canal 145 Mile Race. All because of the nastiest cold my body has ever seen and Christmas.

My first birthday without him felt like there was something missing. The first Christmas felt like shit. I'm not aspiring to be blasphemous, but Christmas is henceforth 'Shit-mas'. We didn't meet up with family this year. Willow and Melanie have the flu, while I'm battling the aforementioned cold. My elderly grandparents are fragile, so we bypassed the visits. We watched Shit-mas movies at home, instead. "We" means "me." River attended his girlfriend's Christmas party, while Willow was in her room for most of *It's a Wonderful Life*, doing God knows what. She hardly leaves her room anymore. Melanie was in the recliner, sleeping through it. I sat rigidly on the sofa, trying to feel sympathy for her, but was selfish and felt none. Willow trudged downstairs as George Bailey screamed, "Merry Christmas" at everything he saw. With her blanket cloaking her head, she was a Disney witch delivering a poison apple. She said, "Wake up." Melanie gazed dazedly at her, and Willow continued talking over the film's best part. "No toilet paper."

"Put the blanket down. You'll bump the tree," Melanie replied. Willow was nowhere near the Shit-mas tree, but still threw her blanket on me. She kept wailing about having to poop until Melanie told her to look in the cupboard. Willow screamed that she already did. George was now in his house, people filtering in to pay him the money they owed. "Look harder, Willow."

The movie's cast started singing "Hark the Herald Angels Sing" as George held his child and smiled lovingly at his wife.

"You're stupid, Mom."

I scowled as Melanie brimmed with newfound energy and chased Willow upstairs. My attention attempted to remain on the TV.

"Hark the herald angels sing
'Glory to the newborn King!
Peace on earth and mercy mild
God and sinners reconciled'"

Willow's door slammed and Mel shouted, "Open it!" while the people in George's house sang "Auld Lang Syne." As they concluded, a bell on George's tree chimed and Little Zuzu said, *"Look, Daddy! Teacher says every time a bell rings, an angel gets its wings."*

"You're a bitch!" I don't know who said it that last time. Maybe it was both, simultaneously. I always cry watching *It's a Wonderful Life*, but it was different this year. Tears were triggered by a question that seemed to be written on each wall.

Has he gotten his wings yet?

December 31, 2012

Hey, Joey Journal!

150 days. After some research, I discovered that 150 is Dunbar's number. According to Wikipedia, this number "is a suggested cognitive limit to the number of people with whom one can maintain stable social relationships."

My jaw dropped when I read this sentence. 150? There are people on this planet with that many stable social relationships? Zero, that's how many stable social relationships I have. And I'm done with that. Done.

I rolled onto my floor at dawn and kicked my legs in the air. Shook 'em about. No need for an alarm, not when every iota of my entity is anticipating the New Year. I wrote resolutions on Post-it notes throughout the day and when I finished, there were thirty-three notes stuck to my wooden headboard. A real array of resolutions. Eat healthy. Bolster my grades. Apply to college. Make *Urinetown* perfection. Break up with my skeeze ball, absentee boyfriend. Normalize my relationship with Jacques. Avoid my burgeoning love for Logan, all because he's right about me being a chicken. Etcetera. Thirty-three Post-its. I pulled out another and wrote, "This will be a productive year" and placed it among the rest. I prefer even numbers.

By three o'clock, I began pacing about, with my mouth muttering. I do this often, to work out my thoughts and practice for future conversations. Sometimes, I simply tell my life's stories. Talking to myself doesn't imply mental instability. Every Dwyer does this. We're mumbling mavericks.

As I write this, it's 4:00 pm. Jacques is throwing his annual party. He goes all out. Sends invitations in the mail. When I got mine, my heart couldn't resist feeling hopeful. Despite this seed of optimism, I still paced and mumbled even more than I usually do. The monologue I gave to my bedroom furniture went as such. "Got this invitation, right? This is the only time of year I get an invitation in the mail. Jacques refuses to send out Facebook invites because he's a cultured soul with penmanship worth flaunting. This is what I love about Jacques. My heart fluttered when I saw his flourishing marks. I felt as if nothing changed. But moments later, my heart sank. I thought. Thought too much. What if that awful doppelganger is there? What if I don't have anything to say to the guests? What if Jacques has only invited me out of obligation? And don't even get me started on Eliot. Don't look at me like that, Alarm Clock. I'm not overthinking this." I proceeded to unplug the device. "Now try and sarcastically shine your numbers!" After collapsing on the bed and realizing I was losing it, I said, "Look, furniture, I won't hurt the rest of you. I'll get it together. Let's just do this already. The party doesn't start until seven. It's around 4:00. Jacques won't mind earliness. Right? Right. His cell went straight to machine since he's spacey. Always forgets to charge his phone. Fine, Bed. I'll get off you. I'll walk over there. I'll help him set up because the only thing that's changed is me."

My God, I hope that last sentence is true. If all goes as planned, I'm coming home from this party with at least one stable social relationship. Jacques, I'm coming for you.

December 31, 2012

Hey, Joey Journal,

　　Still 150 days. Still have zero stable social relationships. Came home hours ago. Melanie didn't notice me sneak back in. The new year is minutes away. When I knocked on their front door, Barb Fagg and her husband exited, carrying luggage. They were bedecked in "out-on-the-town clothes." That's what Barb cheerily called their outfits when I complimented their dapperness. Yep, I call her Barb now, and have been doing so for years. It's her demand. Barb was struggling with clinical depression when Jacques and I met. It took years, but now she farts butterflies. Dan Fagg, who is large in size and even larger at heart, said, "This class act and I are going on a second honeymoon. Bora Bora, baby!"

　　"Aren't you worried about the trouble your boy will get into?"

　　"No," Barb said. "He's the youngest of way too many. We stopped caring two kids back"

　　"Well, don't get too frisky," I said. "Your litter is big enough."

　　While laughing, Barb embraced me, being careful not to crush the taco dip in my arms. Once she freed me, she said, "Your boyfriend is hanging with Jacques in his room. Go on up, and might I add that you nabbed yourself a looker."

　　I entered their foyer and you know that feeling that dismantles one's intestines when something awful is about to happen? No such precognition occurred. I gingerly tiptoed upstairs, planning to surprise them. Something about the new year made me want a cordial break up with Eliot, one that would allow us to be friends afterward. New Year's

Eve is a fake little bitch. The three of us haven't hung out in forever, but somehow, I felt capable of forcing things to become normal. You see, Jacques and I have this game where we flash our butts when the other person isn't expecting it. Once outside his door, I set down the dip and adjusted my skinny jeans and undies. I bit my tongue, as laughter would ruin the execution of the prank. Then I slammed the door open, excited eyes closed. Swiftly, I turned, shaking my bare buttocks. "Gotcha!"

My keister convulsed despite the quiet. I clutched both cheeks, lowered my voice, made my derriere talk. "Gonna call me a dumbass?'" More muteness, so I zipped my pants and said, "What is up with you two?" The boys had something "up" alright, as they were trying to yank their underwear over their own bare behinds. Stillness and stiffness lingered, but it didn't satiate my psyche. The memory of Mrs. Buxton's screaming was beyond present. *"How can I move past walking in on my baby nearly having sex?"* A crucial part of that sentence was cut off. *"With another boy?"*

I grabbed the dip from the hallway, ripped the shrink-wrap off and chucked it at them. It splattered everywhere while I barbarically bellowed, "Suck your own wieners!"

Storming down the Fagg's icy sidewalk, I dealt with two thoughts that swirled about. First thought: *Don't slip, don't slip, don't slip.* Second thought: *What a waste of perfectly good taco dip!*

I stared at the Post-it notes above my bed all night. Two minutes before 2013 began, Eliot called for the twelfth time. His name on my phone was still, *'Dat Booty Tho.'* Both Eliot and Jacques took turns giving calls and texts that went unanswered. Something about knowing I had only a few moments of the year left made me give in. "Hey," said Eliot, slurring the word into shambles.

"Don't ruin 'hey' for me. I'm starting to like that word." That's when I heard him toss his cookies. "You're drunk and probably gay. Attractive combo. My knees are weak." They were, though. Downright decrepit.

Eliot told me he went home immediately after getting caught because he was so embarrassed. "I'm having a bad night just like you. I'm trying to make it better."

"Christ, Eliot. Why not try to make things better months ago?" Consummate silence, so I said, "Stop trying to be hetero, okay? I probably would've liked you better had I known. You know my ideal universe would be just me and a bunch of gay men, don't you?"

"But, Rosie—"

"Stop trying."

As I hung up, my mind formed arrangements. My first plan was to fart on the picture of the two of them on my desk. Certainly had one worked up. Outrage makes gas happen to me. My plans, oh, they're here. Jacques will get a morning helping of eggs. Yes, eggs. As for Eliot, he will get the worst revenge there is. My absolute, unfiltered pity.

January 1, 2013

Hey, Joey Journal!

Day 151 of his absence. Perfect number, seeing as I started the day with Oddfellows Local 151 playing on my iPod and a swig of Bacardi 151. Found the potent rum in the way back of the liquor cabinet. Once my mouth was full, I realized it was absolutely disgusting. I had no choice but to spit it in the sink. *I could never be an alcoholic,* I thought. *Shit. Now how will I meet the challenges that come with adulthood?*

I put the bottle back. As I retrieved my weapon of choice from the refrigerator, my brother walked in. River took to preparing oatmeal and said, "Haven't stayed up that late in ages. Got home real early this morning from Kate's party. When did you get in?"

"Late."

"How was the party?"

"Great."

"Good, Rosie. That's good. Expect to see Jacques soon?"

I shrugged and said, "Going back right now."

He looked so relieved. "Wonderful," said River. "Why do you have a carton of eggs?"

I smiled. "These eggs? I'm gonna scramble them for Jacques."

The microwave beeped as River said, "You two are the best. Let me wolf down my oats. I'll drive you over there."

"Thanks."

I listened to my music as I watched River hunch over his bowl and become a rabid animal. Next thing I knew, he was dropping me off at

Fagg Family Farm and giving me a thumbs up. Once he left, I grew closer to Jacques' home. My naked hand gripped the egg. A little white grenade. His blue stucco house loomed above me, beautiful and threatening, much like the boy inside. I caressed the egg once more before pitching it at his bedroom window. The white grenade didn't go boom. Just crack. Jacques propelled his window open and I paid him no mind, concentrating on what my hands were doing. He shouted the word, "Childish."

I delicately pulled another egg from the carton, fingers memorizing its surface, its smooth exterior easing me. As it smashed on his front door, the sound wasn't smooth. It was unadulterated dynamite. After the second egg bombarded the entrance, Jacques threw the door open and dashed down the lawn. He was shirtless and wearing red silk pajama pants. He clearly just woke up, yet his hair was somehow perfect. It was 11 am. Wild night, no doubt. And although his body shot up over the years, his face was the same as it was when we first met. Perfect picture of a piss ant. Once Jacques was feet away, he decelerated as an out-of-character deep breath was taken. "I'm a jerk," he calmly said, body language offering an armistice. I responded by circling him, snapping my fingers, threatening him *West Side Story* style. He said, "What?" and so I shoved his body into the thick snow. I could only muster a grimace.

"It's terrible," Jacques said, noticeably drowsy as he rose. The way he said the word "terrible" agitated me, because it was obvious he was going to cry. That never happens. Even after my dad died, he couldn't cry. I saw the guilt carved into every crevice of his face when we chilled in an unoccupied room at the funeral home. The tears wouldn't come, and not because he wasn't despairing over the situation. He can't cry in front of anybody for some reason. I think it's something that's sacred to him. Something he needs to do alone, like praying, or taking a crap. And he stood before me this morning, separated from his previous customs, about to cry.

I was shocked, but true to my own character. Impulsive. Rude. Me. His eerie vulnerability was met by a freshly chucked egg, one that torpedoed directly at him. Being limber, Jacques maneuvered out of harm's way. Some straight up Matrix crap. Yolk splashed on Barb's flowerpots, but no flowers were destroyed in the process. Winter slaughtered them way back. Yellow seeped into the snow-capped pots, making it look like someone pissed right in front of Jacques' house. I wish I did that.

His ice solid being partially resulted from his drenched slippers and lost shirt, but the main reason for his immobility was that he'd never witnessed me be this crazy toward him. We've had spats. It's been a friendship marked by chronic scuffling. We've slapped one another often, verbally and physically. Neither of us has ever resorted to egg chucking. Not until now. "How screwy is your mind, psycho?" he said deliberately. Instantly after insanity was insinuated, my eyes inspected the snow I stood in. "Didn't mean it," Jacques said. "I'm a piece of crap."

"You're not merely crap. You're a stink-tastic pile of orangutan dung."

"You read my text? Sent one after my hundredth call."

At one in the morning, I received a rambling apology message. "Words on a screen," I said. "Just words."

"I'll say it. Sorry."

His concession was compassionate. Rare Jacques apologies are typically far from wholehearted. Part of me wanted to hug the sincere bastard, but a bitchier part took control. I said, "Should be, dick-licker." It was an unfledged attempt at an insult, but it worked, seeing as Jacques momentarily lost all ability to hold it together. The boy spewed many diatribes over the years, but the blustering rant that resulted from this comment takes the cake and ravenously devours it.

The following dialogue is a direct quote. I had the tape recorder River gave me in my pocket. Started recording the second I arrived. I replayed it over and over to myself when I got home today. "Wanna know what Mr. Dick-Licker thinks? Not gonna tell you, because heaven knows you only care about your own thoughts, sweetie. Taking back 'sweetie' before you request it. Not because you don't like being called that, but because everyone knows you're not sweet. In your world, everybody is some character. And you're the only character you care about. It's been a saga from the beginning. That's how we got tangled up together. You wanted interesting characters for your life story. Can't get more interesting than the gay sidekick."

"Where's this coming from?" I said.

Jacques eyeballed the snow for a moment, shaking his head. "I—I don't mean this. I mean…I do. I don't know. I haven't been able to say anything out loud since your dad died. Literally. The words can't come out. When things stay in my head too long, they get jumbled until I don't know what's true anymore. Do you get it, Rosie? There's things I wanna say. Don't know when the right time is, if there is such a thing. Right time. Screw it. I shouldn't have been, you know, with Eliot, but you have to hear why."

"It isn't about you," I said, yanking my hat off. Then a muffled scream was vented into it. Out of instinct, he ripped the hat from me and slapped me upside the head. Jacques took in my agape face. From the look on his, it became obvious he knew we're not good enough friends to do those types of things anymore. Jacques was about to speak, but I interrupted and asked him to name one thing. "Name one thing you've done for me during this time to help me, Jacques. Name it."

He said, "It's true that I haven't gone out of my way, but I've done things to reach out. Behind the scenes."

"Name it."

"Rosie, this doesn't make me a saint, but I told everybody to vote you onto homecoming court. A surprise to get you happy."

"Do you realize how that sounds?" Jacques' face proved he was realizing it. I knew it was pity. "I knew it. And getting pity-votes makes me pathetic, but at least I didn't run through the halls, screaming, 'Vote for me or I'll maim you'."

Yep, that's what he did.

Jacques silently seethed. He was Dr. Jacques-ll and Petty Hyde. "That? That was a joke," he said. "I'm well-liked. Sorry that this social trend includes Eliot, but didn't you find it strange that once you introduced us, he only came around when I was invited? The three of us were together all last summer, and the whole time, I felt this distance between the two of you, Rosie. And you two made out occasionally, but you were the initiator. He'd find excuses to stop, saying, 'I'm not into PDA.' Or 'Not in front of Jacques.' One time, he even physically pushed you off and said, 'Hungry? I'm starving.'"

I warned him to stop, but he was glued to the roll his mouth was running on, more so than fat kiddy hands on Rolos. "Heard of a beard?" he said. "He was dating you because he didn't want people knowing he was confused. You're a beard. A Dumbledore status beard. And you're not into him, either. You haven't mentioned Eliot in months. It's all Logan Fields this, Logan Fields that."

"Not fair. I only complain about Logan."

"Reading between lines."

"Read between these lines," I said, holding up my pointer finger, middle finger and index finger.

"Your immaturity is far from chilling."

I caterwauled at my lungs' tippy tops, causing the paperboy to tilt over while walking on the Fagg's winding driveway. I ignored the kid, as did Jacques. I said, "You were doing the deed with my dude. Gay or not, in love with me or not, whether he even tolerates me or not. Facebook says he's mine. You temptress. Could've told me. You're my best friend. You can tell me things."

He said, "Can't. You talk, but don't listen, and it's always been this way."

Sadly, this was accurate and I told him it was horrible.

"It is, but you don't know what it's like being the token gay guy."

That's not what I meant. I meant it was horrible, realizing that I'm an unskilled listener, but I didn't interrupt, tuning in instead.

Jacques said, "Being the only openly gay guy is sometimes worse than being closeted. I feel lonely, but have the added pressure of being some weird entertainment source for randoms who call me their gay best friend. During the last few years, you've started doing that. Then Eliot happened. He pulled me into his parents' bathroom the first time we hung out. You were downstairs, making eggs or something. He asked me how I knew I was gay. Eliot couldn't look me in the eye. Three words into my explanation, he started tearing up. His cheeks flushed. I hugged him, because I knew what was going on in his head. It was special. Then he kissed me. I would've told you right away, but sadly, it felt good being noticed romantically. You know I never had that before. If being with him behind your back hurt at the beginning of summer, imagine how it felt after your dad died. When that happened, I felt the vomit rising in my throat every time I saw you."

He bit his lip in the same way he always does when Bette tells him to be quiet during rehearsal. So, I said, "That's not all. Is it?"

Jacques collapsed in the snow and let his head dangle between his knees. His hand rubbed the back of his neck as he sobbed. I knelt next to him and waited for the response. Finally, Jacques said, "I don't know. Can a person have survivor's guilt when it comes to parents dying?"

"What?"

"My mom, Rosie. Barb. You know about her depression. For years. For so many years. You know the basics of it. The surface. But did you know about the frantic family car rides to the mental hospital? Did you know about me sitting in waiting rooms in the ER too many times during my childhood? Tried to kill herself twice. Survived. Twice. And you've seen her within the last few years. She's healthy and it's a constant struggle to stay that way. Your dad never seemed to have a single problem, and he's the one who died. It scares me. It does. If that man could kill himself, what does that mean for my mom? What does it mean for any of us?"

"I don't know," I said, frowning.

"I put space between us," he said. "Had to. Couldn't say what I just said when he first died. You would've hated me for it."

Jacques and I were connecting. Having a moment for the first time in forever. And I had to demolish our peace with further questioning. "If me hating you is a concern, why did you keep seeing Eliot once it felt wrong?" He got to his feet and so did I. Jacques looked as if he would flee. "If you sprint, I chase. Hard. We both know I'm great at chasing gay boys."

Jacques looked at his soaked slippers and said, "I...we thought you two were over in an unspoken way. He forgot that you two were in a relationship on Facebook. Fuck Facebook."

"Well, we're on the same page now. Changed my status to single last night."

"I feel sick about it," he said. "Please, understand. I was so alone until he came along."

Alone? I forced myself to be calm. "Did I ever tell you about Mouthful and her friends vandalizing my house?" I asked. He didn't answer. "I'm shocked you never found out. My house was vandalized in the seventh grade. You were in Florida."

"River's friends did that."

"Nope. Mouthful and her friends egged the house, toilet-papered the trees, tagged the words 'Rosie is a faggot-loving-whore-face' on the grass, and the words 'Die Rosie Dwyer' on the house. The only reason you didn't hear about it was your trip to Florida being long enough for middle schoolers to move onto new scandals. I think the replacement gossip was Emily Hayes wearing Depends during her period. Monstrous flow."

"I'm sorry," he said, dazed.

"About the vandalism or Emily's monthlies?" Jacques told me not to be dumb, so I said, "Know why they vandalized my place? Same reason I got suspended that year. Hammered her face in. Why? Mouthful said she was gonna vandalize 'Jacob Faggot's house'. I jumped at the chance to battle in the name of Jacques Blain, the person who has made me feel far from alone since the moment I met him. Please, don't tell me you were alone until he came. Don't, Jacob."

"What was that?" he softly asked.

"Jacob, I called you Jacob."

My face was concrete, while Jacob's jaw tipped the Richter scale. My hand rubbed an egg until I transformed into Lenny from *Of Mice and Men*, accidentally squeezing it to death. Yellow goo seeped from its crumbling ivory home, dripping onto the white blanket beneath me. When I released the shells, they rested upon the snow, reminding me of what I'd been feeling like for months. Broken, stripped of color, just plain blending in. I wiped my hand on the snow and trudged down the Faggs' lawn. My eyes burned, striving to halt a flood. My eyelids were the dams and I'll be damned if my dams ever had a damn chance. A tear fell into my mouth, tasting like salt, with a dash of despair. That's what life tastes like. Salt and despair, with a whole mess of goodbye. Goodbye is life's main ingredient.

February 13, 2013

Hey, Joey Journal,

194 days have passed since he died. During this time, his desk in my parents' bedroom has gone untouched. While I briefly had the house to myself over the weekend, I worked up the courage to go in their room and position myself where he once sat. His favorite poem was sitting on top of a mess of books and binders. I stole it and holed up in my room. The poem has been read over a hundred times since I found it. "Sonnet 94" by William Shakespeare.

> *"They that have power to hurt and will do none,*
> *That do not do the thing they most do show,*
> *Who, moving others, are themselves as stone,*
> *Unmoved, cold, and to temptation slow,*
> *They rightly do inherit heaven's graces*
> *And husband nature's riches from expense;*
> *They are the lords and owners of their faces,*
> *Others but stewards of their excellence.*
> *The summer's flower is to the summer sweet,*
> *Though to itself it only live and die,*
> *But if that flower with base infection meet,*
> *The basest weed outbraves his dignity:*
> *For sweetest things turn sourest by their deeds.*
> *Lilies that fester smell far worse than weeds."*

I'm no lily, but I'm a Rosie. Rosie, festering and smelling worse than weeds. A Rosie, knowing this was the last thing he read. I know. While annotating with a shaky hand, my dad wrote on the paper, "I'm so glad something so beautiful is the last thing I'll ever read."

I wonder what this could mean.

For the last month and a half, your location remained uncharted. My last entry was written in a heated flurry, and after writing its final sentence, I chucked you at the wall. Forty-four days ago, on the first of January. You slid behind the TV and took to resting on a mattress made of dust bunnies. I apologize for any detriments I've caused, both physical and emotional. This act of malice went forgotten, leaving me without a place to purge my feelings. I filled my first 'Nonsense Notebook' by January 3rd and completed two more in the time following that date. Since February's start, half a Nonsense Notebook has been at my disposal. However, absurdity has been disenchanting to my wayward soul recently. This discouragement is rooted to me becoming dismayed with life. Life sucks.

And I can't stay on task because thoughts on Barb Fagg keep springing to mind. *What about Barb? I wonder how Barb is. Not that I care about Jacob. Just been thinking about Barb. Nobody ever told me she tried to, you know. Poor Barb. I knew his mom had depression, so I should've figured she tried to kill herself at least once. Jacob never mentioned that. Hardly ever mentioned Barb. When things became sour, Jacob always wanted to hang at my house over his. We only ever acted out Gypsy. We never talked about suicide attempts.*

It's tech week. We take *Urinetown* to audiences starting February 21st. The stress is strangling me. I've been trying to pry Opening Night's fingers from my neck, but my attempts leave me deflated. Speaking of deflation, while I ran to school this morning, a popped red balloon floated by, stopping me in my tracks. Its origin is a mystery. I relished the sight, so random on such a glacial morning. Balloon, go to hell. Wind, help a sister out and pick me up. Self, stop conversing with the inanimate. Insane.

Mackenzie Hemperley hasn't properly memorized her lines, but that's not what's bothering me. I hate seeing her onstage. I do. Bette had her dye her hair blonde. She looks so much like me and operates in a way I wish I could. Mackenzie handles life in such a relaxed manner and has mastered the casual shoulder shrug. I feel like I'm in a movie, one that's like *It's a Wonderful Life*, but instead of seeing how much worse everything could be, I'm seeing how much better the universe would operate if I learned to take deeper breaths. It's a world where my voice is less frantic, shrill, and grating. Jacob Fagg still stands near Mackenzie during water breaks, calls her 'frosh', and runs around with her on his back. He used to do that kind of shit with me. Now he does that shit with a girl who looks like me. I'm forced to watch, and it feels like I have some flesh-eating virus.

Has Jacob told Mackenzie about it? About Barb? Has he vented? He'd probably feel comfortable doing so, since I'm assuming Mackenzie's family is normal and her listening skills are as magical as her voice.

Logan recently broke a set piece during a number. Everybody is leaving props lay helter-skelter. Crew kids are always stoned. We're in far better shape than we were for *Death of a Salesman*, but I can't get the image of Arthur B. Cummings out of my head. The image of that man bathing in his piss and puke lingers behind me everywhere I go, like a dingleberry from hell.

And I'm worried about Jacob's mom.

Then there's Eliot. I haven't told anybody what happened, but people have been asking about my ex, who wasn't ever truly my boyfriend. When a person goes from 'In a Relationship' to 'Single' on Facebook, every human interaction becomes a game of Twenty Questions.

"What happened?"

"Don't wanna talk about it."

"You okay?"

"Don't wanna talk about it."

"He break up with you, or the other way around?"

"Don't wanna talk about it."

"Why not?"

"DON'T WANNA TALK ABOUT IT."

Logan asked about it during today's creative writing class. Bette called it a Wild Card Wednesday. It was the same thing as Peer Review Thursday, the difference being that we had to prepare a piece of writing that nobody would expect from us. We both wrote poems. Shitty poems. Poop stains on the literary world's underpants. Our desks were lined up right next to each other, because sitting as close as humanly possible has become our new thing over the last forty or so days.

"The poem," I said, raising a teasing eyebrow at him. "It's about Mouthful?"

"Dear lord, Rosie, poems don't have to be true."

"Allow me to read it aloud," I said, grinning.

"Don't," he said, smiling even larger than me. "It's bad."

She is smart, and that much is for sure.
When it comes to reading me, she's getting there.
Her—wild in her hair. Child in her eyes. Her.
Me—eyebrows are aerial dancers when she's near.
To be read by another. To be read by a human.
She is delightful and it makes me stupid."

He asked me if I was happy now that he was thoroughly mortified. I slapped my hand to mouth to stop my cruel laugh from coming out. My God, the poem was terrible and the worst part is he tried his best. Logan said, "I'll accept the laughter, only because I know it's my turn to crap on your work. You know your haiku didn't even have the right number of syllables, right?"

"I'm a writer, not a counter."

He rolled his eyes and read it aloud.

"I don't hate the gays, but
I hate how they think they can have everything,
including Cher and my boyfriend."

We communicated with our eyes. His squint asked me if I wanted to talk about it and my eye roll said, *"No, but thanks for not asking me out loud."*

After a deep breath, Logan said. "You actually think my poem is about Mouthful?"

My gut felt like warm bread as I said, "No, I just like teasing you at this point."

"And I just like you at this point." Logan rumpled his entire face. I could tell he was both nervous and excited for my reaction. I mean, it's taken us long enough to get to this point. Then his eyebrows shot up. Aerial dancers. I casually grabbed his hand from underneath our pushed together desks. This has been happening since school started back up. We take turns grabbing each other's hands. On Thursdays, mostly, when we push the desks so that we are sitting right next to one another instead of across. The first time it happened, we didn't realize we laced our fingers for a few moments. When it occurred to us, we gave one another awkward side eye until we both had a laugh. Logan and I haven't discussed it much. That's probably what makes it so fun. He destroyed the fun today. Logan tentatively said, "What we're doing is great, and I don't wanna ruin it, but—"

"Quick tip. Don't ruin it."

My hand tensed as he continued in low tones. "Rosie, I said I liked you. For the first time."

My silence stiffened our muscles until our hand situation became like two battling boa constrictors. I wanted to say I liked him back, but I couldn't help but think about how little I know about Logan. What I learned from Jacob is that with all human beings, there are unseen parts. There are ill feelings and secret boyfriends and Barbs and whatever else there is. If I said I liked Logan right then, would I say too much? I feared saying, *"Like you, Logan? We hardly know each other and I think I'm falling in love with you."*

I sat next to him thinking, *Just tell him you like him. It's an understatement, but it's not untrue. You won't say too much. Say it. 'I like you, Logan.'* I repeated the phrase in my head until it was jumbled. *Like, I Logan you.*

Maybe what Jacob said about himself also applies to me. When things stay in my head too long, they get jumbled until I don't know what's true anymore. My feelings for Logan baked in my gut too long. They're beyond warm. If I pull them out now, they might be charred to bits. I'm not ready to give my blackened parts to another. My hand eased itself away.

"Look," he whispered. "What is it? Eliot?"

"My eyes already told you I don't wanna talk about it," I said and fetched the bathroom pass. Once there, I had a Public Bathroom Silent Sob Session. I didn't know why I was crying. It should've been the best day I've had since my dad died. Knowing that Logan likes me should've made that happen. But I was stressed about the musical and feeling miserable for no reason. Miserable about my dad, sure, but mostly for no reason. At the climax of my bawling, I wondered if Jacob ever sobbed about Barb in the bathroom.

While exiting the facilities, I saw Eliot in the hallway. We were the only people, but I pretended I didn't see him, quickly shoving my face in the fountain. While I gulped water, Eliot tapped me. I wiped droplets from my chin and a compassionate smile became prevalent on his face. "Hey," he said. I wanted to remind him to quit impairing that word, but God pointed his heavenly remote control on me. Pressed mute. I frowned at his outfit. Deep V-neck, gold chain, drop crotch pants. Why did I ever consider him sexy? "We don't gotta talk about that thing, that happened," he said. "When we were sorta dating, or whatever, I couldn't take you to Homecoming. Going to Sadie's together would be a dope way for us to become friends. How 'bout it?"

A pause danced artlessly through the air until I asked, "How 'bout what?"

"Let's go."

"Girls ask the guys."

"That's what I was hoping you'd do."

"Do what, Eliot?"

"Ask me. To the dance."

His voice was feeble and his intentions transparent. Eliot's date bailed on him earlier this week. In an ironic turn of events, she had the flu. I wondered why the confusing boy couldn't stay home and play video games like last time. My face was a flirtatious façade. I stepped toward him, hand stroking his hairy face. "My dearest," I said. "You have a beard. You don't need another one."

Then I smacked him. Triumph tingled in my fingertips, propelling me into a confidently brisk walk back to class. I plopped down next to

Logan and whispered in his ear, "I hate your poetry, but I like you. I do."

We continued the class with our hands meeting in secret under our desks. The warm bread feeling came back to my stomach. It did. But then more crap happened at rehearsal and the warm bread feeling molded. Logan was there, but I didn't want to bother him. He was in focus mode. Things first turned sour when Bette had to make me aware that I have F's in AP Stats and AP Bio. AP classes are weighted, so technically they're D's. Still, I have double D's and not the kind I want. The school is allowing me to stage-manage the remainder of the production. However, if my grades don't improve, I'll be banned from all extracurricular activities. Ha! Like I care. I'm no joiner. Only did this show because Bette guilted me.

On top of that, I have a cold for the third time this winter, goddamn nose spewing snot all day. Then Jacob Fagg spilt his monster sized slushie on my bomber jacket during a rehearsal break. It belonged to my dad when he was my age. Had "Sonnet 94" in the pocket, which ended up getting destroyed. Nobody has noticed we're on the outs, so Jacob apologized real friendly. "Sorry, doll."

Before storming off to find towels, I said, "Don't you even look at me, Jacob Fagg."

But if you want to look at me, you can. And you can maybe tell me more about Barb? Is she okay? Are you okay? This is all in my head. Yep. Bitch faces dominate the real world.

As I frantically wiped my jacket, the German foreign exchange student privately told me people were saying I needed to "take a chill pill." Then Günter requested an explanation of the American slang term. His thick accent brought me no joy like it did when he first came to our school. I explained they were calling me crazy. He said, "I still like you, friend."

He hugged me, lifting me off the ground. Normally, hugs from overweight people are the best. It's like wrapping your arms around a big fluffy mattress. I let my arms fall limply at my sides. You know you've entered a dark place when hugs from flabby German men fail to raise your spirits. Endless upturned thumbs from Bette were also obsolete. I went home around eight. The slush. The ice. The unattended-to dog crap. The neighbor kids' phallic snowman. Everything seen during my walk pissed me off. *What about Barb?* While I trudged into the kitchen, River stood in an apron and pleasantly said, "You're home in time for supper!" I dryly stared, shoulders drooping. "We mixed it up tonight, Rosie."

I couldn't select even a word. *Barb.*

"I'm making bouillon," River declared.

"The hell is that? Doesn't have anything to do with couscous, does it?"

His smile continued as he sat down on a kitchen stool. "Nope. You're bored of that, so I made something exciting."

"What is it?"

"A clear sort of soup," he said. I lunged at the stove, grabbed the soup pot by the handle and made haste toward the sink. He asked me what I was doing as the bouillon went down the drain.

Over the steam, I said, "Clear soup? That's exciting?" Once it was empty, I threw the pot down into the soapy water side of the sink. The heat reacted with the H20 and made a volcanic noise. The sizzling snapped at our senses as Melanie entered and demanded answers.

"She dumped the bouillon, Mom."

I said, "Cry me a river, River!" Then I punched his flat, hard abdomen. I want my chubby brother back. Melanie tried grasping me, but I bolted upstairs. *Barb.* From my room, I could hear her yelling something about me getting a swift kick in the ass if I came back downstairs. I didn't and paced instead. *Barb.* Then I ripped the pages from my scrapbooks and rearranged my furniture. *Barb.* That's when I found you, Joey. Placed you in my desk and wandered around my bedroom until my feet touched every inch. *Barb.* Once I heard each family member get in bed, I allowed thirty minutes to pass and headed downstairs. *Barb.*

And I couldn't stop crying and blubbering and hyperventilating. I turned on the TV. And The 700 Club was playing on *ABC Family*, and they kept showing children in Africa dying from malaria or something. And I despised myself for being depressed over clear soup. And I paced and paced and paced and blubbered and blubbered and blubbered and hyperventilated and hyperventilated and hyperventilated until, through gasps for air, my shaking voice whispered, "I wanna kill myself."

That's the thought that has me by the throat, smothering my oxygen supply, because I now know what Barb's mind was like when she tried. What my dad's mind was like before he did it. I walked to a cabinet in the pantry and stood before all the pills until my eyes zeroed in on three boxes that were labeled with the name Coricidin HBP Cough and Cold Pills. I haven't a clue as to why we need three boxes stored in our house at once, but we do. I remember seeing a special on 20/20 that said kids were popping cough suppressants, including Coricidin HBP. Little red pills. The young people called them Skittles. Some kids overdosed. Some died. Certain options are available over the counter. That's stupid and crazy. Like me.

It was time to down all three boxes and whatever else I could get my hands on. My vibrating fingers tore the first box open. Willow came down to get water and said my name, making me jump. Pills flew everywhere, dancing around my bare feet, a red Skittle rainstorm. When she asked what was wrong, I came into the kitchen, shutting the pantry door behind me. If I'd come down thirty minutes earlier, she would've walked into something far different. Willow would've had an image in her mind, one impossible to erase. Her face was an unforgettable image in itself. Young, unassuming and almost entirely unshaken by the terrors of the world. Well, kind of.

I said I was getting an aspirin and told her to go to bed, but first, I hugged her. Now, I'm telling you about it. And my body is chilled as I write, as if I left my window open on accident. I'm chilled because I'm realizing I have all this power to hurt and I can't say that I have done nothing to hurt myself over the past few months. This must change. Or I might hurt myself to the point of no return.

February 17, 2013

Hey, Joey Journal,

198 days. 198 days wearing robes and joining hands. A choir of days singing, *Time to get happy*. I'm not gonna think about what I almost did the other night. Everybody has those moments. *Time to get happy*. Wrote those words on a Post-It and added it to the resolutions. The note number was uneven. I scrawled on another sticky and it joined the rest. *Have to. It's the only way to be.*

February 24, 2013

Hey, Joey Journal!

205 days. I'm not going to list any special facts about this number. Won't waste my time writing even one word of an anecdote. My dad is probably sitting in some waiting room as we speak. Limbo. I hope his chair causes insufferable butt pain as he looks at the slow ticking eterna l clock. I hope his consultation with God never comes. And he can count. Let's have my dad count every single day that has passed since the day he chose death. Numbers are confining and they are his.

These are the events that brought me to this conclusion.

The week leading to Opening Night is called Hell Week. Hell it was, but some undercurrent of wind swept me up. *Urinetown*'s premiere was glitchless and the gang got a standing ovation. I received an endless amount of back pats. Each new performance only im proved upon the one preceding it. Today was Sunday and we came early to do a tradition called "Cry Circle." The cast and crew became an oval, each person prepared to give a short speech. Bawling naturally ensued.

The speech belonging to Jacob, Lord Almighty. When he stood up, he froze. It was like he had a whole speech planned, but forgot his lines. Mine was also lame, but at least I stammered out a few forgettable words. For the first time since we met, Jacob had stage fright. Before sitting back down, he said, "I can't."

After an awkward silence, Logan jumped up and said, "I can." He proceeded to make everybody get in a huddle around him, then gave the speech from *Invictus*. He put on an accent like Matt Damon's character and said, "Heads up! Look in my eyes. Do you hear? Listen to your country. Seven minutes. Seven minutes! Defense! Defense! Defense! This is it! This our destiny! Kom bokke!"

There was another silence among the theatre kids. I bet that if you surveyed them, the grand majority would say their favorite sports film is *Damn Yankees*. Everybody eventually burst into laughter. I smiled, knowing his speech was the sports pump up he never got to give as the soccer team's bench warmer. After one too many moments of goofiness, I stepped in as stage manager. I said, "Break up the huddle. Prepare to get your asses in the game."

Jacob immediately departed into the hallway outside the theatre's wings. I followed. He was sitting in the corner by a door leading to the teacher parking lot. I sat down next to him. Against the wall. "What was that?" I asked, voice soft. Jacob put his head in his hands. "Not trying to pry. Just curious. You've had your senior year Cry Circle speech written and memorized since freshman year."

He lightly hit the back of his head against the wall and said, "Things change."

"Man, you're telling me."

Trying to keep it together despite his fluctuating voice, Jacques said, "Here's the new speech. Unplanned. I wanna thank you, Rosie Dwyer. You. I wanna thank you. When we first met, we bonded over *West Side Story*. You let me rant and asked me what I liked about it. Other kids were asses. Wouldn't let me rave about musicals. You listened. Sorry I said you don't listen. Fuck. Shit. Bitch. I love you. You listen."

He was forgiven with that. No, I don't forgive people too quickly. I only have discovered that I'm like all people, beautiful and born with a power to hurt. I have chosen to do none. No hurt. None to him. None to myself. It's been almost two months since our battle. Two months of absolute solitude. Two months spent slowly coming around to seeing this situation from his point of view. Two months of formulating questions about Barb. Two months. Time to be happy, right? Time to stop hurting. I embraced him and whispered into his ear, "Love you."

The first act of the Sunday matinee was the run's best. Spirits were high during intermission, cast members already hugging. I was checking the props table when Mackenzie tapped my shoulder. I said, "What's up, Twinsy?"

Normally, we're damn near identical. There was a stark difference today, because her face was green. "Gonna puke, Rosie."

I yanked her into the hallway, wondering why the universe keeps sending me regurgitation. "You've never had nerves before."

"No, I'm sick."

"Mackenzie, soldier through it. One more act, then you're free."

She nodded, holding up a finger, cheeks bloating. I'd seen that expression too often throughout this terrible flu season, so I jumped out of harm's way. With the kid's lunch properly on the tiles, I commanded her to come upstairs and into the drama room. Once there, I called out Bette's name and the Lassie-like woman came running, dressed to the nines. Her suit and beret made her the spitting image of Diane Keaton. She told me the show was fabulous.

"There's a problem."

Mackenzie's cheeks billowed again as she dived toward the wastebasket, slam dunking her vomit into the can. *Swish.*

"What happened?" said Bette. "Shit." She used the wrong word. As Bette said "shit," Mackenzie did just that. Her diarrhea was an anal emission of pure nastiness, leaving every bystander with a toxic taste in their mouth. Spare crew kids evacuated in droves as I walked in circles. "She's sick! It's over."

Bette seized my hunched shoulders and said, "Wrong-o. It ain't over. It goes on."

"That's a cliché."

"It's what must happen. Take her to the bathroom. Grab her next costume from the dressing room. Put it on. Get your ass onstage." I was more worthless than a dog turd on the sidewalk. She said, "Finish the show."

"You insane?"

Bette took a hefty breath, spinning in her yellow swivel chair. Her hands trembled while opening her energy drink and explaining her thought process. "You two are doppelgangers, remember? Go be Hope. You helped me come up with the choreography and blocking. You know it. You can't sing, but worse things have happened. Hope is bound and gagged for most of the second act. Lines aren't a big problem. Even if they were, you know every single one."

"I do."

She gulped her drink, free hand giving a frantic thumbs up. "Ten minutes 'til the top of the act, Rosie."

"No," I said.

"You won't let me down." Her words were an adrenaline shot, so I sprang toward the dressing room. Mackenzie straggled behind, puking once more, barf nearly hitting my heels.

The second act sets in with Günter delivering a monologue as Officer Lockstock. Little intermission time remained. Despite the pinch, I successfully spread the word of the substitution. I told one of the protesters who capture Hope to improvise a line about shaving half my hair off. Even had time to bind and gag myself. Finally, my body took its place as the curtains opened.

The lights were bright. Logan soon sang "Run Freedom Run" and change unhinged me. That song has been performed at every rehearsal. The cast runs about. Dances. But today, I was onstage. An audience member knows what it looks like. The person onstage always feels it.

Logan's character explains during the number that, "Freedom is scary. It's a blast of cool wind that burns your face to wake you up." Those words hit me like a torrential typhoon. Freedom was happening, cool wind burning my face. It's called waking up. Still am. My body took its place to sing "I See a River", the musical's last song. I was so bad. So beautifully bad.

The words flowed. My inner tone deaf Aretha Franklin shimmied out. I sang from my vagina without reminding myself to. I was a train wreck, but oh, what a locomotive it was to ride.

We took our bows as I blacked out, and I only came to once the cast and crew joined the fans in the lobby. Everyone was embracing. After I stopped squeezing the filling out of Günter, I turned around to find a winded Logan. His brow line had a trickle of sweat. We hugged, tightly. When we let go, he backed away so slowly, without turning. The boy asked a question I plan to take with me everywhere. "How does it feel to be a bird?"

Had Logan said that before this day, I'm sure the big bad bird word would've made me smack him upside the head. But today belonged to me. It was mine. And so are birds. My dad has no ownership over them because I'm the one who chose life. Like I said, my dad can count.

Numbers are his.

My grin was too firmly set in place to speak the words, "Logan, being a bird feels luminous."

Open.

March 1, 2013

Hey, Joey Journal!

A whole school week has passed, freedom still blasting my face-space. The days keep getting better and better and better. Better. To celebrate this exponential increase in loveliness, I decided to do a performance art piece during today's lunch period. The night before, I bought red balloons from Walmart and inflated 99 of them and wrote the German word "Luftballon" on each one, in honor of "99 Luftballons" by Nena. And I shoved them into garbage bags. When lunch started, I went off campus to grab everything from home. My balloon hoard, a boom box, a megaphone. Then I ran into the cafeteria and hopped on a table where itty-bitty freshmen were feasting. "What are you doing?" one of them said.

"Performance art, kittens."

Slug-like, they stared. I ignored them and shouted into the megaphone, "Greetings, cafeteria!" I yelled this on repeat until everybody was listening. "Time for performance art."

The lunch chaperones didn't intervene, only because they were my art teacher and my writing teacher and equally intrigued. The silence would've been excruciating if I didn't feel so weightless. I spoke intensely into the megaphone, making sure everybody heard my monologue. "I recently witnessed a popped red balloon whizzing down the sidewalk. It was disturbing because the current season is winter. Balloons are generally associated with summery environments, but I've been thinking. The season isn't the most unsettling thing. I could even deal with the fact that it was popped. What bothered me was knowing that it was just one balloon. By itself, which is devastating. They say misery loves company. I say so do balloons."

I hit play on the boom box. "99 Luftballons" rang through the cafeteria as I emptied the bags. The balloons flew everywhere and kids rushed to grab them. I danced and Günter became overwhelmed, clapping his hands to his jowls. The big guy wobbled over to my table, glee resulting from the song being sung in his native language. Once he was near enough, I pulled him up and we danced. I'm surprised our weight didn't break the table. When the song ended, Philly, my art teacher, briskly approached and said, "Pick up the balloons that went unclaimed by your classmates. Immediately. You can help her, Gunter." She began to turn, but looked back, smiling coyly. "Your art grade just went from an A to an A+."

I physically got down. Figuratively, I'm still high. Four balloons remained on the floor.

March 8! 2012

HEY, JOEY JOURNAL!!!!!!!!!

I THINK IT'S MARCH 8TH. NOT SURE.
HAVEN'T WROTE IN A WEEK! OR TWO! DON'T NO!
CAN'T DITCH MY NONSENSE NOTEBOOKS! RIDING MY LIFE!
RIOTING IN THIS LIFE! GOTTA RITE ABOUT THE LIFE I LEAD!
OR I WILL BE DAMNED AND MY LIFE WILL NOT BE RIGHT!
SEE? THE SNOW, THE BARREN TREES, THE YOU, THE ME, THE
EVERYBODY, ALL BODIES COMBINING! SNOW SHINING! LIKE
A PRECIOUS CRYSTAL EXPLOSION! CRUNCHING BENEATH
MY BARE FEET! NO END TO THIS SENTENCE CALLED LIFE! WE
ARE SENTENCED AND DESTINED TO NEVER REST AND KEEP
ON KEEPIN' ON! BEAT OUR CHESTS LIKE APES! COME HERE!
CLOSER! DON'T FEAR! BE NEAR! NIGHT FALLS, BUT I SAY IT
FELL LONG AGO! I WON'T STOP! TELL ME, MY DEAREST JOEY
JOURNAL—WHERE IS THE FUN IN THAT?! BEING STUPID &
STAGNANT & STILL & AT THE DAMN WILL OF THE DAMNED
WORLD? DONE WITH THAT! BLASTED! BLASTING WIND
BLAZING FACES, PAINTING ME SINNING! MY FACE? NO
LONGER FESTERING AWAY FACE! NO LONGER GRAY FACE!
BECAUSE WIND AND MY GREAT FACE! WINDED AND WOUND
UP! WAKING UP! BECAUSE THE WINDS! NO LONGER
WOUNDED! I AM THE WOKEN! THE ONE! A POPPED BALLOON
FLOATING IN THE WIND, WINNING! THE WIND BENEATH MY
OWN WINGS! AMERICA, OF ME I SING! tried going to the dollar

store to buy a new NOTEBOOK!

circled RANDOM answers on my bio test! I wrote BALL HAIR all over the TEST packet! school bell went RING-A-DING-A-LING…biology test packet turned itself in! threw me arms in the air and waggled 'em.

TORE DOWN POST-IT NOTES! CRUMPLED THEM! BIG BALL! THREW IT OUT THE WINDOW! SCREW RESOLUTIONS! I'M DIVINE.

KIDS PLAYING JENGA DURING LUNCH IN THE ART ROOM! sssslapped at it! TAKE THAT YOU FASCIST BLOCK TOWER!

climbed a tree! jumped out! LANDED ON SIDEWALK! On FEET! WHOA! WHY?!? IMMA BIRD! GOTTA FLY! GOTTA PRACTICE FLYING! before my organs give out and my body masters the art of dying! I'M ELOQUENT AS TITS!

wrote a poem on a giant boulder outside the school WITH A MARKER!

I baked LOGAN some HOMEMADE TWINKIES because HOSTESS TWINKIES are EXTINCT. brought them to SCHOOL! A BELATED present for being awesome in the MUSICAL and I promised I would NOT shove them in his EYE and he was very HAPPY and asked if I was FREE on FRIDAY to BOWL and I said YES!!!!!!!!

ELIOT and JACQUES walked down the hallway! ELIOT bumped into me! THAT BEAUTIFUL BOY knocked my BOOKS down! picked them up! WAS AWKWARD ABOUT IT! And I shouted ELIOT! I DONUT CARE IF YOU'RE GAY or even just KINDA GAY! FLAME ON, GOOD FELLA! YOU BEAUTIFUL FLAMINGO! YOU AND JACQUES MAKE A GREAT COUPLE! And I gave JACQUES a hug! gave ELIOT one too! then I gave BOTH of 'em a hug at the SAME TIME! HUGS ARE MY DRUG! Their mouths hung open! WENT WALKING AND RUNNING AND SPRINTING AND ZOOOOMING! TOOK PICTURES OF EVERYTHING!

ripped the nature sketches from my sketchbooks and threw them off our balcony! The best gallery for nature drawings is the great outdoors!!! And when the wind picks them up…you never know who will find it! I hope Jesus finds the drawings. JESUS! TAKE THE DRAWINGS! BUT DONUT TAKE THE WHEEL! DONUT TAKE IT FROM MY HANDS! WANNA DRIVE MY OWN MY LIFE! RIDE MY OWN LIFE! RIOT IN MY OWN LIFE! WRITE ABOUT MY OWN LIFE! ALRIGHT, RIGHT?

did the workout called INSANITY for a LONG TIME! time for dinner! we ate spaghetti!!! I had four bowls! MY GOD. 4! 4444444444444444444444444! GO SPAGHETTI!

everybody went to bed and I snuck downstairs! MORE SPAGHETTI! COLD NOODLES! And then I went on the computer and looked up the poem called *HOWL!* By ALLEN GINSBERG! read it out loud to myself eight times!

TODAYS THOUGHTS:

I FEEL LIKE BUDDY THE ELF HOPPED UP ON LSD! AND SYRUP! DRANK A WHOLE BOTTLE! put syrup in my spaghetti and RIVER had a good laugh. And so did WILLOW and MEL! AND THEY'RE HAPPY BECAUSE I AM HAPPY! SYRUP!

NOT A SPIRITUAL EXPERIENCE! THIS IS MY SPIRITUAL EXPERIMENT!

THOUGHT SO MANY THOUGHTS THAT I DONUT REMEMBER ALL 'EM! BUT THEY ARE ALL WRITTEN IN MY NONSENSE NOTEBOOKS! BECAUSE I WROTE DOWN ALL MY THOUGHTS TODAY! EVERY SINGLE ONE! TRUE ONES! FALSE ONES! ON THE BACKS OF MY HOMEWORK EVEN!

KEEP TELLING MYSELF THAT IF *IT WANTS TO BE REMEMBERED, IT WILL BE!* BUT WHAT IF I THINK OF SOMETHING GENIUS AND FORGET IT? I COULDN'T BARE IT!

RIVER came downstairs! off to work! asked me if I just woke up! I said YES! even though I got no sleep…I AM waking up in other ways! he smiled and patted me on the head and I donut care if he hasn't done that to my head space since I was TEN! I like feeling young again!

GONNA RUN. GONNA BUY A NEW NOTEBOOK AND *SYRUP!* GONNA RUN TO SCHOOL. GONNA GO BOWLING WITH LOGAN FIELDS. GONNA HAVE THE BEST DAY! Because I AM finally a BIRD.

March 23, 2013

Hey, Joey Journal,

My world altogether changed the day my dad died. I thought a person only gets one day like this. Only one day to make you question who you are as a human. Only one day that forces you to count all the days that come after it. On March 8, 2013, I found one's world can turn on its head more than once. I said numbers were now for my dad to deal with, wherever he is, but I'm taking them back. To stay grounded. It's been fifteen days since the 8th. No. I wouldn't like to state a fact or give an anecdote. I want to rip the Band-Aid off and say what happened. The longer you leave a Band-Aid on, the grimier it becomes. Learned that the hard way.

My last few entries may have suggested I was on a collision course heading to a psychiatric care facility. That's true. It happened during the day I wrote that gobbledygook inside you. March 8, 2013. That morning, I stopped at Walgreens, wearing only red flannel pajamas and black boots, ten dollars balled up in my quaking fist. Freezing my hinder off, I bought a new notebook for nonsense. School is where I went. An uncomfortable amount of crap happened. I'll mention the important crap.

McAdams asked to talk to me after class about my test that was covered in written ball hairs, but when the bell rang, I forgot to stay behind. Honestly, he didn't seem concerned about my mental health. Probably thought I was pulling another stunt, like when I peed in his class the year before.

Art class eventually came, and I was disoriented, seeing as the posters on the wall appeared to be pouncing at me and walking straight became an idiotic task. The sights were sharp, every color richer and brighter than it should've been. The white tiles that made up the walls were blinding. I hopped on a table, removed my boots and interpretive danced on my giant painting. I'd been working on it forever. Christ. People laughed at my performance. Some even filmed me on their phones. Günter said, "Funny girl, Rosie. You must get reality show like a Kardashian."

I grabbed his hand and put it in the painting. "Leave handprints. Take art with you everywhere."

He promised he would as Philly pulled me into her office and told me to sit. I told her I preferred standing. "Sitting is quitting. Standing is taking a stand. Grand. I stand, therefore I am. Understand?"

She insisted I sit and I relented. Plop. "When did you sleep last, Rosie?"

While I wiped paint off my feet, my last journey into unconsciousness was unable to be conceptualized. Philly gave me a health room pass and told me to rest. Soon I was in the office, forgetting what I went there to do. Rhonda, the school nurse who thinks of me as a hypochondriac, looked at me like I was even crazier than usual. That's when I remembered and said, "Hi, I'm suffering from crazy and need sleep. The sleep need is seeping and creeping into my being and—"

"Hall pass?" I dropped the note on the way there, so Rhonda sternly sent me back to class. When I retreated, I explained what happened to Philly, but my statements were accelerated messes. She provided another pass and I tried again, but the nurse's office was locked and the lights were out.

Bette's 7th hour is one of her open periods. *She'll know what to do. She's my respected sage.* As I ran into her room, I urgently told her I needed sleep. She said, "Wanna see Rhonda?"

I recounted my misadventures, and my mouth's pace left me incoherent again. Her advice was to relax on the furniture in the dressing room next door during class, and so I did. My body collapsed on the couch. Sleep wasn't happening. I sobbed. Loudly. The couch was green, and because everything was so sharp, I saw every last stitch and detail.

Every hue in the fabric. Greens, yellows, browns, reds, blues, and colors invisible to the sane eye. Electric ones. The couch was a field and I was a stolid bird. Not a free one, but a decrepit raven wearily soaring over barren wastelands posing as fields. Things aren't always so spectacular from way up high.

After the final bell of the day, Bette entered the dressing room and sat on the couch's edge. First, she tried handing me a glass of water. I told her I didn't need it, and that I hadn't needed water for days. This was because the glass of water was inside me, like in *Urinetown.*

"Oh, Rosie, you don't—"

"The inspiring musical inspired a fire. I know what I wanna be. Wanna be the musical. So much hope. I became Hope. That's all."

Bette asked me if I remember the ending, and I stared up at a bug nipping at a light fixture, fully able to hear it. "Hope dies," she said. "Most of their population dies because hope isn't a sustainable resource."

"Sustainable re-what?" Everything sounded distorted, like when you suck up a Lego brick while vacuuming.

"Hope is good in moderation, but you can't live on it. You okay? What happened?" Her face was concerned. I could see each of her slight wrinkles as if they were craters. And her eyes. They'd always been bright, but had they always been this voltaic?

I started tearing up and said, "Just tired. At least, I should be, right? Can't stop. How'd I let it get this out of control?"

She asked me when I slept last. I said, "That's it! No clue. No idea about sleep or anything because of all my ideas. My head! And I need to write them down. A riot in my head. I feel alive, not dead. And I like it. No, don't know. Don't know. Don't know if I ever slept at all. No idea. Kind of like that. My ideas, though. They're good. Bad ones left. And I really, really, really, reeling—"

"Oh dear, it's just like *A Beautiful Mind*," Bette said.

"What are you talking about, crazy." She told me I was just reminding her of some movie. My foot stomped the ground as my voice interrupted her. "I'm not a movie. I'm a Rosie. The poem. And you—"

She cut me off right back, saying, "You're just...I don't know. Can you please—"

I jumped up and said, "No, I'm fine. Finding the fineness within my fine self. Finding it. Let me go home and sleep and I'll be fine. I'll be fine. I live across the street. Is that fine?"

"No, Rosie, are you sure you wanna?"

"Let me leave. I live across the street. You think I don't know where I live?"

She looked perplexed, but kept trying to rein me in, saying, "Are you sure you can get home?" I nodded, so Bette reluctantly reached into her pocket, pulled out a scrap of paper, and wrote her number on it. "Promise you'll call if you need to talk."

I gave a violent thrust of my head and exited the drama room. Bette followed me into the hallway and yelled, "I'm gonna call your mom this evening. That okay?"

I turned and said, "Whatever destiny leads you to do!"

And she let me leave. Melanie later told me Bette cried at the conference she had with my other teachers the next day, overcome with guilt. I feel guilty that she feels guilty. And look at that, a never-ending cycle.

As I left, the world wasn't just intense, and it wasn't just blurry. It ran together. Everything doubled. Everything stabbed my eyes. Once I got to the intersection where a bird pooped on my head months ago, a hand pulled at my flannel top. "Nice outfit, Rosie."

"La-la-la-Logan," I said, focusing on a bird on a telephone line. "Why is that little guy up there? How does he balance? Does he know the time of year? Does he? Is it March? Why is snow still here? Why? Oh, dear. It's March. I suppose the birds are going to come back now."

"I don't know, probably," he said, stepping in front of me. "Pajamas look mighty good on you, but aren't you cold?" All my thoughts were fast little peregrine falcons, and the only one I could make sense of was the following: *Shush! You've gone insane!* And repeat. He reached into his backpack and said, "Hold up, look what I have." It was the red hoodie. I crawled inside it and put the hood over my blazing red ears. "We still on for bowling, Rosie? Bette told me you couldn't peer review today because you weren't feeling good."

"No! I'm luminous. A-OK. A flower in bloom. Open. We're

bowling tonight. Rosie and Logan sittin' in a tree, B-O-W-L-I-N-G. Bowling. Got it?"

He squinted and tilted his head sideways, as puzzled as Bette had been. Then Logan said, "You seemed spacey in art today. For a while, honestly. You seem out of it now. It's fine if you're not feeling well. We'll raincheck."

"No!" We had to go bowling. It was our destiny. "We must bowl. It's our destiny! Just tired. I'll nap it out when I get home. A promise! I'll kidnappy myself a nappy. Pick me up at five and I'll be so happy." Then something important occurred to me. Anastasia. Was he still seeing Mouthful? I had been aware they weren't together, before my mind went to shit, but I couldn't remember simple details on this day. "What happened to Mouthful?"

He seized my shoulders, playfully shook me and shouted, "Get it through your half-shaved head. Mouthful sucks. This bit of yours is stale. I like you."

I lightly shoved him away and vomited in the snow. We stared at each other blankly for what had to have been ten seconds. "Well, don't look at me like that," I playfully yelled. "Shaking me was a dumb idea!"

I touched my chin and realized there must have been vomit on my face. Didn't want him seeing me so unattractive, so I gave myself a facial in a clean patch of snow. When I came up for air, I said, "There. My face is squeaking clean, so if you ever grow a goddamn penis and decide to kiss me, you won't get my mom's spaghetti on you."

He looked up at the sky and mouthed the word, "What?" Then he slowly brought me in for a hug. As we stood there, hugging, I rambled into his ear. "This isn't what I asked you to do, Logan. You do this kind of thing with Jacques. You're just friends. Maybe you and Jacques are more, though. Wouldn't be the first time somebody I'm into gave it to him, I don't know, I just don't know, I don't know what to think of you or him or this or us or for the love of God, that bird is still up there. Why can't he just learn to move with ease and class, and not ruin all of our lives?"

Next thing I knew, I was sobbing and snotting into his shoulder. "Let's go back to your house," he said softly. "We'll have tea and talk."

I tore myself away from him. "You can't come over to my house until five o'clock. Five. I said five. Five." He asked me why and I told him I had to get ready for bowling. "There's too much to do. Too much."

"Wear what you're wearing. I like it, remember?"

"Bought a whole outfit, Logan. Bought special shoes," I said emphatically.

Some part of him longed to laugh, but he knew something more was going on and suppressed his faint smile. "Can we compromise? Four o'clock?"

"Let's see. Maybe. Gotta shave because I was thinking about fucking you tonight, but I guess that shouldn't take too long. Okay, okay. 4:30. No earlier. 4:30, and I'll be better than I am now, I swear."

His eyes were bulging even before I gave him a mighty kiss on the cheek and bounded into the street, without looking both ways, might I add. Günter's host family nearly hit me, but luckily, Logan pulled me back by my shoulders. "Whoa. Careful, champ," he said. I've never heard his voice sound that stressed.

"Yeah! Definitely," I yelled, crossing the empty street. "Pick me up at 4:30." I heard him following me. "Logan, I said 4:30, goddamit."

When I got home, I forgot to nap. Instead, I took a shower to wash away the crazy. Didn't work. Being bombarded by droplets was the worst feeling in the world. A steaming hot shower is the worst place to be. Once you're in, you want to stay in. It's like a gang. Or a cult. It's difficult to work up the courage to get out and face the cold. I used to believe I could live inside a hot shower for eternity, my languid body becoming wrinkled as a disconnect would form between my problems and me. That's not reality. The sad truth remains this: Showers don't stay warm forever. All showers turn cold. This means you must bring yourself to get out. Gotta face the biting air. As I became drenched while sobbing my eyes out, all that capered in the confines of my cranium was negativity. I thought about warm showers not enduring. I thought about how relationships, and experiences, and life in general all resemble showers. It all comes down fast and heavy and you can't stay warm. You eventually have to get out and move on. This upset me, so I started saying, "Be happy. Be happy. Be happy. It's the only way to be."

Then the water turned cold. I climbed out, despair clobbering my insides while wearing brass knuckles. Then I wrapped myself in a towel and raced to my room. Screamed and moaned into a pillow. Banged my head on the floor, attempting to hammer my brain back to normal. I wandered around my room, nearly naked, drenched, hyperventilating. Then my body attempted to shimmy the crazy out, accompanied by the classical/rap/jazz combinations I made. Dancing made me feel alive, and it made everything worse.

Suddenly, I had the urge to swim, my mind ebbing to my first visit to Eliot's pool, a time when I stayed underwater until I nearly drowned. I had a hankering to feel the early summer air on my limbs. And I craved a diving board, one to spring from. So, I put my yellow bikini on and tied Logan's red hoodie around my neck, like a cape. My iPod headphones were shoved into my ears as I marched to our balcony. It doesn't have rails and is fairly low to the ground. It's a glorified platform, simply an extension of our roof. As the snow torpedoed down, I selected the one appropriate song to accompany the act of jumping off one's balcony. "Jumper" by Third Eye Blind. It appears I'm rather cliché when I've gone off the deep end. Soon, I was walking along the roof's edge, like a tightrope walker, like the bird I saw on the wire, singing along to the song.

The first person to find me on the roof was my neighbor, Stuart. He was trying to get Mr. Bojangles out of his yard. Once he spotted me, he started yelling for me to get down. His voice became white noise that couldn't compete with my gaudy singing. The second person to find me was Willow. She had been playing at a friend's house, but walked home after getting in a quarrel. She was already tearing up because of her fight, and seeing my roof performance didn't improve her emotions one bit. The third person to find me was Logan. He arrived at the Dwyer residence at 4:30 on the dot, ready for bowling. Ready to make our "destiny" a reality. Ready. And I didn't notice him. Days later, during Melanie's daily hospital visit, she told me Logan was there during my meltdown's climax. I buried myself under my sterile white blankets.

The three begged me to stop while I eliminated them from my scope of consciousness. I stood on the edge, belting the song's final lyrics, *"Can you put the past away? I wish you would step back from that ledge my friend. I would understand. "*

      That's when I almost leapt off the roof. I don't know who pulled me into the house or how they did it. Everything that happened between almost flying and laying in the mental hospital that evening is basically a series of bokeh photographs. All I can say for certain is that body and soul came together in their stinging openness, and I'm conflicted by my desire to have this awful feeling back. And I want to make something clear. I never pictured myself landing in the snow. I never pictured myself breaking myself on an ice hard snow bank. I never pictured myself landing. I'm sorry. I should go.

March 24, 2013

Hey, Joey Journal,

Sixteen days since they put me away. Still not in the mood for trivia and anecdotes. It's March 24th. I'm out now and have been since March 17th. Seven days in the real world. During this last week, I went to the hospital each day as a partial patient. I became fully discharged two days ago. It's Sunday. Melanie is letting me stay home from school another week. I once wrote that I've never been afraid at school and that I considered it a sanctuary, but I'm anxious about going back. Everything I did, everything I said, embarrassing.

The hospital's family therapist suggested I take a break from journaling and told me it seems like it's become an excessive hobby. I'm supposed to be drawing or taking photos or literally anything else. "Try new releases," he said. But now that I'm on meds, it's different. I don't feel creative or motivated. I feel like a popped balloon. And I can't watch TV, because every program makes me uncomfortable. Can't even go on the internet. The day I was released, I logged onto Twitter and saw hundreds of asinine tweets posted by me within a span of two weeks. Then I went on Facebook, finding lengthy rants that I thought were poems when I posted them, but honestly, they're the ramblings of a lunatic. Same story with my email. Pressured Speaking is a symptom of my disorder, which means I occasionally have an increased need for communication. This leads me to write and talk in a fast, unintelligible, inordinate manner.

I also posted pictures, wildly edited and flipped upside down. I don't know where they came from and don't fully remember uploading them. While deleting the lot, I felt somewhat better, but people still saw. My unraveling psyche was on display ten whole days while I was locked away. 1083 "friends" were invited to analyze. I'm not even friends with a quarter of those "friends." My social media accounts have been discontinued. Temporarily.

I need to make sense of what happened, so I've chosen to write despite the therapist's advice. However, I'll do so responsibly, composing one short story daily until I'm back in school.

Day 1: Eggs.

Eggs. I'd have rather opened that Styrofoam box to find a live grenade. I didn't have contacts in my eyes because they fell out during my last day in the real world. Maybe I never put them in. Everyone was so panicked, delivering me to the hospital, that they forgot to provide a new pair. Even without 20/20 vision, I knew what my meal was. That yellow color was unmistakable. Eggs. I'm not a picky eater, but seriously, did that daffy dietician completely forget our conversation from the night before?

I must explain that I've had mental hospital eggs before. Because I've been committed to a mental hospital in the past. It wasn't its own big event like it was this time around. It blended in with the day my dad died. You may be wondering why I'm only sharing this crucial piece of information now. Well, this is my goddamn journal, not an autobiography. There are some things I didn't want to talk about in my journal these last few months, and so I didn't. My dad's death has been and still is one of them, and seeing as my first mental hospital visit was entirely a result of my dad's passing, I never jumped at the chance to talk about that August visit in question. This has been a story, but it comes in the form of a journal, the body revealing only the things that were ready to come out. I don't apologize for my journal leaving out details that could've potentially assisted a reader in understanding me as a character, for I am not a character and this document is something that should've never had a reader in the first place. You have a lot of nerve if you've gotten this far.

All of that said, I'm finally in the position where I can reference Hospital Visit #1. It is not with ease that I mention it, but with the uncomfortable knowledge that I must in order for my dismay for the eggs on my first day to make sense.

"Your food preferences?" the dietician asked upon my second hospital arrival, the night before I was greeted by an unwanted breakfast.

"Cool with whatever. Cool runnings. Cool, cool, cool. I wake up tomorrow, find eggs? I'll put a hex on your whole family and flip-the-flipping-flip out."

The dietician nodded as she wrote my admonition on her clipboard. "So, you don't like eggs. Anything else we need to know? Food allergies?"

"Whoa, woman. Shut it. Never said nothing about not liking eggs. Love eggs. Could eat a freaking frittata every night. Just won't eat your eggs. Not the eggs from your ovaries, but you get what I'm saying." Her face suggested she didn't get it. Incredibly inarticulate, I said, "Came here in August and left knowing the food. It's alrighty-then. It's a nut house, not a five-star inn. Ain't a chateau. Still, I won't eat your eggs. Or your rubbery ham. I won't eat your crappy eggs and ham, Sam-I-am. Gave it a try, but I'm ninety-nine percent positive the eggs are made from boxed powder. Why? Another patient told me way back when. Boxed eggs. Not my thing. And no, I'm not allergic to food, but if I said I'm allergic to eggs, would that guarantee I won't be given them?"

My first day in hospital hell, I looked up from my eggs and took in the characters sitting around the table. There was a bone thin Mexican chick and a chubby hipster punk. That morning, I couldn't place Maria. Days later, when my mind became more lucid, I realized the languid Latina was 'Maria Monster', my 6th grade karate nemesis. I recognized the tubby guy right away, though. He was that giggly twit who laughed at me when a bird pooped on my head before the homecoming game. That guy I properly chewed out. That guy. That guy has a name, as he pointed out after I called him "Chubbers" too often. Ronny was polite about it. On the first day, I leaned in his direction and said, "You! Me! Real life?"

Chubbers nodded solemnly. He looked a bit more bloated than usual and his hair was less floppy. It wasn't blue anymore, but a natural auburn shade.

"You get a man period? We must have synced up, Chubbers," I

said, voice too loud for so early in the morning. "They say menses can make us nuts. Except, I don't think I'm bleeding. I hope I'm not bleeding. If I am bleeding, I must've made a bleeding mess." Silence reigned over the table. That's when I looked down and saw my worst nightmare. "My God. The eggs are back, too. Screw it to screw, blow it up in the big ole blue, top o' the morning, good morning to you."

I continued scanning the table. A dangerously thin Asian boy was making origami cranes. He didn't notice me winking at him. I was in a winky mood. On his right was a girl in need of cleavage coverage. It was a hospital, not a brothel. I looked down at my own chest that lay beneath blue paper pajamas. Flat. Instead of pitying myself, I pitied her. Tits McGee would one day have back problems and a pricey breast reduction surgery. Either way, my humor boobs were surely bigger. Looking down at my chest made me wonder how they got me clothed before bringing me here. I couldn't remember. On my other side was a ghostly pale boy. He was about thirteen and tiny. He had shifty eyes and a Crash Bandicoot smile. Mr. Bandicoot was whispering to Tits McGee about how during his last hospitalization, they put him in a straitjacket. Liar. During my first visit, I asked if they were gonna put me in a straitjacket. They said they didn't have one.

"Name is Rosie. Gonna make it rain eggs. That'll teach 'em bastards. That'll teach 'em." They all responded in different ways, except the Asian boy who didn't react and kept folding. I said, "I'm fixing to throw eggs into the heavens, ladies and gents, gents and ladies. They'll fall on the table, so fasten your seatbelts. Guard your origami cranes."

Before I could create an egg rainstorm, an ancient man appeared in the doorway. "My name is Dr. Butterum. I'm filling in for Dr. Patrick. I'm ready to see you, Rosie."

I laughed. *'Dr. Butter'*. That's what I thought his name was, because the "um" part sounded like stammering. I discreetly grabbed the butter packets belonging to me and Crash Bandicoot and held them behind my back. Dr. Butter led the way as I skipped down the hall. Once in his office, I relaxed on the brown leather couch and said, "Got a present for you. Beautiful present. You'll love, love, love it. Yes! Yes for presents!"

The man had a wrinkled, rubbery face. It was difficult to read. Maybe it was hard because I couldn't see straight. He was either extremely bored or analyzing my every movement. Every single detail. With no facial expression, Doc said, "Do you?"

I leapt up, got down on one knee and bestowed him with the butter containers. "Dr. Butter. Will you make me the happiest mental patient in all the land? Be my shrink?"

"My name is Dr. Butterum. I'd love to be your psychiatrist, but you're Dr. Patrick's patient. I'm filling in." I vigorously nodded, and he said, "He's on vacation with his family. When did you last see him?"

Couldn't remember in that moment. I met Dr. Patrick during my first hospital stay, in August. He sent me home after a day, not wanting to medicate me because he believed I wasn't suffering from anything clinical. He said my "outburst" was likely a "product of grief," seeing as my fit happened on the same day as my family's tragedy. He said I needed to be around my family, not strangers. Dr. Patrick also referred me to a therapist named Dr. Jarrod Bosley. Melanie was unable to find an open appointment with him that didn't interfere with our schedules. It got pushed under that pesky rug.

"It's alright if you can't remember," he said. After some more questions, he released me to the group room.

"Bye, bye, bye, Dr. Butter."

"It's Dr. Butterum."

I said, "You have to stop saying 'um'. It makes you sound, um, um-professional."

When I got back to the group room, therapy had already begun. The setting was nothing like what you see in the movies. My surroundings weren't that of some haunted asylum. It looked more like a nice college dormitory, but for the mentally flustered. The group room wasn't gray, nor dreary. The walls were a relaxing blue and a mural of a lake was painted on the far wall. Nice. Bright. Sorta safe. I sat in a chair next to Chubbers and looked around. The boy who liked origami was still doing origami at the table. At the time, I didn't know why the staff was so lenient with him. The staff is never permissive.

When I found out later why they let him do his own thing, I cried during "quiet time." Quiet time is the hour of the day where we had to be in our rooms by ourselves. This is so the early shift workers can exchange notes with night shift workers, in peace. One day, while the kid was in his bedroom during group, somebody asked a nurse why the 'origami kid' was in the hospital. She said, "Normally, we'd let him answer that. Right now, Michael can't speak for himself, and if I were you, I'm sure I'd want answers."

She then went on to explain that the batch of weed the kid smoked was laced with bad shit. My words, not hers. He went into psychosis. I was in psychosis when I came to the hospital, too. However, my psychosis was induced by the chemicals in my brain and by sleep deprivation. They put me on meds. I came back to reality, relatively speaking. That's the difference between Michael and me. The nurse seemed to believe he might not ever exit the state of mind.

Screw talking about that. Sometimes I feel like eating my pen when thinking about Michael. This is about my first day, not his mushed brain. On that day, the nurse hounded Tits McGee with questions. Tits smiled, but was guarded, arms crossed over her lengthy red hair as she gave all the right answers. Once he was done with her, he looked at me, smiled and asked what brought me there. I loudly said, "Back. I'm back."

"What's brought you back?"

I started laughing. Hysterically. Don't know why. Chubbers halted his jiggling knee. Maria grinned and dryly said, "Don't wanna laugh at her, so I'll do it on the inside."

I didn't see other reactions, but I knew everybody was uneasy. I managed to pause my uproar long enough to ask if I could visit the Quiet Room, and the nurse nodded. The first time I was in the hospital, I wanted to go to the Quiet Room. Just once. I longed for the full mental hospital experience. When in Rome. However, even when I've gone off the deep end, I kind of behave. I didn't have a single outburst my first time there. Normally, they only exile kids to the Quiet Room if they yell. The staff never sent me there, because I never let my voice boom. I never shouted meanly, that is. My visit on my first day back was a self-proposed banishment.

I didn't sit and meditate in there, opting for jumping jacks and singing a song. The tune I warbled many a time was "Art is Dead" by Bo Burnham. It's one of his only songs that's serious. The rest of his comedy is different. It's not a joke and you can tell when he sings it. When a person who gets paid to tell jokes stops joking for three whole minutes to sing a serious song and people enjoy it, that's beautiful. I couldn't help but have something that beautiful stuck in my head for days on end. While singing, I cried and smiled simultaneously, until I grew tired and lay face down on the floor.

With eyes struggling to stay open, I tried sorting out where I was and what it meant. I considered my colleagues in craziness and their auras that burned brighter in my mind than auras normally do. Because I was in an elevated mood, my aura descriptions were all positive takes. Shit brown refused to spring to mind, even for the shit people. Asian crane maker—blue. Tits McGee—silver. Bandicoot—yellow. Dr. Butter—green. Chubbers—orange-yellow. Maria Monster—deep red. Me, I'm also red, I suppose. But softer than Maria's red. I'm almost pink. I repeated the colors under my breath multiple times. Then I pinned my cheek to the ground and groaned, "What does this mean?"

And I couldn't figure it out. I've been in the free world for enough time and still can't piece it together. Part of me says not being able to make sense of things is okay, but a small, yet threatening bit of my spirit remains determined to search for the meaning of it all for the rest of my life. *What brought me here? I'm supposed to know that?* That's what I thought to myself. Or shouted. I don't remember.

When I eventually rose, I approached a tiny window on the wall. It was obviously there so the nurses could check on the patient in solitary. There were scratch marks all over it. I imagined some character before me, in blue paper pajamas, digging their nails into the window, trying to scratch it up to the point where the nurses couldn't see through it. The window scratcher failed, seeing as a person could still see through that bad boy if they wanted to. Because of my "When in Rome" mentality, I clawed my nails at the window, putting myself in the lace-free shoes of the little attention attractor who was in the quiet room before me.

March 25th, 2013

Hey, Joey Journal,

Seventeen days since the roof incident. Seventeen. I'm still not in the mood for fun facts or anecdotes, but I need to give some trivia right now. Don't want to, but I need to. Right before drifting into sleep, I often smell chlorine, element 17. I think it's because I was sitting next to a pool the day I got my last phone messages from him. I'm still unprepared to give any more details of his death. However, revealing one thing, revealing chlorine, well, that feels damn good.

You're my friend, Joey. You have a right to know what's wrong with me. Throughout my hospital stay, I craved your weight in my hands. The first night happened on March 8th, seventeen days ago. I left my room to go to the nurse's station, rebuffing sleep. Got there late, because they had to drug test me and cat scan my brain at the real hospital. The fourth time I left my room, the night guard stopped me in the hall and asked if I wanted something to eat. His name was Alfred, and he was as big as he was black. Indigo aura. Calming energy. He had long dreads and a bushy beard, reminiscent of a Black Hagrid. Alfred was the gentlest person I met there. Hell, he might've even been the most laid back person I've met anywhere. Alfred sat me down at a table in the room where the little kids play during the day and microwaved a calzone in the connecting kitchen. When he brought it to me, I pointed to the dollhouse and said, "We play with that tomorrow?"

He casually smiled while sitting across from me. "This room is for little kids. We don't mix little kids with teens. You'll see the group

240

room tomorrow."

"Shame, shame, shaming shame. This room looks like bundles of fun. Bundles."

Alfred affably told me to lower my voice and to eat my food. Then I took a big bite out of the cheesy Hot Pocket while trying to remember my last meal. Spaghetti. It occurred to me that it had been more than a day since I last ate. I tried recalling the meal that came before that meal. I couldn't remember, so I insufflated the Hot Pocket. Mouth stuffed, I said, "Where's Joey Journal? Joey Journal is missing." He told me to swallow first. I did so and tried to talk coherently. "Joey Journal? Where? I need it. Can I have it?"

"Does it have a metal spiral?"

"I think so."

"Journals with spirals aren't allowed."

"Why not?"

His face grew serious as he said, "We've had problems in the past with kids finding ways to be self-destructive with those kinds of journals."

This made me rant about how those kids must be "scary as shit." He shushed me again, but then compassionately said, "Ditch the word 'crazy'. Nobody here is crazy. They're confused, in pain, or lost. Many kids deal with emotional pain by causing themselves pain. We don't want that."

I hummed "99 Luftballons" into my hands, while Alfred leaned back and rubbed his hand along his beard. "Info overload. You're new. There's a lot to digest." He gave a mild grin before saying, "Speaking of digesting, eat."

"I want my journal, Black Hagrid."

He smiled and said, "Black Hagrid? That's a first."

"Joey doesn't hurt. Joey helps. A helping of help, give it to me or I'll yelp, yelp—"

"When your family visits, we can ask them for the journal. You can have it, but we'd have to rip the spiral out."

"Not his spine!" I teared up as I surged and tossed my half-eaten Hot Pocket in the garbage. "It was grand and nice and wonderful and amazing meeting you, Black Hagrid, but I want my room now."

"Okay, rest."

Resting wasn't my intention. I was going to my room to do jumping jacks and had no intentions of sleeping. I didn't tell him that, though, and started departing. As I reached the doorway, Alfred said, "It'll get better."

Promising, mystic, helpful. Alfred was the man. I turned and gave a grateful nod. After leaving my room and wandering the hall twice more, I retired to my bed, forcing my body to lay down for the first time in days. The urge to rise kept arresting me, leaving me rolling the night away. I wanted to write a story about Alfred inside you, Joey, that instant. What kept me bed bound was my remembrance of his words, *"It'll get better."*

I didn't tell you the Hot Pocket story solely to convey how Alfred helped me my first night. I want you, a bundle of papers, to know the power you have over me. That's why I'm going to write responsibly. Endless rants amount to exactly what the premiere adjective implies. Endlessness. Short stories, dear. When I say "short", I mean short.

Day 2: The Diagnosis

Through bleary eyes, I watched Dr. Butter hobble into my room. Behind him was a woman. Her towering height gave away her identity. Melanie carried a plastic bag and I was more excited to see the bag than I was to see her. When she came the previous afternoon, I mostly spoke about the fact that I was marooned without eyewear or clothes options. I didn't like the outfit they put me in before admitting me. "Bad energy. Burn the outfit, Mel." A nurse gave me duds that previous patients accidentally left behind. I was more comfortable than I was in paper pajamas, but still craved my own ensembles. And dammit all, I wanted to see clearly.

Melanie didn't give me my belongings right away. She sat on my bed as I crouched like a suspicious squirrel on a purple platform next to her. I looked at Dr. Butter, his features just as obscured and unreadable as the previous day. I sensed it and held onto my clenched butt. He was about to reveal something huge. He laid it on me easy, but all I heard were a string of words featuring "comorbidity", and "post-traumatic", and "stress", and "disorder", but also "bipolar", and "manic" and "episode." As he explained my symptoms and treatment options, I zoned in and out.

I wasn't angry or ashamed, not at first. My only thought was, *That makes sense.* All I seemed able to do was savor the strangest relief.

"How can she have two disorders?" Melanie said, applying both evenness and punch.

Dr. Butter seemed unfazed, as if this was his best meeting of the day. "Like I said, it's called comorbidity. This is the word used to describe a patient dealing with two conditions. Rosie is tell-tale bipolar. This is caused by the chemicals in her brain. She would've still struggled with the disorder had the event from last summer never happened. I had her file from school sent over. Before the tragedy, there were numerous incidents of impulsive behavior that are far from normal. A teacher claimed she wet her pants on purpose last year. There have also been many fistfights, all started by her. Her erratic behavior displayed at the hospital since she's been here has also made the bipolar disorder clear."

Melanie pursed her lips, thinking momentarily. Then she said, "First of all, don't forget she's in the room. Talk to her like she's here. Okay? And yes, I can understand the bipolar diagnosis. Now, tell me, how does the PTSD play in here?"

"Well, it's a disorder that develops in some people who have lived through traumatic events. It's normal to feel fear after something traumatic happens, but only to a certain extent. Rosie clearly is still reliving her fear. Symptoms usually begin early."

Melanie acted out of character, furrowing her expressive eyebrows, and raising her voice. Because I was in and out, I don't remember the exact words said, but it was something like, "With all due respect, what kind of hospital is this? Rosie was in here right after he died, and the doctor didn't think to warn us to watch out for this? I mean, I have a vague knowledge of PTSD, but I don't know symptoms. Where the hell is that doctor anyway? What's his name again?"

"Dr. Patrick, and he told me he referred you to a therapist."

Mel replied, "It's the way he referred us that's bothering me. He smiled and breezily told me she'd probably start feeling better on her own, when school started back up. 'It's seems like normal grief to me,' he said. For Christ's sake, where's this Patrick guy?"

Dr. Butter didn't want to say, but after a long pause, he let it out.

"Florida. Family vacation."

Mel was about to start laughing, but not her lovely cackle. An exasperated one. Then she said, "How quaint. While my child has an episode that was worsened because of her family falling apart, her doctor is off with his own family in Florida? He's probably wearing Crocs and drinking mojitos, because those are his priorities. Again, what kind of hospital is this? I hate it. I hate being a single mother." Right after she said that, her face drastically transformed. Melanie looked astonished, as if this was the first time she said the term 'single mother' aloud.

Single mother. Crap. She is. I…have been such an ass.

Dr. Butter exited, giving us time to soak it in. Melanie tried comforting me, despite her tears. She said, "It's not bad. Did you hear the doctor when he said PTSD isn't always chronic? Good news, right? And famous people throughout history had bipolar disorder. Churchill, Beethoven, writers and painters, too. See, don't worry. It'll work out. It'll all…uh-huh."

Her caved in brown eyes made it apparent she was the one needing comfort. I wasn't crying, just incessantly repeating myself. "So much sense."

She stayed a long time. During this visit, she found the right moment to give me a card Logan bought me. I wanted to hurl. It reminded me of what happened, including our out there conversation on the street. And I still don't know who pulled me back inside. *Was it him?* I thought. *Don't let it be him.* I studied the card, simultaneously feeling myself temporarily crash landing. He has the handwriting of a toddler. I didn't bother trying to decode the message. The worst part was the generic cover, which had birds on it. I know he picked it with no intentions of upsetting me. Probably only aimed to pick the prettiest card. Logan does things without thinking, which is what I like about him, but he needs to cool it with the birds.

My relationship with birds improved with my mania. Manic people love everything, including symbols with wings and feathers— symbols that swoop in and remind them of people who have passed. Even though I was still manic when I got the card, looking at it made me less manic. In addition to being sweet, his offering sobered me a little. After staring at the card, I impulsively decided there wasn't enough space for me and the folded paper. No space in my room. Rushed into my bathroom and flushed it down the toilet. I clapped my hands over my ears as the toilet swirled. "Sorry, Logan, wherever you are. I'm a bitch."

Melanie attempted to halt me, but she wasn't as fast as my manic self. "I'm sorry," she said as I did snow angels on the ground. "Should've known it was too soon to show you. He's sweet, though. Knocked on the door and asked if he could visit. Told him only family could come to the youth wing. That's when he insisted I pass on the card. Keep him around, will you?"

I kept mum for the rest of her visit. Finally, after thirty minutes passed, Melanie hugged me one last time and left. The plastic bag was gone, but the contents remained scattered on my white blanket. No journal. They didn't let me have you, Joey. I quickly found my glasses, put them in place, and woozily went into my bathroom. There, I eyeballed my reflection, and found my face to be emaciated, eyes bloodshot, hair lawless. I realized my half-shaven hair is like one of my disorders. There are two halves of my head that are polar opposites. But I didn't revel in the symbolism, purely yearning for the appearance of a well-adjusted young girl. My fingers moved my hair's part over a little further to the right, covering up the side I'd been shaving the past few months. A thought emerged and I said it. "Bipolar. PTSD. Crap. Gotta write a memoir."

And although I was the most awake I've ever been, I couldn't help but smell chlorine.

March 26, 2013

Hey, Joey Journal,

Eighteen days since…yeah. Eighteen is the age I am, but not the age I'll forever be. I've never given thought to distant ages. Focusing on my future after receiving news of my disorders is more taxing than ever. It seems like everybody already knows what they're doing after high school wraps. As for me, it's a mystery. I'm not okay with that, but I'm trying to be. I can't navigate my next path until I understand the potholes that threw me off course on my current road. That's why I write. To write is to reflect on the ride.

It's March, but it doesn't feel like spring. The snow is heavily present and it's freezing. What remains of the dying tree outside the kitchen window has my attention. The unfallen parts. Barren branches dance in the wind, quite berserk. I miss being like that. Quite berserk. Mania is wild. It's unhealthy, but it felt amazing until it vanished. Kind of like warm showers. It's nuts, but most of me misses mania. Then I remember everything and retreat into my sweater. Unleashing a muffled scream, I'm a noisy turtle. Can you get extra PTSD from going crazy? Because I'm doing a whole lot of what Dr. Butter calls "re-experiencing", but with memories from being bonkers. Flashbacks. All that jazz.

Mania is a double-edged sword. I lust after extreme happiness, but have a humiliation hangover. Syrup chugging, outing my ex, trying to fly off the roof. Oh, crap. Don't get me started on that roof and my nearly nude body almost flying off it. Here I go.

Day 6: The News

On Day 6, I was the last to leave my room in the morning. I had slumber troubles the night before. Hours before lights out, Melanie made me aware that Logan was there when I almost pounced off my roof. I asked if he was the one who pulled me inside. Strangely, the romantic in me began to hope it was him. Gross, I know. She solemnly said he wasn't the one, but before she could say who it was, I interrupted her. "Shit, Mel. I don't even wanna know which poor soul saved me." I flung myself into the bathroom, slammed the door, and threw my body against it. My hands covered my ears, I said some La-la-la's and screamed at her not to tell me. I did this until visiting time was over.

Embarrassment led to adrenaline, which gave way to late night ambulating. My mind and body drifted into sleep by two am, but when a nurse tried to wake me around six, I entombed my face in my pillow and said, "It's not happening, Doris."

Doris, the nurse, persistently attempted to wake me, like an annoying alarm clock. After I became used to her, I could tune her out. When I finally walked out in sweats and a messy braid, I took in my surroundings. The group room changed every morning. There were always new people added and familiar faces subtracted. Some days, there were heated arguments already taking place between patients, and other days, I found unmitigated silence. On most days, much of the group ravenously ate breakfast before playing a card game called UNO. Because I woke up late on this day, most of them were already in UNO mode.

Inside the UNO circle was Maria. They played around her. She had no cards. All she had was an untouched tray and power to hurt others. She didn't plan on doing none. Maria dryly introduced herself to a new girl who had her nose in a book. She greeted every new face the same. When the new kid looked up from her book, Maria asked if she wanted to know what she was committed for. Her victim of the day cautiously nodded. The Maria Monster smiled menacingly and told her she stabbed her brother because he changed the TV channel on her. The new girl was wide-eyed and terrified. A pause lasted five seconds before being replaced by the groups unified amusement.

Tits McGee's real name is Heather. Heather bit her lip and shook her head as I silently prayed she wouldn't go tattle to the chaperone at a different table. That's how she normally handles situations when people stop playing nice. Leaning on the doorframe, I sent her a message with my eyes. *I'll handle it.* "Don't listen to Maria," I irately said.

"It was a joke." An icy Maria looked at the shy girl and said, "Joking, hon. I'm a joker. Ha. Why so serious?"

I said, "Don't call people 'hon'. It's condescending. And why try to scare her? Being here, being locked up, it's scary enough. How do you get off?"

"Puta, you better not address me again," said a perfectly calm Maria. The new girl, who was beyond uncomfortable, quickly went back to her book.

Heather placed her cards in an upside down fan on the table and leaned forward. She brushed her long red hair behind her ear and tenderly said, "Feeling okay? You seem emotionless."

I undid my hair and fixed my braid, scowl manifesting my face. Then I took a deep breath as my thoughts "raced." That's a term I learned the true meaning of from my talks with Dr. Butter. Racing is when my thoughts go so fast that I can't possibly keep up. Taking deep breaths and making a mental note to "slow down" helps a bit. Not all the way, though. Deepened respiration and repeated mantras aren't magic. Much had been learned by Day 6 of my hospital stay. For example, I was told my fleeting mania would likely combine with emerging melancholia. Drifting into depression after mania is sometimes called "crashing." While carelessly re-braiding my hair, the official crash nipped at me.

Everybody else was done eating, except the origami crane crafter and Maria. Michael was too far gone to eat and Maria had a full-blown eating disorder. That meant she went to the eating disorder unit during much of the day. While other mental mongrels sucked up Lucky Charms, Maria always had to work up the courage to even peel her banana. I went into the lobby and grabbed my tray. When I got back to the room, Heather pulled her feet off the chair they were resting on and said, "Sit with us."

Heather was the perkiest suicidal chick ever. She was as perky as her elephantine tatas. When most people think of suicidal teenagers, they imagine thick eyeliner and scene clothing. That's a stereotype. The depressed kids I met in the hospital weren't inclined to show it through stereotypes. One or two could've potentially been labeled as "emo," but nobody was that one-dimensional and they couldn't be described by a three-letter word. Heather wore "normal" clothes, talked about "normal" adolescent topics, and smiled a "normal" smile. People didn't see misery when they looked at her. People saw a girl constantly trying to prove her happiness to those around her and most of all herself. During group therapy, she constantly said, "I'm feeling much better. Really. I'm ready to go home. I am."

Looking at Heather, I understood what depression looks like. Depression doesn't look like sadness alone. It's an attempt to hide sadness at any cost. "Yoohoo? Rosie," she said. "Sit down, girl. You can play UNO with us when you're done eating. Kay?"

I desperately wanted to know if she was healing or doing a sterling acting job, but didn't say anything about it. My mania was evaporating, and the concept of manners was becoming familiar to me again. I smiled politely back and gave the most courteous "thanks but no thanks" I could summon. Then I sat at across from Greg, our group leader. He was at the only empty table, reading a newspaper and zoning us out. Greg was in his mid-thirties, slightly nerdy, a bit shaky, a tad timid. If he were a superhero, his name would be "Chihuahua Man."

Seeing how rudely some kids treated him, I didn't blame him for being nervous. He was like our resident teacher. Most teachers take a daily beating from their students. Imagine what it would be like for teachers to have a class consisting entirely of mentally unwell kids. No easy task. He mostly had us view videos relating to common teen problems, then would prompt us to "think deeply" about it. Most patients moaned in response to his videos. Someone always had to say something like, *"C'mon. Greg. You showed that episode of If You Really Knew Me the last time I was here."*

Mental hospital kids have much to complain about, and he was the guy we dumped our loaded grievances onto. Same with anger. When we finally tired of grousing, we'd ask if we could play games instead of analyzing our feelings. He always kept his cool. I liked talking to him, as he was the voice of reason in a place that seemed to be without any sense. Hunkering down, I thanked Heather again for the UNO proposition, but told her I needed to catch up on the news. "What are the hot stories, Greg?"

He put down his paper and told me ever so calmly that a new Pope had been chosen. I gave an uninterested nod and said, "Dude, I'm not even Catholic."

"That doesn't mean you can't be updated on the Pope. It's a current event."

"Yes, it's a current event I currently find to be irrelevant."

Greg provided a flustered laugh as his head shook. Then he crossed his thin arms over his mint green polo and looked up at the ceiling through beady glasses. "What else...hmmm. Well, yesterday, I heard on the radio that Twinkies and other Hostess products have a company that wants to purchase them out of bankruptcy."

"Does this mean Twinkies...they're back?"

"Yep."

I ascended and yelled, "Twinkies!"

Of course, nobody understood the metaphorical resonance behind the Resurrection of Twinkies. Ronny, aka Chubbers, began giggling. I glared at him and he put his hands up as he swayed his reddening face. "You barely reacted to the Pope, but the news about Twinkies made you jump for joy." He rubbed his gut, as if there was an infant inside. "And I thought I was addicted to sweets."

I thought he was calling me fat and decided to dump my breakfast.

March 27, 2013

Hey, Joey Journal,

Nineteen days. Nineteen is my least favorite number. My dad once told me there's karmic debt associated with it. Whatever that is and whatever the hell it means, I don't know. It doesn't sound appealing, though. In fact, it makes me anxious. Nineteen. A perfect number for today, because I've been anxious as hell throughout it. It's 4 o'clock, I'm at the library, and the table beneath your covers is more expansive than my needs demand. All I have is you and a tote bag. This table is meant to seat at least two people, preferably more if possible. I'm one person, feeling strangely guilty for claiming a two-person-or-more-table when I'm solo. Melanie decided to run errands today, and I'm still not in school, not until Monday. It's Wednesday. Four more days, if today's excluded.

It's all dark. This crepuscule is something of my own chemicals' creation. I guess life got its hands in there, too. It's not just puberty or Senioritis, not the blues or the mean reds. It's depression and it's part of me. My most callous companion. They said these meds would bring me down before balancing out, and they might not even be the right ones. It's like a meteorologist predicting the weather, a combination of science and a bullshit shot in the dark. Dr. Butter said medicating bipolar patients is especially arduous, because each brain has a unique chemistry. No two cases of Bipolar Disorder are the same. "Patience" is the popular word lately.

So, I'm depressed. Might be for a while, but I can at least try feeling better. It's not all about medicine. My actions matter. That's why

I'm at the library. Earlier, I was lying on the beanbag sack in the living room when I remembered I start school in four days. Nobody was home and I needed help. *Library self-help section*, I thought. I hopped on the bus and traveled briskly to the section. Fingers grazed book spines, until my hand landed on a familiar title. *Why Do Men Have Nipples?* I placed the book to my chest with one hand and my pained face must've made me look like I was having a coronary. I wanted to discover the answer to the cover's question, but couldn't quite open it. It would've made me remember too many things. Reminiscing happened anyhow, about him, him, the other him, her, her, him, me, everyone.

I came there not even to forget this time, but to help myself. And all I could do was remember, which is all I ever do. Then I remembered the other reason I come to the section. To be forgotten. That's not what I wanted this time. I wanted to be remembered, in the same glowing light I'm trying to see everyone else in. The lights that shined above me were the worst in the library. Someone needs to change that flickering bulb. Fully chagrined, I compelled my remembering body to move and went by the window, nabbing the huge table previously described. I'm going to tell another hospital story.

Chubbers and the Maria Monster Have Real Names

Amid Day 8, the anxiety fully hit me. My mind was still fast like when I was manic, but my thoughts weren't exciting. I was thinking about me, and in a terrible light. Arms crossed, I didn't feel like talking in group. It was cold in there, even though I was wearing two pairs of sweatpants and two sweaters. My eyes examined the windows. I couldn't gaze out of them because the blinds were perpetually drawn shut. Clear plastic was built over them so nobody could yank them open.

Greg, the nurses and the therapist attended to almost everybody's problems during group. "Everybody" was a large number on that particular day. Fifteen kids total. Ten residents; five partials. Chubbers had been a partial patient for a few days. He was phosphorescent as he told the group about an outing he shared with his mother. "It was cold as hell, but—"

"Don't say hell," the lady therapist said.

"It was cold as, uh…heck, but it felt good. She used to take me to the batting cages when I was younger, but those trips ended when my dad left during the fourth grade. She didn't have time when she got a job, but we went yesterday. It was fun."

I was jealous he knew the taste of fresh air. Groaning is all I wanted to do, but before I could make an ass out of myself by making rude noises, the therapist addressed me, saying, "What are you thinking, Rosie?"

I shrugged. She smirked, waiting for a verbal response. "Don't know," I said. "Doesn't matter. It's Chubbers' story."

She reminded me that Ronny likes to be called Ronny. Her ashy blonde bob barely moved as she shifted about. That's how stiff her hair was, from all the hair spray. The woman said, "You're normally eager to share, but you're reserved today. Why's that?"

My gaze targeted the lights above, which didn't seem nearly as bright as they were the first day. It was quiet until big boobied Heather said she walked by my room. "You were pacing and whispering to yourself. It seemed like you had a lot to say then."

Heather spoke as politely as possible, but of course, I was pissed. "Listen here, creep. My room is the only private place I have here. If I catch you spying again—"

In this weirdly calm manner, she said, "Your door was open when I was walking to the bubbler. I didn't purposely do anything. Shut up."

The therapist intervened, saying, "Ladies, how about we agree to not look in one another's rooms and to shut our doors when we need privacy?" We sullenly nodded and the therapist asked if I'd like to share what was bothering me the previous night.

"Fine, Nurse Ratchet," I said rapidly. "I was thinking about me. Me, me, me, me, me. Selfish, right? Only thinking about me? Yep, but I wasn't thinking marvelous thoughts. I was thinking about how my classmates must be gossiping about me, about how my family must be worrying about me, and how Logan must be disgusted by all the craziness inside me, and—"

"Who is Logan?" she said.

"Nobody."

She found a weak spot and went in for the kill. "Seems like this 'nobody' means a lot."

"We're not together and never were, if that's what you're insinuating. I'll be lucky if he wants to be my friend after what he saw."

"What did he see?" Chubbers asked. I glared. Told him Logan saw me sing 'Jumper' by Third Eye Blind. Chubbers grinned. "Sorta cheesy, but not bad. Could've been 'I'm Too Sexy' by Right Said Fred."

I told him both songs were gifts from the gods and that he didn't understand. "I was...nearly naked. Wearing a bikini in inclement weather."

"Again, doesn't sound bad," said Chubbers. "Could've been wearing a sunsuit like a toddler."

His ass is obviously as smart as it is fat. I sneered at him and said, "Let me repaint the picture. It was snowing. I was in a bikini and on my roof, singing, and I almost jumped off. Somebody had to wrestle me back inside. No idea who. My little sister, my neighbor, and this guy from school had to watch in horror. Maybe one of them saved me. Don't know." The other days, I told the group I was there for my mania and PTSD, but refused to give specific details before. Everybody fell silent until Heather, or Tits McGee as I prefer to call her, snickered uproariously. My anger was still there from our disagreement about whether she was spying on me, so I couldn't handle laughter from her. I quoted the movie *Heathers* during my icy stare. "What's your damage, Heather?"

Her giggle grew fuller. The therapist commanded her to stop, and she yielded. "That's hilarious." It takes a complete lack of fakeness to laugh in the face of somebody else's hardships. Could it be that Heather didn't have a completely forged existence? My brain denied this possible development as I told her I failed to see the humor. And she said, "It's just funny compared to why some of us are here. Like me. I don't wanna talk about it because you can't put a funny spin on my story, even if you tried."

I contemplated my story while listening to the therapist spew more questions. And I started chuckling as I discovered the whimsy. Next, I cried. See, it was only half-funny. The other half was tragically bonkers. Through gasps for air, I whispered, "Someone open those damn blinds."

Group ran longer than usual. The patients grew impatient and uncomfortable. This was partially because I was sobbing, but even more so because they'd been able to smell our food for five minutes. Greg dismissed the group, walked pensively over to me and knelt.

"Can't stop thinking about that moment and I'm locked in those images," I said. "Is Willow gonna be alright? And I don't really know Stuart, but I'd like to be able to make eye contact during block parties, and—"

He tenderly interrupted, saying, "You tend to ruminate. Know what that means?"

"Course I know. I have a mountainous vocabulary."

Greg grinned and tried not to laugh at my inadvertent humor. "Then you know it means you think about things until your thought process exhausts you. That's part of why you're smart, but sometimes it's toxic. Sometimes you have to move on to the next—"

"Moment?"

"Please try and do that."

I nodded, but as he left, I kept thinking. I silently ate lunch, attempting to chew my thoughts into little bits. It didn't work, so I skulked toward the chair that was farthest from everyone. I drummed on my tummy, thinking, *What does 'you're smart' mean? If I were smart, why would I have two F's? I'm stupid. A stupid, faggot-loving whore face. Like that meanie Mouthful used to call—*

Chubbers was standing above me.

"Yes, Chubbers?"

"Ronny," he reminded me for the umpteenth time. He pulled up a chair, sat directly before me, and smiled without baring his teeth. His grin stretched goofily across his pudgy face. He didn't say anything, so I asked how the 'partial life' was hanging. It was hard to hide how distracted I was. Chubbers said, "Good. Getting discharged later. What're you thinking?"

"Specifically? How I'm nothing. Just mentally off the map. Proof? Somebody once spray-painted something about a 'whore face' on my lawn. But you know, I never told anybody this, after my dad died, she sent me a card. Sent a fucking card, and not one of those short fake ones. It had this heartfelt message and a formal apology. Why am I still mad? Why are people so lovely and so awful at the same time?"

"Wanna talk?"

"No."

His expression was persistent, and it was the type of face that said, *I'm gonna reach out to you, whether you like it or not.*

I cracked my fingers and said, "The topic of discourse?"

"Two topics. For starters, don't worry about Logan Fields."

"How do you know he's the Logan? You don't."

"I do," Chubbers breezily said. "Our moms are sisters. We're not in the same crowd, but we still hang. He's mentioned you. The crap you say. Like 'humor boobs'. Says my mom has a humor D-Cup. One time, I found your stories on his bedside table. He got flustered. Shoved it in his backpack. Said it was 'some dumb Bette assignment'. The pages were wrinkled. Could tell he read it tons. Honestly, the guy is noncommittal when it comes to everything. When we were kids, he could hardly stick to potty training. But with you? Yeah. He gives a damn. Call it cousin telepathy. He came over the day I got out. It was nice. He said he feels crappy about both of us getting down and out. Wishes he pulled his head from his ass and paid attention. Sweet guy."

I said, "That was a dizzying amount of information." His silly smile expanded and he silently told me the conversation only would go where I wanted it to. And so I said, "Chubbers, he's not gonna like me the same way after seeing what he saw."

He swung his head and said, "That's the thing. My cousin's open."

"How can anybody like somebody this crazy?"

Chubbers leaned back, looking like he didn't want to say anything. He did anyways. "If anyone is capable of loving a 'crazy' person, it's him." Then he puffed his cheeks and exhaled. I asked him what he meant and he said, "Shouldn't say."

"Say it."

"Can't. If I were him, I'd prefer telling people myself. His story, Rosie."

I told him that better be the case for everything I said since I was admitted. He nodded ardently. I curled up into a ball on my chair, burying my head into my knees, thinking that was the end of that. Then he said there was something else he wanted to talk about. When I perked up, he said, "Never mind. Probably shouldn't."

His smile reached across his face once more, but this time, it wasn't goofy. It was overly sympathetic. I said, "Screw you and your polite grin, Chubbers. Proceed."

Chubbers tentatively lifted his sweatshirt, untucked his undershirt, and removed a crumpled paper from underneath. I'm sure he would've carried this item in his pocket, but Greg checks the partials' pockets and shoes. One side of the sheet was covered in unfinished math problems, and the other side featured spiraling writing. It crinkled as he flattened it on his jeans with his palm. Chubbers leaned in and softly smiled. "This is a note I wrote before—"

"Santa came last Christmas. That's how that sentence better end."

"Before I tried to kill myself, Rosie."

"A goddamn suicide note?" I was lethal before I caught myself and carefully said, "I appreciate you as a human, but get that away."

"I'm not sharing this to upset you, scare you, or shame you. You've said multiple times in group that you can't remove certain images from your head. Right?" I nodded, and he said, "Same, but with things people say. Can hardly ever get the words out of here," he said, tapping his shaggy head with his pointer finger. "Got worse last summer. Don't know if the drugs and alcohol started the depression, or if I started self-medicating to fix my already depressed self. Ya know?" I furrowed my brow, not sure where this was headed. "Months passed and the words kept filling my head with increasing voracity."

"Sorry to interrupt," I said. "'Voracity.' What a great word." I felt rude, but it was a word worth celebrating. When I first met him, I'd have never guessed he was capable of exceptional word choice.

Chubbers gave a quick 'thanks' before saying, "Months passed, and I had a shit ton of words in my head. They were piling up exponentially." He paused and grinned dumbly as I hid my smile beneath my sweater sleeve. "Another cool word?"

Gave him a thumbs up.

"The words in my head at the beginning of the school year weren't cool. Then the homecoming game came. My friends and I skipped eighth hour. When we came back for the game, we saw a girl get pooped on by a bird. I related to her. Man, that look in her eye. It's something that can only be understood by people like us. The same breed, colleagues in severe suffering."

Fuck me. I went off on him and his friends that day. Don't go there.

"She said words that grabbed me by the balls."

Fuck me harder. I said words. Mean words. He's going there.

"Once she left, I said bye to my friends and walked to my house, in a haze. They didn't bother asking what was wrong. They said, 'Whatever.' Hate that word. Such an easy one. That's the word that bothered me the most."

Fuck yes. My words weren't the worst.

"Once home, I beat my head against my bedroom wall, trying to get the words out. Couldn't. Downed some booze. Couldn't get the words out. Got my drug stash, did some lines."

"Of cocaine?"

His face looked uneasy. "The weed highs weren't enough anymore and...it's dumb. Did the lines. Couldn't get the words out of my head. Went into my closet and wrote the words on the back of an assignment from my pile of unfinished homework. Then I crumpled up the suicide note, threw it at the wall, and grabbed my brother's hunting gun from his room."

Fuck.

"Wasn't loaded, but pretending it was ready was...I don't know. I was still trying to figure out how I'd actually do it. Acting it out oddly calmed me. As I turned it on myself and stared down the barrel, my mom walked in. I was hospitalized for a bit, but when I got home, my friends pulled me back into their crap. That's why I'm here a second time. Skipped school the day I came back here, because new words entered my head. Someone else said them. A random person, but it's my own voice repeating them."

I said, "And the note?"

He looked unsure. I'm not positive he planned this lecture out in the slightest. "Sure you wanna hear?"

My smile wavered, saying, *"Of course, but please realize I'm shitting bricks."*

"Rosie, remember this is for demonstration purposes, not shaming ones."

"Preemptively remembered."

"Here it goes," he said quietly before reading the note aloud, even softer yet, so I'd be the only one to hear. "My attitude was pioneered by James Dean in this movie I've actually seen many times."

FUCK. FUCK. FUCK.

"Bitch just assumes I haven't seen it. Before him, it was, ya know…something a lot of people did. Like some Asian guy who founded stuff. The girl said he must've been high off his ass. Like me, ya know."

Fuck. I mean…fuck. He turned what I said to him that day into a suicide note? Why did a bird have to poop on me? Why?

"No comprende? Depressing, man. Depressing how great movies are shit on by our generation because we're too busy watching *That's My Boy*. Understand? No? Look at me. Something about our generation and it being recycled. Not the sad part. Naw. The sad part is clowns like me don't realize they're recycled. I act like I'm the first ever teen. The first to listen to alternative music, forsake showering, do drugs and be 'different'. I'm not different. A baboon. Recycled matter doesn't matter. Whatever. I hate that word."

I hate myself.

Tears formed in our eyes, until his gracious smile scared his wetness away. I started breathing short breaths. He made eye contact with me, saying, "Don't. The words that bothered me weren't said by you. I grabbed yours, made them mine, repeated them nonstop. Rethinking them screwed me. I was a ticking time bomb looking for the right words to set myself off."

"I'm sorry."

"Words exist," he said, with conviction. "We gotta be careful with them. We can't hold onto painful words and make people into monsters. Same goes for images." I smiled weakly and he smirked back. He took the suicide note and gingerly ripped it into an excess of scraps. Then he reached toward a nearby recycling bin, disposing of the words. "Rosie, you're gonna remember so much, but the most important thing to remember is that you don't have to carry other people's words around underneath your undershirt."

Seconds passed as we reveled in the magic of the world coming full circle. Finally, I said, "Since you're freaky good at memorizing words, why don't you audition for the spring play?"

He perked up. "*A Midsummer's Night Dream*, right? Logan told me I'd make a good Bottom. Normally, I'm a top, but whatever."

The boy giggled as I said, "You're gay?"

"Screwing with you."

"Wouldn't be surprised if you were. I seem to be only capable of befriending gay guys."

He beamed and said, "We're friends? Cool."

"Ronny, we're ready to sign your discharge papers," a nurse called out from the far away doorway.

I couldn't help but tensely warn him once more that if he told Logan what I said or did in the hospital, he'd be done for. Chubbers grinned and said it was my story to tell. As my new friend stood, I told him I'd hug him, but it wasn't allowed. "Air hug?" he said.

I air-hugged the crap out of him. "Ronny, you can hang with my crowd anytime."

He smiled and started walking away. Then he turned, and said, "Thanks for calling me Ronny."

I felt decent for an hour. Room time came, dinnertime came, free time came, time came. I was given time to think and entertained new tragic thoughts with the slow passing of seconds. *I'm a suicide causer. Stop. Ronny didn't tell that story to make you feel guilty. He was trying to help. But what if he wasn't? Stop. What if he wanted this? Stop. For me to spend the night thinking about the crap I said. Stop. Revenge, maybe? Stop.*

My mind…the messed-up telegram.

That's when a girl's raspy voice said, "Why you catatonic?" It was the Maria Monster. She sat next to me. Lord, was she cadaverous. Sorta like me, but thinner, which is frightening. "Zombie ass, what happened?"

"Thoughts are in my head."

"Course," she said. "If you don't have thoughts, all you're gonna have up there is air. An airhead. You wanna be ignorant?"

I wondered why she was talking to me. Maria only ever interacted with the Asian zombie boy, and even then, they never seemed to speak. She always grabbed a seat near him as he made his cranes and if anybody attempted a conversation with her, Maria would tell them they were interrupting an intimate conversation. She told everybody to curtail any attempts to communicate with her. To her, we were all either "loco" or "putas." Early on, Maria made it clear I was both. "Stop staring," she said. "Talk."

"Thought I was loco or a puta or whatever, meaning I shouldn't talk to you."

She fiddled with her big Chaka Khan hair. "Watching Michael was cool for a while. Not gonna lie. Learned a lot from the silence. About myself. About him. I learned that silence could create a lot of fucking origami cranes. But I also learned that when I yell at a silent person for spilling their juice all over my white jeans, they're still gonna be silent. My loudness came back, but his didn't, and that's some scary shit. And I felt like a dick for verbally assaulting somebody who's worse off than me. I'm taking a break from him. I gotta. Just so I can stop being a dick." She cradled an origami crane in her lap. It came from the hoard of paper birds that Michael had been tirelessly crafting. "Stole it. That kid and his cranes. Right? It's goofy, but kinda cool."

After staring at the crane, I dryly said, "But I'm loco. A puta."

"Always have been," she said. "Chica, I remember you. Let's stop avoiding it. Karate classes. You made everybody laugh, mostly at my expense."

"Huh?"

She looked up at the ceiling, smiling in a saddened manner, remembering. "Always calling me Maria Monster, making jokes about my fat self and my snacks. I remember. You were a puta. Didn't like it, but don't worry. My mama is the true reason for my food issues, if I had to pick a reason. She called me Gordita all the time, even though that bruja was the one who was loading me up with Micky D's. And she weighs 350 pounds."

"Sorry about being a bitch."

"Shut up. Hey is for horses, and sorry is for shitheads. You made jokes, but I didn't care. You didn't kiss my big brown ass out of fear. So what? You're the funny sorta loca. That's why everybody likes you."

"Nobody does," I said.

"And nobody ever will if you gonna be such a sad mess."

I threw my head in my palms. That hospital was overrun by youths playing sensei to other youths. I said, "It's the truth. Nobody likes me. I'm a sadness delivery woman. I ruin everything I touch. I flush sentimental cards down toilets. I've delivered sadness to you, Melanie, Logan, Willow, River, Bette, Ronny—"

"I'm not sad. I'm healing. That's enough to be happy about. You were in the 6th grade. If I was still mad about it, I'd basically have a beef with a twelve-year old. That's pathetic, honey."

"Don't call me that."

She returned my menacing stare and said, "Please. I'll call you Empress Turd Waffle Supreme if I want. And all sixth graders are stupid. Don't dwell on that version of you. As for the people you mentioned, the ones with white folk names, I don't know 'em. So, I don't care."

"Not all of them are white. And Ronny was a patient here."

"That fat, giggly shit-biscuit?

"Could you be more insensitive?" She gave a proud nod. "Maria, people like you make me hate this place."

"Why give me the satisfaction? Psh, girl. Fuck the bullshit, just do you." My head jutted toward her. She nobly smiled. "That's my motto. Tight, right? Gonna trademark it when I'm famous and—"

"Repeat it."

"Don't like to overuse it," she said. "If I use it too much, it won't be nearly as dope when I'm famous."

"Please. Say it."

She repeated her motto in an annoyed manner. "Fuck the bullshit, just do you."

I jumped up and breathlessly shouted, "Eureka."

"Sit down, vanilla wafer."

I fell zealously into the chair, eagerly grinning. "You're The Girl's Bathroom Philosopher?"

"I'm what?"

"I sometimes cry in the girl's bathroom. Carved words stopped me once. 'Fuck the bullshit. Just do you.'"

She smiled and leaned back. "I remember doing that. My last day at North, actually."

"You moved?"

She peered down at her crane and her thigh gap and appeared to be meditating. "Remember my Uncle Doug? Well, he's actually my aunt's boyfriend. They've been together forever. I called him my uncle because that's what I thought he was. We've always lived together. His business flopped. We couldn't afford the mortgage on the house. Some of us are living in this crap apartment in Milwaukee."

I remembered Yo Mama's replacing the Dojo, felt guilty for consuming the dairy dessert for a different reason than normal, then said, "Fuck the bullshit. Just do you."

As Maria wearily nodded, Heather daintily yelled, "Y'all up for some UNO?"

Everybody knew I was wholeheartedly against UNO. It was my favorite game before coming to the hospital, but it's the only game anybody ever wanted to play. Maria, on the other hand, didn't like it because it meant being a part of the group. The two of us shot each other disgusted looks. Maria addressed Heather, saying, "Puta, what does it look like? We're fucking the bullshit. We're just doing what we do."

Heather didn't bother decoding Maria's words, shrugging her shoulders and jumping into action with the other UNO players. We both cackled. Once we relaxed, I asked if she also drew the penis on the bathroom stall. She scrunched her face and said, "Fuck I look like?"

I think I finally truly met a girl named Maria.

That night was an uphill battle getting to sleep once again. Finally, I hurled myself out of bed, put on my hospital socks and stormed to the table in the teen area where Black Hagrid was sitting. As I positioned myself crisscross applesauce across the table from him, Black Hagrid smiled at me and put down what he was writing. A form, or maybe a crossword. "What's keeping you up tonight?" he asked.

"Thinking about you," I said. His eyes bulged and I backtracked. "No, not like that. No." An involuntary laugh prevailed before I was calm enough to speak again. "Black Hagrid, this is the last time I'll address you with that nickname."

"Why?"

"Because it's not your name, Alfred. It's what you look like to me, not who you are."

I smiled, as did he. I nodded, as did he. He stayed, I left. I got in bed. I imagine he continued to fill out a form or a crossword. I didn't have time to meditate on the subject and figure out which it was. I was too occupied with slowly becoming unconscious.

March 27, 2013

Hey, Joey Journal,

I'm back from the library now. Still nineteen days. I intended on quitting the writing activity until day twenty comes, but I need to write something down. When I was at the way-too-large library table, I came to a good stopping point and closed you. When I looked up, there was a visitor. It was Logan Fields, who had gotten a buzz cut. His smile wasn't cocked sideways and he was wearing an unzipped green hoodie over his red T-shirt. He looked silly as always, and the fact that he was wearing Christmas colors in March didn't help matters. Logan stared at me like nothing happened. "What's up?" he said, voice severely hushed.

I said nothing and he said, "Saw you and thought I'd say hello. You get my card?"

I buried my eyes in my hand. "Flushed it down the toilet without looking at it."

Logan took a breath, briefly glancing out the window, then back at me. He patiently said, "Doesn't have to be weird." I closed my eyes and put my head on the table. "Remember Ronny? Remember? From the hospital? Related to me? He told me he accidentally hinted at something."

My head skyrocketed up. *I warned that weak tit. Said he would have hell to pay. Seems he's been talking about me. Was he referencing Ronny's suspicion about Logan's feelings toward me?* Logan could tell from my expression that Ronny definitely mentioned something that piqued my curiosity. He half-smiled and said, "I've told him to just talk about it freely. My brother had a psychotic break when I was a kid."

A child walked past with her dad, looking over her shoulder at me the entire hike down the aisle. "He was in the military," Logan whispered, looking around to make sure nobody was lingering about and eavesdropping. "My brother came back to the states when I was like…eight. He had Post Traumatic Stress Disorder. The military knows how to kick a person's psyche to bits. David didn't get proper sleep, got shot in the leg, saw his best friend get blown up. Couldn't cope. Who could, though? He killed himself and I found him. Now I have the mental illness he suffered from. Nobody knows too much about David's death here in Wira. We didn't move here until after it happened. There. You know something about me now. I genuinely hope that helps."

I always thought everything would be better if nobody knew about my dad and I could go through this awful healing process without sympathetic gazes from classmates. I could tell from the sorrowful look in the eyes of Logan Fields that others' ignorance to the life events of another doesn't necessarily improve the situation. I don't know how I could see all of that in only two brown eyes, but I did. A body buried, a soul to never be mentioned again, that's what I yearned for these last few months. Messed-up, but true. Logan's eyes told another story, one of minds. Minds mentioning the dismal memories even when nobody else does.

"Look," he said. "Ronny didn't tell me what you have. In fact, he wouldn't. Said the hospital was like the Italian mob or something, and he couldn't risk being a rat. But I know you well, Rosie. You remind me of…yeah. You've seen someone die, it's not surprising-"

"Sorry about your family," I softly said, "but it's not just that with me. I wish it was only one thing. I have Bipolar Disorder, too."

His face shifted. Logan sat down closer to me, grabbing my hand. "You'll get through it." I peered down at you, Joey. "What's wrong?" Logan asked.

"What's wrong? What you're saying is wrong. You're saying it to make me feel better, but you're secretly thinking, 'Rosie's psychotic. Gotta be nice to her because we've gone through similar shit. What a drag.' So, stop it and leave."

"No." Logan's face fumed as he struggled to keep his voice low.

"I have all these helpful facts and statistics inside my head, Rosie. After all, I was only eight when I walked in on my brother bathing in bloody water after he slit his wrists in the tub. Many helpful one-liners are collected when you spend your childhood in and out of the mental health system as much as I did. I wanna say the phrases, but what use are they going to do? They've already listed them to you while you were in the hospital. You've heard them, yet you're still getting sick pleasure from believing you're the only person to ever go through this. All I'm gonna say is what's useful to you. What you just said…your attitude, attitudes like that drive me up the wall. You're not going to get anywhere with that. Are you determined to go through the rest of your life with your hands over your eyes, yelling, 'I've seen the unimaginable so I'll never see anything again?' Because what you just said is the same. Just different wording."

"Logan, I'm permanently damaged, dammit. And you sound like an after school special. I don't approve."

I wondered how long he practiced that speech in the mirror. Then he interrupted my thoughts with the words, "And you sound like a defeatist. I don't approve."

I threw you into my tote bag, threw the bag over my shoulder, threw my body into standing position and ferociously said, "We're strangers."

Once in the self-help section, Logan clutched my shoulder and whirled me around. "I'm trying to help," he said.

I speedily walked away and he pursued me more. Eventually, this chase turned into moving hide and seek. Finally, I was in the library's lobby, then instinctively ran into the bathroom. I can't stress this enough: To an upset girl, the bathroom is like a sanctum. I entered a stall, locking it behind me. History came knocking on the door, ready to repeat itself. I'll never get used to a boy shimmying his way under the stall while I'm in it. Never. Once the shock passed, I told Logan I hated him. He tried hugging me and insisted I calm down. I didn't. I couldn't. I pushed him against the stall's wall and said, "Get out."

Thank God nobody was there to hear us. My hands were on his chest and he was about to kiss me. The feeling of his keyed-up body made me not mind, and so we made out. It was my first kiss with a straight boy. I could tell the difference. With Eliot, he needed me in the same way his family needed an inground pool. Not a necessity. It proves something to those in the neighborhood. With Logan, he needed water, but only water that came from me. I could be a puddle or Lake Michigan, the Red Sea or a swamp, the Pacific Ocean or the condensation mark left by the bottom of a cup. It didn't matter what form I came in. I was the water and it was enough to satisfy a thirst that's been building for a long time.

His mouth tasted like candy. We spun around until he was pinning me to the stall, fingers occasionally interlacing. When our hands weren't locked, they explored each other's bodies and hair. He accidently touched my head's bald side, and I quickly moved that hand to my cheek because it tickled. He pulled away and smiled, but I tugged him back in. And I felt good; happier than prescription drugs could ever make me feel. I'd describe it further, but writing about kissing is like writing about dancing, or singing about architecture, or whatever that quote is. A kiss done right leaves the kissers hard-pressed to detail all the details.

About a minute passed before I realized what he was doing. Logan Fields has proven himself to be a people pleaser to new extremes. I'm not being irrational. He was so desperate to end a conversation on a positive note, he kissed me to make the realness vanish. I rapidly pushed him off and onto the toilet. My fingers curled around his ear and yanked it. "How dare you try to sedate me with your mouth," I said.

I unlatched the door, grabbed my bag, and ran out of the library. Glad he didn't come after me. He's young. Dealing with me isn't within his capacity. I was glazed over as I stared out the bus window until I heard a voice say, "Looky here, it's ring 'round the Rosie, pocket full of posies." The person sitting across the aisle was Steve. You know, the Steve that never leaves the street. The thought that sprung to mind was rude, but I thought it, nonetheless. *Has Steve always looked this... grubby?* He reeked of booze and his balding gray hair was rumpled and standing on end. Holes were present in his dirty sandals, his sweat-stained grey hoodie, and his grimy jeans. The Holey Trifecta. And his smile had a hole, too. Steve also paired pissed-on socks with his duct-taped sandals. Nothing is wrong with any of this, but there's something wrong with me not fully noticing the state of him before now. I said hello, deflecting my gaze to the headrest in front of me. "You look pretty today. Like a flower. Like a little Rosie."

My cheeks had mascara running down them. I wasn't having a beautiful moment on that bus, and he knew it. I thanked him, regardless. He plopped down next to me. "What's the problem, pretty girl?"

"Nothing."

"Oh, tell me," he said.

I anted up my problem into my closed fist's knuckle. "A stupid boy problem."

Steve leaned in closer to my face, giving me a whiff of the brandy on his lips. "That's why I'm an on-the-road man. I can escape my women problems on the road." I gave a subdued smile as he said, "I'm a hot commodity. Each town I visit, they can only handle Ole Steve-O for so long." Then Steve burped without covering his mouth, might I add. "The rolling stone lifestyle. Some women can't handle it. Unlike my beautiful little Rosie." He grabbed the bottom portion of my left thigh and groggily said, "You can handle it. All this." He gestured to his crotch as the bus driver announced the upcoming stop. I informed Steve that he was making me uneasy. He lazily apologized and zonked out ten seconds later. While the bus driver yielded, I carefully climbed over the sleeping giant and got the hell out of there.

I landed far from my house, so it took me a few seconds to determine my location. It being dark didn't help matters. Once my bearings were caught, I took off, thinking about the Bob Dylan song I once cherished. It asks the listener how it feels to be "on their own, with no direction home." For the first time ever, I was grateful to have both a home and a direction to it.

I'm at the Dwyer residence now, and it's okay. Minutes before starting this entry, I listened to "Like a Rolling Stone" and thoroughly paid attention. I've been misunderstanding the song's aim. It doesn't encourage homelessness. Truthfully, I don't entirely comprehend it. All I know is Bob never sings "To be on your own, with no direction home. That's a great feeling. Go on. Be lonely and directionless." He's asking us to ask ourselves how it feels to be adrift. We must decide for ourselves whether that's a good or bad state of being.

I don't think the lifestyle is appropriate for me after taking an honest look at Steve. My heart goes out to him, but I won't lie. I used to say, "Oh, he's harmless," fearing that I may turn into a cold-hearted bitch. "Positive at all costs" was my mentality when I used to know him. Not all homeless people are like Steve and I'm sure he's not all bad. I just don't want to idolize him, and that doesn't necessarily make me the villain. And I keep thinking about what he said, about escaping his "women problems" on the road. I don't want to escape my "stupid boy problem." Logan isn't a problem. Just a stupid boy who wants to help.

Steve has nothing but the clothes on his back and a misinterpretation of a song. The man thinks being a "rolling stone" means having nobody but the street you're walking on, and I want no part of that. For God's sake! The witch is home with mini-witch in tow. "Go to bed," says the witch to her youngest offspring. "Rosie and I are gonna have a little chat."

I'll handle it, Joey. Don't wait up.

March 28, 2013

Hey, Joey Journal,

Twenty days since I first went to the hospital. My dad's favorite game to play with us kids was Twenty Questions. We'd all stretch out under the tree in the backyard and play the game. He said he loved it because it fostered creativity in us. In his mind, creativity was an unrivaled skill. That's why part of me thinks he'd have seen my whole episode as creativity being mistaken for insanity. Dad would've loved how I unleashed red balloons at school. He would've smiled on so much of it. He got me. Melanie has changed and is unable to understand.

Just in case you're not into working out passive aggressive analogies for yourself, know that the 'witch' from last night was my mom. I would've detailed the argument directly after it happened, but I seem to be unable to do such a thing while spending an evening taking on the persona of Ares, the Greek god of war.

When Mel entered the dining room last night, I didn't look up, gaze focused on my breakneck hand. "Let me finish, Mel."

Next thing I knew, her skeletal fingers snatched you. As she pulled, my hand blew sideways, leaving a pen mark. I then rose to say, "And your deal?"

"My deal? What's your deal?" She aged so much in the last year. I remember when a young Jacques told her she didn't have the skin of a forty-five-year-old. Now, she's fifty-one. Her appearance is catching up with her, wrinkles popping out at me for the first time. And her frizzy poof of hair wasn't thoroughly dark anymore. I spied grays, and thought,

What have I done to this poor woman? A bird pounced out of the cuckoo clock behind her, making a ruckus and announcing it was late. An unexpected bird is still difficult for me to take. She said, "No note. No call? I had to drag your sister all over town. The hell are you doing?"

I said. "Never left notes before. Used to forget about checking in. You've never cared."

"You're sick now and we thought you ran away."

I told her I went to the damn library. She descended into a dining room chair, removed her trench coat and cradled her noggin in it. "Why didn't you answer your phone?"

I smacked my palm to my head as I sat across from her. "Forgot it at home."

"You're never leaving here without telling me. Never."

With that, I was vexed. "Mel, I know why the caged bird sings its fearful trill. It's tired of sitting at home, watching daytime television, in a goddamn cage." I got up and snagged you from the corner and bit the inside of my cheek. "Don't even think about throwing Joey again."

She pounced toward me, emancipating you from my hands. "You're not even supposed to be writing this much."

"But I want to." Journal completely in her clutches, I said, "I have to keep writing to Joey."

She broke down, swaying you in the air. "You can't, Rosie. I hate this. I hate how it absorbs you, how full it is, what you write. And I hate how you named it after—"

"Joey from *Full House*."

"Rosie Dianne, we both know that's a bald-faced lie."

"How dare you read a single page, Mom." I started yanking you from her hands, finding no success, so in the heat of it all, I did something wrong, the forever type of regrettable. Smacked her straight across the face and sprinted to my room to hide from my filth. And when I flew and landed face first on my bed, I hit my chin on the stupid phone I left behind that day. When I turned it on, I found a text from Logan. It said, "Hate texting, Rosie. In person redo when you're ready?"

My texted response read, "Contemplate the meaning of this song carefully." Attached was a link to a Youtube video featuring a song by

Lil Jon and The Eastside Boyz. It's called "Stop Fucking Wit Me." It's rather intense. Minutes later, he came back at me with, "Okay. But I'm lying."

Amidst my wrath, I couldn't help but grin. Smiles made while antagonized make you feel like your lips are concrete and every tooth will fall out. Needless to say, I couldn't sleep last night, drifting off at three in the morning. Slept all day. It's almost eight and I've been in my room all day, avoiding her. I only left to eat meals and she didn't acknowledge me whenever I came down. I don't blame her, but I hate it. She's always right, which completely capsizes me. I hate that. Yep, I shouldn't be journaling, seeing as I spiraled out of control on a spiral notebook. I tried not committing thoughts to paper all day, but I need to talk. I've been texting with Jacques all week, but we run out of things to say. I hate texts like Logan does. I want sleep, but I don't think I can without getting some words out there. I hate that. I hate everything, and most of all, I hate my hateful soul for using the word 'hate' excessively in this entry.

And I wanted to talk about all of this with River, but every time I'm ready to, he's at his girlfriend's place. What's the use of having a brother when said brother doesn't automatically come when you summon him?

Fine. I'll write it out, against my mother's wishes. This is the last story I'll write about the hospital. For now. The reason I often can't ditch my pencil is that I fret about forgetting something important. While unable to curtail my manic jibber jabber, I jotted something unforgettable down. Most of my "notes" were loony nonsense, but this nugget stood out. It was the sane part of me begging my hand and my head to calm down. *If it wants to be remembered, it will be.* I have time to tell the stories that matter, but this final tale needs to be committed to paper, immediately. It'll help me sleep tonight.

Michael

Two nights before I left the hospital, I wrote on printer paper while sitting in the group room by myself. Probably was detailing all the strange people who were passing through, like this one boy who started that morning and told me he was there for an addiction to female empowerment movies. In group, the therapists actually had him talk about this addiction. He couldn't stop watching the films in the *Bring It On* franchise. He forsook sleep to play *Lara Croft Tomb Raider* video games on school nights. And yes—I begged for paper that evening because I'd be a fool not to write these details of my day down.

Then the tip of my pencil busted and it almost echoed and this shattered my comfort. I was in an empty space. I'd been there eight days, but this was the first time I was in the group room solo. The room seemed cramped before, but now the pastel blue walls launched into space, like our universe after the Big Bang—expansive and growing ever outward.

The other nights, my annoyance levels spiked when in there. Everyone talked over each other and made brainless jokes and argued over banal topics. All anyone ever wanted to play was UNO. While on my own in a room that was supposed to feature a "group", my only desires were to partake in the disorganized conversations and hear the dumb jokes and argue over silly issues. And I almost wanted to cry because I had nobody to play UNO with. I myself was UNO. Tried playing myself. Didn't work so hot. I bound the deck with a rubberband before lobbing it at the wall. None of the nurses heard.

The staff had us do "quiet time" at 4 o'clock every day. That's our unaccompanied hour in our individual rooms. This is to prime us patients for what we'll find when we set foot on the pavement outside the hospital. We need to be prepped for a world that often forces us to be alone, even when we don't want to be. For many, that's the problem. We can't handle solitude. When facing ourselves, we self-destruct.

I did my quiet time earlier that day. I wanted people. Even the ones I once considered sub-par. Time slithered by as I pored over the lake mural. Before that night, the painting was soothing, but now it made me feel dehydrated because it sucked up all the moisture. As I was about to go in my room to pace, Michael walked in. He was the zombie-esque Asian boy who received laced weed prior to his stay. Michael haltingly approached the table, eyes converging on his oscillating fingers. He sat two seats away, the cracks of his hands obviously undoing him. Unhurriedly, he palmed the table, attention shifting to the wood's wavering lines. The boy remained slack-jawed, as dazed as Day 1.

Since my first day, I did everything imaginable to engage Michael, with no progress. Breaking through the invisible barrier between us was paramount to me. Perhaps it's because even though his mind was another planet's citizen, I saw myself in him. And if I pulled Old Michael out of the Michael in front of me, I'd feel better. At the time, it wasn't clear why I believed doing this would improve my spirits. Now the fog has come to naught, and answers have altogether arrived. I craved an opportunity to witness someone normalize. If I saw that transformation happen to someone else, my faith in the 'Old Me' would be restored. During the eight days that passed, my hands desperately tried yanking "Old Michael" out of the Michael I met. I failed, but as that boy joined me at the table, awareness became mine.

I failed at finding out who he used to be, but I had a divine chance to get to know the Michael before me. I've come to know that our past selves are a mere concept, and the only versions of us that exist and matter are the people we currently are. I sat back, studied Michael and thought, *He's beautiful, inside and out. Strong, too. That's all.*

Several moments passed before Michael vacantly reached for paper from the stack of blank pages lying near him. Then his hands fumbled about as he folded it into a crane. He did nothing but that for eight full days. Crane after crane after crane. Crane crazy. Honestly, I diverted my gaze the previous days. I was too whacked out to make bird correlations while I was there, so that's not why I couldn't watch. It made me uncomfortable is all. The sight forced me to see the excess humans are capable of. Seeing it in him made me see the excess in me, and realizing excess is a manic person's greatest fear.

I grew tired of sidetracked eyes and was sickened by not watching. So, I sat back as he folded paper after paper into birds. I studied how he created them and thought, *I could do that. I wanna do that. I wanna fill the world with birds.* I picked up a sheet of paper and laid creases in pursuit of creating a crane. The room experienced a second noiseless Big Bang. It collapsed ever inward, and it wasn't such a scary event. We weren't heard. In that silence, I understood that sanctuaries undeniably still endured.

I'm not gifted at writing from my imagination, but can write what I see and I have this desire to do so in a surplus most overwhelming. I saw Michael that night and I didn't commit him to paper. I committed myself to him, to the birds, to that moment.

His fingers speeded and did something different with the last blank page. I sat forward as if I was watching the climax of a Roman Polanski film. Suddenly, Michael lightly tapped my shoulder. I flinched, then calmed. Smiled at him with my eyes. We made eye contact for the first time, his dark eyes boring into mine. Neither of us said anything, but we were communicating. He was thanking me, and I was thanking him back. Slowly, he rose, entered a trance like state, and trudged to his room.

Before I could get up, I halted. A crane overdose expanded over the circular table. And one single origami rose. The word 'open' came to mind and the same with the dinging of Tibetan bowls. I hoisted a crane in one hand and the rose in the other. *You're coming home with me,* I thought. My hands experienced a lightness so delicate; a lightness I now know my soul can once again achieve. A lightness without words. It reminded me of what Logan said the night he drove me home from the library. *"I like instrumental music because it takes the words out of my mind instead of putting them there."*

That's what these paper formations were. Instrumental music. I sunk into a plastic chair and simply let myself blink multiple times. Then my eyes focused on the paper again, my whole being eager to see whether I imagined the rose. It was there, and so was Alfred, standing in the wide entrance. He said, "Bedtime." I looked up at him, calm astonishment rampant in all the tissue in my body. He asked if I needed to talk about anything before going to sleep.

"No," I said. "For real. It's getting better. Goodnight."

"Good for you."

"And goodbye, Alfred, in case this is the last night I see you."

Familiar smiles, familiar nods, and I was right about it being the last time.

Soon I was in bed, around 9:00. I've heard of the calm before the storm, but I knew that I was experiencing the calm that can come after if you want the serenity badly enough. Laying in my hospital bed, I thought, *Art isn't dead, and it never will be.*

March 29, 2013

Hey, Joey Journal,

Twenty-one days now. Twenty-one. That's the century we'll be in until the year 2100. By that time, I'll be lucky if this document still exists. I predict that robots will read and be threatened by the prediction I made to Logan, about robots stealing all the job posts in the world. On Wikipedia, they'll describe me as a famous propagandist. A poor opinion, but others have had worse.

Melanie.

It's Friday. As my mom drove me to my new therapist's office, the tension was palpable. Our fight from two nights ago continued to silently rage between us. Example: I switched the station during a commercial break and her glare was the facial expression equivalent of the *Psycho* theme song. During the meeting's first portion, I talked to Dr. Jarrod Bosley, unescorted. He's different from the psychiatrists I've had. Therapists tend to be as warm and cuddly as Mr. Roger's sweater collection, which contains garments similar to those worn by therapists themselves. When we shook hands, I was jolted by an electric shock buzzer. Although my laugh was nervous, it was the first one to escape my mouth in a week.

He was like a talkative version of Mr. Bean. That's the only way I can describe him.

I clammed up after we finished discussing my hospital experience. Wrenching answers from me was like pulling teeth from the mouth of a shy shark. Bosley told me it seemed liked I had a great deal going through my mind, and then handed me a smooth stone from a bowl of pebbles on the table between us. "A grounding stone," he said. "Whenever you get wound up, reach into your pocket, and the stone will remind you to stay grounded."

Something about the pebble in my pocket made me want to blurt out everything. "My mom and I got in this blowout fight," I said. "The shit hit the ceiling fan. I shouldn't swear, but whatever. Shit flew, two nights ago. We fought about everything. It didn't end well. Both of us went to bed angry. We're still angry. It sucks, Bosley. Sucks, and the suckage has sucked me up." He smiled and told me I wasn't reserved anymore. I let more out. "I'm normally not reserved, but I'm starting to consider my outgoing moments to be just mania. The mania is dwindling, so that means I've lost my fire."

"You have an illness. Two, actually," he said, "Don't let yourself be dictated by them. Mania brings out things like creativity and your bubbly side, but those things are already inside you. They belong to you. Mania temporarily enhances your attributes."

That made me feel better. "This isn't a job interview. You're here to help me, but still, I want us to be chums." He laughed at my word choice and said he was positive that's what we'd become. I said, "Chums. Like I'm a Charlie's Angel, and you're well, you'll be Bosley."

"We'll get along fine, chum."

I nodded and asked him if we could discuss the fight again. He told me to go ahead, and I explained how it was partially over you, my Joey Journal. He kept nodding as I explained who I named you after. Joey Gladstone. He nodded even more when I vented about how my mom thinks I shouldn't write in you anymore. Lots of nodding, then when I was done, he said, "Don't be afraid to write, but you have to find a way to limit how much you write so it doesn't consume you." I hid my face in a chunk of my hair. A smirk came to his face. If anybody else would have sarcastically smirked at me during my spiritless streak, I'd have smacked them. Bos got away with it somehow. After a protracted moment of him realizing that I wasn't going to be an effortless case, Bosley changed subjects. "As for the name of your journal..."

"It came from *Full House*."

"Don't bullshit a bullshitter."

I said, "In truth, I named it after Joey Gladstone. At least I thought I did. Maybe I was pushing my dad from my mind, and he came out slyly in my writing. But 'Joey'? No, we never called him that. He was Joe."

"Write about him any other times?"

"Rarely."

"Ever write about how he died?"

My hands shook as I swayed my head and Bosley asked if I still had my CBT book. CBT stands for Cognitive Behavioral Therapy, and in the hospital, they distribute workbooks revolving around it. It features exercises to help the patients get their thoughts in order. People put off using it, though. It's like hospital homework. Most will do anything to get out of it. "I have it," I said, "but on my second day, I drew weird things in every blank."

"Look at it and do the 'Situation, Thoughts, and Feelings' activity on a piece of paper."

"For what situation?"

"The one where you found him."

I longed to transform into a book and disappear into his shelf of psychological texts. He insisted further that this would help me get closure. Closure. I calmed, tentatively removing bracelets from my tattooed wrist. I reached over the table, showing him the bird flock. "Been wearing clunky bangles to hide a tattoo. Nobody questioned it since accessories are my thing. This tattoo, Bosley. Got it on my birthday. Mel didn't know about it until I was hospitalized. We fought about it during a visit. 'Your grandparents will wring your neck when they see it.' This was ridiculous because she has two tattoos from college and another celebrating her kids. Our baby footprints are on her shoulder blade. Joe had a firework above his ass and who knows what else. You said the word 'closure', and something dawned on me. This tattoo doesn't have that. Birds…birds were his favorite animal. Such a bizarre dude, going on hikes in Safari outfits. And doing bird calls. A bird watcher, through and through. That's what I remember about him the most. So, I have a flock of birds inked on me. That's where you wanna be. A flock. Not by yourself. With your people. But this 'grounding stone' you gave me reminded me that nobody can stay in the sky forever. They must come down. These birds are headed somewhere, and that place isn't the clouds. It's rooted to the ground. A tree. A nest. I need to complete this." I flipped my wrist over and said, "Get my mom to let me finish the tattoo, and I'll do the activity."

The man grinned goofily, crossed his feet and told me I had to promise. I did, wholeheartedly. And it was amazing. He barely said anything. First, he brought my mom in and gave her a chance to say her piece. She said, "Everything has been as good as it could possibly be. You know, everything considered."

Bosley told her there was something I wanted to say. And it all came out. "About the other night. I'm sorry. You were right, Mel. About everything. Especially my journal's name. My subconscious, probably. I've pushed so much under my internal rug, but I'm gonna fix it. There's this CBT activity..." She interrupted to fling herself to my side of the couch and embrace me. When she released, I said, "One condition."

"What's that?"

I re-gave the speech. She smiled, tears running down her face. "Of course we'll get you some tattoo closure."

I turned as energetically toward Bosley as my tired body could. "Whoa. How'd you do that?"

"I didn't," he said. "You did."

March 30, 2013

Hey, Joey Journal,

22 days. In Bingo, 22 is referred to as "two little ducks." I guess that's what this entry is about. Joe and me. Two little ducks, the one who lived and the one who died.

Welcome to "Situations, Thoughts, Feelings." This is how the human mind works. We enter a situation. Thoughts cleave into our craniums. Feelings arrive. There's little we can do about our situations, but we can probe our thoughts and alter them. By consequence, we can amend our moods. Here it is.

SITUATION

It's August 1st and my dad doesn't have a job. He quit mid-July, in a madcap manner. Joe was a comedic actor turned drama teacher, as we already discussed. He loved teaching at Hamilton High in the next town over, and that's the damn truth. However, there was a weird change in him last summer. Kept saying, "I think I might quit and open up my own restaurant." This was weird because he had never mentioned anything about that being his dream. The only meal he could make was a microwaved Lean Cuisine. And on the day Joe quit, he bought a car. A car. My parents weren't drivers, not ever. Cyclists, bus riders, walkers, but not drivers. Not if they could help it. It was a medium-sized hippie van with flowers and a smiling sun painted on it. A junked up 1969 Volkswagen. Cheap, but at the same time, spontaneous, and somehow completely revolting.

Our living situations were interesting on the first of the month. River was still in his apartment in Milwaukee. Melanie, Willow and I were living at home. And Joe probably moved into a motel, temporarily. This was after he found out Mel was cheating. They'd been having marital issues for a while. That's why they went to Florida at the end of my junior year. They told us it was for their 'anniversary'. Every family member knew the two were trying to salvage their shredded marriage. When they got back, Joe told me in private that they bickered the entire trip. Said, "It's gonna be over soon, Rosie."

Two months later, his prediction came true. Maybe it was a self-fulfilled prophecy. Melanie butt-dialed Joe while she was screwing this guy she met at a craft convention. Male crafters are douchebags, but this hipster somehow seduced her into joining him in an extramarital affair. The tryst ended the day she was caught, but it was enough to ruin everything. Joe moved out with little uproar. The night he got in his hippie van, I signaled for him to roll down the window and asked where he was going. He said, "Don't know, kid. Don't know where I'll be. Not now, not ten years from now, or ten years after that. That's what scares me."

"Joe?" He looked everywhere but at me and I said, "Can't you just try harder?"

My dad solemnly looked down. Then he blew a playful kiss, trying to prove he felt better than he looked. Joe reached his hand through the window and shook my hand firmly. "It's been real and it's been nice, kid. But it hasn't been real nice."

I don't know why, but I sternly saluted him, and he did the same to me. As he pulled out of the driveway, he weakly smiled. Willow came running outside moments later, pulling up her jeans, yelling, "He said he was leaving in an hour. I was taking a crap. No." The car was all the way down the road by the time she started rushing after it. I sometimes think that's why he left an hour earlier. Willow's young face could convince anybody to stay, even if it's only for a bit longer. I don't know what makes me feel worse, that kid not getting a proper goodbye, or her not receiving enough hellos. Eight years of hellos from Joe is not enough.

August 3rd came. I was at Eliot's, climbing out of the pool to reread my copy of *The Catcher in Rye*. Eliot and Jacques were roughhousing in the pool as I read the chapter where Holden describes his reaction to his brother's death. He busts every window in his garage, hurting his hand so tremendously, he can no longer make a fist. Then my phone beeped. A text. From my dad. Weird, because he never texted. Like Logan and myself, he hated texting. He saw the advent of texting as a sign of the end of times. Joe preferred staying 'unplugged'.

His uncharacteristic message said, "y wnt n 1 pik u fhones?"

Unreadable almost, but I translated it. *Why won't anyone pick up their phones?* I examined my phone further. Found thirteen missed calls. Then I listened to my voicemail, which was full of messages from him. The first one was composed, but as they continued, he royally unraveled. "Nobody's picking up their phones. I'm home. Why won't anyone come home?"

His voice became more desperate and drunk with each voicemail, until he didn't sound human. The last one was purely moaning and hyperventilating. I imagined he called my mom as well, but Melanie had taken Willow to Six Flags to cheer her up because the poor kid had been crying two straight days about the impending divorce. They were all the way in Illinois.

I was the only one in Wira, too pissed at Melanie over the infidelity to go to an amusement park with her. I sat, soaking wet, staring at the text. As I did this, my nose memorized the smell of chlorine. *'Why won't anyone answer their phones?'* My red sundress was thrown on backward over my sopping swimsuit. Didn't bother putting sandals on. While sprinting home, worry pounded my body as if the feeling was Muhammed Ali and I was its opponent. I ran through the front door, which was wide open. Entering the kitchen, I found the house to be in a state of openness and emptiness that I'm in no way able to explain. Horrified, I immediately yelled, "Dad! Where are you?"

He wasn't in the living room, but there was a piece of paper with almost unintelligible scrawl on it. From what I could decipher, it read, "Sorry. I couldn't do it. I'm getting older. Real old. Still feel like a seventeen-year old. The teacher asked, 'Where do you see yourself ten years from now?' Every time ten years come to pass, I still haven't come up with an answer. The world is caving in and I'm the man, the one who's supposed to carry it on his shoulders. And I can't."

I checked the downstairs bathroom. The upstairs bathroom. Ran down the hallway towards my parents' bedroom. The door was shut and I paused. When I opened it, there was nothing but the usual scene. Yankee candles and the perfect amount of throw pillows and a messy desk belonging to my dad. I exhaled pure relief and mumbled, "He must have taken Mr. Bojangles for a walk. Shit. Where's Mr. B?"

I sprinted through the house, yelling, "Mr. B!" Then I heard barking outside. Opened the back door and walked so slowly, I was practically Native American walking. The incessant barking coming from Mr. Bojangles had lasting effect. When the corgi barks in present day, I contemplate shoving my hand in the blender. That bothers me. That and the ringing of his collar, which Joe had engraved for him. *Spell the word 'dog' backwards.* I was too dazed to hear any of this when I first sprinted home, but once I finally heard it, my ears wanted to detach themselves and find a hiding place. "Mr. Bojangles?" I said. Soon I was in the garage, approaching his car. A boom box was softly playing my parents' original copy of "1-2-3" by Len Barry. Looping.

Then came the horrible image I can't erase from my mind, waiting to swallow me up. My dad wasn't just dead. He was dead and sitting in the driver's seat, and he used car exhaust fumes to achieve this state of being. Asphyxia. His skin was bright red, blotchy, veiny. Burst capillaries or something. His eyes had popped. This image is always with me and it reeks. His hippie van wasn't in stellar condition. Its exhaust smelled of rotten eggs. My hands desperately yanked at the handle, but it was locked from the inside. I needed to get him out. He was obviously dead, and his eyes made that apparent, but I didn't care.

I vomited, then broke all the windows in the garage with a baseball bat because I knew I'd want full use of my fists later. You see, I'm one of those intense writers who writes with their pencil in a curled fist, like I'm doing right now. I need my fists.

Finally, I attacked the driver's side window and tried extracting him from his seat. Bloodied myself up, right good. My neighbor Stuart called the cops when he heard the windows smashing into itty-bitty pieces. He thought there was a criminal in the garage. The police came in as I began using the bat on the boom box. They took me in for questioning. Melanie and Willow were making their way back home from Six Flags when an officer got a hold of her.

I don't remember everything by a perfect timeline. When it's all happening at once, you hardly ever recall it in a wrinkle free, untarnished way. It's kind of like a big...bang. Time is happening chronologically, but it's also happening quicker than you think. It slows down when it's hard, but it hits your body so forcefully and so fast that you can't even formulate a coherent thought on the matter. You simply know you've experienced a big bang all your own. That's all.

When the crime scene was cleared and we were allowed back in, Melanie and Willow cried in the kitchen. They wrapped their long, thin, quaking arms around one another and they wailed. I was so hungry, I was about to drop to my knees. And I thought, *The two people in front of me have frail female arms and that isn't gonna cut it hug wise.* River embraced me, but I couldn't bring myself to hug back. He looks like him. After a long moment of this, he started cooking in the unsophisticated way in which he used to prepare meals. He made microwave pizza rolls for his whole grieving fam.

They didn't notice me sneaking away, completely dry-eyed, nearly expressionless if it weren't for the shuddering of my bottom lip. The only exact time I remember from the beginning of August was midnight. 12:00 glowed ominously on my alarm clock, pricking my eyes like a needle, trying to pry tears out and failing to do so. My family found me mindlessly punching my pillow. They found me mindless. Couldn't get me to stop, and so they took me to the mental hospital. Even during the car ride, I couldn't stop softly punching my reddened cheeks.

Thoughts

When my dad left his job, I thought: Wow, he's peppier than usual. The old man probably noticed he's balding and decided to have a mid-life crisis. He's not Arthur B. Cummings, my pissing, naked, drunken drama teacher. Not even close. No, no, no.

When my dad moved out: No. I want him to stay. I need him to. No.

While reading the text and listening to the voicemails: Shit. Shit. Shit.

While running to my house:

While reading the note:

When I found his body:

While bashing the windows:

While staring at Willow and Melanie bawling:

When I was punching the pillow:

While punching my face during the dark midnight car ride:

While walking into the hospital: Nothing's impossible, but not everything that's possible is wonderful.

Feelings

Powerless. My new bread and butter. Powerless.

Now I'm writing about it, realizing I can't do the second part of the activity. I can't. I can't change the thoughts that were had or not had that day. However, I can change the thoughts I currently have.

Current Situation

I'm in my bedroom, writing about my dad's death.

Current Thoughts

It shouldn't have happened. I tried, but should've tried harder. God tried, but should've tried harder.

Current feelings

Lost and powerless—bread and butter.

I'm going to fix my thoughts, making them more realistic and positive.

Fixed Thoughts

It happened. Can't pretend it didn't. He's gone. There's no bringing him home. I have to remember him in a good light. If he was here, he'd want me to remember the good memories. All the mantras he gave me, like "Confidence is key, kid." His bird calls, for sure. And that damn firework tattoo above his ass. Oh, and that time he accidentally farted at my Aunt Cindy's wedding. It sounded like a bomb went off in his pants. There was a huge silence before he finally said, "Weddings make my colon nervous." Completely straight-faced. Everyone, including the priest, laughed. Most of all, he'd want me to quit blaming myself. There's a stark difference between what we try to do and what ends up happening, and we can't bring ourselves or God into it. We can't do that to ourselves.

How do I feel now?

I don't feel perfect. Hell, I don't even feel real good. But I feel better, and better is always the best.

March 31, 2013

Hey,

Joey Journal is filled up. Not all the way. There are pages left, but I think it's time to move forward. I walked to Walmart around noon. Bought a new notebook. The snow is almost gone and for quite a stretch, warm sun reigned over mammoth puddles. And I'm ready for paper I don't yet know. The same goes for days.

Dad kept journals at my age. He'd write one thing about his day that bothered him, and then four things he was grateful for. He said we can't avoid talking about what's bothering us, but if we put a negative thought against positive ones, it doesn't seem as terrible.

One negative: Willow and I were playing Just Dance around 10:00 am. After a while, my body was exhausted, so I plummeted down next to River on the sofa. He was on the far end, reading the news, as I leaned against the other side. Willow marched over and militantly commanded that I keep playing. I said, "Youngster, please. I'm spent."

She stuck her tongue out before saying, "That hospital made you boring."

Willow climbed over the coffee table and took to jerking my limbs. I told her to hear her elder sister out. She crossed her arms, collapsing dramatically between Riv and I. "Look, Willy, people change. Who you are at eight is completely different than the person you're going to be at eighteen. I'm only changing."

Her eyes zeroed in on her lap as she muttered, "Changing into a boring person."

That was one negative from my day. Now, here are four things I'm grateful for.

First, I'm grateful River was there when Willow called me "boring." I said, "River, back me up. Tell her what you told me way back when." My voice shifted, mocking his philosophical ways. "It's good to change your currents from time to time. Like a river."

Without looking over, he said, "Not all true." His eyes remained on the paper, something he wouldn't have been caught dead with this time last year. "Don't tell Willow she's gonna be entirely different in ten years. Nobody ever transforms into someone absolutely different."

"Look at you. Course they do."

"Naw," said River. His hand tilted his newspaper in my direction, revealing he'd been "reading" cartoons. As he winked, a boisterous bottom burp boomed. "Got another one brewing."

I grabbed the jar of coffee beans on the table and emptied it. Passing the jar over Willow's lap, I told him to put the little guy in safe keeping. River stood and tooted into the jar while Willow stormed off. Once she was in the doorway, she stirred around. "You're not boring. Neither of you are. Just gross."

My brother sealed the jar and cradled it like an infant. "Look," he said. "Willow isn't old enough to understand."

Second, I'm grateful for the daily text messages Jacques has been sending since my first day out of the hospital.

Yesterday, he sent a picture taken before Trick-or-Treating in middle school. As an homage to the musical *Cats,* Jacques was dressed like a pink cat. He was intent on playing a character he devised himself and thought was missing from the cast of the show. Magenta, he called himself. Kids kept calling him "The Pink Panther," enraging him. He flipped them all a bony middle finger, telling them to, "Sit on it." Then they called him other names. Those other names weren't honest mistakes. They were ignorant. I'm thankful we became friends when we did, because I was called names that night, too. We dealt with the crudeness together. If you must know, I dressed like Ruth Bader Ginsburg, and the neighborhood kids dubbed me 'Quaker Bitch'. I'd hope that's not how they'd address the real Ruth.

Jacques and Eliot haven't spoken in two weeks. Jacques is okay with it, though. More than okay, I'd say. The split happened when they were making out in the Faggs' kitchen. Eliot abruptly broke away and said, "This has been bothering me forever. I need to know. Are eggs dairy products?"

Finally, having had enough, Jacques got an egg out from the fridge and held it in front of Eliot. He said, "This is an egg. It isn't a dairy product. You've lived in Wisconsin for a year. Child, this is the dairy state. Therefore, you should know your dairy products. Even if you lived elsewhere, you should know eggs come out of mother-fucking-hens. Look at this egg. Look at it. It's the size of your brain." Jacques cracked the egg over Eliot's head. "That's what I'd like to do to your brain."

"We're over then?" Eliot said.

And they were.

Hanging onto Eliot as my "boyfriend" was like hanging on to a fatty chunk along my side. That's also what leaving Jacques in the doghouse felt like. Like sinking in the ocean because I refused to untie an anchor from my foot. As for Eliot, I've called him to apologize for outing him, but he's screening my calls. Some relationships prove more difficult to mend than others. This is because many bonds are built on faulty foundations.

Today's picture was...special. It featured Logan and Jacques standing with a gap between them, arms wrapped around an invisible person. Below the picture, it read: *Insert Rosie here.* I squinted my eyes and thought, *Hold on. Is that my living room? Shit. That Zen tapestry is so ours.* The picture came in while I was walking home from Walmart. It started drizzling, and my cumbersome umbrella hindered my texting capabilities. I kept it simple, sending a question mark. The next text said, "Excessive couscous consumption causes extreme hotness, because your brother is lookin' fine."

I sprinted home, disturbing countless puddles. My thoughts raced alongside my body. *Please don't let them be at my house! What if they go through my drawers? Oh lord, not my underwear drawer! Hold up. Calm your tits, Dwyer.* My pace sedated to a medium speed as I rolled my tense shoulders. Shook it out.

Third, I'm grateful for Willow…*The Games Master*.

When I came through the door, Logan and Jacques were playing *Just Dance*. While Willow cheered Logan on, the song "Proud Mary" by Tina Turner blared outrageously loud. I dislodged my feet from my rain boots while going unnoticed. As I hung up my jacket, River walked in from the dining room, eating a hot pocket. With a full gullet, he said, "Look. Rosie's home. Let's tackle her."

Willow hurdled over the sofa and tried dragging me to the ground, but failed until the boys were in action. Jacques threw his controller on the couch while River dumped his empty plate on the coffee table. They both lunged at me. Once I was shrieking and strewn across the carpet, Willow called out to Logan, "Cutie, we need your help!"

Willow can't remember names.

"Sorry…can't…stop…dancing!"

Above me was Jacques' face, turning incensed. "The game ended when I left."

Logan said, "No, the song ended...now. Hey! I won."

Jacques attempted to wriggle out from underneath River and was unable to budge. Varied expletives sprung from his mouth. Logan limply lay on top of us, and a strange moment passed before I yelled, "Y'all get off or I'll piss myself."

They hopped up and sat on the living room furniture. I stood in place and nervously said, "Wasn't expecting this. Wish you would've called. Never mind. Yeah… What?"

When you haven't seen many people outside your family in a while, you forget how to speak. Logan said, "It was a surprise. So, um, surprise!"

I calmed down, taking a seat between my two uninvited guests. It was quiet for a moment, until Willow, ever the carefree eight-year old, triumphantly broke the silence. "This is boring. Let's play a game."

"What would you like to play?" Logan said, grinning. He thought she was adorable. I could tell. Willow, a woman of action, didn't need to ponder long. "Here's the plan. We'll play three games of Crocodile Morey. Three. That game gets old fast. Then we'll play hide and seek till it gets boring."

River patted her head and said, "Willow, you're so good at making itineraries. You'll be a camp counselor someday, for sure." We all laughed as Willy nonchalantly cabbage-patched, perfectly somber. Then we circled up and started slapping hands. River won the first round of Crocodile Morey, Jacques won the second, and I won the last one. Logan was the first out during each round. It's because he lives in slow motion. I like that.

Willow, wise beyond her years, was right about the game growing stale after three rounds. When the third round concluded, she capered energetically, saying, "Okay, children. Put your feet in the middle." It was time for the random selection of a person to be "it." Willow pointed at each foot as she sang, "Eenie, meenie, miny, moe. Catch the tiger by the toe. If it hollers, let him go. Eenie, meenie, miny, moe." Her finger landed on Logan's foot.

He kept it there and she told him to pull his foot out. Logan said, "There's more to the rhyme. It ends with 'Not because you're dirty, not because you're clean, just because you kissed the dirty boy behind the dirty magazine.'"

His dance movies perfectly coordinated with the popping of each syllable.

"Cutie, we don't got time for that shit."

I told her to watch it, but we all ended up chuckling. Willow continued her selection process until my foot was the last remaining. I was "It."

I started saying, "I gotta pee first," but they ran off before I could finish. Man, I had to piss. Counted to twenty-five with closed eyes, but couldn't hold it. So, I headed into the downstairs bathroom. Nobody was in sight, so I dropped my trousers and sat on the toilet. My mouth hummed the Harry Potter theme song while I whizzed. It's my routine. Suddenly, laughter echoed, and I flipped out. "Who's in here?"

No response. I flushed the toilet, washed my hands, then whipped the shower curtain open to find Logan, eyes closed, red in the face and stifling giggling. He eased long enough to make fun of me for humming the Harry Potter theme song while peeing.

"Didn't know you were in here, Mister."

He sat down on the tub's edge. So gloomy. He said, "I'm the first eliminated. Aren't I?"

I joined him on the tub. "It's okay if you suck at children's games. You're good at lots of other things."

"Like what?"

"Don't play dumb. You're a decent peer editor. And you won the dance off." He smiled softly while I said, "More importantly, Logan, you're a really good friend."

"Yeah?"

"Yeah. A good friend who keeps reaching out when their friend is being an unresponsive dickhead."

Logan's face and shoulders and spirit slumped. "I wasn't a good friend that night at the library. I was gonna keep texting you, I was, but I decided I was pushing too hard. I'm still pushing too hard, aren't I? You probably think I was taking advantage, but I swear that's—"

"You were trying to help." He patted my shoulder, gracelessly, and I decided to pat his head the same way. "Logan, I'd be lying if I said I didn't have deeply seeded internal urges to call you after I sent you that 'Stop Fucking Wit Me' video. However, I fought with Mel, big time, and yeah, sorry. I forgot. Logan, you panicked. Panic pulls out the crazy in people." Once our hands were to ourselves, he tried figuring out if he wanted to say what was on his mind. I began speaking rapidly. "Say whatever. You're not gonna hurt me. My feelings only get hurt when you censor yourself, and—"

"I like you. Okay? A lot."

"Still?"

"Yes."

I was a saliva-swallowing, eye-bulging, finger-fidgeting sight for sore eyes.

Logan said, "That Mouthful chick was a handful. Most girls are. So are you, but you're a pain in the ass I could get used to."

"Yeah?"

"Oh, yeah. Rosie, before you were hospitalized, you were confusing to the point where I began to think I either was inadequate or you were just an idiot. If it's the last option, you're the most charming idiot I've ever met. Chasing Bette around the writing room, doing your white woman's overbite. Like c'mon, I've seen you put your hand in your armpit to make fart noises, all to give sound effects to one of your stories you read in class. Confusing girl, yes. Daring, though. And during that last play performance, you were understandably terrible, but you were fucking fearless. Not a chicken, at all. And you make me want to be fearless, too. You know that? And, don't look at me like that. Don't look at me like you didn't know." I didn't say anything. Finally, he said, "Fuck it. Fuck fear." He grabbed my head and kissed me. When he pulled away, I started laughing, like a water mammal on drugs.

"That bad?"

"No, it was sweet." My smile grew more and more incredulous. "It's just every time you've hit on me, we've been in a bathroom."

Logan said, "Don't you smell the romance in the air?"

I started laughing and he pulled me in for another kiss. It was the kind that people wait their whole lives for, but rarely find. That was cliché, but see if I care. It's the kind of kiss that people can describe with cliché statements. It was a "Fuck it, Fuck fear" kind of kiss. That's what it was.

But my inner world started feeling euphoric, and it scared me, and I knew it was too soon. So, I broke away. "Friends. Let's be friends. I hope that doesn't confuse you. Friends? For now. I've had the biggest crush on you. You have without a doubt wormed your way into my psyche, but I need to get comfortable with my shit before I can be comfortable with someone else. Understand? Please understand."

His smile was lazy as he nodded and said, "Of course I can be your friend. But we will go bowling someday? Right?"

"Without a doubt, Logan."

I tightly hugged him and, all at once, the bathroom door was ope Arms flailing, Willow said, "This isn't how you play hide and seek."

Logan let go and whispered in my ear, "You have the cutest si ever."

Willow put her hand on her hip. "Heard that. I'm single."

Lastly, I'm grateful for the movie *It's a Wonderful Life*.

We were looking for a movie to watch. When I opened the d

n.

ster

rawer,

Made in the USA
Monee, IL
05 January 2023

24492397R00174